I0651102

J. Bell Pettigew

# Animal locomotion or walking, swimming and flying, with a dissertation on aeronautics

J. Bell Pettigew

**Animal locomotion or walking, swimming and flying, with a dissertation on aeronautics**

ISBN/EAN: 9783742821812

Manufactured in Europe, USA, Canada, Australia, Japa

Cover: Foto ©Andreas Hilbeck / pixelio.de

Manufactured and distributed by brebook publishing software
(www.brebook.com)

J. Bell Pettigew

# Animal locomotion or walking, swimming and flying, with a dissertation on aeronautics

# THE INTERNATIONAL SCIENTIFIC SERIES.

## LIST OF THE VOLUMES ALREADY PUBLISHED.

**THE FORMS OF WATER IN RAIN AND RIVERS, ICE AND GLACIERS.** By J. TYNDALL, L.L.D., F.R.S. With 26 Illustrations. Third Edition. Crown 8vo. 5s.

"One of Professor Tyndall's best scientific treatises."—*Standard.*

"With the clearness and brilliancy of language which have won for him his fame, he considers the subject of ice, snow, and glaciers."—*Morning Post.*

"Before starting for Switzerland next summer every one should study 'The Forms of Water.'"—*Globe.*

"Eloquent and instructive in an eminent degree."—*British Quarterly.*

**PHYSICS AND POLITICS;** or, THOUGHTS ON THE APPLICATION OF THE PRINCIPLES OF "NATURAL SELECTION" AND "INHERITANCE" TO POLITICAL SOCIETY. By WALTER BAGEHOT. Crown 8vo. Second Edition. 4s.

"We can recommend the book as well deserving to be read by thoughtful students of politics."—*Saturday Review.*

"Able and ingenious."—*Spectator.*

"A work of really original and interesting speculation."—*Guardian.*

**FOODS.** By Dr. EDWARD SMITH. Profusely Illustrated. Second Edition. Price 5s.

"A comprehensive résumé of our present chemical and physiological knowledge of the various foods, solid and liquid, which go so far to ameliorate the troubles and vexations of this anxious and wearying existence."—*Chemist and Druggist.*

"Heads of households will find it considerably to their advantage to study its contents."—*Court Express.*

"A very comprehensive book. Every page teems with information. Readable throughout."—*Church Herald.*

**MIND AND BODY: THE THEORIES OF THEIR RELATIONS.** By ALEXANDER BAIN, L.L.D., Professor of Logic at the University of Aberdeen. Four Illustrations. Second Edition. 4s.

**THE STUDY OF SOCIOLOGY.** By HERBERT SPENCER. Crown 8vo. Second Edition. Price 5s.

**ON THE CONSERVATION OF ENERGY.** By Professor BALFOUR STEWART. Fourteen Engravings. Price 5s.

**ANIMAL MECHANICS;** or, **Walking, Swimming, and Flying.** By Dr. J. B. PETTIGREW, M.D. F.R.S. 130 Illustrations. Price 5s.

**RESPONSIBILITY IN MENTAL DISEASE.** By Dr. HENRY MAUDSLEY.

**THE ANIMAL FRAME.** By Prof. E. J. MAREY. 119 Illustrations. Crown 8vo. Price 5s.

**THE NEW CHEMISTRY.** By Prof. JOSIAH P. COOKE, of the Harvard University. Numerous Engravings. Price 5s.

☞ **For List of forthcoming Volumes, see end of the book.**

HENRY S. KING & Co. 65 CORNHILL, and 12 PATERNOSTER ROW.

J. Design.
W. Bollingwell.

WALKING, SWIMMING, AND FLYING.

# ANIMAL LOCOMOTION

OR

# WALKING, SWIMMING, AND FLYING,

WITH A DISSERTATION ON

# AËRONAUTICS.

BY

## J. BELL PETTIGREW, M.D. F.R.S. F.R.S.E. F.R.C.P.E.

LECTURER ON PHYSIOLOGY AT SURGEONS' HALL, EDINBURGH ; PATHOLOGIST TO THE ROYAL
INFIRMARY OF EDINBURGH ;

Extraordinary Member and late President of the Royal Medical Society of Edinburgh ; Croonian Lecturer
to the Royal Society of London for 1860 ; Lecturer to the Royal Institution of Great Britain and
Russell Institution, 1867 ; Lecturer to the Royal College of Surgeons of Edinburgh,
1873 ; Author of numerous Memoirs on Physiological Subjects in the
Philosophical and other Transactions, &c. &c. &c.

*ILLUSTRATED BY 130 ENGRAVINGS ON WOOD.*

Second Edition.

HENRY S. KING & Co.

65 CORNHILL, AND 12 PATERNOSTER ROW, LONDON.

1874.

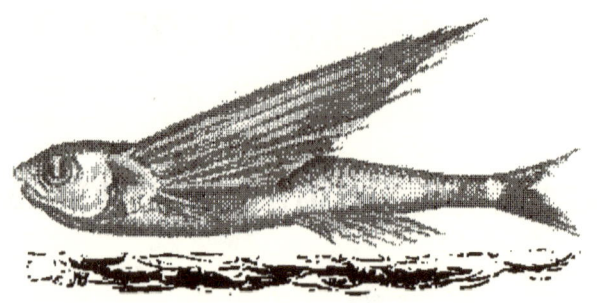

(All Rights reserved.)

# PREFACE.

In the present volume I have endeavoured to explain, in simple language, some difficult problems in "Animal Mechanics." In order to avoid elaborate descriptions, I have introduced a large number of original Drawings and Diagrams, copied for the most part from my Papers and Memoirs "On Flight," and other forms of "Animal Progression." I have drawn from the same sources many of the facts to be found in the present work. My best thanks are due to Mr. W. Ballingall, of Edinburgh, for the highly artistic and effective manner in which he has engraved the several subjects. The figures, I am happy to state, have in no way deteriorated in his hands.

ROYAL COLLEGE OF SURGEONS OF EDINBURGH,
*July* 1873.

# CONTENTS.

---

## ANIMAL LOCOMOTION.

### INTRODUCTION.

| | PAGE |
|---|---|
| Motion associated with the life and well-being of animals, . | 1 |
| Motion not confined to the animal kingdom; all matter in motion; natural and artificial motion; the locomotive, steamboat, etc. A flying machine possible. . . | 2 |
| Weight necessary to flight, . . . | 3 |
| The same laws regulate natural and artificial progression, . | 4 |
| Walking, swimming, and flying correlated, . . . | 5 |
| Flight the poetry of motion, . . . . | 6 |
| Flight a more unstable movement than that of walking and swimming; the travelling surfaces and movements of animals adapted to the earth, the water, and the air, . | 7 |
| The earth, the water, and the air furnish the fulcra for the levers formed by the travelling surfaces of animals, . . | 8 |
| Weight plays an important part in walking, swimming, and flying, . . . . . . | 9 |
| The extremities of animals in walking act as pendulums, and describe figure-of-8 curves, . . . | 0 |
| In swimming, the body of the fish is thrown into figure-of-8 curves, . . . . | 10 |
| The tail of the fish made to vibrate pendulum fashion, . | 11 |
| The tail of the fish, the wing of the bird, and the extremity of the biped and quadruped are screws structurally and functionally. They describe figure-of-8 and waved tracks, | 12 |

PAGE

The body and wing reciprocate in flight; the body rising when
the wing is falling, and vice versâ, . . . . . . 12

Flight the least fatiguing kind of motion. Aërial creatures not
stronger than terrestrial ones, . . . . . 13

Fins, flippers, and wings form mobile helices or screws, . . 14

Artificial fins, flippers, and wings adapted for navigating the
water and air, . . . . . . . . 14

History of the figure-of-8 theory of walking, swimming, and
flying, . . . . . . . . . 15

Priority of discovery on the part of the Author. Admission to
that effect on the part of Professor Marey, . . . 16

Fundamental axioms. Of uniform motion. Motion uniformly
varied, . . . . . . . . . 17

The legs move by the force of gravity. Resistance of fluids.
Mechanical effects of fluids on animals immersed in them.
Centre of gravity, . . . . . . . 18

The three orders of lever, . . . . . . . 19

Passive organs of locomotion. Bones, . . . . 21

Joints, . . . . . . . . . 23

Ligaments. Effects of atmospheric pressure on limbs. Active
organs of locomotion. Muscles; their properties, arrangement, modes of action, etc., . . . . . 24

Muscular cycles. Centripetal and centrifugal movements of
muscles; muscular waves. Muscles arranged in longitudinal, transverse, and oblique spiral lines, . . 25-27

The bones of the extremities twisted and spiral, . . 28

Muscles take precedence of bones in animal movements, . 29

Oblique spiral muscles necessary for spiral bones and joints, . 31

The spiral movements of the spine transferred to the extremities, . . . . . . . . . 33

The travelling surfaces of animals variously modified and
adapted to the media on or in which they move, . 34-36

## PROGRESSION ON THE LAND.

Walking of the Quadruped, Biped, etc., . . . 37

Locomotion of the Horse, . . . . . 39

Locomotion of the Ostrich, . . . . . 45

Locomotion of Man, . . . . . . 51

## PROGRESSION ON AND IN THE WATER.

|                                                                                      | PAGE |
|--------------------------------------------------------------------------------------|------|
| Swimming of the Fish, Whale, Porpoise, etc.,                                         | 60   |
| Swimming of the Seal, Sea-Bear, and Walrus,                                          | 74   |
| Swimming of Man,                                                                     | 78   |
| Swimming of the Turtle, Triton, Crocodile, etc.,                                     | 89   |
| Flight under water,                                                                  | 90   |
| Difference between sub-aquatic and aerial flight,                                    | 92   |
| Flight of the Flying-fish; the kite-like action of the wings,                        | 98   |

## PROGRESSION IN OR THROUGH THE AIR.

|                                                                                      | PAGE |
|--------------------------------------------------------------------------------------|------|
| The wing a lever of the third order,                                                 | 103  |
| Weight necessary to flight,                                                          | 110  |
| Weight contributes to horizontal flight,                                             | 112  |
| Weight, momentum and power to a certain extent synonymous in flight,                 | 114  |
| Air-cells in insects and birds not necessary to flight,                              | 115  |
| How balancing is effected in flight,                                                 | 118  |
| Rapidity of wing movements partly accounted for,                                     | 120  |
| The wing area variable and in excess,                                                | 124  |
| The wing area decreases as the size and weight of the volant animal increases,       | 132  |
| Wings, their form, etc.  All wings screws, structurally and functionally,            | 136  |
| The wing, during its action, reverses its planes, and describes a figure-of-8 track in space, | 140  |
| The wing, when advancing with the body, describes a looped and waved track,          | 143  |
| The margins of the wing, thrown into opposite curves during extension and flexion,   | 146  |
| The tip of the bat and bird's wing describes an ellipse,                             | 147  |
| The wing capable of change of form in all its parts,                                 | 147  |
| The wing during its vibration produces a cross pulsation,                            | 148  |
| Compound rotation of the wing,                                                       | 149  |
| The wing vibrates unequally with reference to a given line,                          | 150  |
| Points wherein the screws formed by the wings differ from those in common use,       | 151  |

viii CONTENTS.

PAGE

The wing at all times thoroughly under control, . . 154
The natural wing when elevated and depressed must move forwards, . . . . . . . 150
The wing ascends when the body descends, and vice versâ, . 159
The wing acts upon yielding fulcra, . . . . 165
The wing acts as a true kite both during the down and up strokes, . . . . . . . 165
Where the kite formed by the wing differs from the boy's kite, 166
The angles formed by the wing during its vibrations, . . 167
The body and wings move in opposite curves, . . . 168


THE WINGS OF INSECTS, BATS, AND BIRDS.

Elytra or wing cases and membranous wings; their shape and uses, . . . . . . . . 170


THE WINGS OF BATS.

The bones of the wing of the bat; the spiral configuration of their articular surfaces, . . . . . 176


THE WINGS OF BIRDS.

The bones of the wing of the bird; their articular surfaces, movements, etc., . . . . . . 178
Traces of design in the wing of the bird; the arrangement of the primary, secondary, and tertiary feathers, etc., . 180
The wing of the bird not always opened up to the same extent in the up stroke, . . . . . . 182
Flexion of the wing necessary to the flight of birds, . 183
Consideration of the forces which propel the wings of insects, . 186
Speed attained by insects, . . . . . 188
Consideration of the forces which propel the wings of bats and birds, . . . . . . . 189
Lax condition of the shoulder-joint in bats and birds, 190
The wing flexed and partly elevated by the action of elastic ligaments; the nature and position of said ligaments in the Pheasant, Snipe, Crested Crane, Swan, etc., . 191

The elastic ligaments more highly differentiated in wings which vibrate rapidly, . . . . . 193
Power of the wing, to what owing, . . . 194
Reasons why the effective stroke should be delivered downwards and forwards, . . . . . 195
The wing acts as an elevator, propeller, and sustainer, both during extension and flexion, . . 197
Flight divisible into four kinds, . . . . 197
The flight of the Albatross compared to the movements of a compass set upon gimbals, . . . 199
The regular and irregular in flight, . . . 201
Mode of ascending, descending, turning, etc., . 201
The flight of birds referable to muscular exertion and weight, 204
Lifting capacity of birds, . . . . . 205

# AËRONAUTICS.

The balloon, . . . . . . . 210
The inclined plane, . . . . 211
The aërial screw, . . . . . 215
Artificial wings (Borelli's views), . . . 219
Marey's views, . . . . . . 226
Chabrier's views, . . . . . 233
Straus-Durckheim's views, . . . . 233
The Author's views; his method of constructing and applying artificial wings, as contra-distinguished from that of Borelli, Chabrier, Durckheim, and Marey, . . 235
The wave wing of the Author, . . . 236
How to construct an artificial wave wing on the insect type, 240
How to construct a wave wing which shall evade the superimposed air during the up stroke, . . 241
Compound wave wing of the Author, . . 242
How to apply artificial wings to the air, . . 245
As to the nature of the forces required for propelling artificial wings, . . . . . . 246

PAGE

Necessity for supplying the roots of artificial wings with elastic
    structures in imitation of the muscles and elastic ligaments
    of flying animals, . . . . . .    247
The artificial wave wing can be driven at any speed—it can
    make its own currents or utilize existing ones, . .    251
Compound rotation of the artificial wave wing. The different
    parts of the wing travel at different speeds, . .    252
How the wave wing creates currents and rises upon them, and
    how the air assists in elevating the wing, . .    253
The artificial wing propelled at various degrees of speed during
    the down and up strokes, . . . . .    255
The artificial wave wing as a propeller, . . .    256
A new form of aërial screw, . . . . .    256
The aërial wave screw operates upon water, . . .    257
The sculling action of the wing, . . . .    231

Concluding Remarks, . .    258

# LIST OF ILLUSTRATIONS.

The Engravings are, with few exceptions, from Photographs, Drawings, and Designs by Mr. Charles Borjeau and the Author. Such as are not original are duly acknowledged.

PAGE

FRONTISPIECE.

In the clutch of the enemy—(*The Graphic*).

The three orders of lever—(*Bishop*), . . . . 19, 20

The skeleton of a Deer—(*Pander and D'Alton*), . . 21

Muscular cycle in the act of flexing the arm, . . . 25

Screws formed by the bones of the wing of the bird, the bones of
    the anterior extremity of the Elephant, and the cast of the
    interior of the left ventricle of the heart, . . . 28

The muscular system of the Horse—(*Bagg*), . . . 30

The feet of the Deer, Ornithorhynchus, Otter, Frog, and Seal, . 34

The Red-throated Dragon, . . . . . 35

The Flying Lemur, . . . . . . 35

The Bat, . . . . . . . 36

Chillingham Bull with extremities describing figure-of-8 move-
    ments, . . . . . . . 37

Double waved tracks described by Man in walking, . . 39

Horse in the act of trotting, . . . . . 41

Footprints of the Horse in the walk, trot, and gallop—(*Gamgee*), 43

Skeleton of the Ostrich—(*Dallas*), . . . . 47

Ostriches pursued by a hunter, . . . . 48

Skeleton of Man, . . . . . . 55

The positions assumed by the extremities and feet in walking,
    —(*Weber*) . . . . . . . 59

Preparing to run—(*Flaxman*), . . . . . 62

The skeleton of a Perch—(*Dallas*), . . . . 65

The Salmon swimming leisurely, . . . . 65

Swimming of the fish according to Borelli, . . . 67

Swimming of the fish according to the Author, . . 68

                                                                          PAGE
The Porpoise and Manatee,    .        .        .        .        .    73
The skeleton of the Dugong—(Dallas),          .        .        .    74
The Seal,      .        .        .        .        .        .        .    74
The Sea-Bear,  .        .        .        .        .        .        .    76
The elliptical, looped, and spiral tracks made in swimming,    .    81
The several attitudes assumed by the extremities in swimming
        in the prone position,    .        .        .        .        .    82
Overhand swimming,    .        .        .        .        .        .    85
Side swimming,          .        .        .        .        .        .    89
Swimming of the Turtle and Triton,    .        .        .        .    89
Swimming of the Little Penguin,        .        .        .        .    91
Sub-aquatic flight or diving,    .        .        .        .        .    94
The feet of the Swan as seen in the open and closed condition,    96
The foot of the Grebe with swimming membrane—(Dallas),    .    97
Double waved track described by the feet of swimming birds, .    97
The flight of the Flying-fish,    .        .        .        .        .    98
The wing a lever of the third order,    .        .        .        .   105
Figure-of-8 vertical track made by the wing in flight,    .        .   107
        Do.       horizontal track,    .        .        .        .   108
Feathers and cork flying forward,        .        .        .        .   112
Diagram illustrating how wings obtain their high speed,        .   120
Butterfly with large wings,    .        .        .        .        .   124
Beetle with small wings,        .        .        .        .        .   125
Partridge with small wings; Heron with large wings,        .   126
The wings of the Hawk and Albatross,        .        .   136, 137
The Green Plover with one wing flexed and the other extended,   138
Blur or impression produced on the eye by the rapidly oscillat-
        ing wing of the insect,    .        .        .        .        .   139
Diagram in which the down and up strokes of the wing of the
        insect are analysed,    .        .        .        .        .   141
Diagrams illustrating the looped and waved tracks described
        by the wing of the insect, bat, and bird,    .        .   144
Figures showing the positions assumed by the wing of the bird
        during the up and down strokes (side view),        .   145
The positions assumed by the wing of the insect as it hastens
        to and fro and describes a figure-of-8 track,        .   141
The figure-of-8 curves made by the wing of the bird in flexion
        and extension,    .        .        .        .        .        .   147
The long and short axes of the wing,    .        .        .        .   149
The waved tracks described by the wing and body of the bird
        as they alternately rise and fall,    .        .        .   157, 163

PAGE

The positions assumed by the wing of the bird during the
down and up strokes (front view), . . . 158
Analysis of the movements of the wing, . . 160, 161
The kite-like action and waved movements of the wing, . 166
The Centaur Beetle and Water Bug, . . . . 171
The Dragon Fly, . . . . . . 172
The screws formed by the wing of the insect, bat, and bird, 174, 175, 176
The muscles, elastic ligaments, and feathers of the wing of the
bird, . . . . . . . 181
The flight of the King-fisher, . . . . . 183
The flight of the Gull, . . . . . 180
The flight of the Owl, . . . . . 198
The flight of the Albatross, . . . . 200
Pigeon and Duck alighting, . . . 203, 204
Hawk and quarry—(*The Graphic*), . . . 206
The Vauxhall Balloon of Mr. Green, . . . 208
Mr. Henson's Flying Machine, . . . . 212
Mr. Stringfellow's Flying Machine, . . . 213
Sir George Cayley's Flying Apparatus, . . . 215
Flying Machine designed by De la Landelle, . . 217
Borelli's Artificial Bird, . . . . 220
Diagrams illustrating the true and false action of the wing, . 228
The sculling action of the wing as seen in the bird, . 231
The artificial wave wing of the Author, . . 237
    Do.    do.    with driving apparatus, . . 239
Various forms of artificial wings by the Author, . . 241
The compound wave wing of the Author, . . 243
Diagrams illustrative of artificial wing movements, . 250
Diagram illustrating the currents produced by the movements
of artificial wings, . . . . . 253
The aërial wave screw of the Author, . . . 256
Swallow in pursuit of insects, . . . . 260

# ANIMAL LOCOMOTION.

IN THE CLUTCH OF THE ENEMY.

Engraved by

# ANIMAL LOCOMOTION.

## INTRODUCTION.

THE locomotion of animals, as exemplified in walking swimming, and flying, is a subject of permanent interest to all who seek to trace in the creature proofs of beneficence and design in the Creator. All animals, however insignificant, have a mission to perform—a destiny to fulfil; and their manner of doing it cannot be a matter of indifference, even to a careless observer. The most exquisite form loses much of its grace if bereft of motion, and the most ungainly animal conceals its want of symmetry in the co-adaptation and exercise of its several parts. The rigidity and stillness of death alone are unnatural. So long as things "live, move, and have a being," they are agreeable objects in the landscape. They are part and parcel of the great problem of life, and as we are all hastening towards a common goal, it is but natural we should take an interest in the movements of our fellow-travellers. As the locomotion of animals is intimately associated with their habits and modes of life, a wide field is opened up, teeming with incident, instruction, and amusement. No one can see a bee steering its course with admirable precision from flower to flower in search of nectar ; or a swallow darting like a flash of light along the lanes in pursuit of insects ; or a wolf panting in breathless haste after a deer ; or a dolphin rolling like a mill-wheel after a shoal of flying fish, without feeling his interest keenly awakened.

A

Nor is this love of motion confined to the animal kingdom.
We admire a cataract more than a canal; the sea is grander
in a hurricane than in a calm ; and the fleecy clouds which
constantly flit overhead are more agreeable to the eye than
a horizon of tranquil blue, however deep and beautiful.   We
never tire of sunshine and shadow when together : we readily
tire of either by itself.   Inorganic changes and movements
are scarcely less interesting than organic ones.   The disaffected
growl of the thunder, and the ghastly lightning flash, scorching
and withering whatever it touches, forcibly remind us that
everything above, below, and around is in motion.    Of absolute rest, as Mr. Grove eloquently puts it, nature gives us
no evidence.   All matter, whether living or dead, whether
solid, liquid, or gaseous, is constantly changing form : in other
words, is constantly moving.   It is well it is so ; for those
incessant changes in inorganic matter and living organisms
introduce that fascinating variety which palls not upon the
eye, the ear, the touch, the taste, or the smell.   If an absolute
repose everywhere prevailed, and plants and animals ceased to
grow ; if day ceased to alternate with night and the fountains
were dried up or frozen; if the shadows refused to creep, the air
and rocks to reverberate, the clouds to drift, and the great race
of created beings to move, the world would be no fitting habi-
tation for man.   In change he finds his present solace and
future hope.   The great panorama of life is interesting because it moves.   One change involves another, and everything which co-exists, co-depends.   This co-existence and
inter-dependence causes us not only to study ourselves, but
everything around us.   By discovering natural laws we are
permitted in God's good providence to harness and yoke
natural powers, and already the giant Steam drags along at
incredible speed the rumbling car and swiftly gliding boat ;
the quadruped has been literally outraced on the land, and the
fish in the sea ; each has been, so to speak, beaten in its own
domain.   That the tramway of the air may and will be traversed by man's ingenuity at some period or other, is, reasoning
from analogy and the nature of things, equally certain.   If
there were no flying things—if there were no insects, bats,
or birds as models, artificial flight (such are the difficulties

attending its realization) might well be regarded an impossibility. As, however, the flying creatures are legion, both as regards number, size, and pattern, and as the bodies of all are not only manifestly heavier than the air, but are composed of hard and soft parts, similar in all respects to those composing the bodies of the other members of the animal kingdom, we are challenged to imitate the movements of the insect, bat, and bird in the air, as we have already imitated the movements of the quadruped on the land and the fish in the water. We have made two successful steps, and have only to make a third to complete that wonderfully perfect and very comprehensive system of locomotion which we behold in nature. Until this third step is taken, our artificial appliances for transit can only be considered imperfect and partial. Those authors who regard artificial flight as impracticable sagely remark that the land supports the quadruped and the water the fish. This is quite true, but it is equally true that the air supports the bird, and that the evolutions of the bird on the wing are quite as safe and infinitely more rapid and beautiful than the movements of either the quadruped on the land or the fish in the water. What, in fact, secures the position of the quadruped on the land, the fish in the water, and the bird in the air, is the life; and by this I mean that prime moving or self-governing power which co-ordinates the movements of the *travelling surfaces* (whether feet, fins, or wings) of all animals, and adapts them to the medium on which they are destined to operate, whether this be the comparatively unyielding earth, the mobile water, or the still more mobile air. Take away this life suddenly —the quadruped falls downwards, the fish (if it be not specially provided with a swimming bladder) sinks, and the bird gravitates of necessity. There is a sudden subsiding and cessation of motion in either case, but the quadruped and fish have no advantage over the bird in this respect. The *savans* who oppose this view exclaim not unnaturally that there is no great difficulty in propelling a machine either along the land or the water, seeing that both these media support it. There is, I admit, no great difficulty now, but there were apparently insuperable difficulties before the locomotive and steam-boat were invented. *Weight,* moreover, instead of being a barrier to

artificial flight is absolutely necessary to it.   This statement
is quite opposed to the commonly received opinion, but is
nevertheless true.   No bird is lighter than the air, and no
machine constructed to navigate it should aim at being specifically lighter.   What is wanted is a reasonable but not cumbrous
amount of weight, and a duplicate (in principle if not in practice) of those structures and movements which enable insects,
bats, and birds to fly.   Until the structure and uses of wings
are understood, the way of " an eagle in the air " must of necessity remain a mystery.   The subject of flight has never,
until quite recently, been investigated systematically or
rationally, and, as a result, very little is known of the laws
which regulate it.   If these laws were understood, and we
were in possession of trustworthy data for our guidance in
devising artificial pinions, the formidable Gordian knot of
flight, there is reason to believe, could be readily untied.

That artificial flight is a possible thing is proved beyond
doubt—1st, by the fact that flight is a natural movement;
and 2d, because the natural movements of walking and swimming have already been successfully imitated.

The very obvious bearing which natural movements have
upon artificial ones, and the relation which exists between
organic and inorganic movements, invest our subject with a
peculiar interest.

It is the blending of natural and artificial progression in
theory and practice which gives to the one and the other its
chief charm.   The history of artificial progression is essentially that of natural progression.   The same laws regulate
and determine both.   The wheel of the locomotive and the
screw of the steam-ship apparently greatly differ from the
limb of the quadruped, the fin of the fish, and the wing of
the bird; but, as I shall show in the sequel, the curves which
go to form the wheel and the screw are found in the travelling
surfaces of all animals, whether they be limbs (furnished with
feet), or fins, or wings.

It is a remarkable circumstance that the undulation or
wave made by the wing of an insect, bat, or bird, when those
animals are fixed or hovering before an object, and when they
are flying, corresponds in a marked manner with the track

described by the stationary and progressive waves in fluids, and likewise with the waves of sound. This coincidence would seem to argue an intimate relation between the instrument and the medium on which it is destined to operate—the wing acting in those very curves into which the atmosphere is naturally thrown in the transmission of sound. Can it be that the animate and inanimate world reciprocate, and that animal bodies are made to impress the inanimate in precisely the same manner as the inanimate impress each other? This much seems certain :—The wind communicates to the water similar impulses to those communicated to it by the fish in swimming; and the wing in its vibrations impinges upon the air as an ordinary sound does. The extremities of quadrupeds, moreover, describe waved tracks on the land when walking and running; so that one great law apparently determines the course of the insect in the air, the fish in the water, and the quadruped on the land.

We are, unfortunately, not taught to regard the travelling surfaces and movements of animals as correlated in any way to surrounding media, and, as a consequence, are apt to consider walking as distinct from swimming, and walking and swimming as distinct from flying, than which there can be no greater mistake. Walking, swimming, and flying are in reality only modifications of each other. Walking merges into swimming, and swimming into flying, by insensible gradations. The modifications which result in walking, swimming, and flying are necessitated by the fact that the earth affords a greater amount of support than the water, and the water than the air.

That walking, swimming, and flying represent integral parts of the same problem is proved by the fact that most quadrupeds swim as well as walk, and some even fly; while many marine animals walk as well as swim, and birds and insects walk, swim, and fly indiscriminately. When the land animals, properly so called, are in the habit of taking to the water or the air; or the inhabitants of the water are constantly taking to the land or the air; or the insects and birds which are more peculiarly organized for flight, spend much of their time on the land and in the water; their organs of locomotion must possess those peculiarities of structure which characterize, as a class, those animals which live on the land, in the water, or in the air respectively.

In this we have an explanation of the gossamer wing of the insect,—the curiously modified hand of the bat and bird, —the webbed hands and feet of the Otter, Ornithorhynchus, Seal, and Walrus,—the expanded tail of the Whale, Porpoise, Dugong, and Manatee,—the feet of the Ostrich, Apteryx, and Dodo, exclusively designed for running,—the feet of the Ducks, Gulls, and Petrels, specially adapted for swimming,— and the wings and feet of the Penguins, Auks, and Guillemots, especially designed for diving. Other and intermediate modifications occur in the Flying-fish, Flying Lizard, and Flying Squirrel; and some animals, as the Frog, Newt, and several of the aquatic insects (the Ephemera or May-fly for example[1]) which begin their career by swimming, come ultimately to walk, leap, and even fly.[2]

Every degree and variety of motion, which is peculiar to the land, and to the water- and air-navigating animals as such, is imitated by others which take to the elements in question secondarily or at intervals.

Of all animal movements, flight is indisputably the finest. It may be regarded as the poetry of motion. The fact that a creature as heavy, bulk for bulk, as many solid substances, can by the unaided movements of its wings urge itself through

[1] The Ephemera in the larva and pupa state reside in the water concealed during the day under stones or in horizontal burrows which they form in the banks. Although resembling the perfect insect in several respects, they differ materially in having longer antennæ, in wanting ocelli, and in possessing horn-like mandibles; the abdomen has, moreover, on each side a row of plates, mostly in pairs, which are a kind of false branchiæ, and which are employed not only in respiration, *but also as paddles.*—Cuvier's Animal Kingdom, p. 576. London, 1840.

[2] Kirby and Spence observe that some insects which are not naturally aquatic, do, nevertheless, swim very well if they fall into the water. They instance a kind of grasshopper (*Acrydium*), which can paddle itself across a stream with great rapidity by the powerful strokes of its hind legs.—(Introduction to Entomology, 5th edit., 1828, p. 360.) Nor should the remarkable discovery by Sir John Lubbock of a swimming insect (*Polynema natans*), which uses its wings *exclusively as fins*, be overlooked.—Linn. Trans. vol. xxiv. p. 135.

the air with a speed little short of a cannon-ball, fills the
mind with wonder. Flight (if I may be allowed the expression) is a more unstable movement than that of walking
and swimming; the instability increasing as the medium to
be traversed becomes less dense. It, however, does not
essentially differ from the other two, and I shall be able to
show in the following pages, that the materials and forces
employed in flight are literally the same as those employed
in walking and swimming. This is an encouraging circumstance as far as artificial flight is concerned, as the same elements and forces employed in constructing locomotives and
steamboats may, and probably will at no distant period,
be successfully employed in constructing flying machines.
Flight is a purely mechanical problem. It is warped in and
out with the other animal movements, and forms a link of a
great chain of motion which drags its weary length over the
land, through the water, and, notwithstanding its weight,
through the air. To understand flight, it is necessary to
understand walking and swimming, and it is with a view to
simplifying our conceptions of this most delightful form of
locomotion that the present work is mainly written. The
chapters on walking and swimming naturally lead up to those
on flying.

In the animal kingdom the movements are adapted either
to the land, the water, or the air; these constituting the three
great highways of nature. As a result, the instruments by
which locomotion is effected are specially modified. This is
necessary because of the different densities and the different
degrees of resistance furnished by the land, water, and air
respectively. On the land the extremities of animals encounter the *maximum* of *resistance*, and occasion the *minimum*
of *displacement*. In the air, the pinions experience the *minimum* of *resistance*, and effect the *maximum* of *displacement*; the
water being intermediate both as regards the degree of
resistance offered and the amount of displacement produced.
The speed of an animal is determined by its shape, mass,
power, and the density of the medium on or in which it
moves. It is more difficult to walk on sand or snow than on
a macadamized road. In like manner (unless the travelling

surfaces are specially modified), it is more troublesome to
swim than to walk, and to fly than to swim.   This arises from
the displacement produced, and the consequent want of support.   The land supplies the fulcrum for the levers formed
by the extremities or travelling surfaces of animals with
terrestrial habits; the water furnishes the fulcrum for the
levers formed by the tail and fins of fishes, sea mammals,
etc.; and the air the fulcrum for the levers formed by the
wings of insects, bats, and birds.   The fulcrum supplied by
the land is immovable; that supplied by the water and air
movable.   The mobility and immobility of the fulcrum constitute the principal difference between walking, swimming,
and flying; the travelling surfaces of animals increasing in
size as the medium to be traversed becomes less dense and
the fulcrum more movable.   Thus terrestrial animals have
smaller travelling surfaces than amphibia, amphibia than fishes,
and fishes than insects, bats, and birds.   Another point to be
studied in connexion with unyielding and yielding fulcra, is
the resistance offered to forward motion.   A land animal is
supported by the earth, and experiences little resistance from
the air through which it moves, unless the speed attained is
high.   Its principal friction is that occasioned by the contact
of its travelling surfaces with the earth.   If these are few, the
speed is generally great, as in quadrupeds.   A fish, or sea mammal, is of nearly the same specific gravity as the water it in-
habits; in other words, it is supported with as little or less effort
than a land animal.   As, however, the fluid in which it moves
is more dense than air, the resistance it experiences in forward
motion is greater than that experienced by land animals, and
by insects, bats, and birds.   As a consequence fishes are for
the most part elliptical in shape; this being the form calculated to cleave the water with the greatest ease.   A flying
animal is immensely heavier than the air.   The support
which it receives, and the resistance experienced by it
in forward motion, are reduced to a minimum.   Flight,
because of the rarity of the air, is infinitely more rapid than
either walking, running, or swimming.   The flying animal
receives support from the air by increasing the size of its
travelling surfaces, which act after the manner of twisted

inclined planes or kites. When an insect, a bat, or a bird
is launched in space, its weight (from the tendency of all
bodies to fall vertically downwards) presses upon the inclined
planes or kites formed by the wings in such a manner as
to become converted directly into a *propelling*, and indirectly
into a *buoying* or supporting power. This can be proved by
experiment, as I shall show subsequently. But for the share
which the weight or mass of the flying creature takes in flight,
the protracted journeys of birds of passage would be impossible. Some authorities are of opinion that birds even sleep
upon the wing. Certain it is that the albatross, that prince
of the feathered tribe, can sail about for a whole hour without
once flapping his pinions. This can only be done in virtue
of the weight of the bird acting upon the inclined planes or
kites formed by the wings as stated.

The weight of the body plays an important part in walking
and swimming, as well as in flying. A biped which advances
by steps and not by leaps may be said to roll over its extremities,[1] the foot of the extremity which happens to be upon
the ground for the time forming the centre of a circle, the
radius of which is described by the trunk in forward motion.
In like manner the foot which is off the ground and swinging
forward pendulum fashion in space, may be said to roll or
rotate upon the trunk, the head of the femur forming the
centre of a circle the radius of which is described by the advancing foot. A double rolling movement is thus established,
the body rolling on the extremity the one instant, the extremity rolling on the trunk the next. During these movements
the body rises and falls. The double rolling movement is
necessary not only to the progression of bipeds, but also to
that of quadrupeds. As the body cannot advance without
the extremities, so the extremities cannot advance without
the body. The double rolling movement is necessary to continuity of motion. If there was only one movement there
would be dead points or halts in walking and running, similar
to what occur in leaping. The continuity of movement necessary to progression in some bipeds (man for instance) is fur-

[1] This is also true of quadrupeds. It is the posterior part of the foot
which is set down first.

ther secured by a pendulum movement in the arms as well as
in the legs, the right arm swinging before the body when the
right leg swings behind it, and the converse. The right leg
and left arm advance simultaneously, and alternate with the
left leg and right arm, which likewise advance together. This
gives rise to a double twisting of the body at the shoulders
and loins. The legs and arms when advancing move in
curves, the convexities of the curves made by the right leg
and left arm, which advance together when a step is being
made, being directed outwards, and forming, when placed
together, a more or less symmetrical ellipse. If the curves
formed by the legs and arms respectively be united, they
form waved lines which intersect at every step. This arises
from the fact that the curves formed by the right and left
legs are found alternately on either side of a given line, the
same holding true of the right and left arms. Walking is
consequently to be regarded as the result of a twisting diagonal
movement in the trunk and in the extremities. Without this
movement, the momentum acquired by the different portions
of the moving mass could not be utilized. As the momentum
acquired by animals in walking, swimming, and flying forms
an important factor in those movements, it is necessary that
we should have a just conception of the value to be attached
to weight when in motion. In the horse when walking, the
stride is something like five feet, in trotting ten feet, but in
galloping eighteen or more feet. The stride is in fact determined by the speed acquired by the mass of the body of the
horse; the momentum at which the mass is moving carrying the limbs forward.[1]

In the swimming of the fish, the body is thrown into double
or figure-of-8 curves, as in the walking of the biped. The twisting of the body, and the continuity of movement which that
twisting begets, reappear. The curves formed in the swimming

---

[1] " According to Salnbell, the celebrated horse Eclipse, when galloping at
liberty, and with its greatest speed, passed over the space of twenty-five feet
at each stride, which he repeated 2½ times in a second, being nearly four
miles in six minutes and two seconds. The race-horse Flying Childers was
computed to have passed over eighty-two feet and a half in a second, or nearly
a mile in a minute."

of the fish are never less than two, a caudal and a cephalic one. They may and do exceed this number in the long-bodied fishes. The tail of the fish is made to vibrate pendulum fashion on either side of the spine, when it is lashed to and fro in the act of swimming. It is made to rotate upon one or more of the vertebræ of the spine, the vertebra or vertebræ forming the centre of a lemniscate, which is described by the caudal fin. There is, therefore, an obvious analogy between the tail of the fish and the extremity of the biped. This is proved by the conformation and swimming of the seal,—an animal in which the posterior extremities are modified to resemble the tail of the fish. In the swimming of the seal the hind legs are applied to the water by a sculling figure-of-8 motion, in the same manner as the tail of the fish. Similar remarks might be made with regard to the swimming of the whale, dugong, manatee, and porpoise, sea mammals, which still more closely resemble the fish in shape. The double curve into which the fish throws its body in swimming, and which gives continuity of motion, also supplies the requisite degree of steadiness. When the tail is lashed from side to side there is a tendency to produce a corresponding movement in the head, which is at once corrected by the complementary curve. Nor is this all; the cephalic curve, in conjunction with the water contained within it, forms the *point d'appui* for the caudal curve, and *vice versa*. When a fish swims, the anterior and posterior portions of its body (supposing it to be a short-bodied fish) form curves, the convexities of which are directed on opposite sides of a given line, as is the case in the extremities of the biped when walking. The mass of the fish, like the mass of the biped, when once set in motion, contributes to progression by augmenting the rate of speed. The velocity acquired by certain fishes is very great. A shark can gambol around the bows of a ship in full sail; and a sword-fish (such is the momentum acquired by it) has been known to thrust its tusk through the copper sheathing of a vessel, a layer of felt, four inches of deal, and fourteen inches of oaken plank.[1]

The wing of the bird does not materially differ from the

[1] A portion of the timbers, etc., of one of Her Majesty's ships, having the

extremity of the biped or the tail of the fish. It is constructed on a similar plan, and acts on the same principle. The tail of the fish, the wing of the bird, and the extremity of the biped and quadruped, are screws structurally and functionally. In proof of this, compare the bones of the wing of a bird with the bones of the arm of a man, or those of the fore-leg of an elephant, or any other quadruped. In either case the bones are twisted upon themselves like the screw of an augur. The tail of the fish, the extremities of the biped and quadruped, and the wing of the bird, when moving, describe waved tracks. Thus the wing of the bird, when it is made to oscillate, is thrown into double or figure-of-8 curves, like the body of the fish. When, moreover, the wing ascends and descends to make the up and down strokes, it rotates within the *facettes* or depressions situated on the scapula and coracoid bones, precisely in the same way that the arm of a man rotates in the glenoid cavity, or the leg in the acetabular cavity in the act of walking. The ascent and descent of the wing in flying correspond to the steps made by the extremities in walking; the wing rotating upon the body of the bird during the down stroke, the body of the bird rotating on the wing during the up stroke. When the wing descends it describes a downward and forward curve, and elevates the body in an upward and forward curve. When the body descends, it describes a downward and forward curve, the wing being elevated in an upward and forward curve. The curves made by the wing and body in flight form, when united, waved lines, which intersect each other at every beat of the wing. The wing and the body act upon each other alternately (the one being active when the other is passive), and the descent of the wing is not more necessary to the elevation of the body than the descent of the body is to the elevation of the wing. It is thus that the weight of the flying animal is utilized, slip avoided, and continuity of movement secured.

As to the actual waste of tissue involved in walking, swimming, and flying, there is much discrepancy of opinion. It is

tusk of a sword-fish imbedded in it, is to be seen in the Hunterian Museum of the Royal College of Surgeons of England.

commonly believed that a bird exerts quite an enormous amount of power as compared with a fish ; a fish exerting a much greater power than a land animal. This, there can be no doubt, is a popular delusion. A bird can fly for a whole day, a fish can swim for a whole day, and a man can walk for a whole day. If so, the bird requires no greater power than the fish, and the fish than the man. The speed of the bird as compared with that of the fish, or the speed of the fish as compared with that of the man, is no criterion of the power exerted. The speed is only partly traceable to the power. As has just been stated, it is due in a principal measure to the shape and size of the travelling surfaces, the density of the medium traversed, the resistance experienced to forward motion, and the part performed by the mass of the animal, when moving and acting upon its travelling surfaces. It is erroneous to suppose that a bird is stronger, weight for weight, than a fish, or a fish than a man. It is equally erroneous to assume that the exertions of a flying animal are herculean as compared with those of a walking or swimming animal. Observation and experiment incline me to believe just the opposite. A flying creature, when fairly launched in space (because of the part which weight plays in flight, and the little resistance experienced in forward motion), sweeps through the air with almost no exertion.[1] This is proved by the sailing flight of the albatross, and by the fact that some insects can fly when two-thirds of their wing area have been removed. (This experiment is detailed further on.) These observations are calculated to show the grave necessity for studying the media to be traversed ; the fulcra which the media furnish, and the size, shape, and movements of the travelling surfaces. The travelling surfaces of animals, as has been already explained, furnish the levers by whose instrumentality the movements of walking, swimming, and flying are effected.

---

[1] A flying creature exerts its greatest power when rising. The effort is of short duration, and inaugurates rather than perpetuates flight. If the volant animal can launch into space from a height, the preliminary effort may be dispensed with as in this case, the weight of the animal acting upon the inclined planes formed by the wings gets up the initial velocity.

By comparing the flipper of the seal, sea-bear, and walrus with the fin and tail of the fish, whale, porpoise, etc.; and the wing of the penguin (a bird which is incapable of flight, and can only swim and dive) with the wing of the insect, bat, and bird, I have been able to show that a close analogy exists between the flippers, fins, and tails of sea mammals and fishes on the one hand, and the wings of insects, bats, and birds on the other; in fact, that theoretically and practically these organs, one and all, form flexible helices or screws, which, in virtue of their rapid reciprocating movements, operate upon the water and air by a wedge-action after the manner of twisted or double inclined planes.  The twisted inclined planes act upon the air and water by means of curved surfaces, the curved surfaces reversing, reciprocating, and engendering a wave pressure, which can be continued indefinitely at the will of the animal.  The wave pressure emanates in the one instance mainly from the tail of the fish, whale, porpoise, etc., and in the other from the wing of the insect, bat, or bird—*the reciprocating and opposite curves* into which the tail and wing are thrown in swimming and flying constituting *the mobile helices, or screws*, which, during their action, produce the precise kind and degree of pressure adapted to fluid media, and to which they respond with the greatest readiness.

In order to prove that sea mammals and fishes swim, and insects, bats, and birds fly, by the aid of curved figure-of-8 surfaces, which exert an intermittent wave pressure, I con structed artificial fish-tails, fins, flippers, and wings, which curve and taper in every direction, and which are flexible and elastic, particularly towards the tips and posterior margins.  These artificial fish-tails, fins, flippers, and wings are slightly twisted upon themselves, and when applied to the water and air by a sculling or figure-of-8 motion, curiously enough reproduce the curved surfaces and movements peculiar to real fish-tails, fins, flippers, and wings, in swimming, and flying.

Propellers formed on the fish-tail and wing model are, I find, the most effective that can be devised, whether for navigating the water or the air.  To operate efficiently on fluid, *i.e.* yielding media, the propeller itself must yield. Of this I am fully satisfied from observation and experiment. The propellers at present employed in navigation are, in my opinion, faulty both in principle and application.

The observations and experiments recorded in the present volume date from 1864. In 1867 I lectured on the subject of animal mechanics at the Royal Institution of Great Britain :[1] in June of the same year (1867) I read a memoir " On the Mechanism of Flight" to the Linnean Society of London ;[2] and in August of 1870 I communicated a memoir " On the Physiology of Wings" to the Royal Society of Edinburgh.[3] These memoirs extend to 200 pages quarto, and are illustrated by 190 original drawings. The conclusions at which I arrived, after a careful study of the movements of walking, swimming, and flying, are briefly set forth in a letter addressed to the French Academy of Sciences in March 1870. This the Academy did me the honour of publishing in April of that year (1870) in the Comptes Rendus, p. 875. In it I claim to have been the first to describe and illustrate the following points, viz. :—

That quadrupeds walk, and fishes swim, and insects, bats, and birds fly by figure-of-8 movements.

That the flipper of the sea bear, the swimming wing of the penguin, and the wing of the insect, bat, and bird, are screws *structurally*, and resemble the blade of an ordinary screw-propeller.

That those organs are screws *functionally*, from their twisting and untwisting, and from their rotating in the direction of their length, when they are made to oscillate.

That they have a reciprocating action, and reverse their planes more or less completely at every stroke.

That the wing describes *a figure-of-8 track* in space when the flying animal is artificially fixed.

That the wing, when the flying animal is progressing at

[1] " On the various modes of Flight in relation to Aëronautics."—Proceedings of the Royal Institution of Great Britain, March 22, 1867.

[2] " On the Mechanical Appliances by which Flight is attained in the Animal Kingdom."—Transactions of the Linnean Society, vol. xxvi.

[3] " On the Physiology of Wings."—Transactions of the Royal Society of Edinburgh, vol. xxvi.

a high speed in a horizontal direction, describes *a looped* and then *a waved track*, from the fact that the figure of 8 is gradually opened out or unravelled as the animal advances.

That the wing acts after the manner of a kite, both during the down and up strokes.

I was induced to address the above to the French Academy from finding that, nearly two years after I had published my views on the figure of 8, looped and wave movements made by the wing, etc., Professor E. J. Marey (College of France, Paris) published a course of lectures, in which the peculiar figure-of-8 movements, first described and figured by me, were put forth as a new discovery. The accuracy of this statement will be abundantly evident when I mention that my first lecture, "On the various modes of Flight in relation to Aëronautics," was published in the Proceedings of the Royal Institution of Great Britain on the 22d of March 1867, and translated into French (Revue des cours scientifiques de la France et de l'Étranger) on the 21st of September 1867; whereas Professor Marey's first lecture, "On the Movements of the Wing in the Insect" (Revue des cours scientifiques de la France et de l'Étranger), did not appear until the 13th of February 1869.

Professor Marey, in a letter addressed to the French Academy in reply to mine, admits my claim to priority in the following terms :—

"J'ai constaté qu'effectivement M. Pettigrew a vu avant moi, et représenté dans son Mémoire, la forme en 8 du parcours de l'aile de l'insecte : que la méthode optique à laquelle j'avais recours est à peu près identique à la sienne. . . . Je m'empresse de satisfaire à cette demande légitime, et de laisser entièrement la priorité sur moi à M. Pettigrew relativement à la question ainsi restreinte."—(Comptes Rendus, May 16, 1870, p. 1093).

The figure-of-8 theory of walking, swimming, and flying, as originally propounded in the lectures, papers, and memoirs referred to, has been confirmed not only by the researches and experiments of Professor Marey, but also by those of M. Senecal, M. de Fastes, M. Ciotti, and others. Its accuracy is no longer a matter of doubt. As the limits of the present volume will not admit of my going into the several arrangements by which locomotion is attained in the animal kingdom as a whole, I will only describe those movements which illustrate in a progressive manner the several kinds of progression on the land, and on and in the water and air.

I propose first to analyse the natural movements of walking, swimming, and flying, after which I hope to be able to show that certain of these movements may be reproduced artificially. The locomotion of animals depends upon mechanical adaptations found in all animals which change locality. These adaptations are very various, but under whatever guise they appear they are substantially those to which we resort when we wish to move bodies artificially. Thus in animal mechanics we have to consider the various orders of levers, the pulley, the centre of gravity, specific gravity, the resistance of solids, semi-solids, fluids, etc. As the laws which regulate the locomotion of animals are essentially those which regulate the motion of bodies in general, it will be necessary to consider briefly at this stage the properties of matter when at rest and when moving. They are well stated by Mr. Bishop in a series of propositions which I take the liberty of transcribing :—

" *Fundamental Axioms.*—First, every body continues in a state of rest, or of uniform motion in a right line, until a change is effected by the agency of some mechanical force. Secondly, any change effected in the quiescence or motion of a body is in the direction of the force impressed, and is proportional to it in quantity. Thirdly, reaction is always equal and contrary to action, or the mutual actions of two bodies upon each other are always equal and in opposite directions.

*Of uniform motion.*—If a body moves constantly in the same manner, or if it passes over equal spaces in equal periods of time, its motion is uniform. The velocity of a body moving uniformly is measured by the space through which it passes in a given time.

The velocities generated or impressed on different masses by the same force are reciprocally as the masses.

*Motion uniformly varied.*—When the motion of a body is

B

uniformly accelerated, the space it passes through during any time whatever is proportional to the square of the time.

In the leaping, jumping, or springing of animals in any direction (except the vertical), the paths they describe in their transit from one point to another in the plane of motion are parabolic curves.

*The legs move by the force of gravity as a pendulum.*—The Professor, Weber, have ascertained, that when the legs of animals swing forward in progressive motion, they obey the same laws as those which regulate the periodic oscillations of the pendulum.

*Resistance of fluids.*—Animals moving in air and water experience in those media a sensible resistance, which is greater or less in proportion to the density and tenacity of the fluid, and the figure, superficies, and velocity of the animal.

An inquiry into the amount and nature of the resistance of air and water to the progression of animals will also furnish the data for estimating the proportional values of those fluids acting as fulcra to their locomotive organs, whether they be fins, wings, or other forms of lever.

The motions of air and water, and their directions, exercise very important influences over velocity resulting from muscular action.

*Mechanical effects of fluids on animals immersed in them.*—When a body is immersed in any fluid whatever, it will lose as much of its weight relatively as is equal to the weight of the fluid it displaces. In order to ascertain whether an animal will sink or swim, or be sustained without the aid of muscular force, or to estimate the amount of force required that the animal may either sink or float in water, or fly in the air, it will be necessary to have recourse to the specific gravities both of the animal and of the fluid in which it is placed.

The specific gravities or comparative weights of different substances are the respective weights of equal volumes of those substances.

*Centre of gravity.*—The centre of gravity of any body is a point about which, if acted upon only by the force of gravity, it will balance itself in all positions; or, it is a point which, if supported, the body will be supported, however it may be situated in other respects; and hence the effects produced by or upon any body are the same as if its whole mass were collected into its centre of gravity.

The attitudes and motions of every animal are regulated by the positions of their centres of gravity, which, in a state of rest, and not acted upon by extraneous forces, must lie in vertical lines which pass through their basis of support. In most animals moving on solids, the centre is supported by variously adapted organs; during the flight of birds and insects it is suspended; but in fishes, which move in a fluid whose density is nearly equal to their specific gravity, the centre is acted upon equally in all directions." [1]

As the locomotion of the higher animals, to which my remarks more particularly apply, is in all cases effected by levers which differ in no respect from those employed in the arts, it may be useful to allude to them in a passing way. This done, I will consider the bones and joints of the skeleton which form the levers, and the muscles which move them.

" *The Lever.*—Levers are commonly divided into three kinds, according to the relative positions of the prop or fulcrum, the power, and the resistance or weight. The straight lever of each order is equally balanced when the power multiplied by its distance from the fulcrum equals the weight, multiplied by its distance, or P the power, and W the weight, are in equilibrium when they are to each other in the inverse ratio of the arms of the lever, to which they are attached. The pressure on the fulcrum however varies.

Fig. 1.

In straight levers of the *first kind*, the fulcrum is between the power and the resistance, as in fig. 1, where F is the fulcrum of the lever AB; P is the power, and W the weight or resistance. We have P : W : : BF : AF, hence

[1] Cyc. of Anat. and Phy., Art. "Motion," by John Bishop, Esq.

P.AF=W.BF, and the pressure on the fulcrum is both the power and resistance, or P+W.

In the second order of levers (fig. 2), the resistance is between the fulcrum and the power; and, as before, P : W :: DF : AF, but the pressure of the fulcrum is equal to W−P, or the weight less the power.

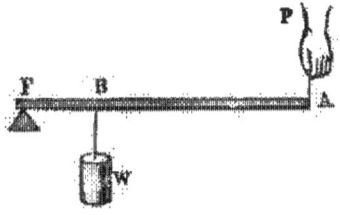

FIG. 2.

In the third order of lever the power acts between the prop and the resistance (fig. 3), where also P : W :: BF : AF, and the pressure on the fulcrum is P−W, or the power less the weight.

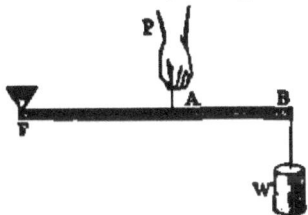

FIG. 3.

In the preceding computations the weight of the lever itself is neglected for the sake of simplicity, but it obviously forms a part of the elements under consideration, especially with reference to the arms and legs of animals.

To include the weight of the lever we have the following equations : $P.AF + \overline{AF}.\frac{1}{2}AF = W.BF + \overline{BF}.\frac{1}{2}BF$; in the first order, where $\overline{AF}$ and $\overline{BF}$ represent the weights of these portions of the lever respectively. Similarly, in the second order $P.AF = W.BF + \overline{AF}.\frac{AF}{2}$, and in the third order $P.AF = W.BF + \overline{BF}.\frac{BF}{2}$.

In this outline of the theory of the lever, the forces have been considered as acting vertically, or parallel to the direction of the force of gravity.

*Passive Organs of Locomotion. Bones.*—The solid frame work or skeleton of animals which supports and protects their more delicate tissues, whether chemically composed of entomoline, carbonate, or phosphate of lime; whether placed internally or externally; or whatever may be its form or dimensions, presents levers and fulcra for the action of the muscular system, in all animals furnished with earthy solids for their support, and possessing locomotive power."[1] The levers and fulcra are well seen in the extremities of the deer, the skeleton of which is selected for its extreme elegance.

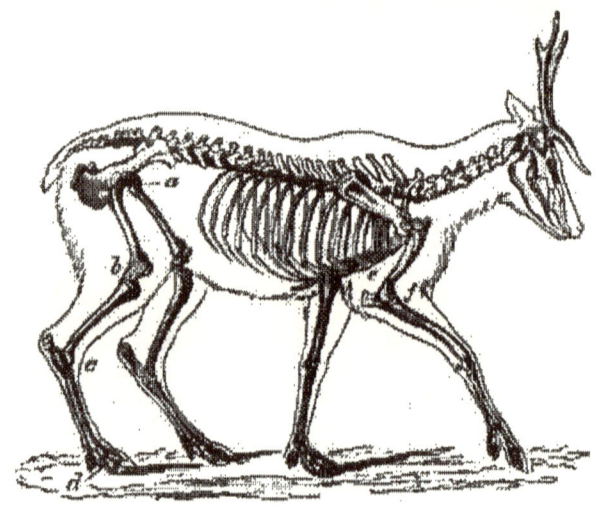

While the bones of animals form levers and fulcra for portions of the muscular system, it must never be forgotten that the earth, water, or air form fulcra for the travelling surfaces of animals as a whole. Two sets of fulcra are therefore always to be considered, viz. those represented by the bones, and those represented by the earth, water, or air respectively. The former when acted upon by the muscles produce motion in different parts of the animal (not necessarily progressive motion); the latter when similarly influenced produce loco-motion. Locomotion is greatly favoured by the tendency which the body once set in motion has to advance in a straight line. The form, strength, density, and elasticity of the skele-ton varies in relation to the bulk and locomotive power of the animal, and to the media in which it is destined to move.

" The number of moveable articulations in a skeleton de-termines the degree of its mobility within itself; and the kind and number of the articulations of the locomotive organs determine the number and disposition of the muscles acting upon them.

The bones of vertebrated animals, especially those which are entirely terrestrial, are much more elastic, hard, and calculated by their chemical elements to bear the shocks and strains incident to terrestrial progression, than those of the aquatic vertebrata; the bones of the latter being more fibrous and spongy in their texture, the skeleton is more soft and yielding.

The bones of the higher orders of animals are constructed according to the most approved mechanical principles. Thus they are convex externally, concave within, and strengthened by ridges running across their discs, as in the scapular and iliac bones; an arrangement which affords large surfaces for the attachment of the powerful muscles of locomotion. The bones of birds in many cases are not filled with marrow but with air,—a circumstance which insures that they shall be very strong and very light.

In the thigh bones of most animals an angle is formed by the head and neck of the bone with the axis of the body, which prevents the weight of the superstructure coming vertically upon the shaft, converts the bone into an elastic arch, and renders it capable of supporting the weight of the body in standing, leaping, and in falling from considerable altitudes.

*Joints.*—Where the limbs are designed to move to and fro simply in one plane, the ginglymoid or hinge-joint is applied; and where more extensive motions of the limbs are requisite, the enarthrodial, or ball-and-socket joint, is introduced. These two kinds of joints predominate in the locomotive organs of the animal kingdom.

The enarthrodial joint has by far the most extensive power of motion, and is therefore selected for uniting the limbs to the trunk. It permits of the several motions of the limbs termed pronation, supination, flexion, extension, abduction, adduction, and revolution upon the axis of the limb or bone about a conical area, whose apex is the axis of the head of the bone, and base circumscribed by the distal extremity of the limb."[1]

The ginglymoid or hinge-joints are for the most part spiral in their nature. They admit in certain cases of a limited degree of lateral rocking. Much attention has been paid to the subject of joints (particularly human ones) by the brothers Weber, Professor Meyer of Zürich, and likewise by Langer, Henke, Meissner, and Goodsir. Langer, Henke, and Meissner succeeded in demonstrating the "screw configuration" of the articular surfaces of the elbow, ankle, and calcaneo-astragaloid joints, and Goodsir showed that the articular surface of the knee-joint consist of "a double conical screw combination." The last-named observer also expressed his belief "that articular combinations with opposite windings on opposite sides of the body, similar to those in the knee-joint, exist in the ankle and tarsal, and in the elbow and carpal joints; and that the hip and shoulder joints consist of single threaded couples, but also with opposite windings on opposite sides of the body." I have succeeded in demonstrating a similar spiral configuration in the several bones and joints of the wing of the bat and bird, and in the extremities of most quadrupeds. The bones of animals, particularly the extremities, are, as a rule, twisted levers, and act after the manner of screws. This arrangement enables the higher

[1] Bishop, *op. cit.*

animals to apply their travelling surfaces to the media on
which they are destined to operate at any degree of obliquity
so as to obtain a maximum of support or propulsion with a
minimum of slip.  If the travelling surfaces of animals did
not form screws structurally and functionally, they could
neither seize nor let go the fulcra on which they act with the
requisite rapidity to secure speed, particularly in water and air.

"*Ligaments.*—The office of the ligaments with respect to
locomotion, is to restrict the degree of flexion, extension, and
other motions of the limbs within definite limits.

*Effect of Atmospheric pressure on Limbs.*—The influence of
atmospheric pressure in supporting the limbs was first noticed
by Dr. Arnott, though it has been erroneously ascribed by
Professor Müller to Weber.  Subsequent experiments made
by Dr. Todd, Mr. Wormald, and others, have fully established
the mechanical influence of the air in keeping the mechanism
of the joints together.  The amount of atmospheric pressure
on any joint depends upon the area or surface presented to
its influence, and the height of the barometer.  According to
Weber, the atmospheric pressure on the hip-joint of a man
is about 26 lbs.  The pressure on the knee-joint is estimated
by Dr. Arnott at 60 lbs."[1]

*Active organs of Locomotion.  Muscles, their Properties, Ar-
rangement, Mode of Action, etc.*—If time and space had permitted, I would have considered it my duty to describe, more
or less fully, the muscular arrangements of all the animals
whose movements I propose to analyse.  This is the more
desirable, as the movements exhibited by animals of the
higher types are directly referable to changes occurring in
their muscular system.  As, however, I could not hope to
overtake this task within the limits prescribed for the present
work, I shall content myself by merely stating the properties
of muscles; the manner in which muscles act; and the manner in which they are grouped, with a view to moving the
osseous levers which constitute the bony framework or skeleton of the animals to be considered.  Hitherto, and by
common consent, it has been believed that whereas a flexor
muscle is situated on one aspect of a limb, and its correspond-

[1] Bishop, *op. cit.*

ing extensor on the other aspect, these two muscles must be opposed to and antagonize each other. This belief is founded on what I regard as an erroneous assumption, viz., that muscles have only the power of shortening, and that when one muscle, say the flexor, shortens, it must drag out and forcibly elongate the corresponding extensor, and the converse. This would be a mere waste of power. Nature never works against herself. There are good grounds for believing, as I have stated elsewhere,[1] that there is no such thing as antagon-

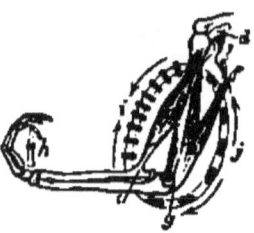

Fig. 5. Shows the muscular system formed by the biceps (a) or flexor muscle, and the triceps (b) or extensor muscle of the human arm. At i the centripetal or shortening action of the biceps is seen, and at j the centrifugal or elongating action of the triceps (vide arrows). The present figure represents the forearm as flexed upon the arm. As a consequence, the long axes of the sarcous elements or ultimate particles of the biceps (i) are arranged in a more or less horizontal direction; the long axes of the sarcous elements of the triceps (j) being arranged in a nearly vertical direction. When the forearm is extended, the long axes of the sarcous elements of the biceps and triceps are reversed. The present figure shows how the bones of the extremities form levers, and how they are moved by muscular action. If, e.g., the biceps (a) shortens and the triceps (b) elongates, they raise the forearm and hand (h) to move towards the shoulder (d). If, on the other hand, the triceps (b) shortens and the biceps (a) elongates, they cause the forearm and hand (h) to move away from the shoulder. In these actions the biceps (a) and triceps (b) are the power; the elbow-joint (g) the fulcrum; and the forearm and hand (h) the weight to be elevated or depressed. If the hand represented a travelling surface which operated on the earth, the water, or the air, it is not difficult to understand how, when it was made to move by the action of the muscles of the arm, it would in turn move the body to which it belonged. d Coracoid process of the scapula, from which the internal or short head of the biceps (a) arises. e Insertion of the biceps into the radius. f Long head of the triceps (b). g Insertion of the triceps into the olecranon process of the ulna.—Original.

ism in muscular movements; the several muscles known as flexors and extensors; abductors and adductors; pronators and supinators, being simply correlated. Muscles, when they

---

[1] "Lectures on the Physiology of the Circulation in Plants, in the Lower Animals, and in Man."—Edinburgh Medical Journal for January and February 1873.

act, operate upon bones or something extraneous to themselves, and not upon each other.  The muscles are folded
round the extremities and trunks of animals with a view to
operating in masses.   For this purpose they are arranged in
cycles, there being what are equivalent to extensor and flexor
cycles, abductor and adductor cycles, and pronator and supinator cycles.  Within these muscular cycles the bones, or
extraneous substances to be moved, are placed, and when one
side of a cycle shortens, the other side elongates.  Muscles
are therefore endowed with a centripetal and centrifugal
action.   These cycles are placed at every degree of obliquity
and even at right angles to each other, but they are so disposed in the bodies and limbs of animals that they always
operate consentaneously and in harmony.  *Vide* fig. 5, p. 25.

There are in animals very few simple movements, *i.e.*
movements occurring in one plane and produced by the action
of two muscles.  Locomotion is for the most part produced
by the consentaneous action of a great number of muscles ;
these or their fibres pursuing a variety of directions.   This is
particularly true of the movements of the extremities in walking, swimming, and flying.

Muscles are divided into the voluntary, the involuntary, and
the mixed, according as the will of the animal can wholly,
partly, or in no way control their movements.   The voluntary
muscles are principally concerned in the locomotion of animals.
They are the power which moves the several orders of levers
into which the skeleton of an animal resolves itself.

The movements of the voluntary and involuntary muscles
are essentially wave-like in character, *i.e.* they spread from
certain centres, according to a fixed order, and in given directions.   In the extremities of animals the centripetal or converging muscular wave on one side of the bone to be moved,
is accompanied by a corresponding centrifugal or diverging
wave on the other side ; the bone or bones by this arrangement
being perfectly under control and moved to a hair's-breadth.
The centripetal or converging, and the centrifugal or diverging
waves of force are, as already indicated, correlated.[1]   Similar
remarks may be made regarding the different parts of the body

[1] Muscles virtually possess a pulling and pushing power; the pushing

of the serpent when creeping, of the body of the fish when swimming, of the wing of the bird when flying, and of our own extremities when walking. In all those cases the moving parts are thrown into curves or waves definitely correlated.

It may be broadly stated, that in every case locomotion is the result of the opening and closing of opposite sides of muscular cycles. By the closing or shortening, say of the flexor halves of the cycles, and the opening or elongation of the extensor halves, the angles formed by the osseous levers are diminished; by the closing or shortening of the extensor halves of the cycles, and the opening or elongation of the flexor halves, the angles formed by the osseous levers are increased. This alternate diminution and increase of the angles formed by the osseous levers produce the movements of walking, swimming, and flying. The muscular cycles of the trunk and extremities are so disposed with regard to the bones or osseous levers, that they in every case produce a maximum result with a minimum of power. The origins and insertions of the muscles, the direction of the muscles and the distribution of the muscular fibres insure, that if power is lost in moving a lever, speed is gained, there being an apparent but never a real loss. The variety and extent of movement is secured by the obliquity of the muscular fibres to their tendons; by the obliquity of the tendons to the bones they are to move; and by the proximity of the attachment of the muscles to the several joints. As muscles are capable of shortening and elongating nearly a fourth of their length, they readily produce the precise kind and degree of motion required in any particular case.[1]

The force of muscles, according to the experiments of Schwann, increases with their length, and *vice versa*. It is a curious circumstance, and worthy the attention of those interested in homologies, that the voluntary muscles of the

power being feeble and obscured by the flaccidity of the muscular mass. In order to push effectually, the pushing substance must be more or less rigid.

[1] The extensor muscles preponderate in mass and weight over the flexors, but this is readily accounted for by the fact, that the extensors, when limbs are to be straightened, always work at a mechanical disadvantage. This is owing to the shape of the bones, the conformation of the joints, and the position occupied by the extensors.

superior and inferior extremities, and more especially of the
trunk, are arranged in longitudinal, transverse, and oblique
spiral lines, and in layers or strata precisely as in the
ventricles of the heart and hollow muscles generally.[1] If,
consequently, I eliminate the element of bone from these
several regions, I reproduce a typical hollow muscle; and
what is still more remarkable, if I compare the bones removed (say the bones of the anterior extremity of a quadruped or bird) with the cast obtained from the cavity of a
hollow muscle (say the left ventricle of the heart of the
mammal), I find that the bones and the cast are twisted
upon themselves, and form elegant screws, the threads or
ridges of which run in the same direction. This affords a
proof that the involuntary hollow muscles supply the type or

Fig. 6.—Wing of bird. Shows how the bones of the arm (a), forearm (b), and
hand (c), are twisted, and form a conical screw. Compare with Figs. 7
and 8.—Original.

Fig. 7.                          Fig. 8.

Fig. 7.—Anterior extremity of elephant. Shows how the bones of the arm (q),
forearm (q's), and foot (o), are twisted to form an osseous screw. Compare
with Figs. 6 and 8.—Original.
Fig. 8.—Cast or mould of the interior of the left ventricle of the heart of a
deer. Shows that the left ventricular cavity is conical and spiral in its
nature. a Portion of right ventricular cavity; b, base of left ventricular
cavity; z, y, spiral grooves occupied by the spiral musculi papillares; fq,
spiral ridges projecting between the musculi papillares. Compare with Figs.
6 and 7.—Original.

pattern on which the voluntary muscles are formed. Fig. 6 represents the bones of the wing of the bird; fig. 7 the bones of the

[1] " On the Arrangement of the Muscular Fibres in the Ventricles of the
Vertebrate Heart, with Physiological Remarks," by the Author.—Philosophical Transactions, 1864.

anterior extremity of the elephant ; and fig. 8 the cast or mould
of the cavity of the left ventricle of the heart of the deer.

It has been the almost invariable custom in teaching
anatomy, and such parts of physiology as pertain to animal
movements, to place much emphasis upon the configuration
of the bony skeleton as a whole, and the conformation of its
several articular surfaces in particular.  This is very natural,
as the osseous system stands the wear and tear of time, while
all around it is in a great measure perishable.  It is the link
which binds extinct forms to living ones, and we naturally
venerate and love what is enduring.  It is no marvel that
Oken, Goethe, Owen, and others should have attempted such
splendid generalizations with regard to the osseous system—
should have proved with such cogency of argument that the
head is an expanded vertebra.  The bony skeleton is a miracle
of design very wonderful and very beautiful in its way.  But
when all has been said, the fact remains that the skeleton,
when it exists, forms only an adjunct of locomotion and
motion generally.  All the really essential movements of an
animal occur in its soft parts.  The osseous system is therefore to be regarded as secondary in importance to the muscular, of which it may be considered a differentiation.  Instead
of regarding the muscles as adapted to the bones, the bones
ought to be regarded as adapted to the muscles.  Bones have
no power either of originating or perpetuating motion.  This
begins and terminates in the muscles.  Nor must it be overlooked, that bone makes its appearance comparatively late in
the scale of being ; that innumerable creatures exist in which
no trace either of an external or internal skeleton is to be
found ; that these creatures move freely about, digest, circu-
late their nutritious juices and blood when present, multiply,
and perform all the functions incident to life.  While the
skeleton is to be found in only a certain proportion of the
animals existing on our globe, the soft parts are to be met

" On the Muscular Arrangements of the Bladder and Prostate, and the
manner in which the Ureters and Urethra are closed," by the Author.—
Philosophical Transactions, 1807.

" On the Muscular Tunics in the Stomach of Man and other Mammalia,"
by the Author.—Proceedings Royal Society of London, 1867

with in all; and this appears to me an all-sufficient reason
for attaching great importance to the movements of soft
parts, such as protoplasm, jelly masses, involuntary and voluntary muscles, etc.[1]  As the muscles of vertebrates are accurately applied to each other, and to the bones, while the bones
are rigid, unyielding, and incapable of motion, it follows that
the osseous system acts as a break or boundary to the muscular
one,—and hence the arbitrary division of muscles into extensors and flexors, pronators and supinators, abductors and adductors.    This division although convenient is calculated to
mislead.  The most highly organized animal is strictly speaking
to be regarded as a living mass whose parts (hard, soft, and

Fig 9.—The Superficial Muscles in the Horse, (after Bagg).

otherwise) are accurately adapted to each other, every part
reciprocating with scrupulous exactitude, and rendering it
difficult to determine where motion begins and where it terminates.  Fig. 9 shows the more superficial of the muscular
masses which move the bones or osseous levers of the horse,
as seen in the walk, trot, gallop, etc.  A careful examination
of these carneous masses or muscles will show that they run

[1] Lectures "On the Physiology of the Circulation in Plants, in the Lower
Animals, and in Man," by the Author.—Edinburgh Medical Journal for September 1872.

longitudinally, transversely, and obliquely, the longitudinal
and transverse muscles crossing each other at nearly right
angles, the oblique ones tending to cross at various angles, as
in the letter X. The crossing is seen to most advantage in
the deep muscles.

In order to understand the twisting which occurs to a
greater or less extent in the bodies and extremities (when
present) of all vertebrated animals, it is necessary to reduce the
bony and muscular systems to their simplest expression. If
motion is desired in a dorsal, ventral, or lateral direction only, a
dorsal and ventral or a right and left lateral set of longitudinal
muscles acting upon straight bones articulated by an ordinary
ball-and-socket joint will suffice. In this case the dorsal,
ventral, and right and left lateral muscles form *muscular cycles ;*
contraction or shortening on the one aspect of the cycle being
accompanied by relaxation or elongation on the other, the
bones and joints forming as it were the diameters of the
cycles, and oscillating in a backward, forward, or lateral
direction in proportion to the degree and direction of the
muscular movements. Here the motion is confined to two
planes intersecting each other at right angles. When, however, the muscular system becomes more highly differentiated,
both as regards the number of the muscles employed, and the
variety of the directions pursued by them, the bones and
joints also become more complicated. Under these circumstances, the bones, as a rule, are twisted upon themselves,
and their articular surfaces present various degrees of spirality
to meet the requirements of the muscular system. Between the
straight longitudinal muscles, therefore, arranged in dorsal and
ventral, and right and left lateral sets, and those which run in a
more or less transverse direction, and between the simple joint
whose motion is confined to one plane and the ball-and-socket
joints whose movements are universal, every degree of obliquity is found in the direction of the muscles, and every possible modification in the disposition of the articular surfaces.
In the fish the muscles are for the most part arranged in
dorsal, ventral, and lateral sets, which run longitudinally; and,
as a result, the movements of the trunk, particularly towards
the tail, are from side to side and sinuous. As, however,

oblique fibres are also present, and the tendons of the longitudinal muscles in some instances cross obliquely towards the
tail, the fish has also the power of tilting or twisting its
trunk (particularly the lower half) as well as the caudal fin.
In a mackerel which I examined, the oblique muscles were
represented by the four lateral masses occurring between the
dorsal, ventral, and lateral longitudinal muscles—two of
these being found on either side of the fish, and corresponding
to the myocommas or "*grand muscle latéral*" of Cuvier. The
muscular system of the fish would therefore seem to be arranged on a fourfold plan,—there being four sets of longitudinal muscles, and a corresponding number of slightly
oblique and oblique muscles, the oblique muscles being spiral
in their nature and tending to cross or intersect at various
angles, an arrest of the intersection, as it appears to me,
giving rise to the myocommas and to that concentric arrangement of their constituent parts so evident on transverse
section. This tendency of the muscular fibres to cross
each other at various degrees of obliquity may also be traced
in several parts of the human body, as, for instance, in the
deltoid muscle of the arm and the deep muscles of the leg.
Numerous other examples of penniform muscles might be
adduced. Although the fibres of the myocommas have a
more or less longitudinal direction, the myocommas themselves pursue an oblique spiral course from before backwards
and from within outwards, *i.e.* from the spine towards the
periphery, where they receive slightly oblique fibres from the
longitudinal dorsal, ventral, and lateral muscles. As the
spiral oblique myocommas and the oblique fibres from the
longitudinal muscles act directly and indirectly upon the
spines of the vertebræ, and the vertebræ themselves to which
they are specially adapted, and as both sets of oblique fibres
are geared by interdigitation to the fourfold set of longitudinal muscles, the lateral, sinuous, and rotatory movements of
the body and tail of the fish are readily accounted for.
The spinal column of the fish facilitates the lateral sinuous
twisting movements of the tail and trunk, from the fact that
the vertebræ composing it are united to each other by a series
of modified universal joints—the vertebræ supplying the cup-

shaped depressions or sockets, the intervertebral substance, the prominence or ball.

The same may be said of the general arrangement of the muscles in the trunk and tail of the Cetacea, the principal muscles in this case being distributed, not on the sides, but on the dorsal and ventral aspects. The lashing of the tail in the whales is consequently from above downwards or vertically, instead of from side to side. The spinal column is jointed as in the fish, with this difference, that the vertebræ (especially towards the tail) form the rounded prominences or ball, the meniscus or cup-shaped intervertebral plates the receptacles or socket.

When limbs are present, the spine may be regarded as being ideally divided, the spiral movements, under these circumstances, being thrown upon the extremities by typical ball-and-socket joints occurring at the shoulders and pelvis. This is peculiarly the case in the seal, where the spirally sinuous movements of the spine are transferred directly to the posterior extremities.[1]

The extremities, when present, are provided with their own muscular cycles of extensor and flexor, abductor and adductor, pronator and supinator muscles,—these running longitudinally and at various degrees of obliquity, and enveloping the hard parts according to their direction—the bones being twisted upon themselves and furnished with articular surfaces which reflect the movements of the muscular cycles, whether these occur in straight lines anteriorly, posteriorly, or laterally, or in oblique lines in intermediate situations. The straight and oblique muscles are principally brought into play in the movements of the extremi-

---

[1] That the movements of the extremities primarily emanate from the spine is rendered probable by the remarkable powers possessed by serpents. "It is true," writes Professor Owen (op. cit. p. 261), "that the serpent has no limbs, yet it can outclimb the monkey, outswim the fish, outleap the jerboa, and, suddenly loosing the close coils of its crouching spiral, it can spring into the air and seize the bird upon the wing." . . . . "The serpent has neither hands nor talons, yet it can outwrestle the athlete, and crush the tiger in the embrace of its ponderous overlapping folds." The peculiar endowments, which accompany the possession of extremities, it appears to me, present themselves in an undeveloped or latent form in the trunk of the reptile.

C

tics of quadrupeds, bipeds, etc. in walking; in the movements of the tails and fins of fishes, whales, etc. in swimming; and in the movements of the wings of insects, bats, and birds in flying. The straight and oblique muscles are usually found together, and co-operate in producing the movements in question; the amount of rotation in a part always increasing as the oblique muscles preponderate. The combination of ball-and-socket and hinge-joints, with their concomitant oblique and longitudinal muscular cycles (the former occurring in their most perfect forms where the extremities are united to the trunk, the latter in the extremities themselves), enable the animal to present, when necessary, an extensive resisting surface the one instant, and a greatly diminished and a comparatively non-resisting one the next. This arrangement secures the subtlety and nicety of motion demanded by the several media at different stages of progression.

*The travelling surfaces of Animals modified and adapted to the medium on or in which they move.*—In those land animals which take to the water occasionally, the feet, as a

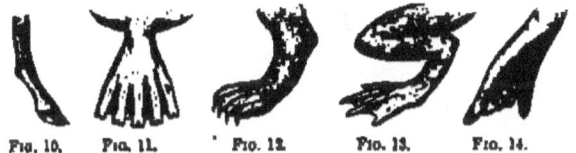

Fig. 10.    Fig. 11.         Fig. 12.         Fig. 13.    Fig. 14.

Fig 10.—Extreme form of compressed foot, as seen in the deer, ox, etc., adapted specially for land transit.—*Original.*
Fig. 11.—Extreme form of expanded foot, as seen in the Ornithorhynchus, etc., adapted more particularly for swimming.—*Original.*
Figs. 12 and 13.—Intermediate form of foot, as seen in the otter (fig. 12), frog (fig. 13), etc. Here the foot is equally serviceable in and out of the water.—*Original.*
Fig. 14.—Foot of the seal, which opens and closes in the act of natation, the organ being folded upon itself during the non-effective or return stroke, and expanded during the effective or forward stroke. Due advantage is taken of this arrangement by the seal when swimming, the animal rotating on its long axis, so as to present the lower portion of the body and the feet obliquely to the water during the return stroke, and the flat, or the greatest available surface of both, during the effective or forward stroke.—*Original.*

rule, are furnished with membranous expansions extending between the toes. Of such the Otter (fig. 12), Ornithorhynchus (fig. 11), Seal (fig. 14), Crocodile, Sea-Bear (fig. 37, p. 76), Walrus, Frog (fig. 13), and Triton, may be cited. The crocodile and triton, in addition to the membranous expansion occurring between the toes, are supplied with a powerful swimming-tail, which adds very materially to the surface engaged in natation. Those animals, one and all, walk awkwardly, it always happening that when the extremities are modified to operate upon two essentially different media (as, for instance, the land and water), the maximum of speed is attained in neither. For this reason those animals which swim the best, walk, as a rule, with the greatest difficulty, and *vice versâ*, as the movements of the auk and seal in and out of the water amply testify.

In addition to those land animals which run and swim, there are some which precipitate themselves, parachute-fashion, from immense heights, and others which even fly. In these the membranous expansions are greatly increased, the ribs affording the necessary support in the Dragon or Flying Lizard (fig. 15), the anterior and posterior extremities and tail, in the Flying Lemur (fig. 16) and Bat (fig. 17, p. 36).

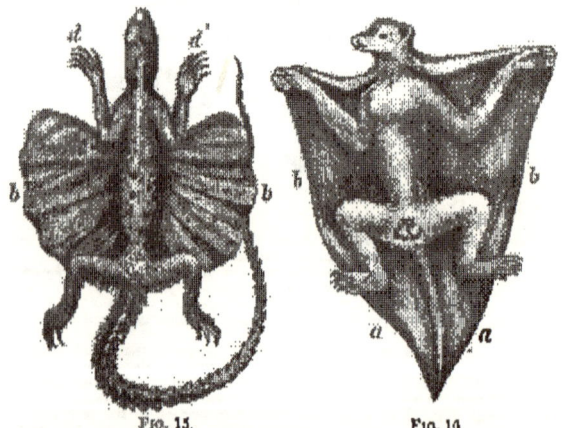

FIG. 15.　　　　　　FIG. 16.

FIG. 15.—The Red-throated Dragon (*Draco hæmatopogon*, Gray) shows a large membranous expansion (*b b*) situated between the anterior (*d d*) and posterior extremities, and supported by the ribs. The dragon by this arrangement can take extensive leaps with perfect safety.—*Original.*

FIG. 16.—The Flying Lemur (*Galeopithecus volans*, Shaw). In the flying lemur the membranous expansion (*a b*) is more extensive than in the Flying Dragon (fig. 15). It is supported by the neck, back, and tail, and by the anterior and posterior extremities. The flying lemur takes enormous leaps; its membranous tunic all but enabling it to fly. The Bat, *Phyllorhina gracilis* (fig. 17), flies with a very slight increase of surface. The surface exposed by the bat exceeds that displayed by many insects and birds. The wings of the bat are deeply concave, and so resemble the wings of beetles and heavy-bodied short-winged birds. The bones of the arm (r), forearm (d), and hand (n, n, n) of the bat (fig. 17) support the anterior or thick margin and the extremity of the wing, and may not inaptly be compared to the nervures in corresponding positions in the wing of the beetle.—*Original.*

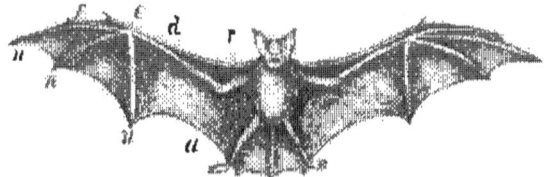

Fig. 17.—The Bat (*Phyllorhina gracilis*, Peters). Here the travelling-surfaces (r d e f, a n n n) are enormously increased as compared with that of the land and water animals generally. Compare with figures from 10 to 14, p. 34. r Arm of bat; d forearm of bat; e f, n n n hand of bat.—*Original.*

Although no lizard is at present known to fly, there can be little doubt that the extinct Pterodactyles (which, according to Professor Huxley, are intermediate between the lizards and crocodiles) were possessed of this power. The bat is interesting as being the only mammal at present endowed with wings sufficiently large to enable it to fly.[1] It affords an extreme example of modification for a special purpose,—its attenuated body, dwarfed posterior, and greatly elongated anterior extremities, with their enormous fingers and outspreading membranes, completely unfitting it for terrestrial progression. It is instructive as showing that flight may be attained, without the aid of hollow bones and air-sacs, by purely muscular efforts, and by the mere diminution and increase of a continuous membrane.

As the flying lizard, flying lemur, and bat (figs. 15, 16, and 17, pp. 35 and 36), connect terrestrial progression with aërial progression, so the auk, penguin (fig. 46, p. 91), and flying-fish (fig. 51, p. 98), connect progression in the water with progression in the air. The travelling surfaces of these anomalous creatures run the movements peculiar to the three highways of nature into each other, and bridge over, as it were, the gaps which naturally exist between locomotion on the land, in the water, and in the air.

[1] The Vampire Bat of the Island of Bonin, according to Dr. Buckland, can also swim ; and this authority was of opinion that the Pterodactyle enjoyed similar advantages.—Eng. Cycl. vol. iv. p. 485.

# PROGRESSION ON THE LAND.

*Walking of the Quadruped, Biped, etc.*—As the earth, because of its solidity, will bear any amount of pressure to which it may be subjected, the size, shape, and weight of animals destined to traverse its surface are matters of little or no consequence. As, moreover, the surface trod upon is rigid or unyielding, the extremities of quadrupeds are, as a rule, terminated by small feet. Fig. 18 (contrast with fig. 17).

Fig. 18.—Chillingham Bull (*Bos Scoticus*). Shows powerful heavy body, and the small extremities adapted for land transit. Also the figure-of-8 movements made by the feet and limbs in walking and running. s, t Curves made by right and left anterior extremities. r, s Curves made by right and left posterior extremities. The right fore and the left hind foot move together to form the waved line (s, s); the left fore and the right hind foot move together to form the waved line (r, t). The curves formed by the anterior (t, s) and posterior (r, s) extremities form ellipses. Compare with fig. 19, p. 39.—*Original*.

In this there is a double purpose—the limited area presented to the ground affording the animal sufficient support and leverage, and enabling it to disentangle its feet with the utmost facility, it being a condition in rapid terrestrial progression that the points presented to the earth be few in number and limited in extent, as this approximates the feet of animals most closely to the wheel in mechanics, where the surface in contact with the plane of progression is reduced to a minimum. When the surface presented to a dense resisting medium is increased, speed is diminished, as shown in the tardy movements of the mollusc, caterpillar, and slowworm, and also, though not to the same extent, in the serpents, some of which move with considerable celerity. In the gecko and common house-fly, as is well known, the travelling surfaces are furnished with suctorial discs, which enable those creatures to walk, if need be, in an inverted position; and "the tree-frogs (*Hyla*) have a concave disc at the end of each toe, for climbing and adhering to the bark and leaves of trees. Some toads, on the other hand, are enabled, by peculiar tubercles or projections from the palm or sole, to clamber up old walls."[1] A similar, but more complicated arrangement, is met with in the arms of the cuttle-fish.

The movements of the extremities in land animals vary considerably.

In the kangaroo and jerboa,[2] the posterior extremities only are used, the animals advancing *per saltum*, i.e. by a series of leaps.[3]

The deer also bounds into the air in its slower movements; in its fastest paces it gallops like the horse, as explained at pp. 40-44. The posterior extremities of the kangaroo are enormously developed as compared with the anterior ones; they are also greatly elongated. The posterior extremities are in excess, likewise, in the horse, rabbit,[4] agouti, and guinea

[1] Comp. Anat. and Phys. of Vertebrates, by Professor Owen, vol. i. pp. 262, 263. Lond. 1866.

[2] The jerboa when pursued can leap a distance of nine feet, and repeat the leaps so rapidly that it cannot be overtaken even by the aid of a swift horse. The bullfrog, a much smaller animal, can, when pressed, clear from six to eight feet at each bound, and project itself over a fence five feet high.

[3] The long, powerful tail of the kangaroo assists in maintaining the equilibrium of the animal prior to the leaps; the posterior extremities and tail forming a tripod of support.

[4] The rabbit occasionally takes several short steps with the fore legs and

pig. As a consequence these animals descend declivities with difficulty. They are best adapted for slightly ascending ground. In the giraffe the anterior extremities are longer and more powerful, comparatively, than the posterior ones, which is just the opposite condition to that found in the kangaroo.

In the giraffe the legs of opposite sides move together and alternate, whereas in most quadrupeds the extremities move diagonally—a remark which holds true also of ourselves in walking and skating, the right leg and left arm advancing together and alternating with the left leg and right arm (fig. 19).

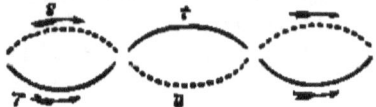

Fig. 19.—Diagram showing the figure-of-8 or double-waved track produced by the alternating of the extremities in man in walking and running ; the right leg (r) and left arm (s) advancing simultaneously to form one step ; and alternating with the left leg (t) and right arm (u), which likewise advances together to form a second step. The continuous line (r, t) gives the waved track made by the legs ; the interrupted line (s, u) that made by the arms. The curves made by the right leg and left arm, and by the left leg and right arm, form ellipses. Compare with fig. 18, p. 37.—Original.

In the hexapod insects, according to Müller, the fore and hind foot of the one side and the middle one of the opposite side move together to make one step, the three corresponding and opposite feet moving together to form the second step. Other and similar combinations are met with in the decapods.

The alternating movements of the extremities are interesting as betokening a certain degree of flexuosity or twisting, either in the trunk or limbs, or partly in the one and partly in the other.

This twisting begets the figure-of-8 movements observed in walking, swimming, and flying. (Compare figs. 6, 7, and 26 r, pp. 28 and 55 ; figs. 18 and 19, pp. 37 and 39 ; figs. 32 and 50, pp. 68 and 97 ; figs. 71 and 73, p. 144 ; and fig. 81, p. 157.)

*Locomotion of the Horse.*—As the limits of the present volume forbid my entering upon a consideration of the movements of all the animals with terrestrial habits, I will describe briefly, and by way of illustration, those of the horse, ostrich,

one long one with the hind legs ; so that it walks with the fore legs, and leaps with the hind ones.

and man.   In the horse, as in all quadrupeds endowed with
great speed, the bones of the extremities are inclined obliquely
towards each other to form angles; the angles diminishing as
the speed increases.   Thus the angles formed by the bones of
the extremities with each other and with the scapulæ and
iliac bones, are less in the horse than in the elephant.   For
the same reason they are less in the deer than in the horse.
In the elephant, where no great speed is required, the limbs
are nearly straight, this being the best arrangement for supporting superincumbent weight.   The angles formed by the
different bones of the wing of the bird are less than in the
fleetest quadruped, the movements of wings being more rapid
than those of the extremities of quadrupeds and bipeds.
These are so many mechanical adaptations to neutralize shock,
to increase elasticity, and secure velocity.   The paces of the
horse are conveniently divided into the walk, the trot, the
amble, and the gallop.   If the horse begins his walk by raising his near fore foot, the order in which the feet are lifted is
as follows :—first the left fore foot, then the right or diagonal
hind foot, then the right fore foot, and lastly the left or
diagonal hind foot.   There is therefore a twisting of the
body and spiral overlapping of the extremities of the horse
in the act of walking, in all respects analogous to what
occurs in other quadrupeds [1] and in bipeds (figs. 18 and 19, pp.
37 and 39).   In the slowest walk Mr. Gamgee observes "that
three feet are in constant action on the ground, whereas in
the free walk in which the hind foot passes the position from
which the parallel fore foot moves, there is a fraction of time
when only two feet are upon the ground, but the interval is
too short for the eye to measure it.   The proportion of time,
therefore, during which the feet act upon the ground, to that
occupied in their removal to new positions, is as three to one
in the slow, and a fraction less in the fast walk.   In the fast
gallop these proportions are as five to three.   In all the paces
the power of the horse is being exerted mainly upon a fore

---

[1] If a cat when walking is seen from above, a continuous wave of movement is observed travelling along its spine from before backwards.   This
movement closely resembles the crawling of the serpent and the swimming of
the eel.

and hind limb, with *the feet implanted in diagonal positions.*
There is also a constant parallel line of positions kept up by
a fore and hind foot, *alternating sides* in each successive move.
These relative positions are renewed and maintained. Thus
each fore limb assumes, as it alights, the advanced position
parallel with the hind, just released and moving; the hind
feet move by turns, in sequence to their diagonal fore, and in
priority to their parallel fellows, which following they maintain for nearly half their course, when the fore in its turn is
raised and carried to its destined place, the hind alighting
midway. All the feet passing over equal distances and keeping the same time, no interference of the one with the other

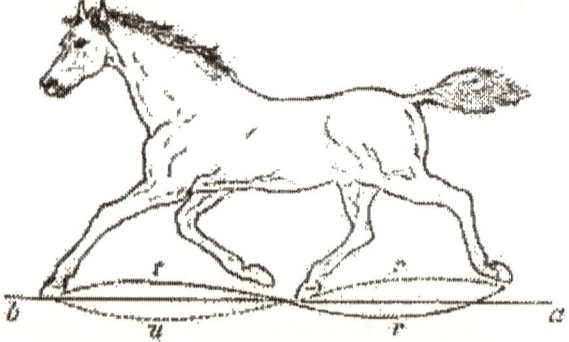

FIG. 20.—Horse in the act of trotting. In this, as in all the other paces,
the body of the horse is levered forward by a diagonal twisting of the trunk
and extremities, the extremities describing a figure-of-8 track (*z u, r t*).
The figure-of-8 is produced by the alternate play of the extremities and feet,
two of which are always on the ground (*z, b*). Thus the right forefoot describes
the curve marked *t*, the left hind foot that marked *r*, the left fore foot that
marked *u*, and the right hind foot that marked *z*. The feet on the ground in
the present instance are the left fore and the right hind. Compare with
figs 18 and 19, pp. 37 and 39.—*Original.*

occurs, and each successive hind foot as it is implanted forms
a new diagonal with the opposite fore, the latter forming the
front of the parallel in one instant, and one of the diagonal
positions in the next: while in the case of the hind, they
assume the diagonal on alighting and become the terminators
of the parallel in the last part of their action."

In the trot, according to Bishop, the legs move in pairs

diagonally. The same leg moves rather oftener during the same period in trotting than in walking, or as six to five. The velocity acquired by moving the legs in pairs, instead of consecutively, depends on the circumstance that in the trot each leg rests on the ground during a short interval, and swings during a long one; whilst in walking each leg swings a short, and rests a long period. The undulations arising from the projection of the trunk in the trot are chiefly in the vertical plane; in the walk they are more in the horizontal.

The gallop has been erroneously believed to consist of a series of bounds or leaps, the two hind legs being on the ground when the two fore legs are in the air, and *vice versâ*, there being a period when all four are in the air. Thus Sainbell in his " Essay on the Proportions of Eclipse," states " that the gallop consists of a repetition of bounds, or leaps, more or less high, and more or less extended in proportion to the strength and lightness of the animal." A little reflection will show that this definition of the gallop cannot be the correct one. When a horse takes a ditch or fence, he gathers himself together, and by a vigorous effort (particularly of the hind legs), throws himself into the air. This movement requires immense exertion and is short-lived. It is not in the power of any horse to repeat these bounds for more than a few minutes, from which it follows that the gallop, which may be continued for considerable periods, must differ very materially from the leap.

The pace known as the amble is an artificial movement, produced by the cunning of the trainer. It resembles that of the giraffe, where the right fore and right hind foot move together to form one step; the left fore and left hind foot moving together to form the second step. By the rapid repetition of these movements the right and left sides of the body are advanced alternately by a lateral swinging motion, very comfortable for the rider, but anything but graceful. The amble is a defective pace, inasmuch as it interferes with the diagonal movements of the limbs, and impairs the continuity of motion which the twisting, cross movement begets. Similar remarks might be made of the gallop if it consisted (which it does not) of a series of bounds or leaps, as each bound would be succeeded by a halt, or dead point, that could not fail seriously to compromise continuous forward motion. In the gallop, as in the slower movements, the horse has never less than two feet on the ground at any instant of time, no two of the four feet being in exactly the same position.

Mr. Gamgee, who has studied the movements of the horse very carefully, has given diagrams of the walk, trot, and gallop, drawn to a scale of the feet of a two-year-old colt in training, which had been walked, trotted, and galloped over the ground for the purpose. The point he sought to determine was the exact distance through which each foot was carried from the place where it was lifted to that where it alighted. The diagrams are reproduced at figures 21, 22, and 23. In figure 23 I have added a continuous waved line to indicate the alternating movements of the extremities; Mr. Gamgee at the time he wrote [1] being, he informs me, unacquainted with the figure-of-8 theory of animal progression as subsequently developed by me. Compare fig. 23 with figs. 18 and 19, pp. 37 and 39; with fig. 50, p. 97; and with figs. 71 and 73, p. 144.

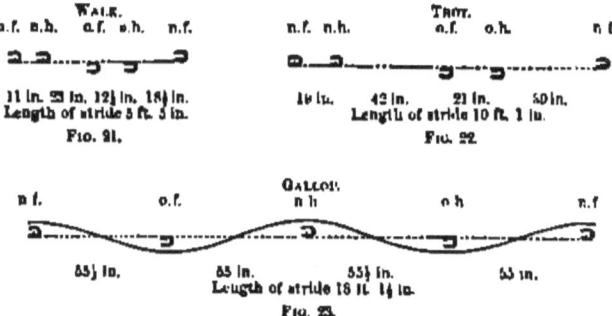

WALK.
n.f. n.h.   o.f. o.h.   n.f.

11 in. 23 in. 12½ in. 18½ in.
Length of stride 5 ft. 3 in.
Fig. 21.

TROT.
n.f. n.h.   o.f. o.h.   n f.

18 in.   42 in.   21 in.   50 in.
Length of stride 10 ft. 1 in.
Fig. 22.

GALLOP.
n f.          o.f.        n h          o h          n.f

55½ in.        55 in.      55½ in.       55 in.
Length of stride 18 ft. 1½ in.
Fig. 23.

In examining figures 21, 22, and 23, the reader will do well to remember that the *near* fore and hind feet of a horse are the *left* fore and hind feet; the *off* fore and hind feet being the *right* fore and hind feet. The terms *near* and *off*

[1] " On the Breeding of Hunters and Roadsters." Prize Essay.—Journal of Royal Agricultural Society for 1863.

are technical expressions, and apply to the left and right sides of the animal. Another point to be attended to in examining the figures in question, is the relation which exists between the fore and hind feet of the near and off sides of the body. In slow walking the near hind foot is planted behind the imprint made by the near fore foot. In rapid walking, on the contrary, the near hind foot is planted from six to twelve or more inches in advance of the imprint made by the near fore foot (fig. 21 represents the distance as eleven inches). In the trot the near hind foot is planted from twelve to eighteen or more inches in advance of the imprint made by the near fore foot (fig. 22 represents the distance as nineteen inches). In the gallop the near hind foot is planted 100 or more inches in advance of the imprint made by the near fore foot (fig. 23 represents the distance as 110½ inches). The distance by which the near hind foot passes the near fore foot in rapid walking, trotting, and galloping, increases in a progressive ratio, and is due in a principal measure to the velocity or momentum acquired by the mass of the horse in rapid motion; the body of the animal carrying forward and planting the limbs at greater relative distances in the trot than in the rapid walk, and in the gallop than in the trot. I have chosen to speak of the near hind and near fore feet, but similar remarks may of course be made of the off hind and off fore feet.

"At fig. 23, which represents the gallop, the distance between two successive impressions produced, say by the near fore foot, is eighteen feet one inch and a half. Midway between these two impressions is the mark of the near hind foot, which therefore subdivides the space into nine feet and six-eighths of an inch, but each of these is again subdivided into two halves by the impressions produced by the off fore and off hind feet. It is thus seen that the horse's body instead of being propelled through the air by bounds or leaps even when going at the highest attainable speed, acts on a system of levers, the mean distance between the points of resistance of which is four feet six inches. The exact length of stride, of course, only applies to that of the particular horse observed, and the rate of speed at which he is going. In the case of any one animal, the greater the speed the longer is the individual stride. In progression, the body moves before a limb is raised from the ground, as is most readily seen when the horse is beginning its slowest action, as in traction." [1]

At fig. 22, which represents the trot, the stride is ten feet one inch. At fig. 21, which represents the walk, it is only five feet five inches. The speed acquired, Mr. Gamgee points out, determines the length of stride; the length of stride being the effect and evidence of speed and not the cause of it. The momentum acquired in the gallop, as already explained, greatly accelerates speed.

"In contemplating length of strides, with reference to the fulcra, allowance has to be made for the length of the feet, which is to be deducted from that of the strides, because the apex, or toe of the horse's hind foot forms the fulcrum in one instant, and the heel of the fore foot in the next, and *vice versa*. This phenomenon is very obvious in the action of the human foot, and is remarkable also for the range of leverage thus afforded in some of the fleetest quadrupeds, of different species. In the hare, for instance, between the point of its hock and the termination of its extended digits, there is a space of upwards of six inches of extent of leverage and variation of fulcrum, and in the fore limb from the *carpus* to the toe-nails (whose function in progression is not to be underrated) upwards of three inches of leverage are found, being about ten inches for each lateral biped, and the double of that for the action of all four feet. Viewed in this way the stride is not really so long as would be supposed if merely estimated from the space between the footprints.

Many interesting remarks might be made on the length of the stride of various animals; the full movement of the greyhound is, for instance, upwards of sixteen feet; that of the hare at least equal; whilst that of the Newfoundland dog is a little over nine feet." [1]

*Locomotion of the Ostrich.*—Birds have been divided by naturalists into eight orders:—the *Natatores*, or Swimming Birds; the *Grallatores*, or Wading Birds; the *Cursores*, or Running Birds; the *Scansores*, or Climbers; the *Rasores*, or

1 Gamgee in Journal of Anatomy and Physiology, vol. III. pp. 375, 376.

Scrapers; the *Columbæ*, or Doves; the *Passeres;* and the *Raptores*, or Birds of Prey.

The first five orders have been classified according to their habits and modes of progression.   The *Natatores* I shall consider when I come to speak of swimming as a form of locomotion, and as there is nothing in the movements of the wading, scraping, and climbing birds,[1] or in the *Passeres*[2] or *Raptores*, requiring special notice, I shall proceed at once to a consideration of the *Cursores*, the best examples of which are the ostrich, emu, cassowary, and apteryx.

The ostrich is remarkable for the great length and development of its legs as compared with its wings (fig. 24).  In this respect it is among birds what the kangaroo is among mammals. The ostrich attains an altitude of from six to eight feet, and is the largest living bird known.   Its great height is due to its attenuated neck and legs.   The latter are very powerful structures, and greatly resemble in their general conformation the posterior extremities of a thoroughbred horse or one of the larger deer—compare with fig. 4, p. 21.   They are expressly made for speed.   Thus the bones of the leg and foot are inclined very obliquely towards each other, the femur being inclined very obliquely to the ilium.   As a consequence the angles made by the several bones of the legs are comparatively small; smaller in fact than in either the horse or deer.

The feet of the ostrich, like those of the horse and deer, are reduced to a minimum as regards size; so that they occasion very little friction in the act of walking and running. The foot is composed of two jointed toes,[3] which spread out when the weight of the body comes upon them, in such a manner as enables the bird to seize and let go the ground with equal facility.   The advantage of such an arrangement in rapid locomotion cannot be over-estimated.   The elasticity and flexibility of the foot contribute greatly to the rapidity

[1] The woodpeckers climb by the aid of the stiff feathers of their tails; the legs and tail forming a firm basis of support.

[2] In this order there are certain birds—the sparrows and thrushes, for example—which advance by a series of vigorous leaps; the leaps being of an intermitting character.

[3] The toes in the emu amount to three.

of movement for which this celebrated bird is famous. The limb of the ostrich, with its large bones placed very obliquely to form a system of powerful levers, is the very embodiment of speed. The foot is quite worthy of the limb, it being in

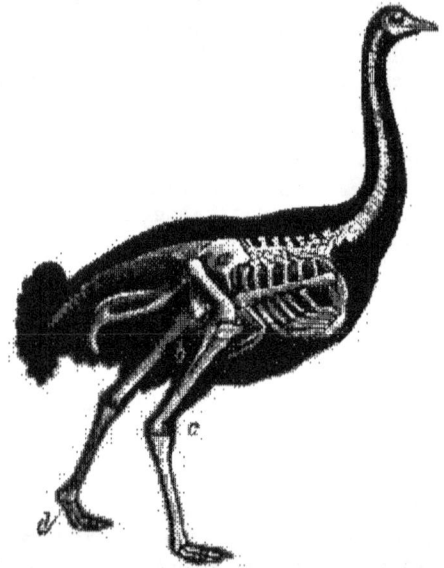

Fig. 24.—Skeleton of the Ostrich. Shows the powerful legs, small feet, and rudimentary wings of the bird; the obliquity at which the bones of the legs and wings are placed, and the comparatively small angles which any two bones make at their point of junction. a Angle made by femur with ilium. b Angle made by tibia and fibula with femur. c Angle made by tarso-metatarsal bone with tibia and fibula. d Angle made by bones of foot with tarso-metatarsal bone. r Bones of wing inclined to each other at nearly right angles. Compare with fig. 4, p. 21, fig. 26, p. 55, and fig. 27, p. 59.—Adapted from Dallas.

some respects the most admirable structure of its kind in existence. The foot of the ostrich differs considerably from that of all other birds, those of its own family excepted. Thus the under portion of the foot is flat, and specially adapted for acting on plane surfaces, particularly solids.[1] The

---

[1] Feet designed for swimming, grasping trees, or securing prey, do not operate to advantage on a flat surface. The awkward waddle of the swan, parrot, and eagle when on the ground affords illustrations.

extremities of the toes superiorly are armed with powerful
short nails, the tips of which project inferiorly to protect the
toes and confer elasticity when the foot is leaving the ground.
The foot, like the leg, is remarkable for its great strength.
The legs of the ostrich are closely set, another feature of
speed.[1]  The wings of the ostrich are in a very rudimentary

FIG. 25.— Ostriches pursued by a Hunter.

condition as compared with the legs.[2]  All the bones are present, but they are so dwarfed that they are useless as organs
of flight.  The angles which the bones of the wing make with
each other, are still less than the angles made by the bones of
the leg.  This is just what we would *a priori* expect, as the
velocity with which wings are moved greatly exceeds that
with which legs are moved.  The bones of the wing of the
ostrich are inclined towards each other at nearly right angles.

[1] In draught horses the legs are much wider apart than in racers; the legs
of the deer being less widely set than those of the racer.
[2] In the apteryx the wings are so very small that the bird is commonly
spoken of as the "wingless bird."

The wings of the ostrich, although useless as flying organs, form important auxiliaries in running. When the ostrich careers along the plain, he spreads out his wings in such a manner that they act as balancers, and so enable him to maintain his equilibrium (fig. 25). The wings, because of the angle of inclination which their under surfaces make with the horizon, and the great speed at which the ostrich travels, act like kites, and so elevate and carry forward by a mechanical adaptation a certain proportion of the mass of the bird already in motion. The elevating and propelling power of even diminutive inclined planes is very considerable, when carried along at a high speed in a horizontal direction. The wings, in addition to their elevating and propelling power, contribute by their short, rapid, swinging movements, to continuity of motion in the legs. No bird with large wings can run well. The albatross, for example, walks with difficulty, and the same may be said of the vulture and eagle. What, therefore, appears a defect in the ostrich, is a positive advantage when its habits and mode of locomotion are taken into account.

Professional runners in many cases at matches reduce the length of their anterior extremities by flexing their arms and carrying them on a level with their chest (fig. 28, p. 62). It would seem that in rapid running there is not time for the arms to oscillate naturally, and that under these circumstances the arms, if allowed to swing about, retard rather than increase the speed. The centre of gravity is well forward in the ostrich, and is regulated by the movements of the head and neck, and the obliquity of the body and legs. In running the neck is stretched, the body inclined forward, and the legs moved alternately and with great rapidity. When the right leg is flexed and elevated, it swings forward pendulum-fashion, and describes a curve whose convexity is directed towards the right side. When the left leg is flexed and elevated, it swings forward and describes a curve whose convexity is directed towards the left side. The curves made by the right and left legs form when united a waved line (vide figs. 18, 19, and 20, pp. 37, 39, and 41). When the right leg is flexed, elevated, and advanced, it rotates upon the iliac

D

portion of the trunk of the bird, the trunk being supported
for the time being by the left leg, which is extended, and in
contact with the ground. When the left leg is flexed, elevated,
and advanced, it in like manner rotates upon the trunk, supported in this instance by the extended right leg. The leg
which is on the ground for the time being supplies the necessary lever, the ground the fulcrum. When the right leg is
flexed and elevated, it rotates upon the iliac portion of the
trunk in a forward direction, the right foot describing the arc of
a circle. When the right leg and foot are extended and fixed
on the ground, the trunk rotates upon the right foot in a forward direction to form the arc of a circle, which is the converse
of that formed by the right foot. If the arcs alternately supplied
by the right foot and trunk are placed in opposition, a more
or less perfect circle is produced, and thus it is that the locomotion of animals is approximated to the wheel in mechanics.
Similar remarks are to be made of the left foot and trunk.
The alternate rolling of the trunk on the extremities, and the
extremities on the trunk, utilizes or works up the inertia of the
moving mass, and powerfully contributes to continuity and
steadiness of action in the moving parts. By advancing the head
neck, and anterior parts of the body, the ostrich inaugurates
the rolling movement of the trunk, which is perpetuated by
the rolling movements of the legs. The trunk and legs of the
ostrich are active and passive by turns. The movements of
the trunk and limbs are definitely co-ordinated. But for this
reciprocation the action of the several parts implicated would
neither be so rapid, certain, nor continuous. The speed of
the ostrich exceeds that of every other land animal, a circumstance due to its long, powerful legs and great stride. It can
outstrip without difficulty the fleetest horses, and is only
captured by being simultaneously assailed from various points,
or run down by a succession of hunters on fresh steeds.
If the speed of the ostrich, which only measures six or eight
feet, is so transcending, what shall we say of the speed of the
extinct *Æpyornis maximus* and *Dinornis giganteus*, which are
supposed to have measured from sixteen to eighteen feet in
height? Incredible as it may appear, the ostrich, with its
feet reduced to a minimum as regards size, and peculiarly

organized for walking and running on solids, can also swim. Mr. Darwin, that most careful of all observers, informs us that ostriches take to the water readily, and not only ford rapid rivers, but also cross from island to island. They swim leisurely, with neck extended, and the greater part of the body submerged.

*Locomotion in Man.*—The speed attained by man, although considerable, is not remarkable. It depends on a variety of circumstances, such as the height, age, sex, and muscular energy of the individual, the nature of the surface passed over, and the resistance to forward motion due to the presence of air, whether still or moving. A reference to the human skeleton, particularly its inferior extremities, will explain why the speed should be moderate.

On comparing the inferior extremities of man with the legs of birds, or the posterior extremities of quadrupeds, say the horse or deer, we find that the bones composing them are not so obliquely placed with reference to each other, neither are the angles formed by any two bones so acute. Further, we observe that in birds and quadrupeds the tarsal and meta-tarsal bones are so modified that there is an actual increase in the number of the angles themselves. In the extremities of birds and quadrupeds there are four angles, which may be increased or diminished in the operations of locomotion. Thus, in the quadruped and bird (fig. 4, p. 21, and fig. 24, p. 47), the femur forms with the ilium one angle ($a$); the tibia and fibula with the femur a second angle ($b$); the cannon or tarso-metatarsal bone with the tibia and fibula a third angle ($c$); and the bones of the foot with the cannon or tarso-metatarsal bone a fourth angle ($d$). In man three angles only are found, marked respectively $a$, $b$, and $c$ (figs. 26 and 27, pp. 55 and 59). The fourth angle ($d$ of figs. 4 and 24) is absent. The absence of the fourth angle is due to the fact that in man the tarsal and metatarsal bones are shortened and crushed together; whereas in the quadruped and bird they are elongated and separated.

As the speed of a limb increases in proportion to the number and acuteness of the angles formed by its several bones, it is not difficult to understand why man should not be so swift

as the majority of quadrupeds. The increase in the number
of angles increases the power which an animal has of shortening and elongating its extremities, and the levers which the
extremities form. To increase the length of a lever is to
increase its power at one end, and the distance through which
it moves at the other; hence the faculty of bounding or leaping possessed in such perfection by many quadrupeds.[1]  If
the wing be considered as a lever, a small degree of motion at
its root produces an extensive sweep at its tip.  It is thus
that the wing is enabled to work up and utilize the thin
medium of the air as a buoying medium.

Another drawback to great speed in man is his erect position.  Part of the power which should move the limbs is
dedicated to supporting the trunk.  For the same reason the
bones of the legs, instead of being obliquely inclined to each
other, as in the quadruped and bird, are arranged in a nearly
vertical spiral line.  This arrangement increases the angle
formed by any two bones, and, as a consequence, decreases
the speed of the limbs, as explained.  A similar disposition of
the bones is found in the anterior extremities of the elephant,
where the superincumbent weight is great, and the speed,
comparatively speaking, not remarkable.  The bones of the
human leg are beautifully adapted to sustain the weight of
the body and neutralize shock.[2]  Thus the femur or thigh
bone is furnished at its upper extremity with a ball-and-socket
joint which unites it to the cup-shaped depression (acetabu-
lum) in the ilium (hip bone).  It is supplied with a neck
which carries the body or shaft of the bone in an oblique
direction from the ilium, the shaft being arched forward and
twisted upon itself to form an elongated cylindrical screw.
The lower extremity of the femur is furnished with spiral
articular surfaces accurately adapted to the upper extremities
of the bones of the leg, viz. the tibia and fibula, and to the
patella.  The bones of the leg (tibia and fibula) are spirally

[1] "The posterior extremities in both the lion and tiger are longer, and the
bones inclined more obliquely to each other than the anterior, giving them
greater power and elasticity in springing."

[2] "The pelvis receives the whole weight of the trunk and superposed
organs, and transmits it to the heads of the femurs."

arranged, the screw in this instance being split up. At the ankle the bones of the leg are applied to those of the foot by spiral articular surfaces analogous to those found at the knee-joint. The weight of the trunk is thus thrown on the foot, not in straight lines, but in a series of curves. The foot itself is wonderfully adapted to receive the pressure from above. It consists of a series of small bones (the tarsal, metatarsal, and phalangeal bones), arranged in the form of a double arch; the one arch extending from the heel towards the toes, the other arch across the foot. The foot is so contrived that it is at once firm, elastic, and moveable,—qualities which enable it to sustain pressure from above, and exert pressure from beneath. In walking, the heel first reaches and first leaves the ground. When the heel is elevated the weight of the body falls more and more on the centre of the foot and toes, the latter spreading out[1] as in birds, to seize the ground and lever the trunk forward. It is in this movement that the wonderful mechanism of the foot is displayed to most advantage, the multiplicity of joints in the foot all yielding a little to confer that elasticity of step which is so agreeable to behold, and which is one of the characteristics of youth. The foot may be said to roll over the ground in a direction from behind forwards. I have stated that the angles formed by the bones of the human leg are larger than those formed by the bones of the leg of the quadruped and bird. This is especially true of the angle formed by the femur with the ilium, which, because of the upward direction given to the crest of the ilium in man, is so great that it virtually ceases to be an angle.

The bones of the superior extremities in man merit attention from the fact that in walking and running they oscillate in opposite directions, and alternate and keep time with the legs, which oscillate in a similar manner. The arms are articulated at the shoulders by ball-and-socket joints to cup-shaped depressions (glenoid cavities) closely resembling those found at the hip-joints. The bone of the arm (humerus) is carried away

[1] The spreading action of the toes is seen to perfection in children. It is more or less destroyed in adults from a faulty principle in boot and shoemaking, the soles being invariably too narrow.

from the shoulder by a short neck, as in the thigh-bone (femur).
Like the thigh-bone it is twisted upon itself and forms a screw.
The inferior extremity of the arm bone is furnished with
spiral articular surfaces resembling those found at the knee.
The spiral articular surfaces of the arm bone are adapted to
similar surfaces existing on the superior extremities of the
bones of the forearm, to wit, the radius and ulna.  These
bones, like the bones of the leg, are spirally disposed with
reference to each other, and form a screw consisting of two
parts.  The bones of the forearm are united to those of
the wrist (carpal) and hand (metacarpal and phalangeal) by
articular surfaces displaying a greater or less degree of
spirality.   From this it follows that the superior extremities
of man greatly resemble his inferior ones ; a fact of considerable importance, as it accounts for the part taken by the
superior extremities in locomotion.  In man the arms do not
touch the ground as in the brutes, but they do not on this
account cease to be useful as instruments of progression.   If
a man walks with a stick in each hand the movements of his
extremities exactly resemble those of a quadruped.

The bones of the human extremities (superior and inferior)
are seen to advantage in fig. 26 ; and I particularly direct
the attention of the reader to the ball-and-socket or universal
joints by which the arms are articulated to the shoulders
($x$, $x'$), and the legs to the pelvis ($a$, $a'$), as a knowledge of
these is necessary to a comprehension of the oscillating or
pendulum movements of the limbs now to be described.  The
screw configuration of the limbs is well depicted in the left
arm ($x$) of the present figure.   Compare with the wing of the
bird, fig. 6, and with the anterior extremity of the elephant,
fig. 7, p. 28.   But for the ball-and-socket joints, and the
spiral nature of the bones and articular surfaces of the extremities, the undulating, sinuous, and more or less continuous
movements observable in walking and running, and the
twisting, lashing, flail-like movements necessary to swimming
and flying, would be impossible.

The leg in the human subject moves by three joints, viz.,
the hip, knee, and ankle joints.  When standing in the erect
position, the hip-joint only permits the limb to move forwards,

the knee-joint backwards, and the ankle-joint neither backwards nor forwards. When the body or limbs are inclined

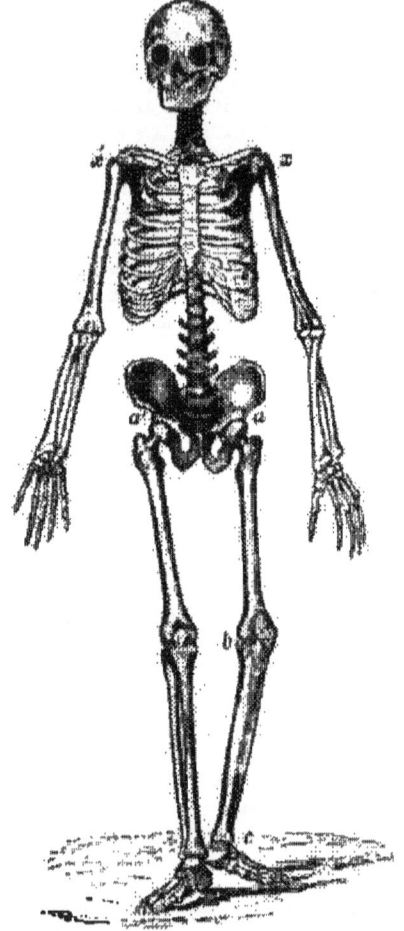

FIG. 26.—Skeleton of Man.  Compare with fig. 4, p. 21, and fig. 24, p. 47.—*Original.*

obliquely, or slightly flexed, the range of motion is increased.

The greatest angle made at the knee-joint is equal to the sums of the angles made by the hip and ankle joints when these joints are simultaneously flexed, and when the angle of inclination made by the foot with the ground equals 30°.

From this it follows that the trunk maintains its erect position during the extension and flexion of the limbs. The step in walking was divided by Borelli into two periods, the one corresponding to the time when both limbs are on the ground ; the other when only one limb is on the ground. In running, there is a brief period when both limbs are off the ground. In walking, the body is alternately supported by the right and left legs, and advanced by a sinuous movement. Its forward motion is quickened when one leg is on the ground, and slowed when both are on the ground. When the limb (say the right leg) is flexed, elevated, and thrown forward, it returns if left to itself (i.e. if its movements are not interfered with by the voluntary muscles) to the position from which it was moved, viz. the vertical, unless the trunk bearing the limb is inclined in a forward direction at the same time. The limb returns to the vertical position, or position of rest, in virtue of the power exercised by gravity, and from its being hinged at the hip by a ball-and-socket joint, as explained. In this respect the human limb when allowed to oscillate exactly resembles a pendulum,—a fact first ascertained by the brothers Weber. The advantage accruing from this arrangement, as far as muscular energy is concerned, is very great, the muscles doing comparatively little work.[1] In beginning to walk, the body and limb which is to take the first step are advanced together. When, however, the body is inclined forwards, a large proportion of the step is performed mechanically by the tendency which the pendulum formed by the leg has to swing forward and regain a vertical position,—an effect produced by the operation of gravity alone. The leg which is advanced swings further forward than is required for the step, and requires to swing back a little before it can be deposited on the ground. The pendulum

[1] The brothers Weber found that so long as the muscles exert the general force necessary to execute locomotion, the velocity depends on the size of the legs and on external forces, but *not on the strength of the muscles.*

movement effects all this mechanically. When the limb has
swung forward as far as the inclination of the body at the
time will permit, it reverses pendulum fashion; the back
stroke of the pendulum actually placing the foot upon the
ground by a retrograde, descending movement. When the
right leg with which we commenced is extended and firmly
placed upon the ground, and the trunk has assumed a nearly
vertical position, the left leg is flexed, elevated, and the trunk
once more bent forward. The forward inclination of the
trunk necessitates the swinging forward of the left leg, which,
when it has reached the point permitted by the pendulum
movement, swings back again to the extent necessary to place
it securely upon the ground. These movements are repeated
at stated and regular intervals. The retrograde movement of
the limb is best seen in slow walking. In fast walking the
pendulum movement is somewhat interrupted from the limb
being made to touch the ground when it attains a vertical
position, and therefore before it has completed its oscillation.[1]
The swinging forward of the body may be said to inaugurate
the movement of walking. The body is slightly bent and
inclined forwards at the beginning of each step. It is
straightened and raised towards the termination of that act.
The movements of the body begin and terminate the steps,
and in this manner regulate them. The trunk rises vertically
at each step, the head describing a slight curve well seen in
the walking of birds. The foot on the ground (say the right
foot) elevates the trunk, particularly its right side, and the
weight of the trunk, particularly its left side, depresses the
left or swinging foot, and assists in placing it on the ground.
The trunk and limbs are active and passive by turns. In
walking, a spiral wave of motion, most marked in an antero-
posterior direction (although also appearing laterally), runs
through the spine. This spiral spinal movement is observable in the locomotion of all vertebrates. It is favoured in
man by the antero-posterior curves (cervical, dorsal, and lum-
bar) existing in the human vertebral column. In the effort
of walking the trunk and limbs oscillate on the ilio-femoral

[1] " In quick walking and running the swinging leg never passes beyond
the vertical which cuts the head of the femur."

articulations (hip-joints). The trunk also rotates in a forward
direction on the foot which is placed upon the ground for the
time being. The rotation begins at the heel and terminates
at the toes. So long as the rotation continues, the body rises.
When the rotation ceases and one foot is placed flat upon the
ground, the body falls. The elevation and rotation of the
body in a forward direction enables the foot which is off
the ground for the time being to swing forward pendulum
fashion ; the swinging foot, when it can oscillate no further
in a forward direction, reversing its course and retrograd-
ing to a slight extent, at which juncture it is deposited on
the ground, as explained. The retrogression of the swinging
foot is accompanied by a slight retrogression on the part of
the body, which tends at this particular instant to regain a
vertical position. From this it follows that in slow walking
the trunk and the swinging foot advance together through a
considerable space, and retire through a smaller space ; that
when the body is swinging it rotates upon the ilio-femoral
articulations (hip-joints) as an axis ; and that when the leg
is not swinging, but fixed by its foot upon the ground, the
trunk rotates upon the foot as an axis. These movements
are correlated and complementary in their nature, and are
calculated to relieve the muscles of the legs and trunk engaged in locomotion from excessive wear and tear.

   Similar movements occur in the arms, which, as has been
explained, are articulated to the shoulders by ball-and-socket
joints (fig. 26, x x', p. 55). The right leg and left arm advance
together to make one step, and so of the left leg and right
arm. When the right leg advances the right arm retires, and
vice versâ. When the left leg advances the left arm retires,
and the converse. There is therefore a complementary swinging of the limbs on each side of the body, the leg swinging
always in an opposite direction to the arm on the same side.
There is, moreover, a diagonal set of movements, also complementary in character : the right leg and left arm advancing
together to form one step ; the left leg and right arm advancing together to form the next. The diagonal movements
beget a lateral twisting of the trunk and limbs ; the oscillation of the trunk upon the limbs or feet, and the oscillation

of the feet and limbs upon the trunk, generate a forward
wave movement, accompanied by a certain amount of vertical
undulation. The diagonal movements of the trunk and
extremities are accompanied by a certain degree of lateral
curvature; the right leg and left arm, when they advance to
make a step, each describing a curve, the convexity of which
is directed to the right and left respectively. Similar curves
are described by the left leg and right arm in making the
second or complementary step. When the curves formed by
the right and left legs or the right and left arms are joined,
they form waved tracks symmetrically arranged on either
side of a given line. The curves formed by the legs and

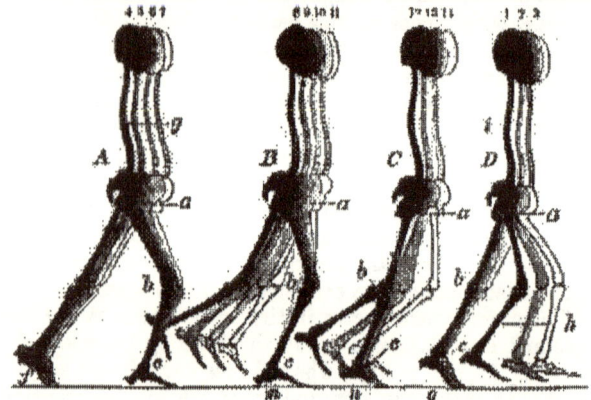

Fig. 27 shows the simultaneous positions of both legs during a step, divided
into four groups. The first group (A), 4 to 7, gives the different positions
which the legs simultaneously assume while both are on the ground; the
second group (B), 8 to 11, shows the various positions of both legs at the
time when the posterior leg is elevated from the ground, but behind the
supported one; the third group (C), 12 to 14, shows the positions which
the legs assume when the swinging leg overtakes the standing one; and
the fourth group (D), 1 to 3, the positions during the time when the swinging leg is propelled in advance of the resting one. The letters a, b, and c
indicate the angles formed by the bones of the right leg when engaged in
making a step. The letters w, n, and o, the positions assumed by the right
foot when the trunk is rolling over it. g Shows the rotating forward of the
trunk upon the left foot (f) as an axis. h Shows the rotating forward of
the left leg and foot upon the trunk (a) as an axis. Compare with fig. 4,
p. 21; with fig. 24, p. 47; and with fig. 29, p. 55.—After Weber.

arms intersect at every step, as shown at fig. 19, p. 39.
Similar curves are formed by the quadruped when walking

(fig. 18, p. 37), the fish when swimming (fig. 32, p. 68), and the bird when flying (figs. 73 and 81, pp. 144 and 157).

The alternate rotation of the trunk upon the limb and the limb upon the trunk is well seen in fig. 27, p. 59.

At *A* of fig. 27 the trunk (*g*) is observed rotating on the left foot (*f*). At *D* of fig. the left leg (*h*) is seen rotating on the trunk (*a*, *i*) : these, as explained, are complementary movements. At *A* of fig. the right foot (*c*) is firmly placed on the ground, the left foot (*f*) being in the act of leaving it. The right side of the trunk is on a lower level than the left, which is being elevated, and in the act of rolling over the foot. At *B* of fig. the right foot (*m*) is still upon the ground, but the left foot having left it is in the act of swinging forward. At *C* of fig. the heel of the right foot (*n*) is raised from the ground, and the left foot is in the act of passing the right. The right side of the trunk is now being elevated. At *D* of fig. the heel of the right foot (*o*) is elevated as far as it can be, the toes of the left foot being depressed and ready to touch the ground. The right side of the trunk has now reached its highest level, and is in the act of rolling over the right foot. The left side of the trunk, on the contrary, is subsiding, and the left leg is swinging before the right one, preparatory to being deposited on the ground.

From the foregoing it will be evident that the trunk and limbs have pendulum movements which are natural and peculiar to them, the extent of which depends upon the length of the parts. A tall man and a short man can consequently never walk in step if both walk naturally and according to inclination.[1]

In traversing a given distance in a given time, a tall man

[1] "The number of steps which a person can take in a given time in walking depends, first, on the length of the leg, which, governed by the laws of the pendulum, swings from behind forwards ; secondly, on the earlier or later interruption which the leg experiences in its arc of oscillation by being placed on the ground. The weight of the swinging leg and the velocity of the trunk serve to give the impulse by which the foot attains a position vertical to the head of the thigh-bone ; but as the latter, according to the laws of the pendulum, requires in the quickest walking a given time to attain that position, or *half* its entire curve of oscillation, it follows that every person has a certain measure for his steps, and a certain number of steps in a given time, which, in his natural gait in walking, he cannot exceed.".

will take fewer steps than a short man, in the same way that a large wheel will make fewer revolutions in travelling over a given space than a smaller one. The relation is a purely mechanical one. The nave of the large wheel corresponds to the ilio-femoral articulation (hip-joint) of the tall man, the spokes to his legs, and portions of the rim to his feet. The nave, spokes, and rim of the small wheel have the same relation to the ilio-femoral articulation (hip-joint), legs and feet of the small man. When a tall and short man walk together, if they keep step, and traverse the same distance in the same time, either the tall man must shorten and slow his steps, or the short man must lengthen and quicken his.

The slouching walk of the shepherd is more natural than that of the trained soldier. It can be kept up longer, and admits of greater speed. In the natural walk, as seen in rustics, the complementary movements are all evoked. In the artificial walk of the trained army man, the complementary movements are to a great extent suppressed. Art is consequently not an improvement on nature in the matter of walking. In walking, the centre of gravity is being constantly changed,—a circumstance due to the different attitudes assumed by the different portions of the trunk and limbs at different periods of time. All parts of the trunk and limbs of a biped, and the same may be said of a quadruped, move when a change of locality is effected. The trunk of the biped and quadruped when walking are therefore in a similar condition to that of the body of the fish when swimming.

In running, all the movements described are exaggerated. Thus the steps are more rapid and the strides greater. In walking, a well-proportioned six-feet man can nearly cover his own height in two steps. In running, he can cover without difficulty a third more.

In fig. 28 (p. 62), an athlete is represented as bending forward prior to running.

The left leg and trunk, it will be observed, are advanced beyond the vertical line (z), and the arms are tucked up like the rudimentary wings of the ostrich, to correct undue oscillation at the shoulders, occasioned by the violent oscillation produced at the pelvis in the act of running.

In order to enable the right leg to swing forward, it is
evident that it must be flexed, and that the left leg must be
extended, and the trunk raised. The raising of the trunk
causes it to assume a more vertical position, and this prevents
the swinging leg from going too far forwards; the swinging

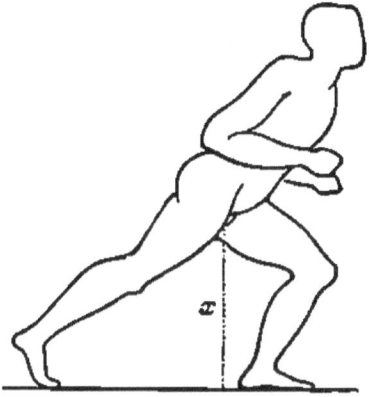

Fig. 28.—Preparing to run, from a design by Flaxman. Adapted. In the original of this figure the right arm is depending and placed on the right
thigh.

leg tending to oscillate in a slightly backward direction as
the trunk is elevated. The body is more inclined forwards
in running than in walking, and there is a period when both
legs are off the ground, no such period occurring in walking.
" In quick walking, the propelling leg acts more obliquely on
the trunk, which is more inclined, and forced forwards more
rapidly than in slow walking. The time when both legs are
on the ground diminishes as the velocity increases, and it
vanishes altogether when the velocity is at a maximum. In
quick running the length of step rapidly increases, whilst the
duration slowly diminishes; but in slow running the length
diminishes rapidly, whilst the time remains nearly the same.
The time of a step in quick running, compared to that in
quick walking, is nearly as two to three, whilst the length of
the steps are as two to one; consequently a person can run in

a given time three times as fast as he can walk. In running, the object is to acquire a greater velocity in progression than can be attained in walking. In order to accomplish this, instead of the body being supported on each leg alternately, the action is divided into two periods, during one of which the body is supported on one leg, and during the other it is not supported at all.

The velocity in running is usually at the rate of about ten miles an hour, but there are many persons who, for a limited period, can exceed this velocity."[1]

> [1] Cyc. of Anat. and Phy., article "Motion."

# PROGRESSION ON AND IN THE WATER.

If we direct our attention to the water, we encounter a medium less dense than the earth, and considerably more dense than the air. As this element, in virtue of its fluidity, yields readily to external pressure, it follows that a certain relation exists between it and the shape, size, and weight of the animal progressing along or through it. Those animals make the greatest headway which are of the same specific gravity, or are a little heavier, and furnished *with extensive surfaces,* which, by a dexterous tilting or twisting (for the one implies the other), or by a sudden contraction and expansion, they apply wholly or in part to obtain the maximum of resistance in the one direction, and the minimum of displacement in the other. The change of shape, and the peculiar movements of the swimming surfaces, are rendered necessary by the fact, first pointed out by Sir Isaac Newton, that bodies or animals moving in water and likewise in air experience a sensible resistance, which is greater or less in proportion to the density and tenacity of the fluid and the figure, superficies, and velocity of the animal.

To obtain the degree of resistance and non-resistance necessary for progression in water, Nature, never at fault, has devised some highly ingenious expedients,—the Syringograde animals advancing by alternately sucking up and ejecting the water in which they are immersed—the Medusæ by a rhythmical contraction and dilatation of their mushroom-shaped disk—the Rotifera or wheel-animalcules by a vibratile action of their cilia, which, according to the late Professor Quekett, twist upon their pedicles so as alternately to increase and diminish the extent of surface presented to the water, as

happens in the feathering of an oar.   A very similar plan is
adopted by the Pteropoda, found in countless multitudes in
the northern seas, which, according to Eschricht, use the
wing-like structures situated near the head after the manner
of a double paddle, resembling in its general features that at
present in use among the Greenlanders.   The characteristic
movement, however, and that adopted in by far the greater
number of instances, is that commonly seen in the fish (figs.
29 and 30)

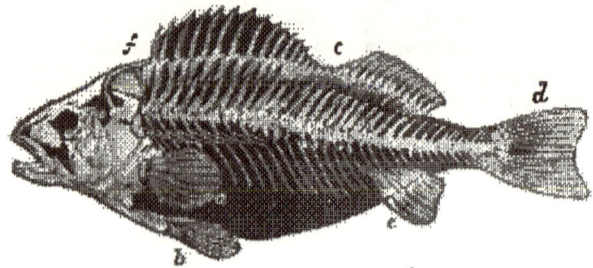

o. 29.—Skeleton of the Perch (*Perca fluviatilis*.  Shows the jointed nature of
the vertebral column, and the facilities afforded for lateral motion, particularly in the tail (d), dorsal (e, f), ventral (b, c), and pectoral (a), fins, which
are principally engaged in swimming.  The extent of the travelling surfaces required for water greatly exceed those required for land.  Compare the
tail and fins of the present figure with the feet of the ox, fig. 18, p. 37.—
(After Dallas.)

Fig. 30.—The Salmon (*Salmo salar*) swimming leisurely  The body, it will be
observed, is bent in two curves, one occurring towards the head, the other
towards the tail.  The shape of the salmon is admirably adapted for cleav-
ing the water.—*Original.*

This, my readers are aware, consists of a lashing, curvilinear, or flail-like movement of the broadly expanded tail, which
oscillates from side to side of the body, in some instances with
immense speed and power.   The muscles in the fish, as has
E

been explained, are for this purpose arranged along the spinal
column, and constitute the bulk of the animal, it being a law
that when the extremities are wanting, as in the water-snake,
or rudimentary, as in the fish, lepidosiren,[1] proteus, and
axolotl, the muscles of the trunk are largely developed.   In
such cases the onus of locomotion falls chiefly, if not entirely,
upon the tail and lower portion of the body.   The operation
of this law is well seen in the metamorphosis of the tad-
pole, the muscles of the trunk and tail becoming modified,
and the tail itself disappearing as the limbs of the perfect
frog are developed.   The same law prevails in certain instances
where the anterior extremities are comparatively perfect,
but too small for swimming purposes, as in the whale,
porpoise, dugong, and manatee, and where both anterior
and posterior extremities are present but dwarfed, as in the
crocodile, triton, and salamander.   The whale, porpoise,
dugong, and manatee employ their anterior extremities in
balancing and turning, the great organ of locomotion being
the tail.   The same may be said of the crocodile, triton, and
salamander, all of which use their extremities in quite a subordinate capacity as compared with the tail.   The peculiar
movements of the trunk and tail evoked in swimming are
seen to most advantage in the fish, and may now be briefly
described.

*Swimming of the Fish, Whale, Porpoise, etc.*—According to
Borelli,[2] and all who have written since his time, the fish in
swimming causes its tail to vibrate on either side of a given
line, very much as a rudder may be made to oscillate by
moving its tiller.   The line referred to corresponds to the
axis of the fish when it is at rest and when its body is straight,
and to the path pursued by the fish when it is swimming.
It consequently represents the axis of the fish and the axis of

---

[1] The *lepidosiren* is furnished with two tapering flexible stem-like bodies,
which depend from the anterior ventral aspect of the animal, the *siren* having
in the same region two pairs of rudimentary limbs furnished with four imperfect toes, while the *proteus* has anterior extremities armed with three toes
each, and a very feeble posterior extremity terminating in two toes.

[2] Borelli, "De motu Animalium," plate 4, fig. 5, sm. 4to, 2 vols.   Rome,
1680.

motion.   According to this theory the tail, when flexed or
curved to make what is termed the back or non-effective
stroke, is forced away from the imaginary line, its curved,
concave, or biting surface being directed outwards.   When,
on the other hand, the tail is extended to make what is termed
the effective or forward stroke, it is urged towards the imaginary line, its convex or non-biting surface being directed
inwards (fig. 31).

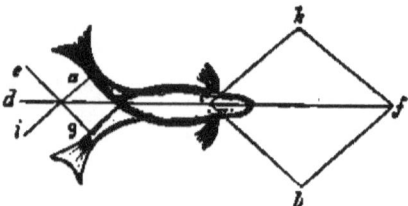

Fig. 31.—Swimming of the Fish.—(After Borelli.)

When the tail strikes in the direction $a\,i$, the head of the
fish is said to travel in the direction $e\,h$.   When the tail
strikes in the direction $g\,e$, the head is said to travel in the
direction $c\,b$; these movements, when the tail is urged with
sufficient velocity, causing the body of the fish to move in
the line $d\,c\,f$.   The explanation is apparently a satisfactory
one; but a careful analysis of the swimming of the living fish
induces me to believe it is incorrect.   According to this, the
commonly received view, the tail would experience a greater
degree of resistance during the back stroke, i.e. when it is
flexed and carried away from the axis of motion ($d\,c\,f$) than
it would during the forward stroke, or when it is extended
and carried towards the axis of motion.   This follows, because
the concave surface of the tail is applied to the water during
what is termed the back or non-effective stroke, and the convex surface during what is termed the forward or effective
stroke.   This is just the opposite of what actually happens,
and led Sir John Lubbock to declare that there was a period
in which the action of the tail dragged the fish backwards,
which, of course, is erroneous.   There is this further difficulty.
When the tail of the fish is urged in the direction $g\,e$, the

head does not move in the direction *c b* as stated, but in the
direction *c h*, the body of the fish describing the arc of a
circle, *a c h*. This is a matter of observation. If a fish when
resting suddenly forces its tail to one side and curves its
body, the fish describes a curve in the water corresponding
to that described by the body. If the concavity of the
curve formed by the body is directed to the right side,
the fish swims in a curve towards that side. To this there
is no exception, as any one may readily satisfy himself, by
watching the movements of gold fish in a vase. Observation
and experiment have convinced me that when a fish swims it
never throws its body into a single curve, as represented at
fig. 31, p. 67, but always into a double or figure-of-8 curve, as
shown at fig. 32.[1]

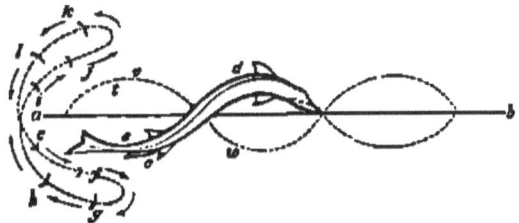

Fig. 82.—Swimming of the Sturgeon. From Nature. Compare with figs. 18
and 19, pp. 37 and 39; fig. 23, p. 43; and figs. 64 to 78, pp. 139, 141, and
144.—*Original.*

The double curve is necessary to enable the fish to present
a convex or non-biting surface (*c*) to the water during flexion
(the back stroke of authors), when the tail is being forced
away from the axis of motion (*a b*), and a concave or biting
surface (*s*) during extension (the forward or effective stroke of
authors), when the tail is being forced with increased energy
towards the axis of motion (*a b*); the resistance occasioned by
a concave surface, when compared with a convex one, being in
the ratio of two to one. The double or complementary curve
into which the fish forces its body when swimming, is necessary to correct the tendency which the head of the fish has
to move in the same direction, or to the same side as that

[1] It is only when a fish is turning that it forces its body into a single curve.

towards which the tail curves. In swimming, the body of
the fish describes a waved track, but this can only be done
when the head and tail travel in opposite directions, and on
opposite sides of a given line, as represented at fig. 32.
The anterior and posterior portions of the fish alternately
occupy the positions indicated at *d c* and *w v;* the fish oscillating on either side of a given line, and gliding along by a
sinuous or wave movement.

I have represented the body of the fish as forced into two
curves when swimming, as there are never less than two.
These I designate the cephalic (*d*) and caudal (*c*) curves, from
their respective positions. In the long-bodied fishes, such as the
eels, the number of the curves is increased, but in every case
the curves occur in pairs, and are complementary. The cephalic
and caudal curves not only complement each other, but they act
as fulcra for each other, the cephalic curve, with the water seized
by it, forming the *point d'appui* for the caudal one, and *vice versâ*.
The fish in swimming lashes its tail from side to side, precisely
as an oar is lashed from side to side in sculling. It therefore
describes a figure-of-8 track in the water (*e f g h i j k l* of
fig. 32). During each sweep or lateral movement the tail is
both extended and flexed. It is extended and its curve
reduced when it approaches the line *a b* of fig. 32, and flexed,
and a new curve formed, when it recedes from the line in
question. The tail is effective as a propeller both during
flexion and extension, so that, strictly speaking, the tail has
no back or non-effective stroke. The terms effective and
non-effective employed by authors are applicable only in a
comparative and restricted sense; the tail always operating,
but being a less effective propeller, when in the act of being
flexed or curved, than when in the act of being extended or
straightened. By always directing the concavity of the tail
(*s* and *t*) towards the axis of motion (*a b*) during extension,
and its convexity (*c* and *v*) away from the axis of motion (*a b*)
during flexion, the fish exerts a maximum of propelling power
with a minimum of slip. In extension of the tail the caudal
curve (*s*) is reduced as the tail travels *towards* the line *a b*.
In flexion a new curve (*v*) is formed as the tail travels *from*
the line *a b*. While the tail travels from *s* in the direction *t*,

the head travels from $d$ in the direction $w$. There is therefore a period, momentary it must be, when both the cephalic
and caudal curves are reduced, and the body of the fish is
straight, and free to advance without impediment. The
different degrees of resistance experienced by the tail in describing its figure-of-8 movements, are represented by the
different-sized curves $e f$, $g h$, $i j$, and $k l$ of fig. 32, p. 68. The
curves $e f$ indicate the resistance experienced by the tail
during flexion, when it is being carried away from and to the
right of the line $a b$. The curves $g h$ indicate the resistance
experienced by the tail when it is extended and carried towards
the line $a b$. This constitutes a half vibration or oscillation of
the tail. The curves $i j$ indicate the resistance experienced
by the tail when it is a second time flexed and carried away
from and to the left of the line $a b$. The curves $k l$ indicate
the resistance experienced by the tail when it is a second
time extended and carried towards the line $a b$. This constitutes a complete vibration. These movements are repeated
in rapid succession so long as the fish continues to swim
forwards. They are only varied when the fish wishes to turn
round, in which case the tail gives single strokes either to
the right or left, according as it wishes to go to the right or
left side respectively. The resistance experienced by the tail
when in the positions indicated by $e f$ and $i j$ is diminished
by the tail being slightly compressed, by its being moved
more slowly, and by the fish rotating on its long axis so as
to present the tail obliquely to the water. The resistance
experienced by the tail when in the positions indicated by
$g h$, $k l$, is increased by the tail being divaricated, by its being
moved with increased energy, and by the fish re-rotating on
its long axis, so as to present the flat of the tail to the water.
The movements of the tail are slowed when the tail is carried
away from the line $a b$, and quickened when the tail is forced
towards it. Nor is this all. When the tail is moved slowly
away from the line $a b$, it draws a current after it which,
being met by the tail when it is urged with increased velocity
towards the line $a b$, enormously increases the hold which the
tail takes of the water, and consequently its propelling power.
The tail may be said to work without slip, and to produce

the precise kind of currents which afford it the greatest leverage. In this respect the tail of the fish is infinitely superior as a propelling organ to any form of screw yet devised. The screw at present employed in navigation ceases to be effective when propelled beyond a given speed. The screw formed by the tail of the fish, in virtue of its reciprocating action, and the manner in which it alternately eludes and seizes the water, becomes more effective in proportion to the rapidity with which it is made to vibrate. The remarks now made of the tail and the water are equally *apropos* of the wing and the air. The tail and the wing act on a common principle. A certain analogy may therefore be traced between the water and air as media, and between the tail and extremities as instruments of locomotion. From this it follows that the water and air are acted upon by curves or wavepressure emanating in the one instance from the tail of the fish, and in the other from the wing of the bird, the reciprocating and opposite curves into which the tail and wing are thrown in swimming and flying constituting *mobile helices* or *screws*, which, during their action, produce the precise kind and degree of pressure adapted to fluid media, and to which they respond with the greatest readiness. The whole body of the fish is thrown into action in swimming ; but as the tail and lower half of the trunk are more free to move than the head and upper half, which are more rigid, and because the tendons of many of the trunk-muscles are inserted into the tail, the oscillation is greatest in the direction of the latter. The muscular movements travel in spiral waves from before backwards; and the waves of force react upon the water, and cause the fish to glide forwards in a series of curves. Since the head and tail, as has been stated, always travel in opposite directions, and the fish is constantly alternating or changing sides, it in reality describes a waved track. These remarks may be readily verified by a reference to the swimming of the sturgeon, whose movements are unusually deliberate and slow. The number of curves into which the body of the fish is thrown in swimming is increased in the long-bodied fishes, as the eels, and decreased in those whose bodies are short or are comparatively devoid of flexibility. In proportion as the curves into which the body is thrown in swimming are diminished, the degree of rotation at the tail or in the fins is augmented, some fishes, as the mackerel, using the tail very much after the manner of a screw in a steam-ship. The fish may thus be said to drill the water in two directions, viz. from behind forwards by a twisting or screwing of the body on its long axis, and from side to side by causing its anterior and posterior portions to assume opposite curves. The pectoral and other fins are also thrown into curves when in action, the movement, as in the body itself, travelling in spiral waves; and it is worthy of remark that the wing of the insect, bat, and bird obeys similar impulses, the pinion, as I shall show presently, being essentially a spiral organ.

The twisting of the pectoral fins is well seen in the common perch (*Perca fluviatilis*), and still better in the 15-spined Stickleback (*Gasterosteus spinosus*), which latter frequently progresses by their aid alone.[1]  In the stickleback, the pectoral fins are so delicate, and are plied with such vigour, that the eye is apt to overlook them, particularly when in motion. The action of the fins can be reversed at pleasure, so that it is by no means an unusual thing to see the stickleback progressing tail first.  The fins are rotated or twisted, and their free margins lashed about by spiral movements which closely resemble those by which the wings of insects are propelled.[2] The rotating of the fish upon its long axis is seen to advantage in the shark and sturgeon, the former of which requires to turn on its side before it can seize its prey,—and likewise

---

[1] The *Syngnathi*, or Pipefishes, swim chiefly by the undulating movement of the dorsal fin.

[2] If the pectoral fins are to be regarded as the homologues of the anterior extremities (which they unquestionably are), it is not surprising that in them the spiral rotatory movements which are traceable in the extremities of quadrupeds, and so fully developed in the wings of bats and birds, should be clearly foreshadowed. "The muscles of the pectoral fins," remarks Professor Owen, "though, when compared with those of the homologous members in higher vertebrates, they are very small, few, and simple, yet suffice for all the requisite movements of the fins—elevating, depressing, advancing, and again laying them prone and flat, by an oblique stroke, upon the sides of the body. The rays or digits of both pectorals and ventrals (the homologues of the posterior extremities) can be divaricated and approximated, and the intervening webs spread out or folded up."—*Op. cit.* vol. 1. p. 252.

in the pipefish, whose motions are unwontedly sluggish. The twisting of the tail is occasionally well marked in the swimming of the salamander. In those remarkable mammals, the whale,[1] porpoise, manatee, and dugong (figs. 33, 34, and 35), the movements are strictly analogous to those of the fish,

FIG. 33.—The Porpoise (*Phocæna communis*). Here the tail is principally engaged in swimming, the anterior extremities being rudimentary, and resembling the pectoral fins of fishes. Compare with fig. 30, p. 65.—*Original.*

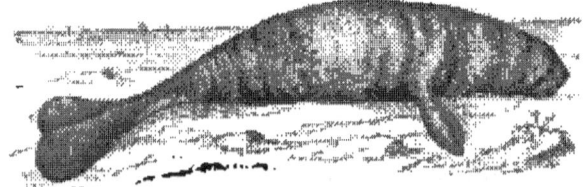

FIG. 34.—The Manatee (*Manatus Americanus*). In this the anterior extremities are more developed than in the porpoise, but still the tail is the great organ of natation. Compare with fig. 33, p. 73, and with fig. 30, p. 65. The shape of the manatee and porpoise is essentially that of the fish.—*Original.*

the only difference being that the tail acts from above downwards or vertically, instead of from side to side or laterally. The anterior extremities, which in those animals are comparatively perfect, are rotated on their long axes, and applied obliquely and non-obliquely to the water, to assist in balancing and turning. Natation is performed almost exclusively by the tail and lower half of the trunk, the tail of the whale exerting prodigious power.

It is otherwise with the Rays, where the hands are princi-

[1] *Vide* "Remarks on the Swimming of the Cetaceans," by Dr. Murie, Proc. Zool. Soc., 1865, pp. 209, 210.

pally concerned in progression, these flapping about in the
water very much as the wings of a bird flap about in the air.
In the beaver, the tail is flattened from above downwards, as
in the foregoing mammals, but in swimming it is made to

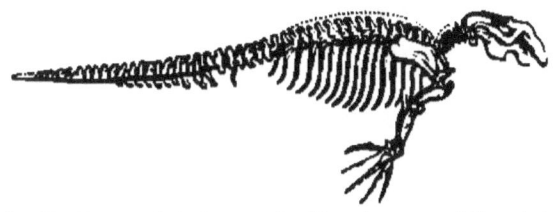

Fig. 35.—Skeleton of the Dugong. In this curious mammal the anterior
extremities are more developed than in the manatee and porpoise, and
resemble those found in the seal, sea-bear, and walrus. They are useful
in balancing and turning, the tail being the effective instrument of propulsion. The vertebral column closely resembles that of the fish, and allows
the tail to be lashed freely about in a vertical direction. Compare with
fig. 29, p. 65.—(After Dallas.)

act upon the water laterally as in the fish. The tail of the
bird, which is also compressed from above downwards, can
be twisted obliquely, and when in this position may be made
to perform the office of a rudder.

*Swimming of the Seal, Sea-Bear, and Walrus.*—In the seal,
the anterior and posterior extremities are more perfect than
in the whale, porpoise, dugong, and manatee; the general

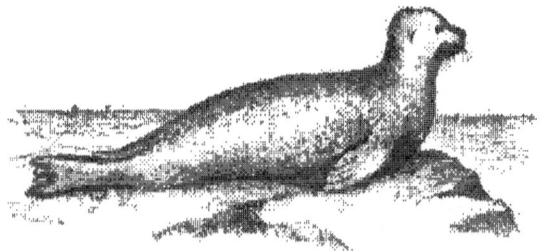

Fig. 36.—The Seal (*Phoca fœtida*, Mull.), adapted principally for water. The
extremities are larger than in the porpoise and manatee. Compare with
figs. 33 and 34, p. 73.—*Original.*

form, however, and mode of progression (if the fact of its
occasionally swimming on its back be taken into account), is
essentially fish-like.

A peculiarity is met with in the swimming of the seal, to which I think it proper to direct attention. When the lower portion of the body and posterior extremities of these creatures are flexed and tilted, as happens during the back and least effective stroke, the naturally expanded feet are more or less completely closed or pressed together, in order to diminish the extent of surface presented to the water, and, as a consequence, to reduce the resistance produced. The feet are opened to the utmost during extension, when the more effective stroke is given, in which case they present their maximum of surface. They form powerful propellers, both during flexion and extension.

The swimming apparatus of the seal is therefore more highly differentiated than that of the whale, porpoise, dugong, and manatee; the natatory tail in these animals being, from its peculiar structure, incapable of lateral compression.[1] It would appear that the swimming appliances of the seals (where the feet open and close as in swimming-birds) are to those of the sea-mammals generally, what the feathers of the bird's wing (these also open and close in flight) are to the continuous membrane forming the wing of the insect and bat.

The anterior extremities or flippers of the seal are not engaged in swimming, but only in balancing and in changing position. When so employed the fore feet open and close, though not to the same extent as the hind ones; the resistance and non-resistance necessary being secured by a partial rotation and tilting of the flippers. By this twisting and untwisting, the narrow edges and broader portions of the flippers are applied to the water alternately. The rotating and tilting of the anterior and posterior extremities, and the opening and closing of the hands and feet in the balancing and swimming of the seal, form a series of strictly progressive and very graceful movements. They are, however, performed so rapidly, and glide into each other so perfectly, as to render an analysis of them exceedingly difficult.

[1] In a few instances the caudal fin of the fish, as has been already stated, is more or less pressed together during the back stroke, the compression and tilting or twisting of the tail taking place synchronously.

In the Sea-Bear (*Otaria jubata*) the anterior extremities attain sufficient magnitude and power to enable the animal to progress by their aid alone; the feet and the lower portions of the body being moved only sufficiently to maintain, correct, or alter the course pursued (fig. 73). The anterior extremities are flattened out, and greatly resemble wings, particularly those of the penguin and auk, which are rudimentary in character. Thus they have a thick and comparatively stiff anterior margin ; and a thin, flexible, and more or less elastic posterior margin. They are screw structures, and when elevated and depressed in the water, twist and untwist, screw-fashion, precisely as wings do, or the tails of the fish, whale, dugong, and manatee.

Fig. 37.—The Sea-Bear (*Otaria jubata*), adapted principally for swimming and diving. It also walks with tolerable facility. Its extremities are larger than those of the seal, and its movements, both in and out of the water, more varied.—*Original.*

This remarkable creature, which I have repeatedly watched at the Zoological Gardens[1] (London), appears to fly in the water, the universal joints by which the arms are attached to the shoulders enabling it, by partially rotating and twisting

---

[1] The unusual opportunities afforded by this unrivalled collection have enabled me to determine with considerable accuracy the movements of the various land-animals, as well as the motions of the wings and feet of birds, both in and out of the water. I have also studied under the most favourable circumstances the movements of the otter, sea-bear, seal, walrus, porpoise, turtle, triton, crocodile, frog, lepidosiren, proteus, axolotl, and the several orders of fishes.

them, to present the palms or flat of the hands to the water the one instant, and the edge or narrow parts the next. In swimming, the anterior or thick margins of the flippers are *directed downwards*, and similar remarks are to be made of the anterior extremities of the walrus, great auk, and turtle.[1]

The flippers are advanced alternately; and the twisting, screw-like movement which they exhibit in action, and which I have carefully noted on several occasions, bears considerable resemblance to the motions witnessed in the pectoral fins of fishes. It may be remarked that the twisting or spiral movements of the anterior extremities are calculated to utilize the water to the utmost—the gradual but rapid operation of the helix enabling the animal to lay hold of the water and disentangle itself with astonishing facility, and with the minimum expenditure of power. In fact, the insinuating motion of the screw is the only one which can contend successfully with the liquid element; and it appears to me that this remark holds even more true of the air. It also applies within certain limits, as has been explained, to the land. The otaria or sea-bear swims, or rather flies, under the water with remarkable address and with apparently equal ease in an upward, downward, and horizontal direction, by muscular efforts alone—an observation which may likewise be made regarding a great number of fishes, since the swimming-bladder or float is in many entirely absent.[2] Compare with figs. 33, 34, 35, and 36, pp. 73 and 74. The walrus, a living specimen of which I had an opportunity of frequently examining, is nearly allied to the seal and sea-bear, but differs from both as regards its manner of swimming. The natation of this rare and singularly interesting animal, as I have taken great pains to satisfy myself, is effected by a mixed movement—the anterior and posterior extremities participating in nearly an equal degree. The anterior extremities or flippers of the walrus, morphologically resemble those of the seal, but physiologically those of the sea-bear; while the posterior extremities

---

[1] This is the reverse of what takes place in flying, the anterior or thick margins of the wings being invariably *directed upwards.*

[2] The air-bladder is wanting in the dermopteri, plagiostomi, and pleuronectidæ.—Owen, *op. cit.* p. 255.

possess many of the peculiarities of the hind legs of the sea-bear, but display the movements peculiar to those of the seal. In other words, the anterior extremities or flippers of the walrus are moved alternately, and reciprocate, as in the sea-bear; whereas the posterior extremities are lashed from side to side by a twisting, curvilinear motion, precisely as in the seal. The walrus may therefore, as far as the physiology of ts extremities is concerned, very properly be regarded as holding an intermediate position between the seals on the one hand, and the sea-bears or sea-lions on the other.

*Swimming of Man.*—The swimming of man is artificial in its nature, and consequently does not, strictly speaking, fall within the scope of the present work. I refer to it principally with a view to showing that it resembles in its general features the swimming of animals.

The human body is lighter than the water, a fact of considerable practical importance, as showing that each has in himself that which will prevent his being drowned, if he will only breathe naturally, and desist from struggling.

The catastrophe of drowning is usually referrible to nervous agitation, and to spasmodic and ill-directed efforts in the extremities. All swimmers have a vivid recollection of the great difficulty experienced in keeping themselves afloat, when they first resorted to aquatic exercises and amusements. In especial they remember the short, vigorous, but flurried, misdirected, and consequently futile strokes which, instead of enabling them to skim the surface, conducted them inevitably to the bottom. Indelibly impressed too are the ineffectual attempts at respiration, the gasping and puffing and the swallowing of water, inadvertently gulped instead of air.

In order to swim well, the operator must be perfectly calm. He must, moreover, know how to apply his extremities to the water with a view to propulsion. As already stated, the body will float if left to itself; the support obtained is, however, greatly increased by projecting it along the surface of the water. This, as all swimmers are aware, may be proved by experiment. It is the same principle which prevents a thin flat stone from sinking when projected with force against the surface of water. A precisely similar result is obtained if the body be placed slantingly in a strong current, and the hands made to grasp a stone or branch. In this case the body is raised to the surface of the stream by the action of the running water, the body remaining motionless. The quantity of water which, under the circumstances, impinges against the body in a given time is much greater than if the body was simply immersed in still water. To increase the area of support, either the supporting medium or the body supported must move. The body is supported in water very much as the kite is supported in air. In both cases the body and the kite are made to strike the water and the air at a slight upward angle. When the extremities are made to move in a horizontal or slightly downward direction, they at once propel and support the body. When, however, they are made to act in an upward direction, as in diving, they submerge the body. This shows that the movements of the swimming surfaces may, according to their direction, either augment or destroy buoyancy. The swimming surfaces enable the seal, sea-bear, otter, ornithorhynchus, bird, etc., to disappear from and regain the surface of the water. Similar remarks may be made of the whale, dugong, manatee, and fish.

Man, in order to swim, must learn the art of swimming. He must serve a longer or shorter apprenticeship to a new form of locomotion, and acquire a new order of movements. It is otherwise with the majority of animals. Almost all quadrupeds can swim the first time they are immersed, as may readily be ascertained by throwing a newly born kitten or puppy into the water. The same may be said of the greater number of birds. This is accounted for by the fact that quadrupeds and birds are lighter, bulk for bulk, than water, but more especially, because in walking and running the movements made by their extremities are precisely those required in swimming. They have nothing to learn, as it were. They are buoyant naturally, and if they move their limbs at all, which they do instinctively, they swim of necessity. It is different with man. The movements made by him in walking and running are not those made by him in swimming; neither is the position resorted to in swimming that which characterizes him on land. The vertical position

is not adapted for water, and, as a consequence, he requires
to abandon it and assume a horizontal one; he requires, in
fact, to throw himself flat upon the water, either upon his
side, or upon his dorsal or ventral aspect. This position
assimilates him to the quadruped and bird, the fish, and
everything that swims; the trunks of all swimming animals
being placed in a prone position. Whenever the horizontal
position is assumed, the swimmer can advance in any direction he pleases. His extremities are quite free, and only
require to be moved in definite directions to produce definite
results. The body can be propelled by the two arms, or the
two legs; or by the right arm and leg, or the left arm and
leg; or by the right arm and left leg, or the left arm and
right leg. Most progress is made when the two arms and
the two legs are employed. An expert swimmer can do
whatever he chooses in water. Thus he can throw himself
upon his back, and by extending his arms obliquely above his
head until they are in the same plane with his body, can
float without any exertion whatever; or, maintaining the
floating position, he can fold his arms upon his chest and by
alternately flexing and extending his lower extremities, can
propel himself with ease and at considerable speed; or, keeping
his legs in the extended position and motionless, he can propel himself by keeping his arms close to his body, and causing
his hands to work like sculls, so as to make figure-of-8 loops
in the water. This motion greatly resembles that made by
the swimming wings of the penguin. It is most effective
when the hands are turned slightly upwards, and a greater or
less backward thrust given each time the hands reciprocate.
The progress made at first is slow, but latterly very rapid,
the rapidity increasing according to the momentum acquired.
The swimmer, in addition to the foregoing methods, can
throw himself upon his face, and by alternately flexing and extending his arms and legs, can float and propel himself for long
periods with perfect safety and with comparatively little exertion. He can also assume the vertical position, and by remaining perfectly motionless, or by treading the water with his
feet, can prevent himself from sinking; nay more, he can turn
a somersault in the water either in a forward or backward

direction. The position most commonly assumed in swimming is the prone one, where the ventral surface of the body
is directed towards the water. In this case the anterior and
posterior extremities are simultaneously flexed and drawn
towards the body slowly, after which they are simultaneously
and rapidly extended. The swimming of the frog conveys an
idea of the movement.[1] In ordinary swimming, when the
anterior and posterior extremities are simultaneously flexed,
and afterwards simultaneously extended, the hands and feet
describe four ellipses; an arrangement which, as explained,
increases the area of support furnished by the moving parts.
The ellipses are shown at fig. 38; the continuous lines representing extension, the dotted lines flexion.

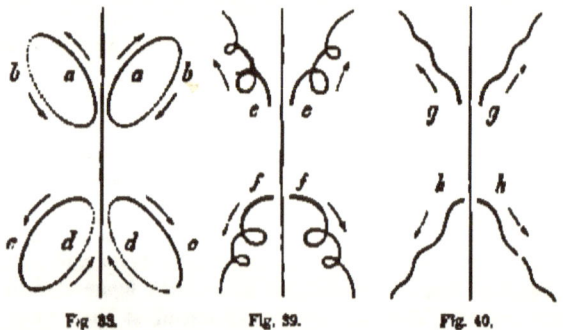

Fig. 38.              Fig. 39.                Fig. 40.

Thus when the arms and legs are pushed away from the
body, the arms describe the inner sides of the ellipses (fig.
38, *a a*), the legs describing the outer sides (*c c*). When the
arms and legs are drawn towards the body, the arms describe
the outer sides of the ellipses (*b b*), the legs describing the
inner sides (*d d*). As the body advances, the ellipses are opened
out and loops formed, as at *e e, f f* of fig. 39. If the speed
attained is sufficiently high, the loops are converted into

---

[1] The frog in swimming leisurely frequently causes its extremities to move
diagonally and alternately. When, however, pursued and alarmed, it folds
its fore legs, and causes its hind ones to move simultaneously and with great
vigour by a series of sudden jerks, similar to those made by man when
swimming on his back.

F

waved lines, as in walking and flying.—(*Vide g g, h h* of fig.
40, p. 81, and compare with fig. 18, p. 37, and figs. 71 and 73,
p. 144.)   The swimming of man, like the walking, swimming,
and flying of animals, is effected by alternately flexing and
extending the limbs, as shown more particularly at fig. 41,
*A, B, C.*

Fig. 41.—*A* shows the arms and legs folded or flexed and drawn towards the
mesial line of the body.—*Original.*
   *B* shows the arms and legs opened out or extended and carried away from
the mesial line of the body.—*Original.*
   *C* shows the arms and legs in an intermediate position, *i.e.* when they are
neither flexed nor extended.   The arms and legs require to be in the position shown at *A* before they can assume that represented at *B*, and they
require to be in the position shown at *B* before they can assume that
represented at *C*.   When the arms and legs are successively assuming the
positions indicated at *A, B,* and *C,* they move in ellipses, as explained.—
*Original.*

By alternately flexing and extending the limbs, the angles
made by their several parts with each other are decreased
and increased,—an arrangement which diminishes and augments the degree of resistance experienced by the swimming
surfaces, which by this means are made to elude and seize
the water by turns.   This result is further secured by the
limbs being made to move more slowly in flexion than in
extension, and by the limbs being made to rotate in the
direction of their length in such a manner as to diminish the
resistance experienced during the former movement, and
increase it during the latter.   When the arms are extended,
the palms of the hands and the inner surfaces of the arms
are directed downwards, and assist in buoying up the
anterior portion of the body.   The hands are screwed
slightly round towards the end of extension, the palms acting

in an outward and backward direction (fig. 41, *B*). In this movement the posterior surfaces of the arms take part; the palms and posterior portions of the arms contributing to the propulsion of the body. When the arms are flexed, the flat of the hands is directed downwards (fig. 41, *C*). Towards the end of flexion the hands are slightly depressed, which has the effect of forcing the body upwards, and hence the bobbing or vertical wave-movement observed in the majority of swimmers.[1]

During flexion the posterior surfaces of the arms act powerfully as propellers, from the fact of their striking the water obliquely in a backward direction. I avoid the terms *back* and *forward* strokes, because the arms and hands, so long as they move, support and propel. There is no period either in extension or flexion in which they are not effective. When the legs are pushed away from the body, or extended (a movement which is effected rapidly and with great energy, as shown at fig. 41, *B*), the soles of the feet, the anterior surfaces of the legs, and the posterior surfaces of the thighs, are directed outwards and backwards. This enables them to seize the water with great avidity, and to propel the body forward. The efficiency of the legs and feet as propelling organs during extension is increased by their becoming more or less straight, and by their being moved with greater rapidity than in flexion; there being a general back-thrust of the limbs as a whole, and a particular back-thrust of their several parts.[2] In this movement the inner surfaces of the legs and thighs act as sustaining organs and assist in floating the posterior part of the body. The slightly inclined position of the body in the water, and the forward motion acquired in swimming, contribute to this result. When the legs and feet are drawn towards the body or flexed, as seen at fig. 41, *C*, *A*,

[1] The professional swimmer avoids bobbing, and rests the side of his head on the water to diminish its weight and increase speed.

[2] The greater power possessed by the limbs during extension, and more especially towards the end of extension, is well illustrated by the kick of the horse; the hind feet dealing a terrible blow when they have reached their maximum distance from the body. Ostlers are well aware of this fact, and in grooming a horse keep always very close to his hind quarters, so that if he does throw up they are forced back but not injured.

their movements are slowed, an arrangement which reduces
the degree of friction experienced by the several parts of the
limbs when they are, as it were, being drawn off the water
preparatory to a second extension.

There are several grave objections to the ordinary or old
method of swimming just described. 1st, The body is laid
prone on the water, which exposes a large resisting surface
(fig. 41, *A, B, C*, p. 82).   2d, The arms and legs are spread
out on either side of the trunk, so that they are applied very
indirectly as propelling organs (fig. 41, *B, C*).   3d, The most
effective part of the stroke of the arms and legs corresponds
to something like a quarter of an ellipse, the remaining three
quarters being dedicated to getting the arms and legs into
position.   This arrangement wastes power and greatly increases friction ; the attitudes assumed by the body at *B* and
*C* of fig. 41 being the worst possible for getting through the
water.   4th, The arms and legs are drawn towards the trunk
the one instant (fig. 41, *A*), and pushed away from it the next
(fig. 41, *B*).   This gives rise to dead points, there being a
period when neither of the extremities are moving.   The
body is consequently impelled by a series of jerks, the swimming mass getting up and losing momentum between the
strokes.

In order to remedy these defects, scientific swimmers have
of late years adopted quite another method.   Instead of
working the arms and legs together, they move first the arm
and leg of one side of the body, and then the arm and leg of
the opposite side.   This is known as the *overhand* movement,
and corresponds exactly with the natural walk of the giraffe,
the amble of the horse, and the swimming of the sea-bear.
It is that adopted by the Indians   In this mode of swimming
the body is thrown more or less on its side at each stroke,
the body twisting and rolling in the direction of its length,
as shown at fig. 42, an arrangement calculated greatly to
reduce the amount of friction experienced in forward motion.

The overhand movement enables the swimmer to throw
himself forward on the water, and to move his arms and legs
in a nearly vertical instead of a horizontal plane ; the extremities working, as it were, above and beneath the trunk,

rather than on either side of it. The extremities are consequently employed in the best manner possible for developing their power and reducing the friction to forward motion caused by their action. This arrangement greatly increases the length of the effective stroke, both of the arms and legs, this being equal to nearly half an ellipse. Thus when the left arm and leg are thrust forward, the arm describes the curve *a b* (fig. 42), the leg *e* describing a similar curve. As the right side of the body virtually recedes when the left side advances, the right arm describes the curve *c d*, while the left arm is describing the curve *a b*; the right leg *f* describing a curve the opposite of that described by *e* (compare arrows). The advancing of the right and left sides of

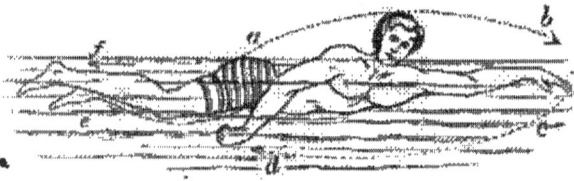

Fig. 42.—Overhand Swimming.—*Original.*

the body alternately, in a nearly straight line, greatly contributes to continuity of motion, the impulse being applied now to the right side and now to the left, and the limbs being disposed and worked in such a manner as in a great measure to reduce friction and prevent dead points or halts. When the left arm and leg are being thrust forward (*a b, e* of fig. 42), the right arm and leg strike very nearly directly backward (*c d, f* of fig. 42). The right arm and leg, and the resistance which they experience from the water consequently form a *point d'appui* for the left arm and leg; the two sides of the body twisting and screwing upon a moveable fulcrum (the water)—an arrangement which secures a maximum of propulsion with a minimum of resistance and a minimum of slip. The propulsive power is increased by the concave surfaces of the hands and feet being directed backwards during the back stroke, and by the arms being made to throw their back water in a slightly outward direction, so as not to impede the advance of the legs. The overhand method of swimming

is the most expeditious yet discovered, but it is fatiguing, and
can only be indulged in for short distances.

An improvement on the foregoing for long distances is
that known as the *side* stroke. In this method, as the term
indicates, the body is thrown more decidedly upon the side.
Either side may be employed, some preferring to swim on the
right side, and some on the left; others swimming alternately
on the right and left sides. In swimming by the side stroke
(say on the left side), the left arm is advanced in a curve,
and made to describe the upper side of an ellipse, as represented at *a b* of fig. 43. This done, the right arm and legs are
employed as propellers, the right arm and legs making a
powerful backward stroke, in which the concavity of the hand

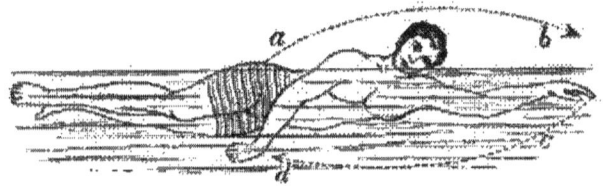

Fig. 43.—Side-stroke Swimming.—Original

is directed backwards and outwards, as shown at *c d* of the
same figure.[1] The right arm in this movement describes
the under side of an ellipse, and acts in a nearly vertical
plane. When the right arm and legs are advanced, some
swimmers lift the right arm out of the water, in order to
diminish friction—the air being more easily penetrated
than the water. The lifting of the arm out of the water
increases the speed, but the movement is neither graceful
nor comfortable, as it immerses the head of the swimmer
at each stroke. Others keep the right arm in the water
and extend the arm and hand in such a manner as to
cause it to cut straight forward. In the side stroke the left
arm (if the operator swims on the left side) acts as a cutwater
(fig. 43, *b*). It is made to advance when the right arm

[1] The outward direction given to the arm and hand enables them to force
away the back water from the body and limbs, and so reduce the friction to
forward motion.

and legs are forced backwards (fig. 43, c d). The right arm
and legs move together, and alternate with the left arm,
which moves by itself. The right arm and legs are flexed
and carried forwards, while the left arm is extended and
forced backwards, and *vice versd*. The left arm always moves
in an opposite direction to the right arm and legs. We have
thus in the side stroke three limbs moving together in the
same direction and keeping time, the fourth limb always
moving in an opposite direction and out of time with the
other three. The limb which moves out of time is the left
one if the operator swims on the left side, and the right one
if he swims on the right side. In swimming on the left
side, the right arm and legs are advanced slowly the one
instant, and forced in a backward direction with great energy
and rapidity the next. Similar remarks are to be made regarding the left arm. When the right arm and legs strike
backwards they communicate to the body a powerful forward
impulse, which, seeing the body is tilted upon its side and
advancing as on a keel, transmits it to a considerable distance.
This arrangement reduces the amount of resistance to forward
motion, conserves the energy of the swimmer, and secures in a
great measure continuity of movement, the body being in the
best possible position for gliding forward between the strokes.

In good side swimming the legs are made to diverge
widely when they are extended or pushed away from the
body, so as to include within them a fluid wedge, the apex of
which is directed forwards. When fully extended, the legs
are made to converge in such a manner that they force the
body away from the wedge, and so contribute to its propulsion. By this means the legs in extension are made to
give what may be regarded a double stroke, viz. an outward
and inward one. When the double move has been made,
the legs are flexed or drawn towards the body preparatory to
a new stroke. In swimming on the left side, the left or
cutwater arm is extended or pushed away from the body in
such a manner that the concavity of the left hand is directed
forwards, and describes the upper half of a vertical ellipse.
It thus meets with comparatively little resistance from the
water. When, however, the left arm is flexed and drawn

towards the body, the concavity of the left hand is directed backwards and made to describe the under half of the ellipse, so as to scoop and seize the water, and thus contribute to the propulsion of the body. The left or cutwater arm materially assists in floating the anterior portions of the body. The stroke made by the left arm is equal to a quarter of a circle, that made by the right arm to half a circle. The right arm, when the operator swims upon the left side, is consequently the more powerful propeller. The right arm, like the left, assists in supporting the anterior portion of the body. In swimming on the left side the major propelling factors are the right arm and hand and the right and left legs and feet. Swimming by the side stroke is, on the whole, the most useful, graceful, and effective yet devised. It enables the swimmer to make headway against wind, wave, and tide in quite a remarkable manner. Indeed, a dexterous side-stroke swimmer can progress when a powerful breast-swimmer would be driven back. In still water an expert non-professional swimmer ought to make a mile in from thirty to thirty-five minutes. A professional swimmer may greatly exceed this. Thus, Mr. J. B. Johnson, when swimming against time, August 5th, 1872, in the fresh-water lake at Hendon, near London, did the full mile in twenty-six minutes. The first half-mile was done in twelve minutes. *Cæteris paribus*, the shorter the distance, the greater the speed. In August 1868, Mr. Harry Parker, a well-known professional swimmer, swam 500 yards in the Serpentine in seven minutes fifty seconds. Among non-professional swimmers the performance of Mr. J. B. Booth is very creditable. This gentleman, in June 1871, swam 440 yards in seven minutes fourteen seconds in the fresh-water lake at Hendon, already referred to. I am indebted for the details regarding time to Mr. J. A. Cowan of Edinburgh, himself acknowledged to be one of the fastest swimmers in Scotland. The speed attained by man in the water is not great when his size and power are taken into account. It certainly contrasts very unfavourably with that of seals, and still more unfavourably with that of fishes. This is due to his small hands and feet, the slow movements of his arms and legs, and the awkward manner in which they are applied to and withdrawn from the water.

*Swimming of the Turtle, Triton, Crocodile, etc.*—The swimming of the turtle differs in some respects from all the other forms of swimming. While the anterior extremities of this

Fig. 44.—The Turtle *Chelonia imbricata*, adapted for swimming and diving, the extremities being relatively larger than in the seal, sea-bear, and walrus. The anterior extremities have a thick anterior margin and a thin posterior one, and in this respect resemble wings. Compare with figs. 36 and 37, pp. 74 and 76.—*Original.*

quaint animal move alternately, and tilt or partially rotate during their action, as in the sea-bear and walrus, the posterior

Fig. 45.—The Crested Newt (*Triton cristatus*, Laur.) In the newt a tail is superadded to the extremities, the tail and the extremities both acting in swimming.—*Original.*

extremities likewise move by turns. As, moreover, the right anterior and left posterior extremities move together, and reciprocate with the left anterior and right posterior ones, the creature has the appearance of walking in the water (fig. 44).

The same remarks apply to the movements of the extremities of the triton (fig. 45, p. 89) and crocodile, when swimming, and to the feebly developed corresponding members in the lepidosiren, proteus, and axolotl, specimens of all of which are to be seen in the Zoological Society's Gardens, London. In the latter, natation is effected principally, if not altogether, by the tail and lower half of the body, which is largely developed and flattened laterally for this purpose, as in the fish.

The muscular power exercised by the fishes, the cetaceans, and the seals in swimming, is conserved to a remarkable extent by the momentum which the body rapidly acquires—the velocity attained by the mass diminishing the degree of exertion required in the individual or integral parts. This holds true of all animals, whether they move on the land or on or in the water or air.

The animals which furnish the connecting link between the water and the air are the diving-birds on the one hand, and the flying-fishes on the other,—the former using their wings for flying above and through the water, as occasion demands; the latter sustaining themselves for considerable intervals in the air by means of their enormous pectoral fins.

*Flight under water, etc.*—Mr. Macgillivray thus describes a flock of red mergansers which he observed pursuing sand-eels in one of the shallow sandy bays of the Outer Hebrides :— " The birds seemed to move under the water with almost as much velocity as in the air, and often rose to breathe at a distance of 200 yards from the spot at which they had dived."[1]

In birds which fly indiscriminately above and beneath the water, the wing is provided with stiff feathers, and reduced to a minimum as regards size. In subaqueous flight the wings may act by themselves, as in the guillemots, or in conjunction with the feet, as in the grebes.[2] To convert the

---

[1] History of British Birds, vol. i. p. 48.

[2] The guillemots in diving do not use their feet ; so that they literally fly under the water. Their wings for this purpose are reduced to the smallest possible dimensions consistent with flight. The loons, on the other hand, while they employ their feet, rarely, if ever, use their wings. The subaqueous progression of the grebe resembles that of the frog.—Cuvier's Animal Kingdom, Lond. 1840, pp. 252, 253.

wing into a powerful oar for swimming, it is only necessary
to extend and flex it in a slightly backward direction, the
mere act of extension causing the feathers to roll down, and
giving to the back of the wing, which in this case communicates the more effective stroke, the angle or obliquity necessary for sending the animal forward.   This angle, I may
observe, corresponds with that made by the foot during extension, so that, if the feet and wings are both employed,
they act in harmony.   If proof were wanting that it is the
back or convex surface of the wing which gives the more
effective stroke in subaquatic flight, it would be found in the
fact that in the penguin and great auk, which are totally incapable of flying out of the water, the wing is actually twisted

Fig. 46.—The Little Penguin (*Aptenodytes minor*, Linn.), adapted exclusively
for swimming and diving.  In this quaint bird the wing forms a perfect
screw, and is employed as such in swimming and diving.  Compare with
fig. 37, p. 70, and fig. 44, p. 89.—*Original.*

round in order that the concave surface, which takes a better
hold of the water, may be directed backwards (fig. 46).[1]   The
thick margin of the wing when giving the effective stroke
is turned downwards, as happens in the flippers of the
sea-bear, walrus, and turtle.   This, I need scarcely remark, is
precisely the reverse of what occurs in the ordinary wing in
aërial flight.   In those extraordinary birds (great auk and
penguin) the wing is covered with short, bristly-looking
feathers, and is a mere rudiment and exceedingly rigid, the

[1] In the swimming of the crocodile, turtle, triton, and frog, the concave
surfaces of the feet of the anterior extremities are likewise turned backwards.

movement which wields it emanating, for the most part, from
the shoulder, where the articulation partakes of the nature of
a universal joint. The wing is beautifully twisted upon itself,
and when it is elevated and advanced, it rolls up from the
side of the bird at varying degrees of obliquity, till it makes
a right angle with the body, when it presents a *narrow* or
*cutting edge* to the water. The wing when fully extended,
as in ordinary flight, makes, on the contrary, an angle of
something like 30° with the horizon. When the wing is
depressed and carried backwards,[1] the angles which its under
surface make with the surface of the water are gradually
increased. The wing of the penguin and auk propels both
when it is elevated and depressed. It acts very much after
the manner of a screw; and this, as I shall endeavour to
show, holds true likewise of the wing adapted for aërial flight.

*Difference between Subaquatic and Aërial Flight.*—The difference between subaquatic flight or diving, and flight proper,
may be briefly stated. In aërial flight, the most effective
stroke is delivered *downwards* and *forwards* by the under,
concave, or biting surface of the wing which is turned in this
direction; the less effective stroke being delivered in an upward and forward direction by the upper, convex, or non-
biting surface of the wing. In subaquatic flight, on the
contrary, the most effective stroke is delivered *downwards* and
*backwards*, the least effective one upwards and forwards. In
aërial flight the long axis of the body of the bird and the
short axis of the wings are inclined slightly upwards, and make
a *forward* angle with the horizon. In subaquatic flight the
long axis of the body of the bird, and the short axis of the
wings are inclined slightly downwards and make a *backward*
angle with the surface of the water. The wing acts more or less
efficiently in every direction, as the tail of the fish does. The
difference noted in the direction of the down stroke in flying
and diving, is rendered imperative by the fact that a bird which
flies in the air is heavier than the medium it navigates, and
must be supported by the wings; whereas a bird which flies
under the water or dives, is lighter than the water, and must

[1] The effective stroke is also delivered during flexion in the shrimp, prawn, and lobster.

force itself into it to prevent its being buoyed up to the surface. However paradoxical it may seem, *weight* is necessary
to aërial flight, and *levity* to subaquatic flight. A bird destined
to fly above the water is provided with travelling surfaces, so
fashioned and so applied (they strike *from above, downwards*
and *forwards*), that if it was lighter than the air, they would
carry it off into space without the possibility of a return ; in
other words, the action of the wings would carry the bird
obliquely upwards, and render it quite incapable of flying
either in a horizontal or downward direction. In the same
way, if a bird destined to fly under the water (auk and penguin) was not lighter than the water, such is the configuration
and mode of applying its travelling surfaces (they strike *from
above, downwards* and *backwards*), they would carry it in the
direction of the bottom without any chance of return to the
surface. In aërial flight, weight is the power which nature
has placed at the disposal of the bird for regulating its altitude and horizontal movements, a cessation of the play of its
wings, aided by the inertia of its trunk, enabling the bird to
approach the earth. In subaquatic flight, levity is a power
furnished for a similar but opposite purpose ; this, combined
with the partial slowing or stopping of the wings and feet,
enabling the diving bird to regain the surface at any moment.
Levity and weight are auxiliary forces, but they are necessary
forces when the habits of the aërial and aquatic birds and the
form and mode of applying their travelling surfaces are taken
into account. If the aërial flying bird was lighter than the air,
its wings would require *to be twisted round* to resemble the diving
wings of the penguin and auk. If, on the other hand, the diving
bird (penguin or auk) was heavier than the water, its wings
would require to resemble aërial wings, and they would require
to strike in an opposite direction to that in which they strike
normally. From this it follows that *weight* is necessary to the
bird (as at present constructed) destined to navigate the air,
and *levity* to that destined to navigate the water. If a bird
was made very large and very light, it is obvious that the
diving force at its disposal would be inadequate to submerge
it. If, again, it was made very small and very heavy, it is
equally plain that it could not fly. Nature, however, has

struck the just balance; she has made the diving bird, which
flies under the water, relatively much heavier than the bird

FIG. 47.—At *A* the penguin is in the act of diving, and it will be observed that the anterior or thick margin of the wing is directed downwards and forwards, while the posterior margin is directed upwards and backwards. This has the effect of directing the under or ventral concave surface of the wing upwards and backwards, the most effective stroke being delivered in a downward and backward direction. The efficacy of the wing in counteracting levity is thus obvious. At *B* the penguin is in the act of regaining the surface of the water, and in this case the wing is articulated in one position, or made to strike downwards and forwards like the aerial wing, the margins and under surface of the pinion being reversed for this purpose. The pinion now is not to depress but to elevate the body. These movements are facilitated by the alternate play of the feet. (Compare fig. 47 with fig. 57, p. 78.)

which flies in the air, and has curtailed the travelling surfaces
of the former, while she has increased those of the latter.

For the same reason, she has furnished the diving bird with a certain degree of buoyancy, and the flying bird with a certain amount of weight—levity tending to bring the one to the surface of the water, weight the other to the surface of the earth, which is the normal position of rest for both. The action of the subaquatic or diving wing of the king penguin is well seen at p. 94, fig. 47.

From what has been stated it will be evident that the wing acts very differently in and out of the water; and this is a point deserving of attention, the more especially as it seems to have hitherto escaped observation. In the water the wing, when most effective, strikes *downwards* and *backwards*, and acts as an auxiliary of the foot; whereas in the air it strikes *downwards* and *forwards*. The oblique surfaces, spiral or otherwise, presented by animals to the water and air are therefore made to act in opposite directions, as far as the down strokes are concerned. This is owing to the greater density of the water as compared with the air,—the former supporting or nearly supporting the animal moving upon or in it; the latter permitting the creature to fall through it in a downward direction during the ascent of the wing. To counteract the tendency of the bird in motion to fall downwards and forwards, the down stroke is delivered in this direction; the kite-like action of the wing, and the rapidity with which it is moved causing the mass of the bird to pursue a more or less horizontal course. I offer this explanation of the action of the wing in and out of the water after repeated and careful observation in tame and wild birds, and, as I am aware, in opposition to all previous writers on the subject.

The rudimentary wings or paddles of the penguin (the movements of which I had an opportunity of studying in a tame specimen) are principally employed in swimming and diving. The feet, which are of moderate size and strongly webbed, are occasionally used as auxiliaries. There is this difference between the movements of the wings and feet of this most curious bird, and it is worthy of attention. The wings act together, or synchronously, as in flying birds; the feet, on the other hand, are moved alternately. The wings are wielded with great energy, and, because of their

semi-rigid condition, are incapable of expansion.  They therefore present their maximum and minimum of surface by
a partial rotation or tilting of the pinion, as in the walrus,
sea-bear, and turtle.  The feet, which are moved with less
vigour, are, on the contrary, rotated or tilted to a very slight
extent, the increase and diminution of surface being secured
by the opening and closing of the membranous expansion or
web between the toes.  In this latter respect they bear a certain analogy to the feet of the seal, the toes of which, as has
been explained, spread out or divaricate during extension,
and the reverse.  The feet of the penguin entirely differ
from those of the seal, in being worked separately, the
foot of one side being flexed or drawn towards the body,

Fig. 48.—Swan, in the act of swimming, the right foot being fully expanded,
and about to give the effective stroke, which is delivered outwards, downwards, and backwards, as represented at r of fig. 50; the left foot being closed,
and about to make the return stroke, which is delivered in an inward, upward, and forward direction, as shown at s of fig. 50.  In rapid swimming
the swan flexes its legs simultaneously and somewhat slowly; it then
vigorously extends them.—*Original.*

while its fellow is being extended or pushed away from it.
The feet, moreover, describe definite curves in opposite directions, the right foot proceeding from within outwards, and
from above downwards during extension, or when it is fully
expanded and giving the effective stroke ; the left one, which
is moving at the same time, proceeding from without inwards and from below upwards during flexion, or when it is
folded up, as happens during the back stroke.  In the acts of
extension and flexion the legs are slightly rotated, and the

feet more or less tilted. The same movements are seen in the feet of the swan, and in those of swimming birds generally (fig. 48).

One of the most exquisitely constructed feet for swimming and diving purposes is that of the grebe (fig. 49). This foot

Fig. 49.—Foot of Grebe (*Podiceps*). In this foot each toe is provided with its swimming membrane; the membrane being closed when the foot is flexed, and expanded when the foot is extended. Compare with foot of swan (fig. 48), where the swimming membrane is continued from the one toe to the other.—(After Dallas.)

consists of three swimming toes, each of which is provided with a membranous expansion, which closes when the foot is being drawn towards the body during the back stroke, and opens out when it is being forced away from the body during the effective stroke.

Fig. 50.—Diagram representing the double-waved track described by the feet of swimming birds. Compare with figs. 18 and 19, pp. 87 and 89, and with fig. 32, p. 68.—*Original.*

In swimming birds, each foot describes one side of an ellipse when it is extended and thrust from the body, the other side of the ellipse being described when the foot is flexed and drawn towards the body. The curve described by the right foot when pushed from the body is seen at the arrow *r* of fig. 50; that formed by the left foot when drawn towards the body, at the arrow *s* of the same figure. The curves formed by the feet during extension and flexion produce, when united in the act of swimming, waved lines, these constituting a chart for the movements of the extremities of swimming birds.

There is consequently an obvious analogy between the swimming of birds and the walking of man (compare fig. 50, p. 97, with fig. 19, p. 39); between the walking of man and the walking of the quadruped (compare figs. 18 and 19, pp. 37 and 39); between the walking of the quadruped and the swimming of the walrus, sea-bear, and seal; between the swimming of the seal, whale, dugong, manatee, and porpoise, and that of the fish (compare fig. 32, p. 68, with figs. 18 and 19, pp. 37 and 39); and between the swimming of the fish and the flying of the insect, bat, and bird (compare all the foregoing figures with figs. 71, 73, and 81, pp. 144 and 157).

*Flight of the Flying-fish ; the kite-like action of the Wings, etc.*—Whether the flying-fish uses its greatly expanded pectoral fins

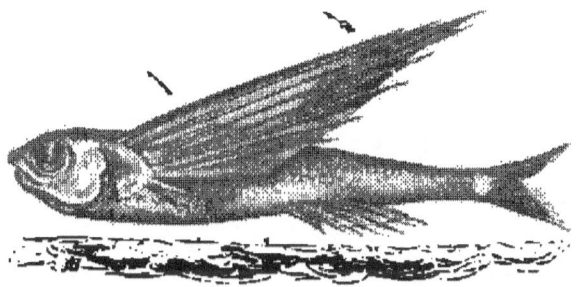

Fig. 51.—The Flying-fish (*Exocœtus exiliens*, Linn.), with wings expanded and elevated in the act of flight (*vide* arrows) This anomalous and interesting creature is adapted both for swimming and flying. The swimming-tail is consequently retained, and the pectoral fins, which act as wings, are enormously increased in size.—*Original.*

as a bird its wings, or only as parachutes, has not, so far as I am aware, been determined by actual observation.   Most observers are of opinion that these singular creatures glide up the wind, and do not beat it after the manner of birds; so that their flight (or rather leap) is indicated by the arc of a circle, the sea supplying the chord.   I have carefully examined the structure, relations, and action of those fins, and am satisfied in my own mind that they act as true pinions within

certain limits, their inadequate dimensions and limited range
alone preventing them from sustaining the fish in the air for
indefinite periods.  When the fins are fully flexed, as happens
when the fish is swimming, they are arranged along the sides
of the body ; but when it takes to the air, they are raised
above the body and make a certain angle with it.  In being
raised they are likewise inclined forwards and outwards, the
fins rotating on their long axes until they make an angle of
something like 30° with *the horizon*—this being, as nearly as
I can determine, the greatest angle made by the wings during
the down stroke in the flight of insects and birds.

The pectoral fins, or pseudo-wings of the flying-fish, like
all other wings, act after the manner of kites—the angles of
inclination which their under surfaces make with the horizon
varying according to the degree of extension, the speed acquired, and the pressure to which they are subjected by being
carried against the air.  When the flying-fish, after a preliminary rush through the water (in which it acquires initial
velocity), throws itself into the air, it is supported and carried
forwards by the kite-like action of its pinions ;—this action
being identical with that of the boy's kite when the boy runs,
and by pulling upon the string causes the kite to glide upwards and forwards.  In the case of the boy's kite *a pulling
force* is applied to the kite in front.  In the case of the flying-
fish (and everything which flies) *a similar force* is applied to
the kites formed by the wings by the weight of the flying
mass, which always tends to fall vertically downwards.
Weight supplies a motor power in flight similar to that
supplied by the leads in a clock.  In the case of the boy's
kite, the hand of the operator furnishes the power; in
flight, a large proportion of the power is furnished by
the weight of the body of the flying creature.  It is a
matter of indifference how a kite is flown, so long as its
under surface is made to impinge upon the air over which
it passes.[1]  A kite will fly effectually when it is neither
acted upon by the hand nor a weight, provided always
there is a stiff breeze blowing.  In flight one of two things

[1] "On the Various Modes of Flight in relation to Aëronautics."  By the
Author.—Proceedings of the Royal Institution of Great Britain, March 1867.

is necessary. Either the under surface of the wings must be carried rapidly against still air, or the air must rush violently against the under surface of the expanded but motionless wings. Either the wings, the body bearing them, or the air, must be in rapid motion ; one or other must be active. To this there is no exception. To fly a kite in still air the operator must run. If a breeze is blowing the operator does not require to alter his position, the breeze doing the entire work. It is the same with wings. In still air a bird, or whatever attempts to fly, must flap its wings energetically until it acquires initial velocity, when the flapping may be discontinued ; or it must throw itself from a height, in which case the initial velocity is acquired by the weight of the body acting upon the inclined planes formed by the motionless wings. The flapping and gliding action of the wings constitute the difference between ordinary flight and that known as skimming or sailing flight. The flight of the flying-fish is to be regarded rather as an example of the latter than the former, the fish transferring the velocity acquired by the vigorous lashing of its tail in the water to the air,—an arrangement which enables it to dispense in a great measure with the flapping of the wings, which act by a combined parachute and wedge action. In the flying-fish the flying-fin or wing attacks the air *from beneath*, whilst it is being raised above the body. It has no downward stroke, the position and attachments of the fin preventing it from descending beneath the level of the body of the fish. In this respect the flying-fin of the fish differs slightly from the wing of the insect, bat, and bird. The gradual expansion and raising of the fins of the fish, coupled with the fact that the fins never descend below the body, account for the admitted absence of beating, and have no doubt originated the belief that the pectoral fins are merely passive organs. If, however, they do not act as true pinions within the limits prescribed, it is difficult, and indeed impossible, to understand how such small creatures can obtain the momentum necessary to project them a distance of 200 or more yards, and to attain, as they sometimes do, an elevation of twenty or more feet above the water. Mr. Swainson, in crossing the line in 1816, zealously attempted

to discover the true action of the fins in question, but the flight of the fish is so rapid that he utterly failed. He gives it as his opinion that flight is performed in two ways,—first by a spring or leap, and second by the spreading of the pectoral fins, which are employed in propelling the fish in a forward direction, either by flapping or by a motion analogous to the skimming of swallows. He records the important fact, that the flying-fish can change its course after leaving the water, which satisfactorily proves that the fins are not simply passive structures. Mr. Lord, of the Royal Artillery,[1] thus writes of those remarkable specimens of the finny tribe:—
" There is no sight more charming than the flight of a shoal of flying-fish, as they shoot forth from the dark green wave in a glittering throng, like silver birds in some gay fairy tale, gleaming brightly in the sunshine, and then, with a mere touch on the crest of the heaving billow, again flitting onward reinvigorated and refreshed."

Before proceeding to a consideration of the graceful and, in some respects, mysterious evolutions of the denizens of the air, and the far-stretching pinions by which they are produced, it may not be out of place to say a few words in recapitulation regarding the extent and nature of the surfaces by which progression is secured on land and on or in the water. This is the more necessary, as the travelling-surfaces employed by animals in walking and swimming bear a certain, if not a fixed, relation to those employed by insects, bats, and birds in flying. On looking back, we are at once struck with the fact, remarkable in some respects, that the travelling-surfaces, whether feet, flippers, fins, or pinions, are, as a rule, increased in proportion to the tenuity of the medium on which they are destined to operate. In the ox (fig. 18, p. 37) we behold a ponderous body, slender extremities, and unusually small feet. The feet are slightly expanded in the otter (fig. 12, p. 34), and considerably so in the ornithorhynchus (fig. 11, p. 34). The travelling-area is augmented in the seal (fig. 14, p. 34; fig. 36, p. 74), penguin (figs. 46 and 47, pp. 91 and 94), sea-bear (fig. 37, p. 76), and turtle (fig. 44, p. 89). In the triton (fig. 45, p. 89) a huge swimming-tail is added to the

[1] Nature and Art, November 1866, p. 173.

feet—the tail becoming larger, and the extremities (anterior) diminishing, in the manatee (fig. 34, p. 73) and porpoise (fig. 33, p. 73), until we arrive at the fish (fig. 30, p. 65), where not only the tail but *the lower half of the body* is actively engaged in natation. Turning from the water to the air, we observe a remarkable modification in the huge pectoral fins of the flying-fish (fig. 51, p. 98), these enabling the creature to take enormous leaps, and serving as pseudo-pinions. Turning in like manner from the earth to the air, we encounter the immense tegumentary expansions of the flying-dragon (fig. 15, p. 35) and galeopithecus (fig. 16, p. 35), the floating or buoying area of which greatly exceeds that of some of the flying beetles.

In those animals which fly, as bats (fig. 17, p. 36), insects (figs. 57 and 58, p. 124 and 125), and birds (figs. 59 and 60, p. 126), the travelling surfaces, because of the extreme tenuity of the air, are prodigiously augmented ; these in many instances greatly exceeding the actual area of the body. While, therefore, the movements involved in walking, swimming, and flying are to be traced in the first instance to the shortening and lengthening of the muscular, elastic, and other tissues operating on the bones, and their peculiar articular surfaces; they are to be referred in the second instance to the extent and configuration of the travelling areas—these on all occasions being accurately adapted to the capacity and strength of the animal and the density of the medium on or in which it is intended to progress. Thus the land supplies the resistance, and affords the support necessary to prevent the small feet of land animals from sinking to dangerous depths, while the water, immensely less resisting, furnishes the peculiar medium requisite for buoying the fish, and for exposing, without danger and to most advantage, the large surface contained in its ponderous lashing tail,—the air, unseen and unfelt, furnishing that quickly yielding and subtle element in which the greatly expanded pinions of the insect, bat, and bird are made to vibrate with lightning rapidity, discoursing, as they do so, a soft and stirring music very delightful to the lover of nature.

THE atmosphere, because of its great tenuity, mobility, and comparative imponderability, presents little resistance to bodies passing through it at low velocities. If, however, the speed be greatly accelerated, the passage of even an ordinary cane is sensibly impeded.

This comes of the action and reaction of matter, the resistance experienced varying according to the density of the atmosphere and the shape, extent, and velocity of the body acting upon it. While, therefore, scarcely any impediment is offered to the progress of an animal in motion, it is often exceedingly difficult to compress the air with sufficient rapidity and energy to convert it into a suitable fulcrum for securing the onward impetus. This arises from the fact that bodies moving in the air experience the *minimum of resistance* and occasion the *maximum of displacement*. Another and very obvious difficulty is traceable to the great disparity in the weight of air as compared with any known solid, this in the case of water being nearly as 1000 to 1. According to the density of the medium so is its buoying or sustaining power.

*The Wing a Lever of the Third Order.*—To meet the peculiarities stated above, the insect, bat, and bird are furnished with extensive surfaces in the shape of pinions or wings, which they can apply with singular velocity and power, as levers of the third order (fig. 3, p. 20),[1] at various angles, or by alternate slow and sudden movements, to obtain the

---

[1] In this form of lever the power is applied between the fulcrum and the weight to be raised. The mass to be elevated is the body of the insect, bat, or bird,—the force which resides in the living pinion (aided by the inertia of the trunk) representing the power, and the air the fulcrum.

necessary degree of resistance and non-resistance. Although
the third order of lever is particularly inefficient when the
fulcrum is *rigid* and *immobile*, it possesses singular advantages
when these conditions are reversed, *i.e.* when the fulcrum, as
happens with the air, is *elastic* and *yielding*. In this case a
very slight movement at the root of the pinion, or that end
of the lever directed towards the body, is succeeded by an
immense sweep of the extremity of the wing, where its elevating and propelling power is greatest. This arrangement insures that the large quantity of air necessary for propulsion
and support shall be compressed under the most favourable
conditions.

It follows from this that those insects and birds are endowed
with the greatest powers of flight whose wings are the longest.
The dragon-fly and albatross furnish examples. The former
on some occasions dashes along with amazing velocity and
wheels with incredible rapidity; at other times it suddenly
checks its headlong career and hovers or fixes itself in the air
after the manner of the kestrel and humming-birds. The flight
of the albatross is also remarkable. This magnificent bird, I am
informed on reliable authority, sails about with apparent un-
concern for hours together, and rarely deigns to flap its enormous pinions, which stream from its body like ribbons to the
extent, in some cases, of seven feet on either side.

The manner in which the wing levers the body upwards
and forwards in flight is shown at fig. 52.

In this fig. $ff'$ represent the moveable fulcra furnished by
the air; $pp'$ the power residing in the wing, and $b$ the body
to be flown. In order to make the problem of flight more
intelligible, I have prolonged the lever formed by the wing
beyond the body ($b$), and have applied to the root of the wing
so extended the weight $ww'$. $x$ represents the universal
joint by which the wing is attached to the body. When the
wing ascends, as shown at $p$, the air (= fulcrum $f$) resists its
upward passage, and forces the body ($b$), or its representative
($w$), slightly downwards. When the wing descends, as shown
at $p'$, the air (= fulcrum $f'$) resists its downward passage,
and forces the body ($b$), or its representative ($w'$), slightly
upwards. From this it follows, that when the wing rises the

body falls, and *vice versâ*; the wing describing the arc of a large circle (*f f'*), the body (*b*), or the weights representing it (*w w'*) describing the arc of a much smaller circle.   The body,

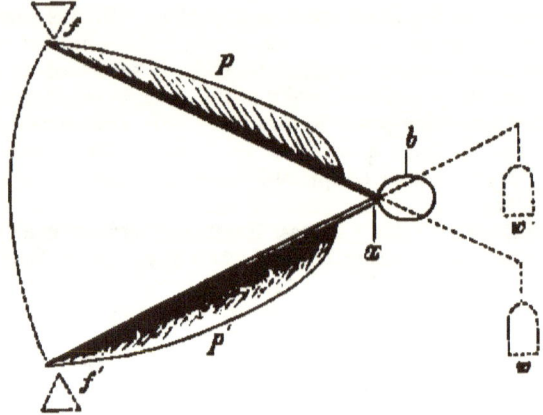

Fig. 52.

therefore, as well as the wing, rises and falls in flight.   When the wing descends it elevates the body, the wing being active and the body passive; when the body descends it elevates the wing, the body being active and the wing passive.   The elevator muscles, and the reaction of the air on the under surface of the wing, contribute to its elevation.   It is in this manner that weight forms a factor in flight, the wing and the weight of the body reciprocating and mutually assisting and relieving each other.   This is an argument for employing four wings in artificial flight, the wings being so arranged that the two which are up shall always by their fall mechanically elevate the two which are down.   Such an arrangement is calculated greatly to conserve the driving power, and, as a consequence, to reduce the weight.   It is the upper or dorsal surface of the wing which more especially operates upon the air during the up stroke, and the under or ventral surface which operates during the down stroke.   The wing, which at the beginning of the down stroke has its surfaces and margins (anterior and posterior) arranged in nearly the same plane with

the horizon,[1] rotates upon its anterior margin as an axis during
its descent and causes its under surface to make a gradually
increasing angle with the horizon, the posterior margin (fig.
53, c) in this movement descending beneath the anterior
one. A similar but opposite rotation takes place during the
up stroke. The rotation referred to causes the wing to twist
on its long axis screw-fashion, and to describe a figure-of-8
track in space, one-half of the figure being described during
the ascent of the wing, the other half during its descent.
The twisting of the wing and the figure-of-8 track described
by it when made to vibrate, are represented at fig. 53.
The rotation of the wing on its long axis as it ascends and
descends causes the under surface of the wing to act as a
kite, both during the up and down strokes, provided always
the body bearing the wing is in forward motion. But the
upper surface of the wing, as has been explained, acts when
the wing is being elevated, so that both the upper and under
surfaces of the wing are efficient during the up stroke. When
the wing ascends, the upper surface impinges against the air;
the under surface impinging at the same time from its being
carried obliquely forward, after the manner of a kite, by the
body, which is in motion. During the down stroke, the
under surface only acts. The wing is consequently effective
both during its ascent and descent, its slip being nominal in
amount. The wing acts as a kite, both when it ascends and
descends. It acts more as a propeller than an elevator during
its ascent; and more as an elevator than a propeller during
its descent. It is, however, effective both in an upward and
downward direction. The efficiency of the wing is greatly increased by the fact that when it ascends it draws a current of
air up after it, which current being met by the wing during
its descent, greatly augments the power of the down stroke.
In like manner, when the wing descends it draws a current
of air down after it, which being met by the wing during its
ascent, greatly augments the power of the up stroke. These
induced currents are to the wing what a stiff autumn breeze is
to the boy's kite. The w__g is endowed with this very re-

[1] In some cases the posterior margin is slightly elevated above the horizon
(fig. 53, g).

markable property, that it creates the current on which it rises
and progresses. It literally flies on a whirlwind of its own
forming.

These remarks apply more especially to the wings of bats
and birds, and those insects whose wings are made to vibrate
in a more or less vertical direction. The action of the wing
is readily imitated, as a reference to fig. 53 will show.

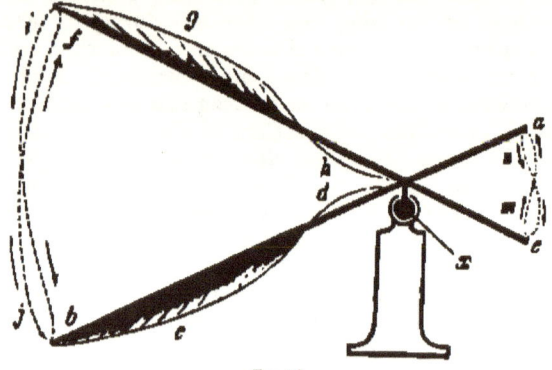

Fig. 53.

If, for example, I take a tapering elastic reed, as represented
at *a b*, and supply it with a flexible elastic sail (*c d*), and a
ball-and-socket joint (*x*), I have only to seize the reed at *a*
and cause it to oscillate upon *x* to elicit all the wing movements. By depressing the root of the reed in the direction
*n e*, the wing flies up as a kite in the direction *j f*. During
the upward movement the wing flies upwards and forwards,
and describes a double curve. By elevating the root of the
reed in the direction *m a*, the wing flies down as a kite in
the direction *i b*. During the downward movement the
wing flies downwards and forwards, and describes a double
curve. These curves, when united, form a waved track,
which represents progressive flight. During the rise and fall
of the wing a large amount of tractile force is evolved, and
if the wings and the body of the flying creature are inclined
slightly upwards, kite-fashion, as they invariably are in ordinary flight, the whole mass of necessity moves upwards and

forwards. To this there is no exception. A sheet of paper
or a card will float along if its anterior margin is slightly
raised, and if it be projected with sufficient velocity. The
wings of all flying creatures when made to vibrate, twist and
untwist, the posterior thin margin of each wing twisting
round the anterior thick one, like the blade of a screw. The
artificial wing represented at fig. 53 (p. 107) does the same, *c d*
twisting round *a b*, and *g h* round *e f*. The natural and artificial wings, when elevated and depressed, describe a figure-of-8
track in space when the bodies to which they are attached
are stationary. When the bodies advance, the figure-of-8 is
opened out to form first a looped and then a waved track. I
have shown how those insects, bats, and birds which flap
their wings in a more or less vertical direction evolve tractile
or propelling power, and how this, operating on properly
constructed inclined surfaces, results in flight. I wish now
to show that flight may also be produced by a very oblique
and almost horizontal stroke of the wing, as in some insects,
*e.g.* the wasp, blue-bottle, and other flies. In those insects
the wing is made to vibrate with a figure-of-8 sculling

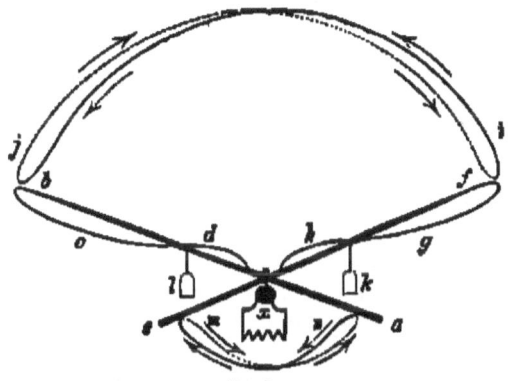

Fig. 54.

motion in a very oblique direction, and with immense energy.
This form of flight differs in no respect from the other, unless
in the direction of the stroke, and can be readily imitated, as
a reference to fig. 54 will show.

In this figure (54) the conditions represented at fig. 53 (p. 107) are exactly reproduced, the only difference being that in the present figure the wing is applied to the air in a more or less horizontal direction, whereas in fig. 53 it is applied in a more or less vertical direction.   The letters in both figures are the same.   The insects whose wings tack upon the air in a more or less horizontal direction, have an extensive range, each wing describing nearly half a circle, these half circles corresponding to the area of support.   The body of the insect is consequently the centre of a circle of motion.   It corresponds to *x* of the present figure (fig. 54).   When the wing is seized by the hand at *a*, and the root made to travel in the direction *n c*, the body of the wing travels in the direction *j f*.   While so travelling it flies upwards in a double curve, kite-fashion, and elevates the weight *l*.   When it reaches the point *f*, it reverses suddenly to prepare for a return stroke, which is produced by causing the root of the wing to travel in the direction *m a*, the body and tip travelling in the direction *i b*. During the reverse stroke, the wing flies upwards in a double curve, kite-fashion, and elevates the weight *k*   The more rapidly these movements are repeated, the more powerful the wing becomes, and the greater the weight it elevates.   This follows because of the reciprocating action of the wing,—the wing, as already explained, always drawing a current of air after it during the one stroke, which is met and utilized by it during the next stroke.   The reciprocating action of the wing here referred to is analogous in all respects to that observed in the flippers of the seal, sea-bear, walrus, and turtle; the swimming wing of the penguin; and the tail of the whale, dugong, manatee, porpoise, and fish.   If the muscles of the insect were made to act at the points *a c*, the body of the insect would be elevated as at *k l*, by the reciprocating action of the wings.   The amount of tractile power developed in the arrangement represented at fig. 53 (p. 107), can be readily ascertained by fixing a spring or a weight acting over a pulley to the anterior margin (*a b* or *e f*) of the wing; weights acting over pulleys being attached to the root of the wing (*a* or *c*).

The amount of elevating power developed in the arrangement represented at fig. 54, can also be estimated by

causing weights acting over pulleys to operate upon the root
of the wing (*a* or *e*), and watching how far the weights (*k* or *l*)
are raised.   In these calculations allowance is of course to be
made for friction.   The object of the two sets of experiments
described and figured, is to show that the wing can exert a
tractile power either in a nearly horizontal direction or in a
nearly vertical one, flight being produced in both cases.   I
wish now to show that a body not supplied with wings or
inclined surfaces will, if left to itself, fall vertically downwards; whereas, if it be furnished with wings, its vertical fall
is converted into oblique downward flight.   These are very
interesting points.   Experiment has shown me that a wing
when made to vibrate vertically produces horizontal traction;
when made to vibrate horizontally, vertical traction; the
vertical fall of a body armed with wings producing oblique
traction.   The descent of weights can also be made to propel
the wings either in a vertical or horizontal direction; the
vibration of the wings upon the air in natural flight causing
the weights (body of flying creature) to move forward.
This shows the very important part performed by weight in
all kinds of flight.

*Weight necessary to Flight.*—However paradoxical it may
seem, a certain amount of weight is indispensable in flight.

In the first place, it gives peculiar efficacy and energy to
the up stroke, by acting upon the inclined planes formed
by the wings in the direction of the plane of progression.
The power and the weight may thus be said to reciprocate,
the two sitting, as it were, side by side, and blending their
peculiar influences to produce a common result.

Secondly, it adds momentum,—a heavy body, when once
fairly under weigh, meeting with little resistance from the
air, through which it sweeps like a heavy pendulum.

Thirdly, the mere act of rotating the wings on and off
the wind during extension and flexion, with a slight down-
word stroke, apparently represents the entire exertion on the
part of the volant animal, the rest being performed by weight
alone.

This last circumstance is deserving of attention, the more
especially as it seems to constitute the principal difference

between a living flying thing and an aërial machine. If a flying-machine was constructed in accordance with the principles which we behold in nature, the weight and the propelling power of the machine would be made to act upon the sustaining and propelling surfaces, whatever shape they assumed, and these in turn would be made to operate upon the air, and *vice versâ*. In the aërial machine, as far as yet devised, there is no sympathy between the weight to be elevated and the lifting power, whilst in natural flight the wings and the weight of the flying creature act in concert and reciprocate; the wings elevating the body the one instant, the body by its fall elevating the wings the next. When the wings elevate the body they are active, the body being passive. When the body elevates the wings it is active, the wings being passive. The force residing in the wings, and the force residing in the body (weight is a force when launched in space and free to fall in a vertical direction) cause the mass of the volant animal to oscillate vertically on either side of an imaginary line—this line corresponding to the path of the insect, bat, or bird in the air. While the wings and body act and react upon each other, the wings, body, and air likewise act and react upon each other. In the flight of insects, bats, and birds, *weight* is to be regarded as an independent moving power, this being made to act upon the oblique surfaces presented by the wings in conjunction with the power expended by the animal—the latter being, by this arrangement, conserved to a remarkable extent. Weight, assisted by the elastic ligaments or springs, which recover all wings in flexion, is to be regarded as the mechanical expedient resorted to by nature in supplementing the efforts of all flying things.[1] Without this, flight would be of short duration, laboured, and uncertain, and the almost miraculous journeys at present performed by the denizens of the air impossible.

---

[1] Weight, as is well known, is the sole moving power in the clock—the pendulum being used merely to regulate the movements produced by the descent of the leads. In watches, the onus of motion is thrown upon a *spiral spring;* and it is worthy of remark that the mechanician has seized upon, and ingeniously utilized, two forces largely employed in the animal kingdom.

*Weight contributes to Horizontal Flight.*—That the weight of
the body plays an important part in the production of flight
may be proved by a very simple experiment.

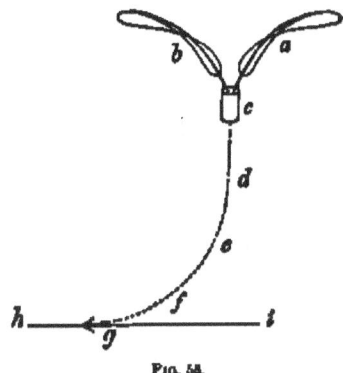

FIG. 55.

If I take two primary feathers and fix them in an ordinary
cork, as represented at fig. 55, and allow the apparatus to
drop from a height, I find the cork does not fall vertically
downwards, but *downwards* and *forwards* in a curve. This
follows, because the feathers *a, b* are twisted flexible inclined
planes, which arch in an upward direction. They are in fact
true wings in the sense that an insect wing in one piece is a
true wing. (Compare *a, b, c* of fig. 55, with *g, g', s* of fig. 82,
p. 156.) When dragged downwards by the cork (*c*), which
would, if left to itself, fall vertically, they have what is virtually a down stroke communicated to them. Under these
circumstances a struggle ensues between the cork tending to
fall vertically and the feathers tending to travel in an upward
direction, and, as a consequence, the apparatus describes the
curve *d e f g* before reaching the earth *h, i.* This is due to
the action and reaction of the feathers and air upon each
other, and to the influence which gravity exerts upon the
cork. The forward travel of the cork and feathers, as compared with the space through which they fall, is very great.
Thus, in some instances, I found they advanced as much as a
yard and a half in a descent of three yards. Here, then, is

an example of flight produced by purely mechanical appliances. The winged seeds fly in precisely the same manner. The seeds of the plane-tree have, *e.g.* two wings which exactly resemble the wings employed for flying; thus they taper from the root towards the tip, and from the anterior margin towards the posterior margin, the margins being twisted and disposed in different planes to form true screws. This arrangement prevents the seed from falling rapidly or vertically, and if a breeze is blowing it is wafted to a considerable distance before it reaches the ground.   Nature is uniform and consistent throughout.  She employs the same principle, and very nearly the same means, for flying a heavy, solid seed which she employs for flying an insect, a bat, or a bird.

When artificial wings constructed on the plan of natural ones, with stiff roots, tapering semi-rigid anterior margins, and thin yielding posterior margins, are allowed to drop from a height, they describe double curves in falling, the roots of the wings reaching the ground first.    This circumstance proves the greater buoying power of the tips of the wings as compared with the roots.   I might refer to many other experiments made in this direction, but these are sufficient to show that weight, when acting upon wings, or, what is the same thing, upon elastic twisted inclined planes, must be regarded as an independent moving power.   But for this circumstance flight would be at once the most awkward and laborious form of locomotion, whereas in reality it is incomparably the easiest and most graceful.   The power which rapidly vibrating wings have in sustaining a body which tends to fall vertically downwards, is much greater than one would naturally imagine, from the fact that the body, which is always beginning to fall, is never permitted actually to do so.    Thus, when it has fallen sufficiently far to assist in elevating the wings, it is at once elevated by the vigorous descent of those organs.   The body consequently never acquires the downward momentum which it would do if permitted to fall through a considerable space uninterruptedly. It is easy to restrain even a heavy body when beginning to fall, while it is next to impossible to check its progress when

H

it is once fairly launched in space and travelling rapidly in a downward direction.

*Weight, Momentum, and Power, to a certain extent, synonymous in Flight.*—When a bird rises it has little or no momentum, so that if it comes in contact with a solid resisting surface it does not injure itself. When, however, it has acquired all the momentum of which it is capable, and is in full and rapid flight, such contact results in destruction. My friend Mr. A. D. Bartlett informed me of an instance where a wild duck terminated its career by coming violently in contact with one of the glasses of the Eddystone Lighthouse. The glass, which was fully an inch in thickness, was completely smashed. Advantage is taken of this circumstance in killing sea-birds, a bait being placed on a board and set afloat with a view to breaking the neck of the bird when it stoops to seize the carrion. The additional power due to momentum in heavy bodies in motion is well illustrated in the start and progress of steamboats. In these the *slip*, as it is technically called, decreases as the speed of the vessel increases; the strength of a man, if applied by a hawser attached to the stern of a moderate-sized vessel, being sufficient to retard, and, in some instances prevent, its starting. In such a case the power of the engine is almost entirely devoted to " slip " or in giving motion to the fluid in which the screw or paddle is immersed. It is consequently not the power residing in the paddle or screw which is cumulative, but the momentum inhering in the mass. In the bird, the momentum, *alias* weight, is made to act upon the inclined planes formed by the wings, these adroitly converting it into sustaining and propelling power. It is to this circumstance, more than any other, that the prolonged flight of birds is mainly due, the inertia or dead weight of the trunk aiding and abetting the action of the wings, and so relieving the excess of exertion which would necessarily devolve on the bird. It is thus that the power which in living structures resides in the mass is conserved, and the mass itself turned to account. But for this reciprocity, no bird could retain its position in the air for more than a few minutes at a time. This is proved by the comparatively brief upward flight of the lark and the hovering of the hawk when hunting. In both these cases the body is exclusively sustained by the action of the wings, the weight of the trunk taking no part in it; in other words, the weight of the body does not contribute to flight by adding its momentum and the impulse which momentum begets. In the flight of the albatross, on the other hand, the momentum acquired by the moving mass does the principal portion of the work, the wings for the most part being simply rotated on and off the wind to supply the proper angles necessary for the inertia or mass to operate upon. It appears to me that in this blending of active and passive power the mystery of flight is concealed, and that no arrangement will succeed in producing flight artificially which does not recognise and apply the principle here pointed out.

*Air-cells in Insects and Birds not necessary to Flight.*—The boasted levity of insects, bats, and birds, concerning which so much has been written by authors in their attempts to explain flight, is delusive in the highest degree.

Insects, bats, and birds are as heavy, bulk for bulk, as most other living creatures, and flight can be performed perfectly by animals which have neither air-sacs nor hollow bones; air-sacs being found in animals never designed to fly. Those who subscribe to the heated-air theory are of opinion that the air contained in the cavities of insects and birds is so much lighter than the surrounding atmosphere, that it must of necessity contribute materially to flight. I may mention, however, that the quantity of air imprisoned is, to begin with, so infinitesimally small, and the difference in weight which it experiences by increase of temperature so inappreciable, that it ought not to be taken into account by any one endeavouring to solve the difficult and important problem of flight. The Montgolfier or fire-balloons were constructed on the heated-air principle; but as these have no analogue in nature, and are apparently incapable of improvement, they are mentioned here rather to expose what I regard a false theory than as tending to elucidate the true principles of flight.

When we have said that cylinders and hollow chambers increase the area of the insect and bird, and that an insect

and bird so constructed is stronger, weight for weight, than
one composed of solid matter, we may dismiss the subject;
flight being, as I shall endeavour to show by-and-by, not so
much a question of levity as one of weight and power intelligently directed, upon properly constructed flying surfaces.

The bodies of insects, bats, and birds are constructed on
strictly mechanical principles,—lightness, strength, and dura-
bility of frame being combined with power, rapidity, and
precision of action.  The cylindrical method of construction
is in them carried to an extreme, the bodies and legs of
insects displaying numerous unoccupied spaces, while the
muscles and solid parts are tunnelled by innumerable air-
tubes, which communicate with the surrounding medium by
a series of apertures termed spiracles.

A somewhat similar disposition of parts is met with in
birds, these being in many cases furnished not only with
hollow bones, but also (especially the aquatic ones) with a
liberal supply of air-sacs.  They are likewise provided with a
dense covering of feathers or down, which adds greatly to
their bulk without materially increasing their weight.  Their
bodies, moreover, in not a few instances, particularly in birds
of prey, are more or less flattened.  The air-sacs are well
seen in the swan, goose, and duck; and I have on several
occasions minutely examined them with a view to determine
their extent and function.  In two of the specimens which I
injected, the material employed had found its way not only
into those usually described, but also into others which ramify
in the substance of the muscles, particularly the pectorals.
No satisfactory explanation of the purpose served by these
air-sacs has, I regret to say, been yet tendered.  According
to Sappey,[1] who has devoted a large share of attention to the
subject, they consist of a membrane which is neither serous
nor mucous, but partly the one and partly the other; and as
blood-vessels in considerable numbers, as my preparations

[1] Sappey enumerates fifteen air-sacs,—the *thoracic*, situated at the lower
part of the neck, behind the sternum; *two cervical*, which run the whole
length of the neck to the head, which they supply with air; *two pairs of
anterior*, and *two pairs of posterior diaphragmatic*; and *two pairs of abdo-
minal.*

show, ramify in their substance, and they are in many cases
covered with muscular fibres which confer on them a rhythmic
movement, some recent observers (Mr. Drosier [1] of Cambridge,
for example) have endeavoured to prove that they are ad-
juncts of the lungs, and therefore assist in aërating the blood.
This opinion was advocated by John Hunter as early as
1774,[2] and is probably correct, since the temperature of birds
is higher than that of any other class of animals, and because
they are obliged occasionally to make great muscular exertions both in swimming and flying.  Others have viewed the
air-sacs in connexion with the hollow bones frequently, though
not always, found in birds,[3] and have come to look upon the
heated air which they contain as being more or less essential
to flight.  That the air-cells have absolutely nothing to do with
flight is proved by the fact that some excellent fliers (take the
bats, e.g.) are destitute of them, while birds such as the
ostrich and apteryx, which are incapable of flying, are provided with them.  Analogous air-sacs, moreover, are met
with in animals never intended to fly; and of these I may
instance the great air-sac occupying the cervical and axillary regions of the orang-outang, the float or swimming-
bladder in fishes, and the pouch communicating with the
trachea of the emu.[4]

[1] "On the Functions of the Air-cells and the Mechanism of Respiration in
Birds," by W. H. Drosier, M.D., Caius College.—Proc. Camb. Phil. Soc.,
Feb. 12, 1866.
[2] "An Account of certain Receptacles of Air in Birds which communicate
with the Lungs, and are lodged among the Fleshy Parts and in the Hollow
Bones of these Animals."—Phil. Trans., Lond. 1774.
[3] According to Dr. Crisp the swallow, martin, swifts, and many birds of
passage have no air in their bones (Proc. Zool. Soc., Lond. part xxv. 1857, p.
13).  The same author, in a second communication (pp. 215 and 216), adds
that the glossy starling, spotted flycatcher, whin-chat, wood-wren, willow-wren,
black-headed bunting, and canary, five of which are birds of passage, have
likewise no air in their bones.  The following is Dr. Crisp's summary:—Out
of ninety-two birds examined he found " air in many of the bones, five
(Falconidæ); air in the humeri and not in the inferior extremities, thirty-
nine ; no air in the extremities and probably none in the other bones, forty-
eight."
[4] Nearly allied to this is the great gular pouch of the bustard.  Specimens
of the air-sac in the orang, emu, and bustard, and likewise of the air-sacs of

The same may be said of the hollow bones,—some really admirable fliers, as the swifts, martins, and snipes, having their bones filled with marrow, while those of the wingless running birds alluded to have air. Furthermore and finally, a living bird weighing 10 lbs. weighs the same when dead, plus a very few grains; and all know what effect a few grains of heated air would have in raising a weight of 10 lbs. from the ground.

*How Balancing is effected in Flight, the Sound produced by the Wing, etc.*—The manner in which insects, bats, and birds balance themselves in the air has hitherto, and with reason, been regarded a mystery, for it is difficult to understand how they maintain their equilibrium when the wings are beneath their bodies. Figs. 67 and 68, p. 141, throw considerable light on the subject in the case of the insect. In those figures the space (*a, g*) mapped out by the wing during its vibrations is entirely occupied by it; *i.e.* the wing (such is its speed) is in every portion of the space at nearly the same instant, the space representing what is practically a solid basis of support. As, moreover, the wing is jointed to the upper part of the body (thorax) by a universal joint, which admits of every variety of motion, the insect is always suspended (very much as a compass set upon gimbals is suspended); the wings, when on a level with the body, vibrating in such a manner as to occupy a circular area (*vide r d b f* of fig. 56, p. 120), in the centre of which the body (*a e c*) is placed. The wings, when vibrating above and beneath the body occupy a conical area; the apex of the cone being directed upwards when the wings are below the body, and downwards when they are above the body. These points are well seen in the bird at figs. 82 and 83, p. 158. In fig. 82 the inverted cone formed by the wings when above the body is represented, and in fig. 83 that formed by the wings when below the body is given. In these figures it will be observed that the body, from the insertion of the roots of the wings into its upper portion, is always suspended, and this, of course, is equivalent to suspending the centre of gravity. In the bird and

the swan and goose, as prepared by me, may be seen in the Museum of the Royal College of Surgeons of England.

bat, where the stroke is delivered more vertically than in the insect, the *basis of support* is increased by the tip of the wing folding inwards and backwards in a more or less horizontal direction at the end of the down stroke; and outwards and forwards at the end of the up stroke. This is accompanied by the rotation of the outer portion of the wing upon the wrist as a centre, the tip of the wing, because of the ever varying position of the wrist, describing an ellipse. In insects whose wings are broad and large (butterfly), and which are driven at a comparatively low speed, the balancing power is diminished. In insects whose wings, on the contrary, are long and narrow (blow-fly), and which are driven at a high speed, the balancing power is increased. It is the same with short and long winged birds, so that the function of balancing is in some measure due to the form of the wing, and the speed with which it is driven; the long wing and the wing vibrated with great energy increasing the capacity for balancing. When the body is light and the wings very ample (butterfly and heron), the reaction elicited by the ascent and descent of the wing displaces the body to a marked extent. When, on the other hand, the wings are small and the body large, the reaction produced by the vibration of the wing is scarcely perceptible. Apart, however, from the shape and dimensions of the wing, and the rapidity with which it is urged, it must never be overlooked that all wings (as has been pointed out) are attached to the bodies of the animals bearing them by some form of universal joint, and in such a manner that the bodies, whatever the position of the wings, are accurately balanced, and swim about in a more or less horizontal position, like a compass set upon gimbals. To such an extent is this true, that the position of the wing is a matter of indifference. Thus the pinion may be above, beneath, or on a level with the body; or it may be directed forwards, backwards, or at right angles to the body. In either case the body is balanced mechanically and without effort. To prove this point I made an artificial wing and body, and united the one to the other by a universal joint. I found, as I had anticipated, that in whatever position the wing was placed, whether above, beneath, or on

a level with the body, or on either side of it, the body almost
instantly attained a position of rest. The body was, in fact,
equally suspended and balanced from all points.

*Rapidity of Wing Movements partly accounted for.*—Much
surprise has been expressed at the enormous rapidity with
which some wings are made to vibrate. The wing of the
insect is, as a rule, very long and narrow. As a consequence,
a comparatively slow and very limited movement at the root

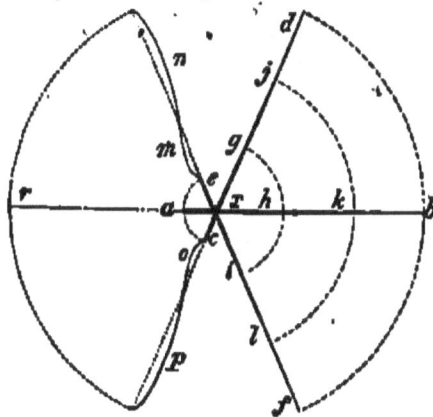

Fig. 56.[1]

confers great range and immense speed at the tip; the speed
of each portion of the wing increasing as the root of the wing
is receded from. This is explained on a principle well understood in mechanics, viz. that when a rod hinged at one end
is made to move in a circle, the tip or free end of the rod
describes a much wider circle *in a given time* than a portion
of the rod nearer the hinge. This principle is illustrated at

[1] In this diagram I have purposely represented the right wing by a straight
*rigid* rod. The natural wing, however, is curved, *flexible*, and *elastic*. It
likewise *moves in curves*, the curves being most marked towards the end of
the up and down strokes, as shown at *m n, o p*. The curves, which are
double figure-of-8 curves, are obliterated towards the middle of the strokes (*a r*).
This remark holds true of all natural wings, and of all artificial wings properly
constructed. The curves and the reversal thereof are necessary to give continuity of motion to the wing during its vibrations, and what is not less
important, to enable the wing alternately to seize and dismiss the air.

fig. 56.    Thus if *a b* of fig. 56 be made to represent the
rod hinged at *x*, it travels through the space *d b f* in the
same time it travels through *j·k l;* and through *j k l* in the
same time it travels through *g h i;* and through *g h i* in the
same time it travels through *e a c*, which is the area occupied
by the thorax of the insect.    If, however, the part of the rod
*b* travels through the space *d b f* in the same time that the part
*a* travels through the space *e a c*, it follows of necessity that
the portion of the rod marked *a* moves very much slower
than that marked *b*.    The muscles of the insect are applied
at the point *a*, as short levers (the point referred to corresponding to the thorax of the insect), so that a comparatively slow
and limited movement at the root of the wing produces the
marvellous speed observed at the tip ; the tip and body of the
wing being those portions which occasion the blur or impression produced on the eye by the rapidly oscillating pinion (figs.
64, 65, and 66, p. 139),  But for this mode of augmenting
the speed originally inaugurated by the muscular system, it is
difficult to comprehend how the wings could be driven at the
velocity attributed to them.    The wing of the blow-fly is
said to make 300 strokes per second, i.e. 18,000 per minute.
Now it appears to me that muscles to contract at the rate of
18,000 times in the minute would be exhausted in a very
few seconds, a state of matters which would render the continuous flight of insects impossible.  (The heart contracts only
between sixty and seventy times in a minute.)  I am, therefore,
disposed to believe that the number of contractions made by
the thoracic muscles of insects has been greatly overstated ;
the high speed at which the wing is made to vibrate being
due.less to the separate and sudden contractions of the muscles
at its root than to the fact that the speed of the different
parts of the wing is increased in a direct ratio as the several
parts are removed from the driving point, as already explained.    Speed is certainly a matter of great importance
in wing movements, as the elevating and propelling power of
the pinion depends to a great extent upon the rapidity with
which it is urged.    Speed, however, may be produced in two
ways—either by a series of separate and opposite movements,
such as is witnessed in the action of a piston, or by a series

of separate and opposite movements acting upon an instrument so designed, that a movement applied at one part increases in rapidity as the point of contact is receded from, as happens in the wing. In the piston movement the motion is uniform, or nearly so; all parts of the piston travelling at very much the same speed. In the wing movements, on the contrary, the motion is gradually accelerated towards the tip of the pinion, where the pinion is most effective as an elevator, and decreased towards the root, where it is least effective—an arrangement calculated to reduce the number of muscular contractions, while it contributes to the actual power of the wing. This hypothesis, it will be observed, guarantees to the wing a very high speed, with comparatively few reversals and comparatively few muscular contractions.

In the bat and bird the wings do not vibrate with the same rapidity as in the insect, and this is accounted for by the circumstance, that in them the muscles do not act exclusively at the root of the wing. In the bat and bird the muscles run along the wing towards the tip for the purpose of flexing or folding the wing prior to the up stroke, and for opening out and expanding it prior to the down stroke.

As the wing must be folded or flexed and opened out or expanded every time the wing rises and falls, and as the muscles producing flexion and extension are long muscles with long tendons, which act at long distances as long levers, and comparatively slowly, it follows that the great short muscles (pectorals, etc.) situated at the root of the wing must act slowly likewise, as the muscles of the thorax and wing of necessity act together to produce one pulsation or vibration of the wing. What the wing of the bat and bird loses in speed it gains in power, the muscles of the bat and bird's wing acting directly upon the points to be moved, and under the most favourable conditions. In the insect, on the contrary, the muscles act indirectly, and consequently at a disadvantage. If the pectorals only moved, they would act as short levers, and confer on the wing of the bat and bird the rapidity peculiar to the wing of the insect.

The tones emitted by the bird's wing would in this case

be heightened. The swan in flying produces a loud whistling sound, and the pheasant, partridge, and grouse a sharp whirring noise like the stone of a knife-grinder.

It is a mistake to suppose, as many do, that the tone or note produced by the wing during its vibrations is a true indication of the number of beats made by it in any given time. This will be at once understood when I state, that a long wing will produce a higher note than a shorter one driven at the same speed and having the same superficial area, from the fact that the tip and body of the long wing will move through a greater space in a given time than the tip and body of the shorter wing. This is occasioned by all wings being jointed at their roots, the sweep made by the different parts of the wing in a given time being longer or shorter in proportion to the length of the pinion. It ought, moreover, not to be overlooked, that in insects the notes produced are not always referable to the action of the wings, these, in many cases, being traceable to movements induced in the legs and other parts of the body.

It is a curious circumstance, that if portions be removed from the posterior margins of the wings of a buzzing insect, such as the wasp, bee, blue-bottle fly, etc., the note produced by the vibration of the pinions is raised in pitch. This is explained by the fact, that an insect whose wings are curtailed requires to drive them at a much higher speed in order to sustain itself in the air. That the velocity at which the wing is urged is instrumental in causing the sound, is proved by the fact, that in slow-flying insects and birds no note is produced; whereas in those which urge the wing at a high speed, a note is elicited which corresponds within certain limits to the number of vibrations and the form of the wing. It is the posterior or thin flexible margin of the wing which is more especially engaged in producing the sound; and if this be removed, or if this portion of the wing, as is the case in the bat and owl, be constructed of very soft materials, the character of the note is altered. An artificial wing, if properly constructed and impelled at a sufficiently high speed, emits a drumming noise which closely resembles the note produced by the vibration of short-winged, heavy-bodied

birds, all which goes to prove that sound is a concomitant of
rapidly vibrating wings.

*The Wing area Variable and in Excess.*—The travelling-
surfaces of insects, bats, and birds greatly exceed those of
fishes and swimming animals; the travelling-surfaces of swimming animals being greatly in excess of those of animals which
walk and run. The wing area of insects, bats, and birds
varies very considerably, flight being possible within a com-

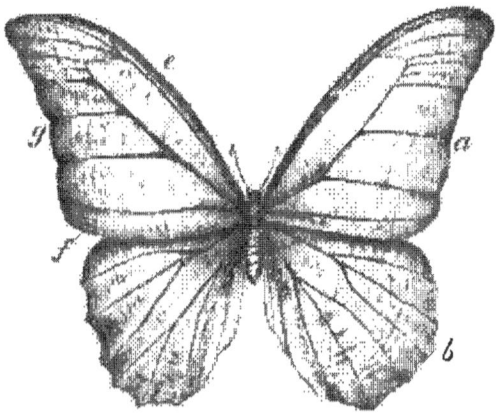

Fig. 57.—Shows a butterfly with comparatively very large wings. The nervures
are seen to great advantage in this specimen: and the enormous expanse of
the pinions readily explains the irregular flight of the insect on the principle
of recoil. *a* Anterior wing. *b* Posterior wing. *e* Anterior margin of wing.
*f* Ditto posterior margin. *g* Ditto outer margin. Compare with beetle, fig.
58.—*Original.*

paratively wide range. Thus there are light-bodied and large-
winged insects and birds—as the butterfly (fig. 57) and heron
(fig. 60, p. 126); and others whose bodies are comparatively
heavy, while their wings are insignificantly small—as the
sphinx moth and Goliath beetle (fig. 58) among insects, and
the grebe, quail, and partridge (fig. 59, p. 126) among birds.

The apparent inconsistencies in the dimensions of the body
and wings are readily explained by the greater muscular development of the heavy-bodied short-winged insects and birds, and
the increased power and rapidity with which the wings in them
are made to oscillate. In large-winged animals the movements

are slow; in small-winged ones comparatively very rapid.   This shows that flight may be attained by a heavy, powerful animal with comparatively small wings, as well as by a lighter one with enormously enlarged wings.   While there is apparently no fixed relation between the area of the wings and the animal to be raised, there is, unless in the case of sailing birds,[1] an unvarying relation between the weight of

Fig. 58.—Under-surface of large beetle (*Goliathus micans*), with deeply concave and comparatively small wings (compare with butterfly, fig. 57), shows that the nervures (r, d, e, f, n, u, w) of the wings of the beetle are arranged along the anterior margins and throughout the substance of the wings generally, very much as the bones of the arm, forearm, and hand, are in the wings of the bat, to which they bear a very marked resemblance, both in their shape and mode of action.   The wings are folded upon themselves at the point e during repose.   Compare letters of this figure with similar letters of fig. 17, p. 30.—*Original*.

the animal, the area of its wings, and the number of oscillations made by them in a given time.   The problem of flight thus resolves itself into one of weight, power, velocity, and small surfaces; *versus* buoyancy, debility, diminished speed,

[1] In birds which skim, sail, or glide, the pinion is greatly elongated or ribbon-shaped, and the weight of the body is made to operate upon the inclined planes formed by the wings, in such a manner that the bird when it has once got fairly under weigh, is in a measure self-supporting.   This is especially the case when it is proceeding against a slight breeze—the wind and the inclined planes resulting from the upward inclination of the wings reacting upon each other, with this very remarkable result, that the mass of the bird moves steadily forwards in a more or less horizontal direction.

and extensive surfaces,—weight in either case being a *sine
quâ non.*  In order to utilize the air as a means of transit,
the body in motion, whether it moves iu virtue of the life it
possesses, or because of a force superadded, must be heavier

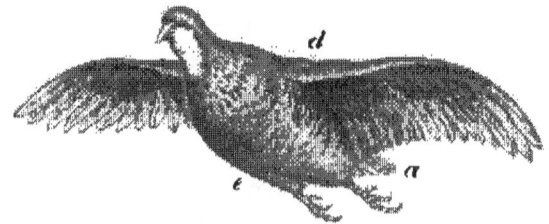

Fig. 59.—The Red-legged Partridge (*Perdix rubra*) with wings fully extended
as in rapid flight, shows deeply concave form of the wings, how the primary
and secondary feathers overlap and support each other during extension,
and how the anterior or thick margins of the wings are directed upwards
and forwards, and the posterior or thin ones downwards and backwards.
The wings in the partridge are wielded with immense velocity and power.
This is necessary because of their small size as compared with the great
dimensions and weight of the body.
    If a horizontal line be drawn across the feet (a, e' to represent the horizon,
and another from the tip of the tail (a) to the root of the wing (d), the angle
at which the wing strikes the air is given.  The body and wings when taken
together form a kite.  The wings in the partridge are rounded and broad.
Compare with heron, fig. 60.—*Original.*

than the air.  It must tread and rise upon the air as a swimmer upon the water, or as a kite upon the wind.  It must
act against gravity, and elevate and carry itself forward at
the expense of the air, and by virtue of the force which

Fig. 60.—The Grey Heron (*Ardea cinerea*) in full flight.  In the heron the
wings are deeply concave, and unusually large as compared with the size of
the bird.  The result is that the wings are moved very leisurely, with a slow,
heavy, and almost solemn beat.  The heron figured weighed under 3 lbs.;
and the expanse of wing was considerably greater than that of a wild goose
which weighed over 9 lbs.  Flight is consequently more a question of power
and weight than of buoyancy and surface.  d, e, f Anterior thick strong
margin of right wing.  c, a, b Posterior thin flexible margin, composed of
primary (b), secondary (a), and tertiary (c) feathers.  Compare with partridge, fig. 59.—*Original.*

resides in it.  If it were rescued from the law of gravity on
the one hand, and bereft of independent movement on the
other, it would float about uncontrolled and uncontrollable,
as happens in the ordinary gas-balloon.

That no fixed relation exists between the area of the wings and the size and weight of the body, is evident on comparing the dimensions of the wings and bodies of the several orders of insects, bats, and birds. If such comparison be made, it will be found that the pinions in some instances diminish while the bodies increase, and the converse. No practical good can therefore accrue to aërostation from elaborate measurements of the wings and trunks of any flying thing ; neither can any rule be laid down as to the extent of surface required for sustaining a given weight in the air. The wing area is, as a rule, considerably in excess of what is actually required for the purposes of flight. This is proved in two ways. First, by the fact that bats can carry their young without inconvenience, and birds elevate surprising quantities of fish, game, carrion, etc. I had in my possession at one time a tame barn-door owl which could lift a piece of meat a quarter of its own weight, after fasting four-and-twenty hours ; and an eagle, as is well known, can carry a moderate-sized lamb with facility.

The excess of wing area is proved, secondly, by the fact that a large proportion of the wings of most volant animals may be removed without destroying the power of flight. I instituted a series of experiments on the wings of the fly, dragon-fly, butterfly, sparrow, etc., with a view to determining this point in 1867. The following are the results obtained:—

*Blue-bottle Fly.*—*Experiment* 1. Detached posterior or thin half of each wing in its long axis. Flight perfect.

*Exp.* 2. Detached posterior *two-thirds* of either wing in its long axis. Flight still perfect. I confess I was not prepared for this result.

*Exp.* 3. Detached one-third of anterior or thick margin of either pinion obliquely. Flight imperfect.

*Exp.* 4. Detached one-half of anterior or thick margin of either pinion obliquely. The power of flight completely destroyed. From experiments 3 and 4 it would seem that the anterior margin of the wing, which contains the principal nervures, and which is the most rigid portion of the pinion, cannot be mutilated with impunity.

*Exp.* 5. Removed one-third from the extremity of either

wing transversely, *i.e.* in the direction of the short axis of
the pinion.   Flight perfect.

*Exp.* 6.  Removed *one-half* from either wing transversely, as
in experiment 5.   Flight very slightly (if at all) impaired.

*Exp.* 7.  Divided either pinion in the direction of its long
axis into three equal parts, the anterior nervures being contained in the anterior portion.   Flight perfect.

*Exp.* 8.  Notched two-thirds of either pinion obliquely from
behind.   Flight perfect.

*Exp.* 9.  Notched anterior third of either pinion transversely.
The power of flight destroyed.   Here, as in experiment 4,
the mutilation of the anterior margin was followed by loss of
function.

*Exp.* 10.  Detached posterior two-thirds of right wing in
its long axis, the left wing being untouched.   Flight perfect.
I expected that this experiment would result in loss of
balancing-power; but this was not the case.

*Exp.* 11.  Detached half of right wing transversely, the left
one being normal.   The insect flew irregularly, and came to
the ground about a yard from where I stood.   I seized it
and detached the corresponding half of the left wing, after
which it flew away, as in experiment 6.

*Dragon-Fly.—Exp.* 12.  In the dragon-fly either the first or
second pair of wings may be removed without destroying the
power of flight.    The insect generally flies most steadily
when the posterior pair of wings are detached, as it can balance better; but in either case flight is perfect, and in no
degree laboured.

*Exp.* 13.  Removed one-third from the posterior margin of
the first and second pairs of wings.   Flight in no wise impaired.

If more than a third of each wing is cut away from the
posterior or thin margin, the insect can still fly, but with
effort.

Experiment 13 shows that the posterior or thin flexible
margins of the wings may be dispensed with in flight.   They
are more especially engaged in propelling.   Compare with
experiments 1 and 2.

*Exp.* 14.  The extremities or tips of the first and second
pair of wings may be detached to the extent of one-third,

without diminishing the power of flight.    Compare with experiments 5 and 6.

If the mutilation be carried further, flight is laboured, and in some cases destroyed.

*Exp.* 15.  When the front edges of the first and second pairs of wings are notched or when they are removed, flight is completely destroyed.    Compare with experiments 3, 4, and 9.

This shows that a certain degree of stiffness is required for the front edges of the wings, the front edges indirectly supporting the back edges.    It is, moreover, on the front edges of the wings that the pressure falls in flight, and by these edges the major portions of the wings are attached to the body.    The principal movements of the wings are communicated to these edges.

*Butterfly.*—*Exp.* 16.  Removed posterior halves of the first pair of wings of white butterfly.    Flight perfect.

*Exp.* 17.  Removed posterior halves of first and second pairs of wings.    Flight not strong but still perfect.    If additional portions of the posterior wings were removed, the insect could still fly, but with great effort, and came to the ground at no great distance.

*Exp.* 18.  When the tips (outer sixth) of the first and second pairs of wings were cut away, flight was in no wise impaired.    When more was detached the insect could not fly.

*Exp.* 19.  Removed the posterior wings of the brown butterfly.    Flight unimpaired.

*Exp.* 20.  Removed in addition a small portion (one-sixth) from the tips of the anterior wings.    Flight still perfect, as the insect flew upwards of ten yards.

*Exp.* 21.  Removed in addition a portion (one-eighth) of the posterior margins of anterior wings.    The insect flew imperfectly, and came to the ground about a yard from the point where it commenced its flight.

*House Sparrow.*—The sparrow is a heavy small-winged bird, requiring, one would imagine, all its wing area.    This, however, is not the case, as the annexed experiments show.

*Exp.* 22.  Detached the half of the secondary feathers of either pinion in the direction of the long axis of the wing, the primaries being left intact.    Flight as perfect as before

I

the mutilation took place. In this experiment, one wing was operated upon before the other, in order to test the balancing-power. The bird flew perfectly, either with one or with both wings cut.

*Exp.* 23. Detached the half of the secondary feathers and a fourth of the primary ones of either pinion in the long axis of the wing. Flight in no wise impaired. The bird, in this instance, flew upwards of 30 yards, and, having risen a considerable height, dropped into a neighbouring tree.

*Exp.* 24. Detached nearly the half of the primary feathers in the long axis of either pinion, the secondaries being left intact. When one wing only was operated upon, flight was perfect; when both were tampered with, it was still perfect, but slightly laboured.

*Exp.* 25. Detached rather more than a third of both primary and secondary feathers of either pinion in the long axis of the wing. In this case the bird flew with evident exertion, but was able, notwithstanding, to attain a very considerable altitude.

From experiments 1, 2, 7, 8, 10, 13, 16, 22, 23, 24, and 25, it would appear that great liberties may be taken with the posterior or thin margin of the wing, and the dimensions of the wing in this direction materially reduced, without destroying, or even vitiating in a marked degree, the powers of flight. This is no doubt owing to the fact indicated by Sir George Cayley, and fully explained by Mr. Wenham, that in all wings, particularly long narrow ones, the elevating power is transferred to the anterior or front margin. These experiments prove that the upward bending of the posterior margins of the wings during the down stroke is not necessary to flight.

*Exp.* 26. Removed alternate primary and secondary feathers from either wing, beginning with the first primary. The bird flew upwards of fifty yards with very slight effort, rose above an adjoining fence, and wheeled over it a second time to settle on a tree in the vicinity. When one wing only was operated upon, it flew irregularly and in a lopsided manner.

*Exp.* 27. Removed alternate primary and secondary feathers from either wing, beginning with the *second primary.* Flight,

from all I could determine, perfect. When one wing only
was cut, flight was irregular or lopsided, as in experiment 26.

From experiments 26 and 27, as well as experiments 7
and 8, it would seem that the wing does not of necessity
require to present an 'unbroken or continuous surface to the
air, such as is witnessed in the pinion of the bat, and that the
feathers, when present, may be separated from each other
without destroying the utility of the pinion. In the raven
and many other birds the extremities of the first four or
five primaries divaricate in a marked manner. A similar
condition is met with in the *Alauda hexadactyla*, where the
delicate feathery-looking processes composing the wing are
widely removed from each other. The wing, however, *ceteris
paribus*, is strongest when the feathers are not separated from
each other, and when they *overlap*, as then they are arranged
so as mutually to support each other.

*Exp.* 28. Removed half of the primary feathers from either
wing transversely, *i.e.* in the direction of the short axis of the
wing. Flight very slightly, if at all, impaired when only one
wing was operated upon. When both were cut, the bird flew
heavily, and came to the ground at no very great distance.
This mutilation was not followed by the same result in experiments 6 and 11. On the whole, I am inclined to believe
that the area of the wing can be curtailed with least injury
in the direction of its long axis, by removing successive portions from its posterior margin.

*Exp.* 29. The carpal or wrist-joint of either pinion rendered immobile by lashing the wings to slender reeds, the
elbow-joints being left free. The bird, on leaving the hand,
fluttered its wings vigorously, but after a brief flight came
heavily to the ground, thus showing that a certain degree of
twisting and folding, or flexing of the wings, is necessary to
the flight of the bird, and that, however the superficies and
shape of the pinions may be altered, the movements thereof
must not be interfered with. I tied up the wings of a pigeon
in the same manner, with a precisely similar result.

The birds operated upon were, I may observe, caught in a
net, and the experiments made within a few minutes from
the time of capture.

Some of my readers will probably infer from the foregoing, that the figure-of-8 curves formed along the anterior and posterior margins of the pinions are not necessary to flight, since the tips and posterior margins of the wings may be removed without destroying it. To such I reply, that the wings are flexible, elastic, and composed of a congeries of curved surfaces, and that so long as a portion of them remains, they form, or tend to form, figure-of-8 curves in every direction.

Captain F. W. Hutton, in a recent paper "On the Flight of Birds" (*Ibis*, April 1872), refers to some of the experiments detailed above, and endeavours to frame a theory of flight, which differs in some respects from my own. His remarks are singularly inappropriate, and illustrate in a forcible manner the old adage, "A little knowledge is a dangerous thing." If Captain Hutton had taken the trouble to look into my memoir "On the Physiology of Wings," communicated to the Royal Society of Edinburgh, on the 2d of August 1870,[1] fifteen months before his own paper was written, there is reason to believe he would have arrived at very different conclusions. Assuredly he would not have ventured to make the rash statements he has made, the more especially as he attempts to controvert my views, which are based upon anatomical research and experiment, without making any dissections or experiments of his own.

*The Wing area decreases as the Size and Weight of the Volant Animal increases.*—While, as explained in the last section, no definite relation exists between the weight of a flying animal and the size of its flying surfaces, there being, as stated, heavy bodied and small-winged insects, bats, and birds, and the converse; and while, as I have shown by experiment, flight is possible within a wide range, the wings being, as a rule, in excess of what are required for the purposes of flight; still it appears, from the researches of M. de Lucy, that there is a general law, to the effect that the larger the volant animal the smaller by comparison are its flying surfaces. The existence of such a law is very encouraging as far as artificial

"On the Physiology of Wings, being an Analysis of the Movements by which Flight is produced in the Insect, Bat, and Bird."—Trans. Roy. Soc. of Edinburgh, vol. xxvi.

flight is concerned, for it shows that the flying surfaces of a large, heavy, powerful flying machine will be comparatively small, and consequently comparatively compact and strong. This is a point of very considerable importance, as the object desiderated in a flying machine is elevating capacity.

M. de Lucy has tabulated his results, which I subjoin :[1]—

| INSECTS. | | BIRDS. | |
|---|---|---|---|
| Names. | Referred to the kilogramme = 2 lbs. 3 oz. 3 dwt. 2 gr. Avoird. = 2 lbs. 3 oz. 4.428 gr. | Names. | Referred to the kilogramme. |
| | yds. ft. in. | | yds. ft. in. |
| Gnat, | 11 8 92 | Swallow, | 1 1 104½ |
| Dragon-fly (small), | 7 2 56 | Sparrow, | 0 5 142½ |
| Coccinella (Lady-bird), | 5 13 87 | Turtle-dove, | 0 4 100½ |
| Dragon-fly (common), | 5 2 89 | Pigeon, | 8 2 113 |
| Tipula, or Daddy-long-legs, | 3 5 11 | Stork, | 0 2 20 |
| Bee, | 1 2 74½ | Vulture, | 0 1 116 |
| Meat-fly, | 1 3 54½ | Crane of Australia, | 0 0 139 |
| Drone (blue), | 1 2 29 | | |
| Cockchafer, | 1 2 50 | | |
| Lucanus } Stag-beetle (female), | 1 1 59½ | | |
| cervus } Stag-beetle (male), | 0 3 83 | | |
| Rhinoceros-beetle, | 0 6 122½ | | |

"It is easy, by aid of this table, to follow the order, always decreasing, of the surfaces, in proportion as the winged animal increases in size and weight. Thus, in comparing the insects with one another, we find that the gnat, which weighs 460 times less than the stag-beetle, has fourteen times more of surface. The lady-bird weighs 150 times less than the stag-beetle, and possesses five times more of surface. It is the same with the birds. The sparrow weighs about ten times less than the pigeon, and has twice as much surface. The pigeon weighs about eight times less than the stork, and has twice as much surface. The sparrow weighs 339 times less than the Australian crane, and possesses seven times more surface. If now we compare the insects and the birds, the gradation will become even much more striking. The gnat, for example, weighs 97,000 times

[1] "On the Flight of Birds, of Bats, and of Insects, in reference to the subject of Aërial Locomotion," by M. de Lucy, Paris.

less than the pigeon, and has forty times more surface; it weighs 3,000,000 times less than the crane of Australia, and possesses 149 times more of surface than this latter, the weight of which is about 9 kilogrammes 500 grammes (25 lbs. 5 oz. 9 dwt. troy, 20 lbs. 15 oz. 2½ dr. avoirdupois).

The Australian crane is the heaviest bird that I have weighed. It is that which has the smallest amount of surface, for, referred to the kilogramme, it does not give us a surface of more than 899 square centimetres (139 square inches), that is to say about an eleventh part of a square metre. But every one knows that these grallatorial animals are excellent birds of flight. Of all travelling birds they undertake the longest and most remote journeys. They are, in addition, the eagle excepted, the birds which elevate themselves the highest, and the flight of which is the longest maintained."[1]

Strictly in accordance with the foregoing, are my own measurements of the gannet and heron. The following details of weight, measurement, etc., of the gannet were supplied by an adult specimen which I dissected during the winter of 1869. Entire weight, 7 lbs. (minus 3 ounces); length of body from tip of bill to tip of tail, three feet four inches; head and neck, one foot three inches; tail, twelve inches; trunk, thirteen inches; girth of trunk, eighteen inches; expanse of wing from tip to tip across body, six feet; widest portion of wing across primary feathers, six inches; across secondaries, seven inches; across tertiaries, eight inches. Each wing, when carefully measured and squared, gave an area of 19½ square inches. The wings of the gannet, therefore, furnish a supporting area of three feet three inches square. As the bird weighs close upon 7 lbs., this gives something like thirteen square inches of wing for every 36½ ounces of body, i.e. one foot one square inch of wing for every 2 lbs. 4½ oz. of body.

The heron, a specimen of which I dissected at the same time, gave a very different result, as the subjoined particulars will show. Weight of body, 3 lbs. 3 ounces; length of body from tip of bill to tip of tail, three feet four inches; head and neck, two feet; tail, seven inches; trunk, nine inches; girth

[1] M. de Lucy, *op. cit.*

of body, twelve inches; expanse of wing from tip to tip across
the body, five feet nine inches; widest portion of wing across
primary and tertiary feathers, eleven inches; across secondary
feathers, twelve inches.

Each wing, when carefully measured and squared, gave an
area of twenty-six square inches. The wings of the heron,
consequently, furnish a supporting area of four feet four inches
square. As the bird only weighs 3 lbs. 3 ounces, this gives
something like twenty-six square inches of wing for every
$25\frac{1}{2}$ ounces of bird, or one foot $5\frac{1}{4}$ inches square for every
1 lb. 1 ounce of body.

In the gannet there is only one foot one square inch of
wing for every 2 lbs. $4\frac{1}{2}$ ounces of body. The gannet has,
consequently, less than half of the wing area of the heron.
The gannet's wings are, however, long narrow wings (those
of the heron are broad), which extend transversely across the
body; and these are found to be the most powerful—the
wings of the albatross—which measure fourteen feet from tip
to tip (and only one foot across), elevating 18 lbs. without
difficulty. If the wings of the gannet, which have a superficial area of three feet three inches square, are capable of
elevating 7 lbs., while the wings of the heron, which have a
superficial area of four feet four inches, can only elevate 3 lbs.,
it is evident (seeing the wings of both are twisted levers, and
formed upon a common type) that the gannet's wings must
be vibrated with greater energy than the heron's wings; and
this is actually the case. The heron's wings, as I have ascertained from observation, make 60 down and 60 up strokes
every minute; whereas the wings of the gannet, when the
bird is flying in a straight line to or from its fishing-ground,
make close upon 150 up and 150 down strokes during the
same period. The wings of the divers, and other short-winged,
heavy-bodied birds, are urged at a much higher speed, so that
comparatively small wings can be made to elevate a comparatively heavy body, if the speed only be increased sufficiently.[1]   Flight, therefore, as already indicated, is a ques-

[1] The grebes among birds, and the beetles among insects, furnish examples
where small wings, made to vibrate at high speeds, are capable of elevating
great weights.

tion of power, speed, and small surfaces *versus* weight. Elaborate measurements of wing, area, and minute calculations of speed, can consequently only determine the minimum of wing for elevating the maximum of weight—flight being attainable within a comparatively wide range.

*Wings, their Form, etc.; all Wings Screws, structurally and functionally.*—Wings vary considerably as to their general contour; some being falcated or scythe-like, some oblong, some rounded or circular, some lanceolate, and some linear.[1]

All wings are constructed upon a common type. They are in every instance carefully graduated, the wing tapering

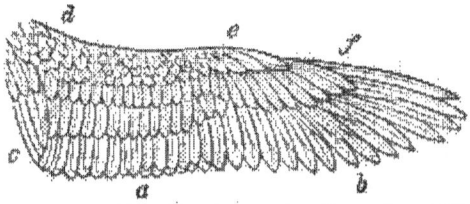

Fig. 61.—Right wing of the Kestrel, drawn from the specimen, while being held against the light. Shows how the primary (b), secondary (a), and tertiary c feathers overlap and buttress or support each other in every direction. Each set of feathers has its coverts and subcoverts, the wing being concave from within outwards, and from before backwards. d, e, f anterior or thick margin of wing. b, a, c posterior or thin margin. The wing of the kestrel is intermediate as regards form, it being neither rounded as in the partridge (fig. 96, p. 176), nor ribbon-shaped as in the albatross (fig. 62), nor pointed as in the swallow. The feathers of the kestrel's wing are unusually symmetrical and strong. Compare with figs. 62, 94, and 96, pp. 174, 175, and 176.—*Original.*

from the root towards the tip, and from the anterior margin in the direction of the posterior margin. They are of a generally triangular form, and twisted upon themselves in the direction of their length, to form a helix or screw. They are convex above and concave below, and more or less flexible and elastic throughout, the elasticity being greatest at the tip and along the posterior margin. They are also moveable in all their parts. Figs. 61, 62, 63 (p. 138), 59 and 60 (p. 126), 96 and 97 (p. 176), represent typical bird wings; figs. 17 (p. 36), 94 and 95 (p. 175), typical bat wings; and figs. 57 and 58 (p. 125), 89 and 90 (p. 171), 91 (p. 172), 92 and 93 (p. 174), typical insect wings.

[1] "The wing is short, broad, convex, and rounded in grouse, partridges, and other rasores; long, broad, straight, and pointed in most pigeons. In the peregrine falcon it is acuminate, the second quill being longest, and the first

In all the wings which I have examined, whether in the insect, bat, or bird, the wing is recovered, flexed, or drawn towards the body by the action of elastic ligaments, these structures, by their mere contraction, causing the wing, when fully extended and presenting its maximum of surface, to resume its position of rest and plane of least resistance. The principal effort required in flight is, therefore, made during extension, and at the beginning of the down stroke. The elastic ligaments are variously formed, and the amount of contraction which they undergo is in all cases accurately adapted to the size and form of the wing, and the rapidity with which it is worked; the contraction being greatest in the short-winged and heavy-bodied insects and birds, and

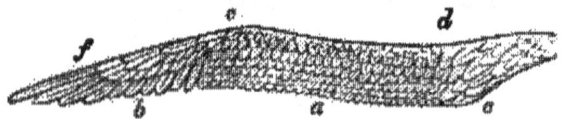

Fig. 82.—Left wing of the albatross.  d, e, f Anterior or thick margin of pinion. b, a, c Posterior or thin margin, composed of the primary (b), secondary (a), and tertiary (c) feathers.  In this wing the first primary is the longest, the primary coverts and subcoverts being unusually long and strong.  The secondary coverts and subcoverts occupy the body of the wing ;r,fl, and are so numerous as effectually to prevent any escape of air between them during the return or up stroke.  This wing, which I have in my possession, measures over six feet in length. – Original.

least in the light-bodied and ample-winged ones, particularly such as skim or glide.  The mechanical action of the elastic ligaments, I need scarcely remark, insures an additional period of repose to the wing at each stroke ; and this is a point of some importance, as showing that the lengthened and laborious flights of insects and birds are not without their stated intervals of rest.

All wings are furnished at their roots with some form of universal joint which enables them to move not only in an

little shorter ; and in the swallows this is still more the case, the first quill being the longest, the rest rapidly diminishing in length."— Macgillivray, Hist. Brit. Birds, vol. i. p. 82.  " The hawks have been classed as noble or ignoble, according to the length and sharpness of their wings ; and the falcons, or long-winged hawks, are distinguished from the short-winged ones by the second feather of the wing being either the longest or equal in length to the third, and by the nature of the stoop made in pursuit of their prey."— Falconry in the British Isles, by F. H. Salvin and W. Brodrick. Lond. 1855, p. 28.

upward, downward, forward, or backward direction, but also at various intermediate degrees of obliquity. All wings obtain their leverage by presenting oblique surfaces to the air, the degree of obliquity gradually increasing in a direction from behind forwards and downwards during extension and the down stroke, and gradually decreasing in an opposite direction during flexion and the up stroke.

In the insect the oblique surfaces are due to the conformation of the shoulder-joint, this being furnished with a system of check-ligaments, and with horny prominences or stops, set,

Fig. 63.—The Lapwing, or Green Plover (*Vanellus cristatus*, Meyer), with one wing (c b, d' e' f') fully extended, and forming a long lever ; the other (d e f, c b) being in a flexed condition and forming a short lever. In the extended wing the anterior or thick margin (d' e' f') is directed *upwards* and *forwards* (*vide* arrow), the posterior or thin margin (c, b) *downwards* and *backwards*. The reverse of this happens during flexion, the anterior or thick margin (d, e, f) being directed *downwards* and *forwards* (*vide* arrow), the posterior or thin margin (c b) bearing the rowing-feathers *upwards* and *backwards*. The wings therefore twist in opposite directions during extension and flexion ; and this is a point of the utmost importance in the action of all wings, as it enables the volant animal to rotate the wings on and off the air, and to present at one time (in extension) resisting, kite-like surfaces, and at another (in flexion) knife-like and comparatively non-resisting surfaces. It rarely happens in flight that the wing (d e f, c b) is so fully flexed as in the figure. As a consequence, the under surface of the wing is, as a rule, inclined upwards and forwards, even in flexion, so that it acts as a kite in extension and flexion, and during the up and down strokes.—*Original.*

as nearly as may be, at right angles to each other. The check-ligaments and horny prominences are so arranged that when the wing is made to vibrate, it is also made to rotate in the direction of its length, in the manner explained.

In the bat and bird the oblique surfaces are produced by the spiral configuration of the articular surfaces of the bones of the wing, and by the rotation of the bones of the arm, forearm, and hand, upon their long axes. The reaction of the air also assists in the production of the oblique surfaces.

That the wing twists upon itself structurally, not only in the insect, but also in the bat and bird, any one may readily satisfy himself by a careful examination; and that it twists upon itself during its action I have had the most convincing and repeated proofs (figs. 64, 65, and 66). The twisting in question

FIG. 64.

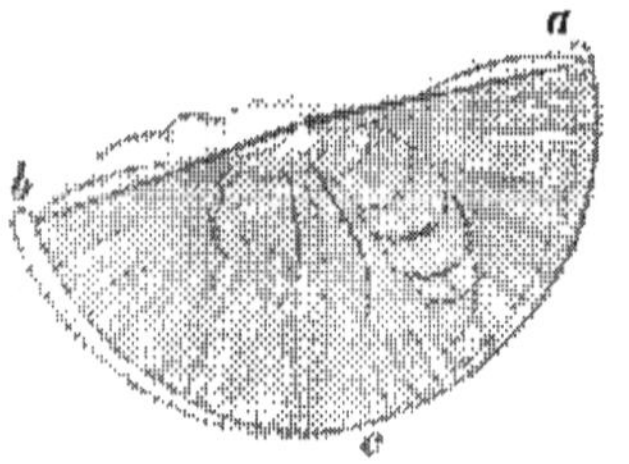

FIG. 65. 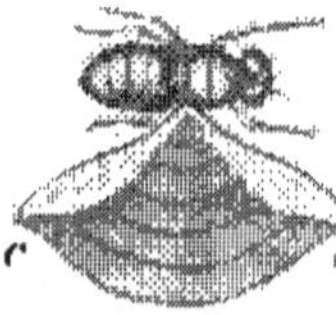                          FIG. 66.

FIG. 64 shows left wing (a, b) of wasp in the act of twisting upon itself, the tip of the wing describing a figure-of-8 track (a, c, b). From nature.—*Original.*
FIGS. 65 and 66 show right wing of blue-bottle fly rotating on its anterior margin, and twisting to form double or figure-of-8 curves (a b, c d). From nature.—*Original.*

is most marked in the posterior or thin margin of the wing, the anterior and thicker margin performing more the part of an axis. As a result of this arrangement, the anterior or thick margin cuts into the air quietly, and as it were by stealth, the posterior one producing on all occasions a violent commotion, especially perceptible if a flame be exposed behind the vibrating wing. Indeed, it is a matter for surprise that the spiral conformation of the pinion, and its spiral mode of action, should have eluded observation so long; and I shall be pardoned for dilating upon the subject when I state my conviction that it

forms the fundamental and distinguishing feature in flight,
and must be taken into account by all who seek to solve
this most involved and interesting problem by artificial means.
The importance of the twisted configuration or screw-like
form of the wing cannot be over-estimated.    That this
shape is intimately associated with flight is apparent from
the fact that the rowing feathers of the wing of the bird are
every one of them distinctly spiral in their nature ; in fact,
one entire rowing feather is equivalent—morphologically and
physiologically—to one entire insect wing.    In the wing of
the martin, where the bones of the pinion are short and in
some respects rudimentary, the primary and secondary feathers
are greatly developed, and banked up in such a manner that
the wing as a whole presents the same curves as those displayed by the insect's wing, or by the wing of the eagle where
the bones, muscles, and feathers have attained a maximum
development.  The conformation of the wing is such that it
presents a waved appearance in every direction—the waves
running longitudinally, transversely, and obliquely.    The
greater portion of the pinion may consequently be removed
without materially affecting either its form or its functions.
This is proved by making sections in various directions, and
by finding, as has been already shown, that in some instances
as much as two-thirds of the wing may be lopped off without
visibly impairing the power of flight.    The spiral nature of
the pinion is most readily recognised when the wing is seen
from behind and from beneath, and when it is foreshortened.
It is also well marked in some of the long-winged oceanic
birds when viewed from before (figs. 82 and 83, p. 158), and
cannot escape detection under any circumstances, if sought
for,—the wing being essentially composed of a congeries of
curves, remarkable alike for their apparent simplicity and the
subtlety of their detail.

*The Wing during its action reverses its Planes, and describes a
Figure-of-8 track in space.*—The twisting or rotating of the
wing on its long axis is particularly observable during extension and flexion in the bat and bird, and likewise in the
insect, especially the beetle, cockroach, and such as fold
their wings during repose.    In these in extreme flexion

the anterior or thick margin of the wing is directed downwards, and the posterior or thin one upwards. In the act of extension, the margins, in virtue of the wing rotating upon its long axis, reverse their positions, the anterior or thick margins describing a spiral course from below upwards, the posterior or thin margin describing a similar but opposite course from above downwards. These conditions, I need scarcely observe, are reversed during flexion. The movements of the margins during flexion and extension may be represented with a considerable degree of accuracy by a figure-of-8 laid horizontally.

In the bat and bird the wing, when it ascends and descends, describes a nearly vertical figure-of-8. In the insect, the wing, from the more oblique direction of the stroke,

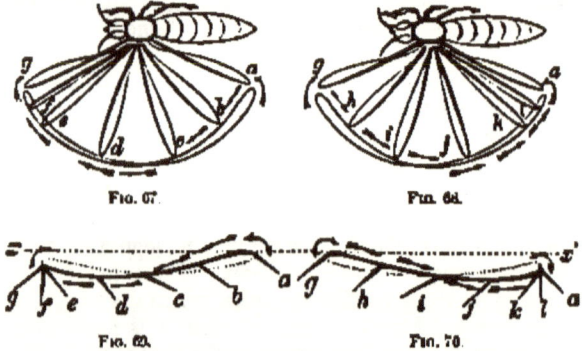

Fig. 67.    Fig. 68.

Fig. 69.    Fig. 70.

Figs. 67, 68, 69, and 70 show the area mapped out by the left wing of the wasp when the insect is fixed and the wing made to vibrate. These figures illustrate the various angles made by the wing as it hastens to and fro, how the wing reverses and reciprocates, and how it twists upon itself and describes a figure-of-8 track in space. Figs. 67 and 69 represent the forward or down stroke; figs. 68 and 70 the backward or up stroke. The terms forward and back stroke are here employed with reference to the head of the insect.—*Original.*

describes a nearly horizontal figure-of-8. In either case the wing reciprocates, and, as a rule, reverses its planes. The down and up strokes, as will be seen from this account, cross each other, as shown more particularly at figs. 67, 68, 69, and 70.

In the wasp the wing commences the down or forward stroke at *a* of figs. 67 and 69, and makes an angle of some-

thing like 45° with the horizon ($z\ z'$).    At $b$ (figs. 67 and 69)
the angle is slightly diminished, partly because of a rotation
of the wing along its anterior margin (long axis of wing),
partly from increased speed, and partly from the posterior
margin of the wing yielding to a greater or less extent.

At $c$ the angle is still more diminished from the same
causes.

At $d$ the wing is slowed slightly, preparatory to reversing,
and the angle made with the horizon ($z$) increased.

At $e$ the angle, for the same reason, is still more increased;
while at $f$ the wing is at right angles to the horizon.    It is,
in fact, in the act of reversing.

At $g$ the wing is reversed, and the up or back stroke
commenced.

The angle made at $g$ is, consequently, the same as that
made at $a$ (45°), with this difference, that the anterior margin
and outer portion of the wing, instead of being directed *forwards*, with reference to the head of the insect, are now
directed *backwards*.

During the up or backward stroke all the phenomena are
reversed, as shown at $g\ h\ i\ j\ k\ l$ of figs. 68 and 70 (p. 141); the
only difference being that the angles made by the wing with
the horizon are somewhat less than during the down or forward
stroke—a circumstance which facilitates the forward travel
of the body, while it enables the wing during the back stroke
still to afford a considerable amount of support.    This
arrangement permits the wing to travel backwards while the
body is travelling forwards; the diminution of the angles
made by the wing in the back stroke giving very much the
same result as if the wing were striking in the direction of
the travel of the body.    The slight upward inclination of the
wing during the back stroke permits the body to fall downwards and forwards to a slight extent at this peculiar juncture, the fall of the body, as has been already explained,
contributing to the elevation of the wing.

The pinion acts as a helix or screw in a more or less horizontal direction from behind forwards, and from before backwards; but it likewise acts as a screw in a nearly vertical
direction.    If the wing of the larger domestic fly be viewed

during its vibrations from above, it will be found that the blur or impression produced on the eye by its action is more or less concave (fig. 60, p. 139). This is due to the fact that the wing is spiral in its nature, and because during its action it twists upon itself in such a manner as to describe a double curve,—the one curve being directed upwards, the other downwards. The double curve referred to is particularly evident in the flight of birds from the greater size of their wings. The wing, both when at rest and in motion, may not inaptly be compared to the blade of an ordinary screw propeller as employed in navigation. Thus the general outline of the wing corresponds closely with the outline of the blade of the propeller, and the track described by the wing in space is twisted upon itself propeller fashion. The great velocity with which the wing is driven converts the impression or blur into what is equivalent to a solid for the time being, in the same way that the spokes of a wheel in violent motion, as is well understood, completely occupy the space contained within the rim or circumference of the wheel (figs. 64, 65, and 66, p. 139).

The figure-of-8 action of the wing explains how an insect, bat, or bird, may fix itself in the air, the backward and forward reciprocating action of the pinion affording support, but no propulsion. In these instances, the backward and forward strokes are made to counterbalance each other.

*The Wing, when advancing with the Body, describes a Looped and Waved Track.*—Although the figure-of-8 represents with considerable fidelity the twisting of the wing upon its long axis during extension and flexion, and during the down and up strokes when the volant animal is playing its wings before an object, or still better, when it is artificially fixed, it is otherwise when it is free and progressing rapidly. In this case the wing, in virtue of its being carried forward by the body in motion, describes first a looped and then a waved track. This looped and waved track made by the wing of the insect is represented at figs. 71 and 72, and that made by the wing of the bat and bird at fig. 73, p. 144.

The loops made by the wing of the insect, owing to the more oblique stroke, are more horizontal than those made by

the wing of the bat and bird. The principle is, however, in
both cases the same, the loops ultimately terminating in a
waved track. The impulse is communicated to the insect
wing at the heavy parts of the loops *a b c d e f g h i j k l m n*
of fig. 71 ; the waved tracks being indicated at *p q r s t* of
the same figure. The recoil obtained from the air is represented at corresponding letters of fig. 72, the body of the

Fig. 71.

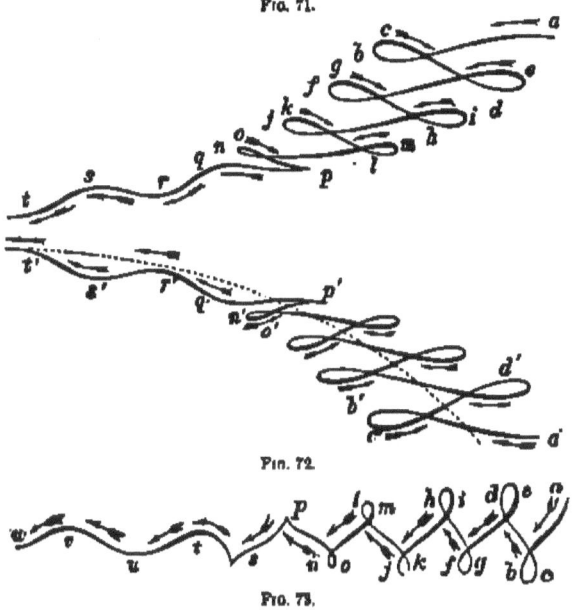

Fig. 72.

Fig. 73.

insect being carried along the curve indicated by the dotted
line. The impulse is communicated to the wing of the bat
and bird at the heavy part of the loops *a b c d e f g h i j k l m n o*
of fig. 73, the waved track being indicated at *p s t u v w* of
this figure. When the horizontal speed attained is high, the
wing is successively and rapidly brought into contact with
innumerable columns of undisturbed air. It, consequently, is
a matter of indifference whether the wing is carried at a high
speed against undisturbed air, or whether it operates upon air

travelling at a high speed (as, *e.g.* the artificial currents produced by the rapidly reciprocating action of the wing). The result is the same in both cases, inasmuch as a certain quantity of air is worked up under the wing, and the necessary degree of support and progression extracted from it. It is, therefore, quite correct to state, that as the horizontal speed of the body increases, the reciprocating action of the wing decreases; and *vice versâ*. In fact the reciprocating and non-reciprocating action of the wing in such cases is purely a matter of speed. If the travel of the wing is greater than the horizontal travel of the body, then the figure-of-8 and the reciprocating power of the wing will be more or less perfectly developed, according to circumstances. If, however, the horizontal travel of the body is greater than that of the wing, then it follows that no figure of-8 will be described by the wing; that the wing will not reciprocate to any marked

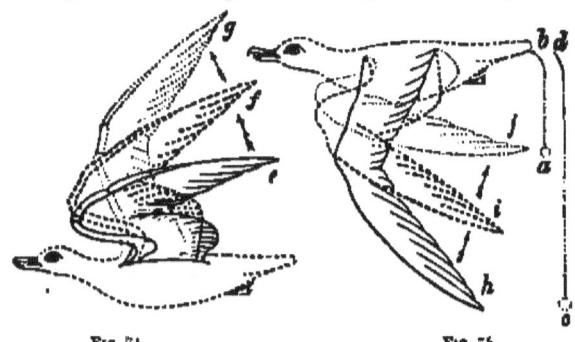

FIG. 74.                          FIG. 75.

Figs. 74 and 75 show the more or less perpendicular direction of the stroke of the wing in the flight of the bird (gull)—how the wing is gradually extended as it is elevated (*s f g* of fig. 74)—how it descends as a long lever until it assumes the position indicated by *h* of fig. 75—how it is flexed towards the termination of the down stroke, as shown at *h i j* of fig. 75, to convert it into a short lever (*a b*), and prepare it for making the up stroke. The difference in the length of the wing during flexion and extension is indicated by the short and long levers *a b* and *c d* of fig. 75. The sudden conversion of the wing from a long into a short lever at the end of the down stroke is of great importance, as it robs the wing of its momentum, and prepares it for reversing its movements. Compare with figs. 82 and 83, p. 158.—*Original.*

extent; and that the organ will describe a waved track, the curves of which will become less and less abrupt, *i.e.* longer and longer in proportion to the speed attained. The more

K.

vertical direction of the loops formed by the wing of the bat
and bird will readily be understood by referring to figs.
74 and 75 (p. 145), which represent the wing of the bird
making the down and up strokes, and in the act of being extended and flexed. (Compare with figs. 64, 65, and 66, p.
139 ; and figs. 67, 68, 69, and 70, p. 141.)

The down and up strokes are compound movements,—the
termination of the down stroke embracing the beginning of
the up stroke; the termination of the up stroke including the
beginning of the down stroke. This is necessary in order
that the down and up strokes may glide into each other in
such a manner as to prevent jerking and unnecessary retarda-
tion.

*The Margins of the Wing thrown into opposite Curves during
Extension and Flexion.*—The anterior or thick margin of the
wing, and the posterior or thin one, form different curves,
similar in all respects to those made by the body of the
fish in swimming (see fig. 32, p. 68). These curves may,
for the sake of clearness, be divided into axillary and distal
curves, the former occurring towards the root of the wing,
the latter towards its extremity. The curves (axillary and
distal) found on the anterior margin of the wing are
always the converse of those met with on the posterior
margin, *i.e.* if the convexity of the anterior axillary curve
be directed downwards, that of the posterior axillary curve
is directed upwards, and so of the anterior and posterior
distal curves. The two curves (axillary and distal), occurring
on the anterior margin of the wing, are likewise antagonistic,
the convexity of the axillary curve being always directed
downwards, when the convexity of the distal one is directed
upwards, and *vice versâ.* The same holds true of the axillary
and distal curves occurring on the posterior margin of the
wing. The anterior axillary and distal curves completely
reverse themselves during the acts of extension and flexion,
and so of the posterior axillary and distal curves (figs. 76, 77,
and 78). This antagonism in the axillary and distal curves
found on the anterior and posterior margins of the wing is
referable in the bat and bird to changes induced in the bones
of the wing in the acts of flexion and extension. In the

insect it is due to a twisting which occurs at the root of the wing and to the reaction of the air.

Fig. 76.    Fig. 77.    Fig. 78.

Fig. 76.—Curves seen on the anterior (*d e f*) and posterior (*c a b*) margin in the wing of the bird in flexion.—*Original.*

Fig. 77.—Curves seen on the anterior margin (*d e f*) of the wing in semi-extension. In this case the curves on the posterior margin (*b c*) are obliterated.—*Original.*

Fig. 78.—Curves seen on the anterior (*d e f*) and posterior (*c a b*) margin of the wing in extension. The curves of this fig. are the converse of those seen at fig. 76. Compare these figs. with fig. 79 and fig. 33, p. 68.—*Original.*

*The Tip of the Bat and Bird's Wing describes an Ellipse.*— The movements of the wrist are always the converse of those occurring at the elbow-joint. Thus in the bird, during extension, the elbow and bones of the forearm are elevated, and describe one side of an ellipse, while the wrist and bones of the hand are depressed, and describe the side of another and opposite ellipse. These movements are reversed during flexion, the elbow being depressed and carried backwards, while the wrist is elevated and carried forwards (fig. 79).

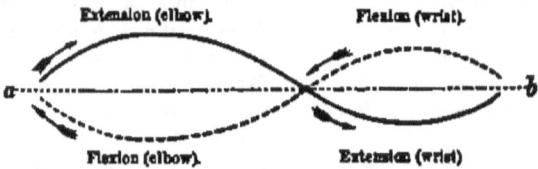

Extension (elbow).    Flexion (wrist).

Flexion (elbow).    Extension (wrist)

Fig. 79.—(*a b*) Line along which the wing travels during extension and flexion. The body of the fish in swimming describes similar curves to those described by the wing in flying.—(*Vide* fig. 32, p. 68.)

*The Wing capable of Change of Form in all its Parts.*—From this description it follows that when the different portions of the anterior margin are elevated, corresponding portions of the posterior margin are depressed ; the different parts of the wing moving in opposite directions, and playing, as it were, at cross purposes for a common good; the object being to rotate or screw the wing down upon the wind at a gradually increasing angle during extension, and to rotate it in an

opposite direction and withdraw it at a gradually decreasing
angle during flexion. It also happens.that the axillary and
distal curves co-ordinate each other and bite alternately, the
distal curve posteriorly seizing the air in extreme extension
with its concave surface (while the axillary curve relieves
itself by presenting its convex surface) ; the axillary curve, on
the other hand, biting during flexion with its concave surface
(while the distal one relieves itself by presenting its convex
one). The wing may therefore be regarded as exercising a
fourfold function, the pinion in the bat and bird being made
to move from within outwards, and from above downwards
in the down stroke, during extension; and from without
inwards, and from below upwards, in the up stroke, during
flexion.

*The Wing during its Vibration produces a Cross Pulsation.*—
The oscillation of the wing on two separate axes—the one
running parallel with the body of the bird, the other at right
angles to it (fig. 80, *a b, c d*)—is well worthy of attention, as showing that the wing attacks the air, on which it
operates in every direction, and at almost the same moment,
viz. from within outwards, and from above downwards,
during the down stroke; and from without inwards, and
from below upwards, during the up stroke. As a corollary
to the foregoing, the wing may be said to agitate the air
in two principal directions, viz. from within outwards and
downwards, or the converse ; and from behind forwards, or
the converse ; the agitation in question producing two powerful pulsations, a vertical and a horizontal. The wing when
it ascends and descends produces artificial currents which
increase its elevating and propelling power. The power of
the wing is further augmented by similar currents developed
during its extension and flexion. The movement of one part
of the wing contributes to the movement of every other part
in continuous and uninterrupted succession. As the curves
of the wing glide into each other when the wing is in motion,
so the one pulsation merges into the other by a series of
intermediate and lesser pulsations.

The vertical and horizontal pulsations occasioned by the
wing in action may be fitly represented by wave-tracks running

at right angles to each other, the vertical wave-track being the more distinct.

*Compound Rotation of the Wing.*—To work the tip and posterior margin of the wing independently and yet simultaneously, two axes are necessary, one axis (the short axis) corresponding to the root of the wing and running across it; the second (the long axis) corresponding to the anterior margin of the wing, and running in the direction of its length. The long and short axes render the movements of the wing eccentric in character. In the wing of the bird the movements of the primary or rowing feathers are also eccentric, the shaft of each feather being placed nearer the anterior than the posterior margin; an arrangement which enables the feathers to open up and separate during flexion and the up stroke, and approximate and close during extension and the down one.

These points are illustrated at fig. 80, where *a b* represents

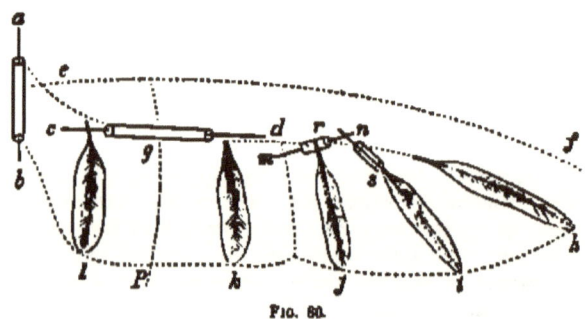

Fig. 80.

the short axis (root of wing) with a radius *e f*; *c d* representing the long axis (anterior margin of wing) with a radius *g p*.

Fig. 80 also shows that, in the wing of the bird, the individual, primary, secondary, and tertiary feathers have each what is equivalent to a long and a short axis. Thus the primary, secondary, and tertiary feathers marked *h, i, j, k, l* are capable of rotating on their long axes (*r s*), and upon their short axes (*m n*). The feathers rotate upon their long axes in a direction from below upwards during the down stroke, to make the wing impervious to air; and from above down-

wards during the up stroke, to enable the air to pass through
it. The primary, secondary, and tertiary feathers have thus
a distinctly valvular action.[1] The feathers rotate upon their
short axes (*m n*) during the descent and ascent of the wing,
the tip of the feathers rising slightly during the descent of
the pinion, and falling during its ascent. The same movement virtually takes place in the posterior margin of the
wing of the insect and bat.

*The Wing vibrates unequally with reference to a given Line.*—
The wing, during its vibration, descends further below the
body than it rises above it. This is necessary for *elevating
purposes.* In like manner the posterior margin of the wing
(whatever the position of the organ) descends further below
the anterior margin than it ascends above it. This is requisite for *elevating and propelling purposes;* the under surface
of the wing being always presented at a certain upward angle
to the horizon, and acting as a true kite (figs. 82 and 83, p.
158. Compare with fig. 116, p. 231). If the wing oscil-
lated equally above and beneath the body, and if the posterior margin of the wing vibrated equally above and below
the line formed by the anterior margin, much of its elevating
and propelling power would be sacrificed. The tail of the
fish oscillates on either side of a given line, but it is otherwise with the wing of a flying animal. The fish is of nearly
the same specific gravity as the water, so that the tail may
be said only to propel. The flying animal, on the other
hand, is very much heavier than the air, so that the wing requires both to propel and *elevate.* The wing, to be effective as
an *elevating organ,* must consequently be vibrated rather below
than above the centre of gravity; at all events, the intensity
of the vibration should occur rather below that point. In
making this statement, it is necessary to bear in mind that
the centre of gravity is *ever varying,* the body rising and falling
in a series of curves as the wings ascend and descend.

To *elevate* and *propel,* the posterior margin of the wing must
rotate round the anterior one; the posterior margin being, as
a rule, always on a lower level than the anterior one. By
the oblique and more vigorous play of the wings *under* rather
than *above* the body, each wing expends its entire energy in

---

[1] The degree of valvular action varies according to circumstances.

pushing the body *upwards* and *forwards.* It is necessary that the wings descend further than they ascend; that the wings be *convex* on their upper surfaces, and *concave* on their under ones; and that the concave or biting surfaces be brought more violently in contact with the air during the down stroke than the convex ones during the up stroke. The greater range of the wing below than above the body, and of the posterior margin below than above a given line, may be readily made out by watching the flight of the larger birds. It is well seen in the upward flight of the lark. In the hovering of the kestrel over its quarry, and the hovering of the gull over garbage which it is about to pick up, the wings play above and on a level with the body rather than below it; but these are exceptional movements for special purposes, and as they are only continued for a few seconds at a time, do not affect the accuracy of the general statement.

*Points wherein the Screws formed by the Wings differ from those employed in navigation.*—1. In the blade of the ordinary screw the integral parts are rigid and unyielding, whereas, in the blade of the screw formed by the wing, they are mobile and plastic (figs. 93, 95, 97, pp. 174, 175, 176). This is a curious and interesting point, the more especially as it does not seem to be either appreciated or understood. The mobility and plasticity of the wing is necessary, because of the tenuity of the air, and because the pinion is an *elevating* and *sustaining organ*, as well as a *propelling* one.

2. The vanes of the ordinary two-bladed screw are short, and have a comparatively limited range, the range corresponding to their area of revolution. The wings, on the other hand, are long, and have a comparatively wide range; and during their elevation and depression rush through an extensive space, the slightest movement at the root or short axis of the wing being followed by a gigantic up or down stroke at the other (fig. 56, p. 120; figs. 64, 65, and 66, p. 139; figs. 82 and 83, p. 158). As a consequence, the wings as a rule act upon successive and undisturbed strata of air. The advantage gained by this arrangement in a thin medium like the air, where the quantity of air to be compressed is necessarily great, is simply incalculable.

3. In the ordinary screw the blades follow each other in rapid succession, so that they travel over nearly the same space, and operate upon nearly the same particles (whether water or air), in nearly the same interval of time. The limited range at their disposal is consequently not utilized, the action of the two blades being confined, as it were, to the same plane, and the blades being made to precede or follow each other in such a manner as necessitates the work being virtually performed only by one of them. This is particularly the case when the motion of the screw is rapid and the mass propelled is in the act of being set in motion, *i.e.* before it has acquired momentum. In this instance a large percentage of the moving or driving power is inevitably consumed in slip, from the fact of the blades of the screw operating on nearly the same particles of matter. The wings, on the other hand, do not follow each other, but have a distinct reciprocating motion, *i.e.* they dart first in one direction, and then in another and opposite direction, in such a manner that they make during the one stroke the current on which they rise and progress the next. The blades formed by the wings and the blur or impression produced on the eye by the blades when made to vibrate rapidly are widely separated,—the one blade and its blur being situated on the right side of the body and corresponding to the right wing, the other on the left and corresponding to the left wing. The right wing traverses and completely occupies the right half of a circle, and compresses all the air contained within this space; the left wing occupying and working up all the air in the left and remaining half. The range or sweep of the two wings, when urged to their extreme limits, corresponds as nearly as may be to one entire circle[1] (fig. 56, p. 120). By separating the blades of the screw, and causing them to reciprocate, a double result is produced, since the blades always act upon independent columns of air, and in no instance overlap or double upon each other. The advantages possessed by this

[1] Of this circle, the thorax may be regarded as forming the centre, the abdomen, which is always heavier than the head, tilting the body slightly in an upward direction. This tilting of the trunk favours flight by causing the body to act after the manner of a kite.

arrangement are particularly evident when the motion is rapid. If the screw employed in navigation be driven beyond a certain speed, it cuts out the water contained within its blades; the blades and the water revolving as a solid mass. Under these circumstances, the propelling power of the screw is diminished rather than increased. It is quite otherwise with the screws formed by the wings; these, because of their reciprocating movements, becoming more and more effective in proportion as the speed is increased. As there seems to be no limit to the velocity with which the wings may be driven, and as increased velocity necessarily results in increased elevating, propelling, and sustaining power, we have here a striking example of the manner in which nature triumphs over art even in her most ingenious, skilful, and successful creations.

4. The vanes or blades of the screw, as commonly constructed, are fixed at a given angle, and consequently always strike at the same degree of obliquity. The speed, moreover, with which the blades are driven, is, as nearly as may be, uniform. In this arrangement power is lost, the two vanes striking after each other in the same manner, in the same direction, and almost at precisely the same moment,—no provision being made for increasing the angle, and the propelling power, at one stage of the stroke, and reducing it at another, to diminish the amount of slip incidental to the arrangement. The wings, on the other hand, are driven at a varying speed, and made to attack the air at a great variety of angles; the angles which the pinions make with the horizon being gradually increased by the wings being made to rotate on their long axes during the down stroke, to increase the *elevating* and *propelling* power, and gradually decreased during the up stroke, to reduce the resistance occasioned by the wings during their ascent. The latter movement increases the *sustaining* area by placing the wings in a more horizontal position. It follows from this arrangement that every particle of air within the wide range of the wings is separately influenced by them, both during their ascent and descent,—the elevating, propelling, and sustaining power being by this means increased to a maximum, while the slip or waftage is reduced to a minimum.

These results are further secured by the undulatory or waved track described by the wing during the down and up strokes. It is a somewhat remarkable circumstance that the wing, when not actually engaged as a propeller and elevator, acts as a *sustainer* after the manner of a parachute. This it can readily do, alike from its form and the mode of its application, the double curve or spiral into which it is thrown in action enabling it to lay hold of the air with avidity, in whatever direction it is urged. I say " in whatever direction," because, even when it is being recovered or drawn off the wind during the back stroke, it is climbing a gradient which arches above the body to be elevated, and so prevents it from falling. It is difficult to conceive a more admirable, simple, or effective arrangement, or one which would more thoroughly economize power. Indeed, a study of the spiral configuration of the wing, and its spiral, flail-like, lashing movements, involves some of the most profound problems in mathematics, —the curves formed by the pinion as a pinion anatomically, and by the pinion in action, or physiologically, being exceedingly elegant and infinitely varied ; these running into each other, and merging and blending, to consummate the triple function of *elevating, propelling,* and *sustaining.*

Other differences might be pointed out ; but the foregoing embrace the more fundamental and striking. Enough, moreover, has probably been said to show that it is to wing-structures and wing-movements the aëronaut must direct his attention, if he would learn "the way of an eagle in the air," and if he would rise upon the whirlwind in accordance with natural laws.

*The Wing at all times thoroughly under control.*—The wing is moveable in all parts, and can be wielded intelligently even to its extremity ; a circumstance which enables the insect, bat, and bird to rise upon the air and tread it as a master—to subjugate it in fact. The wing, no doubt, abstracts an upward and onward recoil from the air, but in doing this it exercises a selective and controlling power ; it seizes one current, evades another, and creates a third ; it feels and paws the air as a quadruped would feel and paw a treacherous yielding surface. It is not difficult to comprehend why this should be so.  If the flying creature is living, endowed with volition, and capable of directing its own course, it is surely more reasonable to suppose that it transmits to its travelling surfaces the peculiar movements necessary to progression, than that those movements should be the result of impact from fortuitous currents which it has no means of regulating.  That the bird, *e.g.* requires to control the wing, and that the wing requires to be in a condition to obey the behests of the will of the bird, is pretty evident from the fact that most of our domestic fowls can fly for considerable distances when they are young and when their wings are flexible; whereas when they are old and the wings stiff, they either do not fly at all or only for short distances, and with great difficulty.  This is particularly the case with tame swans.  This remark also holds true of the steamer or race-horse duck (*Anas brachy-ptera*), the younger specimens of which only are volant.  In older birds the wings become too rigid and the bodies too heavy for flight.  Who that has watched a sea-mew struggling bravely with the storm, could doubt for an instant that the wings and feathers of the wings are under control ?  The whole bird is an embodiment of animation and power.  The intelligent active eye, the easy, graceful, oscillation of the head and neck, the folding or partial folding of one or both wings, nay more, the slight tremor or quiver of the individual feathers of parts of the wings so rapid, that only an experienced eye can detect it, all confirm the belief that the living wing has not only the power of directing, controlling, and utilizing natural currents, but of creating and utilizing artificial ones.  But for this power, what would enable the bat and bird to rise and fly in a calm, or steer their course in a gale ?  It is erroneous to suppose that anything is left to chance where living organisms are concerned, or that animals endowed with volition and travelling surfaces should be denied the privilege of controlling the movements of those surfaces quite independ-ently of the medium on which they are destined to operate. I will never forget the gratification afforded me on one occasion at Carlow (Ireland) by the flight of a pair of magnificent swans.  The birds flew towards and past me, my attention having been roused by a peculiarly loud whistling noise

made by their wings. They flew about fifteen yards from the
ground, and as their pinions were urged not much faster than
those of the heron,[1] I had abundant leisure for studying their
movements. The sight was very imposing, and as novel as it
was grand. I had seen nothing before, and certainly have
seen nothing since that could convey a more elevated conception of the prowess and guiding power which birds may
exert. What particularly struck me was the perfect command
they seemed to have over themselves and the medium they
navigated. They had their wings and bodies visibly under
control, and the air was attacked in a manner and with an
energy which left little doubt in my mind that it played quite
a subordinate part in the great problem before me. The
necks of the birds were stretched out, and their bodies to a
great extent rigid. They advanced with a steady, stately
motion, and swept past with a vigour and force which greatly
impressed, and to a certain extent overawed, me. . Their
flight was what one could imagine that of a flying machine
constructed in accordance with natural laws would be.[2]

   *The Natural Wing, when elevated and depressed, must move
forwards.*—It is a condition of natural wings, and of artificial
wings constructed on the principle of living wings, that when

---

[1] I have frequently timed the beats of the wings of the Common Heron
(*Ardea cinerea*) in a heronry at Warren Point. In March 1869 I was placed
under unusually favourable circumstances for obtaining trustworthy results.
I timed one bird high up over a lake in the vicinity of the heronry for fifty
seconds, and found that in that period it made fifty down and fifty up strokes ;
*i.e.* one down and one up stroke per second. I timed another one in the
heronry itself. It was snowing at the time (March 1869), but the birds, notwithstanding the inclemency of the weather and the early time of the year,
were actively engaged in hatching, and required to be driven from their
nests on the top of the larch trees by knocking against the trunks thereof with
large sticks. One unusually anxious mother refused to leave the immediate
neighbourhood of the tree containing her tender charge, and circled round and
round it right overhead. I timed this bird for ten seconds, and found that
she made ten down and ten up strokes ; *i.e.* one down and one up stroke
per second precisely as before. I have therefore no hesitation in affirming
that the heron, in ordinary flight, makes exactly sixty down and sixty up
strokes per minute. The heron, however, like all other birds when pursued
or agitated, has the power of greatly augmenting the number of beats made
by its wings.

[2] The above observation was made at Carlow on the Barrow in October
1867, and the account of it is taken from my note-book.

forcibly elevated or depressed, even in a strictly vertical
direction, they inevitably dart forward. This is well shown
in fig. 81.

Fig. 81.

If, for example, the wing is suddenly depressed in *a vertical
direction*, as represented at *a b*, it at once darts downwards
and forwards in a curve to *c*, thus converting the vertical
down stroke into *a down oblique forward stroke.* If, again, the
wing be suddenly elevated in a strictly vertical direction, as
at *c d*, the wing as certainly darts upwards and forwards in
a curve to *e*, thus converting the vertical up stroke into an
*upward oblique forward stroke.* The same thing happens when
the wing is depressed from *e* to *f*, and elevated from *g* to *h*.
In both cases the wing describes a waved track, as shown at
*e g, g i*, which clearly proves that the wing strikes *downwards
and forwards* during the down stroke, and *upwards and forwards*
during the up stroke. The wing, in fact, is always advancing ;
its under surface attacking the air like a boy's kite. If, on
the other hand, the wing be forcibly depressed, as indicated
by the heavy waved line *a c*, and left to itself, it will as surely
rise again and describe a waved track, as shown at *c e*. This
it does by rotating on its long axis, and in virtue of its flexibility and elasticity, aided by the recoil obtained from the
air. In other words, it is not necessary to elevate the wing
forcibly in the direction *c d* to obtain the upward and forward
movement *c e*. One single impulse communicated at *a* causes
the wing to travel to *e*, and a second impulse communicated
at *e* causes it to travel to *i*. It follows from this that a series
of vigorous down impulses would, *if a certain interval were
allowed to elapse between them*, beget a corresponding series of
up impulses, in accordance with the law of action and reaction ; the wing and the air under these circumstances being
alternately active and passive. I say if a certain interval
were allowed to elapse between every two down strokes, but

this is practically impossible, as the wing is driven with such velocity that there is positively no time to waste in waiting for the purely mechanical ascent of the wing. That the

FIG. 82.

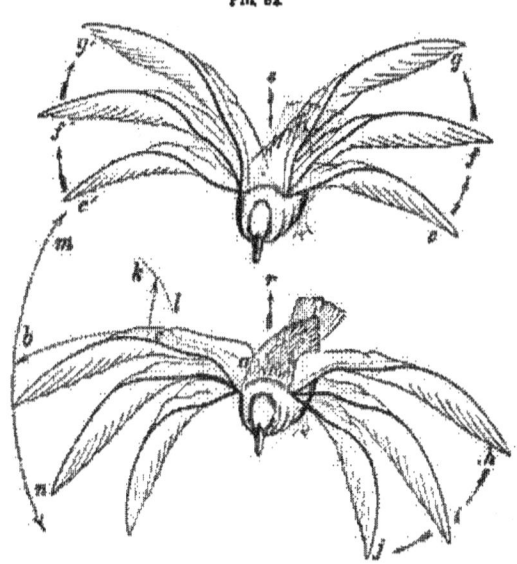

FIG. 83.

Figs. 82 and 83 show that when the wings are elevated (e, f, g of fig. 82) the body falls (s of fig. 82); and that when the wings are depressed (h, i, j of fig. 83) the body is elevated (r of fig. 83). Fig. 82 shows that the wings are elevated as short levers (c) until towards the termination of the up stroke, when they are gradually expanded (f, g) to prepare them for making the down stroke. Fig. 83 shows that the wings descend as long levers (k) until towards the termination of the down stroke, when they are gradually folded or flexed (i, l) to rob them of their momentum and prepare them for making the up stroke. Compare with figs. 74 and 75, p. 145. By this means the air beneath the wings is vigorously seized during the down stroke, while that above it is avoided during the up stroke. The concavo-convex form of the wings and the forward travel of the body contribute to this result. The wings, it will be observed, act as a parachute both during the up and down strokes. Compare with fig. 55, p. 112. Fig. 83 shows, in addition, the compound rotation of the wing, how it rotates upon a as a centre, with a radius m b n, and upon a c b as a centre, with a radius k l. Compare with fig. 80, p. 149.—Original.

ascent of the pinion is not, and ought not to be entirely due to the reaction of the air, is proved by the fact that in flying creatures (certainly in the bat and bird) **there are distinct** elevator muscles and elastic ligaments delegated to the performance of this function. The reaction of the air is therefore only one of the forces employed in elevating the wing; the others, as I shall show presently, are vital and vito-mechanical in their nature. The falling downwards and forwards of the body when the wings are ascending also contribute to this result.

*The Wing ascends when the Body descends, and vice versâ.—* As the body of the insect, bat, and bird falls forwards in a curve when the wing ascends, and is elevated in a curve when the wing descends, it follows that the trunk of the animal is urged along a waved line, as represented at 1, 2, 3, 4, 5 of fig. 81, p. 157; the waved line *a c e g i* of the same figure giving the track made by the wing. I have distinctly seen the alternate rise and fall of the body and wing when watching the flight of the gull from the stern of a steam-boat.

The direction of the stroke in the insect, as has been already explained, is much more horizontal than in the bat or bird (compare figs. 82 and 83 with figs. 64, 65, and 66, p. 139). In either case, however, the down stroke must be delivered in a more or less forward direction. This is necessary for support and propulsion. A horizontal to-and-fro movement will elevate, and an up-and-down vertical movement propel, but an oblique forward motion is requisite for progressive flight.

In all wings, whatever their position during the intervals of rest, and whether in one piece or in many, this feature is to be observed in flight. The wings are slewed downwards and forwards, *i.e.* they are carried more or less in the direction of the head during their descent, and reversed or carried in an opposite direction during their ascent. In stating that the wings are carried away from the head during the back stroke, I wish it to be understood that they do not therefore necessarily travel backwards in space when the insect is flying forwards. On the contrary, the wings, as a rule, move forward in curves, both during the down and up strokes. The fact is, that the wings at their roots are hinged and geared to the trunk so loosely, that the body is free to oscillate in a forward or backward direction, or in an up, down, or oblique direction. As a consequence of this freedom of movement,

and as a consequence likewise of the speed at which the insect
is travelling, the wings during the back stroke are for the
most part actually travelling forwards. This is accounted for
by the fact, that the body falls downwards and forwards in a
curve during the up or return stroke of the wings, and because the horizontal speed attained by the body is as a rule
so much greater than that attained by the wings, that the
latter are never allowed time to travel backward, the lesser
movement being as it were swallowed up by the greater. For
a similar reason, the passenger of a steam-ship may travel
rapidly in the direction of the stern of the vessel, and yet be
carried forward in space,—the ship sailing much quicker than
he can walk. While the wing is descending, it is rotating
upon its root as a centre (short axis). It is also, and this is
a most important point, rotating upon its anterior margin
(long axis), in such a manner as to cause the several parts
of the wing to assume various angles of inclination with the
horizon.

Figs. 84 and 85 supply the necessary illustration.

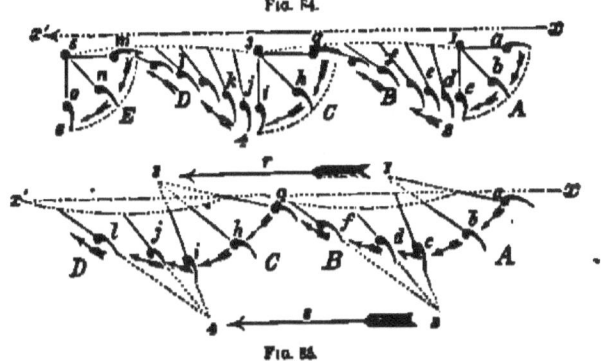

FIG. 84.

FIG. 85.

In flexion, as a rule, the under surface of the wing (fig. 84
*a*) is arranged in the same plane with the body, both being in
a line with or making a slight angle with the horizon (*x x*).[1]

---

[1] It happens occasionally in insects that the posterior margin of the wing
is on a higher level than the anterior one towards the termination of the up
stroke. In such cases the posterior margin is suddenly rotated in a downward

When the wing is made to descend, it gradually, in virtue of its simultaneously rotating upon its long and short axes, makes a certain angle with the horizon as represented at *b*. The angle is increased at the termination of the down stroke as shown at *c*, so that the wing, particularly its posterior margin, during its descent (*A*), is screwed or crushed down upon the air with its concave or biting surface directed forwards and towards the earth.  The same phenomena are indicated at *a b c* of fig. 85, but in this figure the wing is represented as travelling more decidedly forwards during its descent, and this is characteristic of the down stroke of the insect's wing—the stroke in the insect being delivered in a very oblique and more or less horizontal direction (figs. 64, 65, and 66, p. 139; fig. 71, p. 144).  The forward travel of the wing during its descent has the effect of diminishing the angles made by the under surface of the wing with the horizon.  Compare *b c d* of fig. 85 with the same letters of fig. 84.

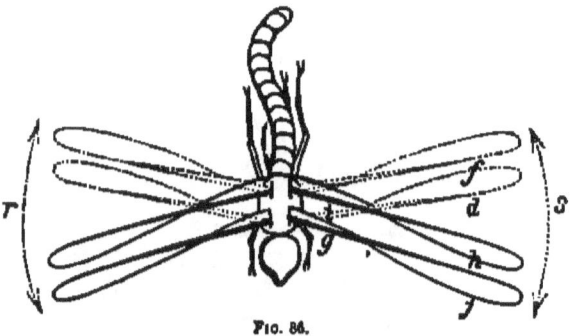

FIG. 86.

At fig. 88 (p. 166) the angles for a similar reason are still further diminished.  This figure (88) gives a very accurate idea of the kite-like action of the wing both during its descent and ascent.

The downward screwing of the posterior margin of the

and forward direction at the beginning of the down stroke—the downward and forward rotation securing additional elevating power for the wing.  The posterior margin of the wing in bats and birds, unless they are flying downwards, never rises above the anterior one, either during the up or down stroke.

L

wing during the down stroke is well seen in the dragon-fly, represented at fig. 86, p. 161.

Here the arrows r s indicate the range of the wing.   At the beginning of the down stroke the upper or dorsal surface of the wing (i d f) is inclined slightly upwards and forwards.   As the wing descends the posterior margin (i f) twists and rotates round the anterior margin (i d), and greatly increases the angle of inclination as seen, at i j, g h.   This rotation of the posterior margin (i j) round the anterior margin (g h) has the effect of causing the different portions of the under surface of the wing to assume various angles of inclination with the horizon, the wing attacking the air like a boy's kite. The angles are greatest towards the root of the wing and least towards the tip.   They accommodate themselves to the speed at which the different parts of the wing travel—a small angle with a high speed giving the same amount of buoying power as a larger angle with a diminished speed.   The screwing of the under surface of the wing (particularly the posterior margin) in a downward direction during the down stroke is necessary to insure the necessary upward recoil; the wing being made to swing downwards and forwards pendulum fashion, for the purpose of elevating the body, which it does by acting upon the air as a long lever, and after the manner of a kite.   During the down stroke the wing is active, the air passive. In other words, the wing is depressed by a purely vital act.

The down stroke is readily explained, and its results upon the body obvious.   The real difficulty begins with the up or return stroke.   If the wing was simply to travel in an upward and backward direction from c to a of fig. 84, p. 160, it is evident that it would experience much resistance from the superimposed air, and thus the advantages secured by the descent of the wing would be lost.   What really happens is this.   The wing does not travel upwards and *backwards* in the direction c b a of fig. 84 (the body, be it remembered, is advancing) but upwards and *forwards* in the direction c d e f g.   This is brought about in the following manner.   The wing is at right angles to the horizon (x x') at c.   It is therefore caught by the air at the point (2) because of the more or less horizontal travel of the body; the elastic ligaments and other structures combined with the resistance experienced from the air rotating the posterior or thin margin of the pinion in an upward direction, as shown at *d e f g* and *d f g* of figs. 84 and 85, p. 160. The wing by this partly vital and partly mechanical arrangement is rotated off the wind in such a manner as to keep its dorsal or non-biting surface directed upwards, while its concave or biting surface is directed downwards. The wing, in short, has its planes so arranged, and its angles so adjusted to the speed at which it is travelling, that it darts up a gradient like a true kite, as shown at *c d e f g* of figs. 84 and 85, p. 160, or *g h i* of fig. 88, p. 166. The wing consequently elevates and propels during its *ascent* as well as during its *descent*. It is, in fact, a kite during both the down and up strokes. The ascent of the wing is greatly assisted by the *forward travel*, and *downward and forward fall* of the body. This view will be readily understood by supposing, what is really the case, that the wing is more or less fixed by the air in space at the point indicated by 2 of figs. 84 and 85, p. 160; the body, the instant the wing is fixed, falling downwards and forwards in a curve, which, of course, is equivalent to placing the wing above, and, so to speak, behind the volant animal—in other words, to elevating the wing preparatory to a second down stroke, as seen at *g* of the figures referred to (figs. 84 and 85). The ascent and descent of the wing is always very much greater than that of the body, from the fact of the pinion acting as a long lever. The peculiarity of the wing consists in its being a flexible lever which acts upon yielding fulcra (the air), the body participating in, and to a certain extent perpetuating, the movements originally produced

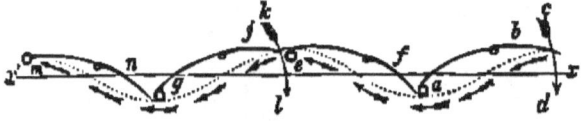

Fig. 87.

by the pinion. The part which the body performs in flight is indicated at fig. 87. At *a* the body is depressed, the wing being elevated and ready to make the down stroke at *b*. The wing descends in the direction *c d*, but the moment it begins to descend the body moves *upwards and forwards* (see arrows) in a curved line to *e*. As the wing is attached to the body the wing is made gradually to assume the position *f*. The body (*e*), it will be observed, is now on a higher level than the wing (*f*); the under surface of the latter being so adjusted that it strikes upwards and forwards as a kite. It is thus that the wing sustains and propels during the up stroke. The body (*e*) now falls *downwards and forwards* in a curved line to *g*, and in doing this it elevates or assists in elevating the wing to *j*. The pinion is a second time depressed in the direction *k l*, which has the effect of forcing the body along a waved track and in *an upward direction* until it reaches the point *m*. The ascent of the body and the descent of the wing take place simultaneously (*m n*). The body and wing, are alternately above and beneath a given line *z z'*.

A careful study of figs. 84, 85, 86, and 87, pp. 160, 161, and 163, shows the great importance of the twisted configuration and curves peculiar to the natural wing. If the wing was not curved in every direction it could not be rolled on and off the wind during the down and up strokes, as seen more particularly at fig. 87, p. 163. This, however, is a vital point in progressive flight. The wing (*b*) is rolled on to the wind in the direction *b a*, its under concave or biting surface being crushed hard down with the effect of elevating the body to *e*. The body falls to *g*, and the wing (*f*) is rolled off the wind in the direction *f j*, and elevated until it assumes the position *j*. The elevation of the wing is effected partly by the fall of the body, partly by the action of the elevator muscles and elastic ligaments, and partly by the reaction of the air, operating on its under or concave biting surface. The wing is therefore to a certain extent resting during the up stroke.

The concavo-convex form of the wing is admirably adapted for the purposes of flight. In fact, the power which the wing possesses of always keeping its concave or under surface directed *downwards* and *forwards* enables it to seize the air at every stage of both the up and down strokes so as to supply a persistent buoyancy. The action of the natural wing is accompanied by remarkably little slip—the elasticity of the

organ, the resiliency of the air, and the shortening and
elongating of the elastic ligaments and muscles all co-operating
and reciprocating in such a manner that the descent of the
wing elevates the body; the descent of the body, aided by the
reaction of the air and the shortening of the elastic ligaments
and muscles, elevating the wing. The wing during the up
stroke *arches above the body* after the manner of a parachute,
and prevents the body from falling. The sympathy which
exists between the parts of a flying animal and the air on
which it depends for support and progress is consequently of
the most intimate character.

The up stroke (*B, D* of figs. 84 and 85, p. 160), as will
be seen from the foregoing account, is a compound movement
due in some measure to recoil or resistance on the part of the
air; to the shortening of the muscles, elastic ligaments, and
other vital structures; to the elasticity of the wing; and to
the falling of the body in a downward and forward direction.
The wing may be regarded as rotating during the down
stroke upon 1 of figs. 84 and 85, p. 160, which may be taken
to represent the long and short axes of the wing; and during
the up stroke upon 2, which may be taken to represent the
yielding fulcrum furnished by the air. A second pulsation is
indicated by the numbers 3 and 4 of the same figures (84, 85).

*The Wing acts upon yielding Fulcra.*—The chief peculiarity
of the wing, as has been stated, consists in its being a twisted
flexible lever specially constructed to act upon yielding
fulcra (the air). The points of contact of the wing with the
air are represented at *a b c d e f g h i j k l* respectively of
figs. 84 and 85, p. 160; and the imaginary points of rotation
of the wing upon its long and short axes at 1, 2, 3, and 4 of
the same figures. The assumed points of rotation advance from
1 to 3 and from 2 to 4 (*vide* arrows marked *r* and *s*, fig. 85);
these constituting the steps or pulsations of the wing. The
actual points of rotation correspond to the little loops *a b c d
f g h i j l* of fig. 85. The wing descends at *A* and *C*, and
ascends at *B* and *D*.

*The Wing acts as a true Kite both during the Down and Up
Strokes.*—If, as I have endeavoured to explain, the wing, even
when elevated and depressed in a strictly vertical direction,
inevitably and invariably darts forward, it follows as a con-

sequence that the wing, as already partly explained, flies
forward as a true kite, both during the down and up strokes,
as shown at *c d e f g h i j k l m* of fig. 88; and that its under
concave or biting surface, in virtue of the forward travel
communicated to it by the body in motion, is closely applied
to the air, both during its ascent and descent—a fact hitherto
overlooked, but one of considerable importance, as showing
how the wing furnishes a persistent buoyancy, alike when it
rises and falls.

Fig. 88.

In fig. 88 the greater impulse communicated during the
down stroke is indicated by the double dotted lines. The
angle made by the wing with the horizon (*a b*) is constantly
varying, as a comparison of *c* with *d*, *d* with *e*, *e* with *f*, *f*
with *g*, *g* with *h*, and *h* with *i* will show ; these letters having
reference to supposed transverse sections of the wing. This
figure also shows that the *convex* or non-biting surface of the
wing is always directed upwards, so as to avoid unnecessary
resistance on the part of the air to the wing during its ascent ;
whereas the *concave* or biting surface is always directed downwards, so as to enable the wing to contend successfully with
gravity.

*Where the Kite formed by the Wing differs from the Boy's Kite.*
—The natural kite formed by the wing differs from the artificial kite only in this, that the former is capable of being
moved in all its parts, and is more or less flexible and elastic,
the latter being comparatively rigid. The flexibility and
elasticity of the kite formed by the natural wing is rendered
necessary by the fact that the wing is articulated or hinged
at its root ; its different parts travelling at various degrees of
speed in proportion as they are removed from the axis of
rotation. Thus the tip of the wing travels through a much
greater space in a given time than a portion nearer the root.
If the wing was not flexible and elastic, it would be impossible
to reverse it at the end of the up and down strokes, so as to

produce a continuous vibration. The wing is also practically hinged along its anterior margin, so that the posterior margin of the wing travels through a greater space in a given time than a portion nearer the anterior margin (fig. 80, p. 149). The compound rotation of the wing is greatly facilitated by the wing being flexible and elastic. This causes the pinion to twist upon its long axis during its vibration, as already stated. The twisting is partly a vital, and partly a mechanical act; that is, it is occasioned in part by the action of the muscles, in part by the reaction of the air, and in part by the greater momentum acquired by the tip and posterior margin of the wing, as compared with the root and anterior margin; the speed acquired by the tip and posterior margin causing them to reverse always subsequently to the root and anterior margin, which has the effect of throwing the anterior and posterior margins of the wing into figure-of-8 curves. It is in this way that the posterior margin of the outer portion of the wing is made to incline forwards at the end of the down stroke, when the anterior margin is inclined backwards; the posterior margin of the outer portion of the wing being made to incline backwards at the end of the up stroke, when a corresponding portion of the anterior margin is inclined forwards (figs. 69 and 70, g, a, p. 141; fig. 86, j, f, p. 161).

*The Angles formed by the Wing during its Vibrations.*—Not the least interesting feature of the compound rotation of the wing—of the varying degrees of speed attained by its different parts—and of the twisting or plaiting of the posterior margin around the anterior,—is the great variety of kite-like surfaces developed upon its dorsal and ventral aspects. Thus the tip of the wing forms a kite which is inclined upwards, forwards, and outwards, while the root forms a kite which is inclined upwards, forwards, and inwards. The angles made by the tip and outer portions of the wing with the horizon are less than those made by the body or central part of the wing, and those made by the body or central part less than those made by the root and inner portions. The angle of inclination peculiar to any portion of the wing increases as the speed peculiar to said portion decreases, and *vice versâ*. The wing is consequently mechanically perfect; the angles made by its

several parts with the horizon being accurately adjusted to
the speed attained by its different portions during its travel
to and fro. From this it follows that the air set in motion
by one part of the wing is seized upon and utilized by
another; the inner and anterior portions of the wing supplying, as it were, currents for the outer and posterior portions.
This results from the wing always forcing the air outwards
and backwards. These statements admit of direct proof, and
I have frequently satisfied myself of their exactitude by experiments made with natural and artificial wings.

In the bat and bird, the twisting of the wing upon its long
axis is more of a vital and less of a mechanical act than in
the insect; the muscles which regulate the vibration of the
pinion in the former (bat and bird), extending quite to the
tip of the wing (fig. 95, p. 175; figs. 82 and 83, p. 158).

*The Body and Wings move in opposite Curves.*—I have stated
that the wing advances in a waved line, as shown at *a c e g i*
of fig. 81, p. 157; and similar remarks are to be made of
the body as indicated at 1, 2, 3, 4, 5 of that figure. Thus,
when the wing descends in the curved line *a c*, it elevates
the body in a corresponding but minor curved line, as at
1, 2; when, on the other hand, the wing ascends in the
curved line *c e*, the body descends in a corresponding but
smaller curved line (2, 3), and so on *ad infinitum.* The undulations made by the body are so trifling when compared
with those made by the wing, that they are apt to be
overlooked. They are, however, deserving of attention, as
they exercise an important influence on the undulations made
by the wing; the body and wing swinging forward alternately,
the one rising when the other is falling, and *vice versâ.*
Flight may be regarded as the resultant of three forces :—the
*muscular and elastic force,* residing in the wing, which causes
the pinion to act as a true kite, both during the down and up
strokes; the *weight of the body,* which becomes a force the
instant the trunk is lifted from the ground, from its tendency
to fall downwards and forwards ; and *the recoil obtained from
the air* by the rapid action of the wing. These three forces
may be said to be active and passive by turns.

When a bird rises from the ground it runs for a short

distance, or throws its body into the air by a sudden leap, the wings being simultaneously elevated. When the body is fairly off the ground, the wings are made to descend with great vigour, and by their action to continue the upward impulse secured by the preliminary run or leap. The body then falls in a curve downwards and forwards; the wings, partly by the fall of the body, partly by the reaction of the air on their under surface, and partly by the shortening of the elevator muscles and elastic ligaments, being placed above and to some extent behind the bird—in other words, elevated. The second down stroke is now given, and the wings again elevated as explained, and so on in endless succession; the body falling when the wings are being elevated, and *vice versâ* (fig. 81, p. 157). When a long-winged oceanic bird rises from the sea, it uses the tips of its wings as levers for forcing the body up; the points of the pinions suffering no injury from being brought violently in contact with the water. A bird cannot be said to be flying until the trunk is swinging forward in space and taking part in the movement. The hawk, when fixed in the air over its quarry, is simply supporting itself. To fly, in the proper acceptation of the term, implies to support and propel. This constitutes the difference between a bird and a balloon. The bird can elevate *and carry itself forward*, the balloon can simply elevate itself, and must rise and fall in a straight line in the absence of currents. When the gannet throws itself from a cliff, the inertia of the trunk at once comes into play, and relieves the bird from those herculean exertions required to raise it from the water when it is once fairly settled thereon. A swallow dropping from the eaves of a house, or a bat from a tower, afford illustrations of the same principle. Many insects launch themselves into space prior to flight. Some, however, do not. Thus the blow-fly can rise from a level surface when its legs are removed. This is accounted for by the greater amplitude and more horizontal play of the insect's wing as compared with that of the bat and bird, and likewise by the remarkable reciprocating power which the insect wing possesses when the body of the insect is not moving forwards (figs. 67, 68, 69, and 70 p. 141). When a beetle attempts

to fly from the hand, it extends its front legs and flexes
the back ones, and tilts its head and thorax upwards, so
as exactly to resemble a horse in the act of rising from the
ground.  This preliminary over, whirr go its wings with immense velocity, and in an almost horizontal direction, the
body being inclined more or less vertically.  The insect rises
very slowly, and often requires to make several attempts
before it succeeds in launching itself into the air.  I could
never detect any pressure communicated to the hand when
the insect was leaving it, from which I infer that it does not
leap into the air.  The bees, I am disposed to believe, also
rise without anything in the form of a leap or spring.  I
have often watched them leaving the petals of flowers, and
they always appeared to me to elevate themselves by the steady
play of their wings, which was the more necessary, as the surface from which they rose was in many cases a yielding surface.

### THE WINGS OF INSECTS, BATS, AND BIRDS.

*Elytra or Wing-cases, Membranous Wings—their shape and
uses.*—The wings of insects consist either of one or two pairs.
When two pairs are present, they are divided into an anterior or upper pair, and a posterior or under pair.  In some
instances the anterior pair are greatly modified, and present
a corneous condition.  When so modified, they cover the
under wings when the insect is reposing, and have from
this circumstance been named elytra, from the Greek ἔλυτρον,
a sheath.  The anterior wings are dense, rigid, and opaque
in the beetles (fig. 89, r); solid in one part and membran-
aceous in another in the water-bugs (fig. 90, r); more or less
membranous throughout in the grasshoppers; and completely
membranous in the dragon-flies (fig. 91, e e, p. 172).  The
superior or upper wings are inclined at a certain angle when
extended, and are indirectly connected with flight in the
beetles, water-bugs, and grasshoppers.  They are actively
engaged in this function in the dragon-flies and butterflies.
The elytra or anterior wings are frequently employed as *sus-
tainers* or *gliders* in flight,[1] the posterior wings acting more

[1] That the elytra take part in flight is proved by this, that when they
are removed, flight is in many cases destroyed.

particularly as *elevators* and *propellers*.   In such cases the elytra
are twisted upon themselves after the manner of wings.

FIG. 69.

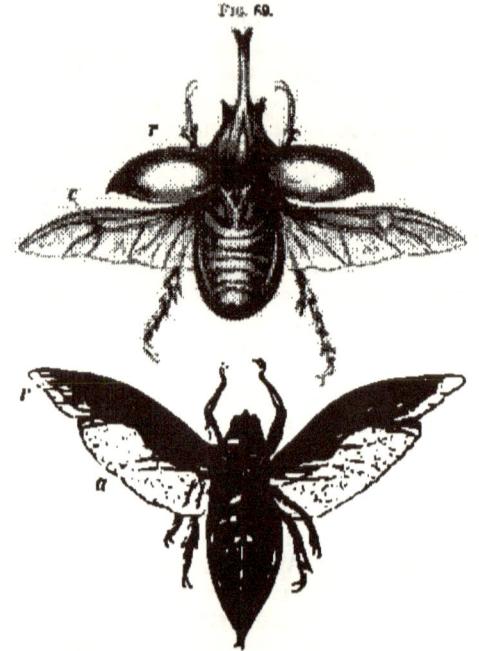

FIG. 90.

FIG. 89.—The Centaur Beetle (*Augusoma centaurus*), seen from above.  Shows
elytra (*r*) and membranous wings (*e*) in the extended state.  The nervures
are arranged and jointed in such a manner that the membranous wings can
be folded (*e*) transversely across the back beneath the elytra during repose.
When so folded, the anterior or thick margins of the membranous wings are
directed outwards and slightly downwards, the posterior or thin margins
inwards and slightly upwards.   During extension the positions of the margins are reversed by the wings twisting and rotating upon their long axes, the
anterior margins, as in bats and birds, being directed upwards and forwards,
and making a very decided angle with the horizon.   The wings in the beetles
are insignificantly small when compared with the area of the body.   They
are, moreover, finely twisted upon themselves, and possess great power as
propellers and elevators.—*Original.*

FIG. 90.—The Water-Bug (*Genus belostoma*).   In this insect the superior wings
(elytra or wing covers *r*) are semi-membranous.   They are geared to the
membranous or under wings (*a*) by a hook, the two acting together in flight.
When so geared the upper and under wings are delicately curved and
twisted.   They moreover taper from within outwards, and from before backwards.—*Original.*

The wings of insects present different degrees of opacity—
those of the moths and butterflies being non-transparent;
those of the dragon-flies, bees, and common flies presenting a
delicate, filmy, gossamer-like appearance. The wings in every
case are composed of a duplicature of the integument or in-

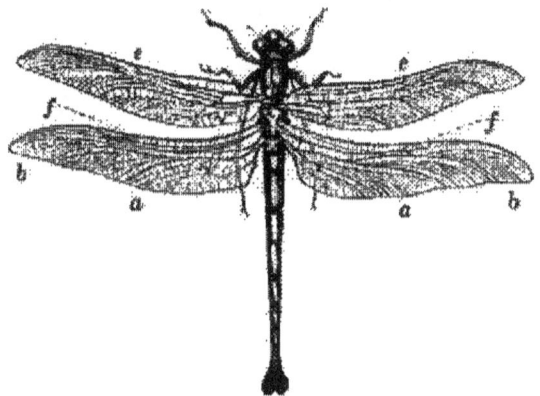

Fig. 91.—The Dragon-fly (*Petalura gigantea*). In this insect the wings are
finely curved and delicately transparent, the nervures being most strongly
developed at the roots of the wings and along the anterior margins (e e, f f,
and least so at the tips (b b), and along the posterior margins (a a). The
anterior pair (e e) are analogous in every respect to the posterior (f f). Both
make a certain angle with the horizon, the anterior pair (e e), which are principally used as elevators, making a smaller angle than the posterior pair
(f f), which are used as drivers. The wings of the dragon-fly make the proper
angles for flight even in repose, so that the insect can take to wing instantly.
The insect flies with astonishing velocity.—*Original*

vesting membrane, and are strengthened in various directions
by a system of hollow, horny tubes, known to entomologists
as the neuræ or nervures. The nervures taper towards the
extremity of the wing, and are strongest towards its root and
anterior margin, where they supply the place of the arm in
bats and birds. They are variously arranged. In the beetles
they pursue a somewhat longitudinal course, and are jointed to
admit of the wing being folded up transversely beneath the
elytra.[1] In the locusts the nervures diverge from a common
centre, after the manner of a fan, so that by their aid the wing
is crushed up or expanded as required; whilst in the dragon-fly,

[1] The wings of the May-fly are folded longitudinally and transversely, so
that they are crumpled up into little squares.

where no folding is requisite, they form an exquisitely reti-
culated structure.   The nervures, it may be remarked, are
strongest in the beetles, where the body is heavy and the
wing small.   They decrease in thickness as those conditions
are reversed, and entirely disappear in the minute chalcis and
psilus.[1]   The function of the nervures is not ascertained; but
as they contain spiral vessels which apparently communicate
with the trachess of the trunk, some have regarded them as
being connected with the respiratory system; whilst others
have looked upon them as the receptacles of a subtle fluid,
which the insect can introduce and withdraw at pleasure to
obtain the requisite degree of expansion and tension in the
wing.   Neither hypothesis is satisfactory, as respiration and
flight can be performed in their absence.   They appear to
me, when present, rather to act as mechanical stays or
stretchers, in virtue of their rigidity and elasticity alone,—
their arrangement being such that they admit of the wing
being folded in various directions, if necessary, during flexion,
and give it the requisite degree of firmness during extension.
They are, therefore, in every respect analogous to the skeleton
of the wing in the bat and bird.   In those wings which,
during the period of repose, are folded up beneath the elytra,
the mere extension of the wing in the dead insect, where no
injection of fluid can occur, causes the nervures to fall into
position, and the membranous portions of the wing to unfurl
or roll out precisely as in the living insect, and as happens in
the bat and bird.   This result is obtained by the spiral arrangement of the nervures at the root of the wing; the anterior nervure occupying a higher position than that further back, as in
the leaves of a fan.   The spiral arrangement occurring at
the root extends also to the margins, so that wings which fold
up or close, as well as those which do not, are twisted upon
themselves, and present a certain degree of convexity on their
superior or upper surface, and a corresponding concavity on
their inferior or under surface; their free edges supplying
those fine curves which act with such efficacy upon the air,
in obtaining the maximum of resistance and the minimum
of displacement; or what is the same thing, the maximum
of support with the minimum of slip (figs. 92 and 93).

[1] Kirby and Spence, vol. II. 5th ed., p. 352.

The wings of insects can be made to oscillate within given areas anteriorly, posteriorly, or centrally with regard to the plane of the body; or in intermediate positions with regard to it and a perpendicular line. The wing or wings of the one

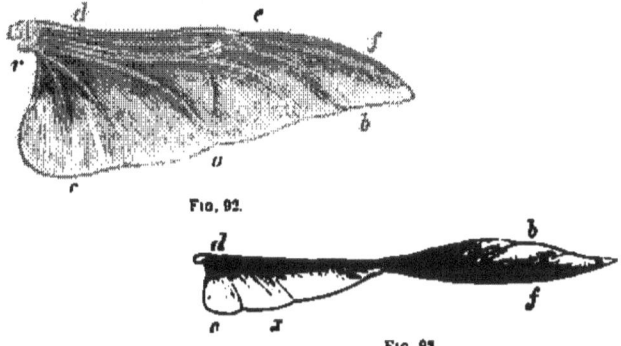

Fio. 92.

Fio. 93.

Fig. 92.—Right wing of Beetle (*Goliathus micans*), dorsal surface. This wing somewhat resembles the kestrel's (fig. 61, p. 156) in shape. It has an anterior thick margin, *d e f*, and a posterior thin one, *b n e*. Strong nervures run along the anterior margin (*a*) until they reach the joint (*e*), where the wing folds upon itself during repose. Here the nervures split up and divaricate and gradually become smaller and smaller until they reach the extremity of the wing (*f*) and the posterior or thin margin (*h*); other nervures radiate in graceful curves from the root of the wing. These also become finer as they reach the posterior or thin margin (*e a*). *r*, Root of the wing with its complex compound joint. The wing of the beetle bears a certain analogy to that of the bat, the nervures running along the anterior margin (*d*) of the wing, resembling the humerus and forearm of the bat (fig. 94, *d*, p. 175), the joint of the beetle's wing (*e*) corresponding to the carpal or wrist-joint of the bat's wing (fig. 94, *e*), the terminal or distal nervures of the beetle (*f b*) to the phalanges of the bat (fig. 94, *f b*). The parts marked *f b* may in both instances be likened to the primary feathers of the bird, that marked *a* to the secondary feathers, and *e* to the tertiary feathers. In the wings of the beetle and bat no air can possibly escape through them during the return or up stroke.—*Original.*

Fig. 93.—Right wing of the Beetle (*Goliathus micans*), as seen from behind and from beneath. When so viewed, the anterior or thick margin (*d f*) and the posterior or thin margin (*b e c*) are arranged in different planes, and form a true helix or screw. Compare with figs. 95 and 97.—*Original.*

side can likewise be made to move independently of those of the opposite side, so that the centre of gravity, which, in insects, bats, and birds, is suspended, is not disturbed in the endless evolutions involved in ascending, descending, and wheeling. The centre of gravity varies in insects according to the shape of the body, the length and shape of the limbs and antennæ, and the position, shape, and size of the pinions. It is corrected in some by curving the body, in others by bending or straightening the limbs and antennæ, but principally in all by the judicious play of the wings themselves.

The wing of the bat and bird, like that of the insect, is concavo-convex, and more or less twisted upon itself (figs. 94, 95, 96, and 97).

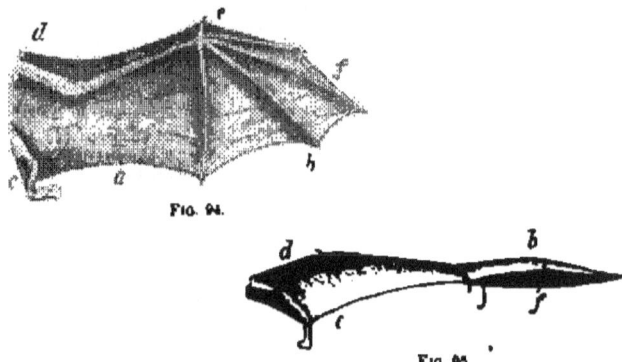

FIG. 94.

FIG. 95.

FIG. 94.—Right wing of the Bat (*Phyllorhina gracilis*), dorsal surface. *d e f*, Anterior or thick margin of the wing, supported by the bones of the arm, forearm, and hand (first and second phalanges); *c a b*, posterior or thin margin, supported by the remaining phalanges, by the side of the body, and by the foot.—*Original.*
FIG. 95.—Right wing of the Bat (*Phyllorhina gracilis*), as seen from behind and from beneath. When so regarded, the anterior or thick margin (*d f*) of the wing displays different curves from those seen on the posterior or thin margin (*b c*); the anterior and posterior margins being arranged in different planes, as in the blade of a screw propeller.—*Original.*

The twisting is in a great measure owing to the manner in which the bones of the wing are twisted upon themselves, and the spiral nature of their articular surfaces; the long axes of the joints always intersecting each other at nearly right angles. As a result of this disposition of the articular surfaces, the wing is shot out or extended, and retracted or flexed in a variable plane, the bones of the wing rotating in the direction of their length during either movement. This secondary action, or the revolving of the component bones upon their own axes, is of the greatest importance in the movements of the wing, as it communicates to the hand and forearm, and

consequently to the membrane or feathers which they bear,
the precise angles necessary for flight. It, in fact, insures
that the wing, and the curtain, sail, or fringe of the wing
shall be screwed into and down upon the air in extension,
and unscrewed or withdrawn from it during flexion. The
wing of the bat and bird may therefore be compared to a
huge gimlet or auger, the axis of the gimlet representing the
bones of the wing; the flanges or spiral thread of the gimlet
the frenum or sail (figs. 95 and 97).

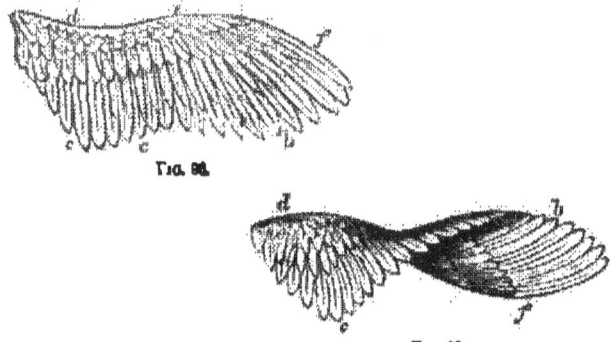

Fig. 95.

Fig. 97.

Fig. 96.—Right wing of the Red-legged Partridge (*Perdix rubra*), dorsal
aspect. Shows extreme example of short rounded wing; contrast with the
wing of the albatross (fig. 62, p. 137), which furnishes an extreme example
of the long ribbon-shaped wing *d t f*; anterior margin; *b a e*, posterior
ditto, consisting of primary (*b*) secondary (*a*), and tertiary (*e*) feathers,
with their respective coverts and subcoverts; the whole overlapping and
mutually supporting each other. This wing, like the kestrel's (fig. 91, p.
180), was drawn from a specimen held against the light, the object being to
display the mutual relation of the feathers to each other, and how the
feathers overlap.—*Original.*
Fig. 97.—Right wing of Red-legged Partridge (*Perdix rubra*), seen from behind and from beneath, as in the beetle (fig. 98) and bat (fig. 95) The same
lettering and explanation does for all three.—*Original.*

## THE WINGS OF BATS.

*The Bones of the Wing of the Bat—the spiral configuration
of their articular surfaces.*—The bones of the arm and hand
are especially deserving of attention. The humerus (fig.
17, *r*, p. 36) is short and powerful, and twisted upon itself
to the extent of something less than a quarter of a turn.

As a consequence, the long axis of the shoulder-joint is nearly at right angles to that of the elbow-joint. Similar remarks may be made regarding the radius (the principal bone of the forearm) (*d*), and the second and third metacarpal bones with their phalanges (*e f*), all of which are greatly elongated, and give strength and rigidity to the anterior or thick margin of the wing.    The articular surfaces of the bones alluded to, as well as of the other bones of the hand, are spirally disposed with reference to each other, the long axes of the joints intersecting at nearly right angles.    The object of this arrangement is particularly evident when the wing of the living bat, or of one recently dead, is extended and flexed as in flight.

In the flexed state the wing is greatly reduced in size, its under surface being nearly parallel with the plane of progression.    When the wing is fully extended its under surface makes a certain angle with the horizon, the wing being then in a position to give the down stroke, which is delivered *downwards* and *forwards*, as in the insect.    When extension takes place the elbow-joint is depressed and carried forwards, the wrist elevated and carried backwards, the metacarpo-phalangeal joints lowered and inclined forwards, and the distal phalangeal joints slightly raised and carried backwards. The movement of the bat's wing in extension is consequently a spiral one, the spiral running alternately from below upwards and forwards, and from above downwards and backwards (compare with fig. 79, p. 147).    As the bones of the arm, forearm, and hand rotate on their axes during the extensile act, it follows that the posterior or thin margin of the wing is rotated in a downward direction (the anterior or thick one being rotated in an opposite direction) until the wing makes an angle of something like 30° with the horizon, which, as I have already endeavoured to show, is the greatest angle made by the wing in flight.    The action of the bat's wing at the shoulder is particularly free, partly because the shoulder-joint is universal in its nature, and partly because the scapula participates in the movements of this region.    The freedom of action referred to enables the bat not only to rotate and twist its wing as a whole, with a view to dimin-

M

ishing and increasing the angle which its under surface makes
with the horizon, but to elevate and depress the wing, and
move it in a forward and backward direction.  The rotatory
or twisting movement of the wing is an essential feature in
flight, as it enables the bat (and this holds true also of the
insect and bird) to balance itself with the utmost exactitude,
and to change its position and centre of gravity with marvellous dexterity.  The movements of the shoulder-joint are
restrained within certain limits by a system of check-ligaments,
and by the coracoid and acromian processes of the scapula.
The wing is recovered or flexed by the action of elastic ligaments which extend between the shoulder, elbow, and wrist.
Certain elastic and fibrous structures situated between the
fingers and in the substance of the wing generally take part
in flexion.  The bat flies with great ease and for lengthened
periods.  Its flight is remarkable for its softness, in which
respect it surpasses the owl and the other nocturnal birds.
The action of the wing of the bat, and the movements of
its component bones, are essentially the same as in the bird.

## THE WINGS OF BIRDS.

*The Bones of the Wing of the Bird—their Articular Sur-
faces, Movements, etc.*—The humerus, or arm-bone of the
wing, is supported by three of the trunk-bones, viz. the
scapula or shoulder-blade, the clavicle or collar-bone, also
called the *furculum*,[1] and the coracoid bone,—these three
converging to form a *point d'appui*, or centre of support for
the head of the humerus, which is received in *facettes* or
depressions situated on the scapula and coracoid.  In order
that the wing may have an almost unlimited range of motion,
and be wielded after the manner of a flail, it is articulated to
the trunk by a somewhat lax universal joint, which permits

---

[1] The furcula are usually united to the anterior part of the sternum by
ligament; but in birds of powerful flight, where the wings are habitually
extended for gliding and sailing, as in the frigate-bird, the union is osseous in
its nature.  "In the frigate-bird the furcula are likewise anchylosed with
the coracoid bones."—Comp. Anat. and Phys. of Vertebrates, by Prof. Owen,
vol. II. p. 66.

vertical, horizontal, and intermediate movements.[1]  The long axis of the joint is directed vertically; the joint itself somewhat backwards.  It is otherwise with the elbow-joint, which is turned forwards, and has its long axis directed horizontally, from the fact that the humerus is twisted upon itself to the extent of nearly a quarter of a turn.  The elbow-joint is decidedly spiral in its nature, its long axis intersecting that of the shoulder-joint at nearly right angles.  The humerus articulates at the elbow with two bones, the radius and the ulna, the former of which is pushed from the humerus, while the other is drawn towards it during extension, the reverse occurring during flexion.  Both bones, moreover, while those movements are taking place, revolve to a greater or less extent upon their own axes.  The bones of the forearm articulate at the wrist with the carpal bones, which being spirally arranged, and placed obliquely between them and the metacarpal bones, transmit the motions to the latter in a curved direction.  The long axis of the wrist-joint is, as nearly as may be, at right angles to that of the elbow-joint, and more or less parallel with that of the shoulder.  The metacarpal or hand-bones, and the phalanges or finger-bones are more or less fused together, the better to support the great primary feathers, on the efficiency of which flight mainly depends.  They are articulated to each other by double hinge-joints, the long axes of which are nearly at right angles to each other.

As a result of this disposition of the articular surfaces, the wing is shot out or extended and retracted or flexed in a variable plane, the bones composing the wing, particularly those of the forearm, rotating on their axes during either movement.

This secondary action, or the revolving of the component bones upon their own axes, is of the greatest importance in the movements of the wing, as it communicates to the hand

---

[1] "The os humeri, or bone of the arm, is articulated by a small rounded surface to a corresponding cavity formed between the coracoid bone and the scapula, in such a manner as to allow great freedom of motion."—Macgillivray's Brit. Birds, vol. i. p. 33.

"The arm is articulated to the trunk by a ball-and-socket joint, permitting all the freedom of motion necessary for flight."—Cyc. of Anat. and Phys., vol. iii. p. 424.

and forearm, and consequently to the primary and secondary
feathers which they bear, the precise angles necessary for
flight; it in fact insures that the wing, and the curtain or
fringe of the wing which the primary and secondary feathers
form, shall be screwed into and down upon the air in extension, and unscrewed or withdrawn from it during flexion.
The wing of the bird may therefore be compared to a huge
gimlet or auger; the axis of the gimlet representing the
bones of the wing, the flanges or spiral thread of the gimlet
the primary and secondary feathers (fig. 63, p. 138, and fig.
97, p. 176).

*Traces of Design in the Wing of the Bird—the arrangement of
the Primary, Secondary, and Tertiary Feathers, etc.*—There are
few things in nature more admirably constructed than the
wing of the bird, and perhaps none where design can be more
readily traced. Its great strength and extreme lightness, the
manner in which it closes up or folds during flexion, and
opens out or expands during extension, as well as the manner
in which the feathers are strung together and overlap each
other in divers directions to produce at one time a solid
resisting surface, and at another an interrupted and comparatively non-resisting one, present a degree of fitness to which
the mind must necessarily revert with pleasure. If the
feathers of the wing only are contemplated, they may be conveniently divided into three sets of three each (on both sides
of the wing)—an upper or dorsal set (fig. 61, *d, e, f*, p. 136), a
lower or ventral set (*c, a, b*), and one which is intermediate.
This division is intended to refer the feathers to the bones of
the arm, forearm, and hand, but is more or less arbitrary in
its nature. The lower set or tier consists of the primary (*b*),
secondary (*a*), and tertiary (*c*) feathers, strung together by
fibrous structures in such a way that they move in an outward or inward direction, or turn upon their axes, at precisely
the same instant of time,—the middle and upper sets of
feathers, which overlap the primary, secondary, and tertiary
ones, constituting what are called the "coverts" and "subcoverts." The primary or rowing feathers are the longest and
strongest (*b*), the secondaries (*a*) next, and the tertiaries third
(*c*). The tertiaries, however, are occasionally longer than the

secondaries. The tertiary, secondary, and primary feathers increase in strength from within outwards, i.e. from the body

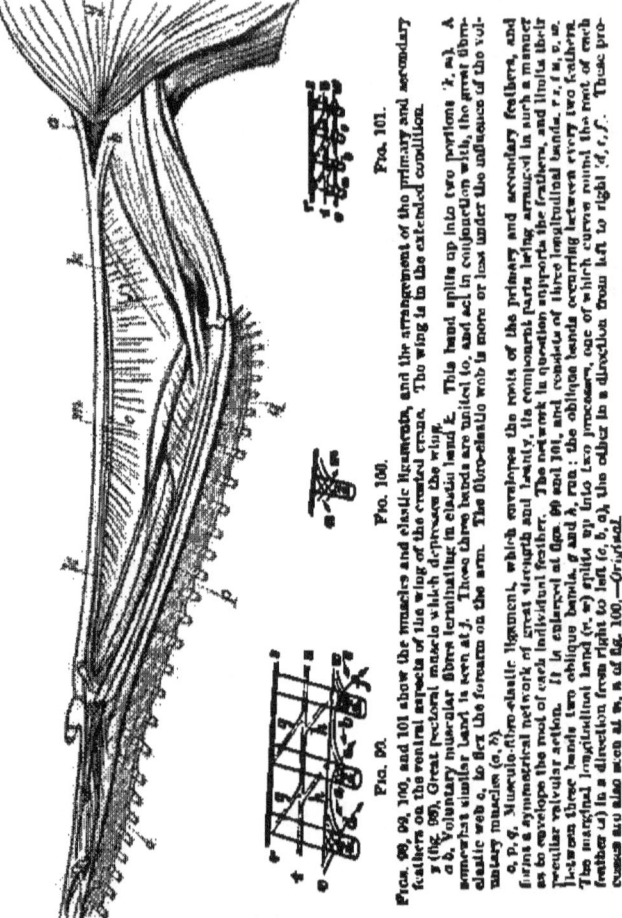

FIG. 101.

FIG. 100.

FIG. 99.

FIGS. 98, 99, 100, and 101 show the muscles and elastic ligaments, and the arrangement of the primary and secondary feathers on the ventral aspects of the wing of the crested crane. The wing is in the extended condition.

a, b, Voluntary muscular fibres terminating in elastic band E. This band splits up into two portions (?, m). A somewhat similar band is seen at j. These three bands are united to, and act in conjunction with, the great fibro-elastic web c, to flex the forearm on the arm. The fibro-elastic web is more or less under the influence of the voluntary muscles (a, b).

c, p, q, Musculo-fibro-elastic ligament, which envelopes the roots of the primary and secondary feathers, and forms a symmetrical network of great strength and beauty, its component parts being arranged in such a manner as to envelope the root of each individual feather. The network in question supports the feathers, and limits their peculiar valvular action. It is enlarged at figs. 99 and 101, and consists of three longitudinal bands, r, s, t, u, v, w. Between these bands two oblique bands, g and h, run: the oblique bands occurring between every two feathers. The marginal longitudinal band (r, w) splits up into two processes, one of which curves round the root of each feather u) in a direction from right to left (e, b, a), the other in a direction from left to right (d, e, f. These processes are also seen at m, n of fig. 100.—Original.

towards the extremity of the wing, and so of the several sets of wing-coverts. This arrangement is necessary, because the

strain on the feathers during flight increases in proportion to
their distance from the trunk.

The manner in which the roots of the primary, secondary,
and tertiary feathers are geared to each other in order to
rotate in one direction in flexion, and in another and opposite
direction in extension, is shown at figs. 98, 99, 100, and 101,
p. 181. In flexion the feathers open up and permit the air
to pass between them. In extension they flap together and
render the wing as air-tight as that of either the insect or bat.
The primary, secondary, and tertiary feathers have consequently a valvular action.

*The Wing of the Bird not always opened up to the same extent
in the Up Stroke.*—The elaborate arrangements and adaptations
for increasing the area of the wing, and making it impervious
to air during the down stroke, and for decreasing the area
and opening up the wing during the up stroke, although
necessary to the flight of the heavy-bodied, short-winged
birds, as the grouse, partridge, and pheasant, are by no means
indispensable to the flight of the long-winged oceanic birds,
unless when in the act of rising from a level surface; neither
do the short-winged heavy birds require to fold and open up
the wing during the up stroke to the same extent in all cases,
less folding and opening up being required when the birds
fly against a breeze, and when they have got fairly under
weigh. All the oceanic birds, even the albatross, require to
fold and flap their wings vigorously when they rise from the
surface of the water. When, however, they have acquired a
certain degree of momentum, and are travelling at a tolerable
horizontal speed, they can in a great measure dispense with
the opening up of the wing during the up stroke—nay, more,
they can in many instances dispense even with flapping.
This is particularly the case with the albatross, which (if a
tolerably stiff breeze be blowing) can sail about for an hour
at a time without once flapping its wings. In this case the
wing is wielded in one piece like the insect wing, the bird
simply screwing and unscrewing the pinion on and off the
wind, and exercising a restraining influence—the breeze doing
the principal part of the work. In the bat the wing is
jointed as in the bird, and folded during the up stroke. As,

however, the bat's wing, as has been already stated, is covered
by a continuous and more or less elastic membrane, it follows
that it cannot be opened up to admit of the air passing
through it during the up stroke.   Flight in the bat is therefore
secured by alternately diminishing and increasing the area of
the wing during the up and down strokes—the wing rotating
upon its root and along its anterior margin, and presenting a
variety of kite-like surfaces, during its ascent and descent, precisely as in the bird (fig. 80, p. 149, and fig. 83, p. 158).

Fig. 102.—Shows the upward inclination of the body and the flexed condition
of the wings in *b*, *a f*; *a' b'*, *e f*   in the flight of the kingfisher.   The body
and wings when taken together form a kite.   Compare with fig. 59, p.
120, where the wings are fully extended.

*Flexion of the Wing necessary to the Flight of Birds.*—Considerable diversity of opinion exists as to whether birds do or
do not flex their wings in flight.   The discrepancy is owing
to the great difficulty experienced in analysing animal movements, particularly when, as in the case of the wings, they are
consecutive and rapid.   My own opinion is, that the wings
are flexed in flight, but that all wings are not flexed to the
same extent, and that what holds true of one wing does not
necessarily hold true of another.   To see the flexing of the
wing properly, the observer should be either immediately
above the bird or directly beneath it.   If the bird be con-

templated from before, behind, or from the side, the up and down strokes of the pinion distract the attention and complicate the movement to such an extent as to render the observation of little value. In watching rooks proceeding leisurely against a slight breeze, I have over and over again satisfied myself that the wings are flexed during the up stroke, the mere extension and flexion, with very little of a down stroke, in such instances sufficing for propulsion. I have also observed it in the pigeon in full flight, and likewise in the starling, sparrow, and kingfisher (fig. 102, p. 183).

It occurs principally at the wrist-joint, and gives to the wing the peculiar quiver or tremor so apparent in rapid flight, and in young birds at feeding-time. The object to be attained is manifest. By the flexing of the wing in flight, the "*remiges*," or rowing feathers, are opened up or thrown out of position, and the air permitted to escape—advantage being thus taken of the peculiar action of the individual feathers and the higher degree of differentiation perceptible in the wing of the bird as compared with that of the bat and insect.

In order to corroborate the above opinion, I extended the wings of several birds as in rapid flight, and fixed them in the outspread position by lashing them to light unyielding reeds. In these experiments the shoulder and elbow-joints were left quite free—the wrist or carpal and the metacarpal joints only being bound. I took care, moreover, to interfere as little as possible with the action of the elastic ligament or alar membrane which, in ordinary circumstances, recovers or flexes the wing, the reeds being attached for the most part to the primary and secondary feathers. When the wings of a pigeon were so tied up, the bird could not rise, although it made vigorous efforts to do so. When dropped from the hand, it fell violently upon the ground, notwithstanding the strenuous exertions which it made with its pinions to save itself. When thrown into the air, it fluttered energetically in its endeavours to reach the dove-cot, which was close at hand; in every instance, however, it fell, more or less heavily, the distance attained varying with the altitude to which it was projected.

Thinking that probably the novelty of the situation and

the strangeness of the appliances confused the bird, I allowed
it to walk about and to rest without removing the reeds.   I
repeated the experiment at intervals, but with no better
results.   The same phenomena, I may remark, were witnessed in
the sparrow; so that I think there can be no doubt that a certain degree of flexion in the wings is indispensable to the flight
of all birds—the amount varying according to the length and
form of the pinions, and being greatest in the short broad-
winged birds, as the partridge and kingfisher, less in those
whose wings are moderately long and narrow, as the gulls, and
many of the oceanic birds, and least in the heavy-bodied long
and narrow-winged sailing or gliding birds, the best example
of which is the albatross.   The degree of flexion, moreover,
varies according as the bird is rising, falling, or progressing
in a horizontal direction, it being greatest in the two former,
and least in the latter.

It is true that in insects, unless perhaps in those which
fold or close the wing during repose, no flexion of the pinion
takes place in flight; but this is no argument against this
mode of diminishing the wing-area during the up stroke
where the joints exist; and it is more than probable that when
joints are present they are added to augment the power of
the wing during its active state, *i.e.* during flight, quite as
much as to assist in arranging the pinion on the back or side of
the body when the wing is passive and the animal is reposing.
The flexion of the wing is most obvious when the bird is
exerting itself, and may be detected in birds which skim or
glide when they are rising, or when they are vigorously flapping their wings to secure the impetus necessary to the gliding
movement.   It is less marked at the elbow-joint than at the
wrist; and it may be stated generally that, as flexion *decreases*, the twisting flail-like movement of the wing at the
shoulder *increases*, and *vice versâ*,—the great difference between
sailing birds and those which do not sail amounting to this,
that in the sailing birds the wing is worked from the shoulder
by being alternately rolled on and off the wind, as in insects;
whereas, in birds which do not glide, the spiral movement
travels along the arm as in bats, and manifests itself during
flexion and extension in the bending of the joints and in the

rotation of the bones of the wing on their axes. The spiral conformation of the pinions, to which allusion has been so frequently made, is best seen in the heavy-bodied birds, as the turkey, capercailzie, pheasant, and partridge; and here also the concavo-convex form of the wing is most perceptible. In the light-bodied, ample-winged birds, the amount of twisting is diminished, and, as a result, the wing is more or less flattened, as in the sea-gull (fig. 103).

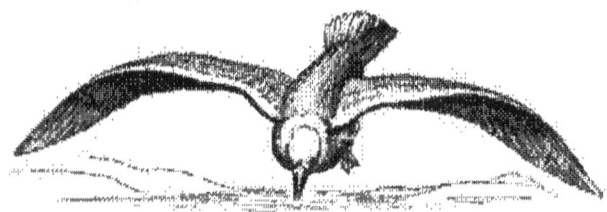

Fig. 103.—Shows the twisted levers or screws formed by the wings of the gull. Compare with fig. 63, p. 107, with figs. 76, 77, and 78, p. 147, and with figs. 64 and 65, p. 158.—*Original.*

*Consideration of the Forces which propel the Wings of Insects.* —In the thorax of insects the muscles are arranged in two principal sets in the form of a cross—*i.e.* there is a powerful vertical set which runs from above downwards, and a powerful antero-posterior set which runs from before backwards. There are likewise a few slender muscles which proceed in a more or less oblique direction. The antero-posterior and vertical sets of muscles are quite distinct, as are likewise the oblique muscles. Portions, however, of the vertical and oblique muscles terminate at the root of the wing in jelly-looking points which greatly resemble rudimentary tendons, so that I am inclined to believe that the vertical and oblique muscles exercise a direct influence on the movements of the wing. The shortening of the antero-posterior set of muscles (indirectly assisted by the oblique ones) elevates the dorsum of the thorax by causing its anterior extremity to approach its posterior extremity, and by causing the thorax to bulge out or expand laterally. This change in the thorax necessitates the descent of the wing. The shortening of the vertical set (aided by the oblique ones) has a precisely opposite effect,

and necessitates its ascent.  While the wing is ascending and
descending the oblique muscles cause it to rotate on its long
axis, the bipartite division of the wing at its root, the spiral
configuration of the joint, and the arrangement of the elastic
and other structures which connect the pinion with the body,
together with the resistance it experiences from the air, conferring on it the various angles which characterize the down
and up strokes.  The wing may therefore be said to be depressed by the shortening of the antero-posterior set of
muscles, aided by the oblique muscles, and elevated by the
shortening of the vertical and oblique muscles, aided by the
elastic ligaments, and the reaction of the air.  If we adopt
this view we have a perfect physiological explanation of the
phenomenon, as we have a complete circle or cycle of motion,
the antero-posterior set of muscles shortening when the
vertical set of muscles are elongating, and *vice versâ*.  This, I
may add, is in conformity with all other muscular arrangements, where we have what are usually denominated extensors and flexors, pronators and supinators, abductors and
adductors, etc., but which, as I have already explained (pp.
24 to 34), are simply the two halves of a circle of muscle and
of motion, an arrangement for securing diametrically opposite
movements in the travelling surfaces of all animals.

Chabrier's account, which I subjoin, virtually supports this
hypothesis :—

" It is generally through the intervention of the proper
motions of the dorsum, which are very considerable during
flight, that the wings or the elytra are moved equally and
simultaneously.  Thus, when it is elevated, it carries with it
the internal side of the base of the wings with which it is
articulated, from which enanes the depression of the external
side of the wing ; and when it approaches the sternal portion
of the trunk, the contrary takes place.  During the depression of the wings, the dorsum is curved from before backwards, or in such a manner that its anterior extremity is
brought nearer to its posterior, that its middle is elevated,
and its lateral portions removed further from each other.
The reverse takes place in the elevation of the wings ; the
anterior extremity of the dorsum being removed to a greater

distance from the posterior, its middle being depressed, and
its sides brought nearer to each other.  Thus its bending in
one direction produces a diminution of its curve in the direction normally opposed to it; and by the alternations of this
motion, assisted by other means, the body is alternately compressed and dilated, and the wings are raised and depressed
by turns."[1]

In the *libellulæ* or dragon-flies, the muscles are inserted
into the roots of the wings as in the bat and bird, the only
difference being that in the latter the muscles creep along the
wings to their extremities.

In all the wings which I have examined, whether in the
insect, bat, or bird, the wings are recovered, flexed, or
drawn towards the body by the action of elastic ligaments,
these structures, by their mere contraction, causing the
wings, when fully extended and presenting their maximum
of surface, to resume their position of rest, and plane of
least resistance.   The principal effort required in flight
would therefore seem to be made during extension and
the down stroke.   The elastic ligaments are variously formed,
and the amount of contraction which they undergo is in
all cases accurately adapted to the size and form of the
wings, and the rapidity with which they are worked—the
contraction being greatest in the short-winged and heavy-
bodied insects and birds, and least in the light-bodied and
ample-winged ones, particularly in such as skim or glide.
The mechanical action of the elastic ligaments, I need scarcely
remark, insures a certain period of repose to the wings
at each stroke, and this is a point of some importance, as
showing that the lengthened and laborious flights of insects
and birds are not without their stated intervals of rest.

*Speed attained by Insects.*—Many instances might be quoted
of the marvellous powers of flight possessed by insects as a
class.  The male of the silkworm-moth (*Attacus Paphia*) is
stated to travel more than 100 miles a day;[2] and an anonymous writer in Nicholson's Journal[3] calculates that the common house-fly (*Musca domestica*), in ordinary flight, makes 600

[1] Chabrier, as rendered by E. F. Bennett, F.L.S., etc.
[2] Linn. Trans. vii. p. 40.           [3] Vol. iii. p. 36.

strokes per second, and advances twenty-five feet, but that the rate of speed, if the insect be alarmed, may be increased six or seven fold, so that under certain circumstances it can outstrip the fleetest racehorse. Every one when riding on a warm summer day must have been struck with the cloud of flies which buzz about his horse's ears even when the animal is urged to its fastest paces; and it is no uncommon thing to see a bee or a wasp endeavouring to get in at the window of a railway car in full motion. If a small insect like a fly can outstrip a racehorse, an insect as large as a horse would travel very much faster than a cannon-ball. Leeuwenhoek relates a most exciting chase which he once beheld in a menagerie about 100 feet long between a swallow and a dragon-fly (*Mordella*). The insect flew with incredible speed, and wheeled with such address, that the swallow, notwithstanding its utmost efforts, completely failed to overtake and capture it.[1]

*Consideration of the Forces which propel the Wings of Bats and Birds.*—The muscular system of birds has been so frequently and faithfully described, that I need not refer to it further than to say that there are muscles which by their action are capable of elevating and depressing the wings, and of causing them to move in a forward and backward direction, and obliquely. They can also extend or straighten and bend, or flex the wings, and cause them to rotate in the direction of their length during the down and up strokes. The muscles principally concerned in the elevation of the wings are the smaller pectoral or breast muscles (*pectorales minor*); those chiefly engaged in depressing the wings are the larger pectorals (*pectorales major*). The pectoral muscles correspond to the fleshy mass found on the breast-bone or sternum, which in flying birds is boat-shaped, and furnished with a keel. These muscles are sometimes so powerful and heavy that they outweigh all the other muscles of the body.

---

[1] "The hobby falcon, which abounds in Bulgaria during the summer months, hawks *large dragonflies*, which it seizes with the foot and devours whilst in the air. It also kills swifts, larks, turtle-doves, and bee-birds, although more rarely."—Falconry in the British Isles, by Francis Henry Salvin and William Brodrick. Lond, 1855.

The power of the bird is thus concentrated for the purpose of moving the wings and conferring steadiness upon the volant mass. In birds of strong flight the keel is very large, in order to afford ample attachments for the muscles delegated to move the wings. In birds which cannot fly, as the members of the ostrich family, the breast-bone or sternum has no keel.[1]

The remarks made regarding the muscles of birds, apply with very slight modifications to the muscles of bats. The muscles of bats and birds, particularly those of the wings, are geared to, and act in concert with, elastic ligaments or membranes, to be described presently.

*Lax condition of the Shoulder-Joint in Bats, Birds, etc.*—The great laxity of the shoulder-joint in bats and birds, readily admits of their bodies falling downwards and forwards during the up stroke. This joint, as has been already stated, admits of movement in every direction, so that the body of the bat or bird is like a compass set upon gimbals, *i.e.* it swings and oscillates, and is equally balanced, whatever the position of the wings. The movements of the shoulder-joint in the bird, bat, and insect are restrained within certain limits by a system of check ligaments and prominences; but in each case the range of motion is very great, the wings being permitted to swing forwards, backwards, upwards, downwards, or at any degree of obliquity. They are also permitted to rotate along their anterior margin, or to twist in the direction of their length to the extent of nearly a quarter of a turn. This great freedom of movement at the shoulder-joint enables the insect, bat, and bird to rotate and balance upon two centres—the one running in the direction of the length of the body, the other at right angles or across the body, *i.e.* in the direction of the length of the wings.

In the bird the head of the humerus is convex and somewhat oval (not round), the long axis of the oval being directed from above downwards, *i.e.* from the dorsal towards the ventral aspect of the bird. The humerus can, therefore, *glide up and down* in the *facettes* occurring on the articular ends of the

<hr>

[1] One of the best descriptions of the bones and muscles of the bird is that given by Mr. Macgillivray in his very admirable, voluminous, and entertaining work, entitled History of British Birds. Lond. 1837

coracoid and scapular bones with great facility, much in the same way that the head of the radius glides upon the distal end of the humerus.  But the humerus has another motion ; it moves *like a hinge from before backwards, and* vice versâ. The axis of the latter movement is almost at right angles to that of the former.  As, however, the shoulder-joint is connected by long ligaments to the body, and can be drawn away from it to the extent of one-eighth of an inch or more, it follows that *a third and twisting movement can be performed*, the twisting admitting of rotation to the extent of something like a quarter of a turn.  In raising and extending the wing preparatory to the downward stroke two opposite movements are required, viz. one from before backwards, and another from below upwards.  As, however, the axes of these movements are at nearly right angles to each other, a spiral or twisting movement is necessary to run the one into the other—to turn the corner, in fact.

From what has been stated it will be evident that the movements of the wing, particularly at the root, are remarkably free, and very varied.  A directing and restraining, as well as a propelling force, is therefore necessary.

The guiding force is to be found in the voluntary muscles which connect the wing with the body in the insect, and which in the bat and bird, in addition to connecting the wing with the body, extend along the pinion even to its tip. It is also to be found in the musculo-elastic and other ligaments, seen to advantage in the bird.

*The Wing flexed and partly elevated by the Action of Elastic Ligaments—the Nature and Position of such Ligaments in the Pheasant, Snipe, Crested Crane, Swan, etc.*—When the wing is drawn away from the body of the bird by the hand the posterior margin of the pinion formed by the primary, secondary, and tertiary feathers rolls down to make a variety of inclined surfaces with the horizon (*c b*, of fig. 63, p. 138). When, however, the hand is withdrawn, even in the dead bird, the wing instantly folds up ; and in doing so reduces the amount of inclination in the several surfaces referred to (*c b, d e f* of the same figure).  The wing is folded by the action of certain elastic ligaments, which are put upon

the stretch in extension, and which recover their original form
and position in flexion (fig. 98, c, p. 181). This simple experiment shows that the various inclined surfaces requisite
for flight are produced by the mere acts of extension and
flexion in the dead bird. It is not, however, to be inferred
from this circumstance that flight can be produced without
voluntary movements any more than ordinary walking. The
muscles, bones, ligaments, feathers, etc., are so adjusted with
reference to each other that if the wing is moved at all,
it must move in the proper direction—an arrangement which
enables the bird to fly without thinking, just as we can
walk without thinking. There cannot, however, be a doubt
that the bird has the power of controlling its wings both
during the down and up strokes; for how otherwise could
it steer and direct its course with such precision in obtaining its food? how fix its wings on a level with or above
its body for skimming purposes? how fly in a curve? how
fly with, against, or across a breeze? how project itself from
a rock directly into space, or how elevate itself from a level
surface by the laboured action of its wings?

The wing of the bird is elevated to a certain extent in
flight by the reaction of the air upon its under surface; but
it is also elevated by muscular action—by the contraction of
the elastic ligaments, and by the body falling downwards and
forwards in a curve.

That muscular action is necessary is proved by the fact
that the pinion is supplied with distinct elevator muscles.[1]
It is further proved by this, that the bird can, and always

[1] Mr. Macgillivray and C. J. L. Krarup, a Danish author, state that the
wing is elevated by a vital force, viz. by the contraction of the *pectoralis
minor*. This muscle, according to Krarup, acts with one-eighth the intensity
of the *pectoralis major* (the depressor of the wing). He bases his statement
upon the fact that in the pigeon the pectoralis minor or elevator of the wing
weighs one-eighth of an ounce, whereas the pectoralis major or depressor of
the wing weighs seven-eighths of an ounce. It ought, however, to be borne in
mind that the volume of a muscle does not necessarily determine the precise
influence exerted by its action; for the tendon of the muscle may be made to
act upon a long lever, and, under favourable conditions, for developing its
powers, while that of another muscle may be made to act upon a short lever,
and, consequently, under unfavourable conditions.—On the Flight of Birds,
p. 30. Copenhagen, 1869.

does, elevate its wings prior to flight, quite independently of the air.   When the bird is fairly launched in space the elevator muscles are assisted by the tendency which the body has to fall downwards and forwards : by the reaction of the air; and by the contraction of the elastic ligaments.  The air and the elastic ligaments contribute to the elevation of the wing, but both are obviously under control—they, in fact, form links in a chain of motion which at once begins and terminates in the muscular system.

That the elastic ligaments are subsidiary and to a certain extent under the control of the muscular system in the same sense that the air is, is evident from the fact that voluntary muscular fibres run into the ligaments in question at various points (*a*, *b* of fig. 98, p. 181).   The ligaments and muscular fibres act in conjunction, and fold or flex the forearm on the arm.   There are others which flex the hand upon the forearm.   Others draw the wing towards the body.

The elastic ligaments, while occupying a similar position in the wings of all birds, are variously constructed and variously combined with voluntary muscles in the several species.

*The Elastic Ligaments more highly differentiated in Wings which vibrate rapidly.*—The elastic ligaments of the swan are more complicated and more liberally supplied with voluntary muscle than those of the crane, and this is no doubt owing to the fact that the wings of the swan are driven at a much higher speed than those of the crane.   In the snipe the wings are made to vibrate very much more rapidly than in the swan, and, as a consequence, we find that the fibro-elastic bands are not only greatly increased, but they are also geared to a much greater number of voluntary muscles, all which seems to prove that the musculo-elastic apparatus employed for recovering or flexing the wing towards the end of the down stroke, becomes more and more highly differentiated in proportion to the rapidity with which the wing is moved.[1]   The reason for this is obvious.   If the wing is to be worked at a higher speed, it must, as a consequence, be more rapidly flexed and

[1] A careful account of the musculo-elastic structures occurring in the wing of the pigeon is given by Mr. Macgillivray in his History of British Birds, pp. 37, 38.

N

extended. The rapidity with which the wing of the bird is extended and flexed is in some instances exceedingly great ; so great, in fact, that it escapes the eye of the ordinary observer. The speed with which the wing darts in and out in flexion and extension would be quite inexplicable, but for a knowledge of the fact that the different portions of the pinion form angles with each other, these angles being instantly increased or diminished by the slightest quiver of the muscular and fibro-elastic systems. If we take into account the fact that the wing of the bird is recovered or flexed by the combined action of voluntary muscles and elastic ligaments ; that it is elevated to a considerable extent by voluntary muscular effort ; and that it is extended and depressed entirely by muscular exertion, we shall have difficulty in avoiding the conclusion that the wing is thoroughly under the control of the muscular system, not only in flexion and extension, but also throughout the entire down and up strokes.

An arrangement in every respect analogous to that described in the bird is found in the wing of the bat, the covering or web of the wing in this instance forming the principal elastic ligament (fig. 17, p. 36).

*Power of the Wing—to what owing.*—The shape and power of the pinion depend upon one of three circumstances—to wit, the length of the humerus,[1] the length of the cubitus or forearm, and the length of the primary feathers. In the swallow the humerus, and in the humming-bird the cubitus, is very short, the primaries being very long ; whereas in the albatross the humerus or arm-bone is long and the primaries short. When one of these conditions is fulfilled, the pinion is usually greatly elongated and scythe-like (fig. 62, p. 137) —an arrangement which enables the bird to keep on the wing for immense periods with comparatively little exertion, and to wheel, turn, and glide about with exceeding ease and grace. When the wing is truncated and rounded (fig. 96, p.

[1] "The humerus varies extremely in length, being very short in the swallow, of moderate length in the gallinaceous birds, longer in the crows, very long in the gannets, and unusually elongated in the albatross. In the golden eagle it is also seen to be of great length."--Macgillivray's British Birds, vol. I. p. 30.

176), a form of pinion usually associated with a heavy body, as in the grouse, quail, diver, and grebe, the muscular exertion required, and the rapidity with which the wing moves are very great; those birds, from a want of facility in turning, flying either in a straight line or making large curves. They, moreover, rise with difficulty, and alight clumsily and somewhat suddenly. Their flight, however, is perfect while it lasts.

The goose, duck (fig. 107, p. 204), pigeon (fig. 106, p. 203) and crow, are intermediate both as regards the form of the wing and the rapidity with which it is moved.

The heron (fig. 60, p. 126) and humming-bird furnish extreme examples in another direction,—the heron having a large wing with a leisurely movement, the humming-bird a comparatively large wing with a greatly accelerated one.

But I need not multiply examples; suffice it to say that flight may be attained within certain limits by every size and form of wing, if the number of its oscillations be increased in proportion to the weight to be raised.

*Reasons why the effective Stroke should be delivered downwards and forwards.*—The wings of all birds, whatever their form, act by alternately presenting oblique and comparatively non-oblique surfaces to the air,—the mere extension of the pinion, as has been shown, causing the primary, secondary, and tertiary feathers to roll down till they make an angle of 30° or so with the horizon, in order to prepare it for giving the effective stroke, which is delivered, with great rapidity and energy, in a *downward* and *forward* direction. I repeat, "downwards and forwards;" for a careful examination of the relations of the wing in the dead bird, and a close observation of its action in the living one, supplemented by a large number of experiments with natural and artificial wings, have fully convinced me that the stroke is invariably delivered in this direction.[1]   If the wing did not strike

---

[1] *Prevailing Opinions as to the Direction of the Down Stroke.*—Mr. Macgillivray, in his History of British Birds, published in 1837, states (p. 34) that in flexion the wing is drawn upwards, forwards, and inwards, but that during extension, when the effective stroke is given, it is made to strike outwards, downwards, and *backwards*. The Duke of Argyll holds a similar opinion. In speaking of the hovering of birds, he asserts that,

downwards and *forwards*, it would act at a manifest disadvantage :—

1*st.* Because it would present the back or convex surface of the wing to the air——a convex surface dispersing or dissipating the air, while a concave surface gathers it together or focuses it.

2*d.* In order to strike backwards effectually, the concavity of the wing would also require to be turned backwards; and this would involve the depression of the anterior or thick margin of the pinion, and the elevation of the posterior or thin one, during the down stroke, which never happens.

3*d.* The strain to which the pinion is subjected in flight would, if the wing struck *backwards*, fall, not on the anterior or strong margin of the pinion formed by the bones and muscles, but on the posterior or weak margin formed by the tips of the primary, secondary, and tertiary feathers—which is not in accordance with the structure of the parts.

4*th.* The feathers of the wing, instead of being closed, as they necessarily are, by a downward and *forward* movement,

---

"If a bird, by altering the axis of its own body, can direct its wing stroke in some degree *forwards*, it will have the effect of *stopping* instead of promoting progression;" and that, "Except for the purpose of *arresting* their flight, birds can never strike except *directly downwards*—that is, directly against the opposing force of gravity."—Good Words, Feb. 1865, p. 132.

Mr. Bishop, in the Cyc. of Anat. and Phys., vol. iii. p. 425, says, "In consequence of the planes of the wings being disposed either *perpendicularly* or *obliquely backwards* to the direction of their motion, a corresponding impulse is given to their centre of gravity." Professor Owen, in like manner, avers that "a downward stroke would only tend to raise the bird in the air; to carry it forwards, the wings require to be moved in an oblique plane, so as to *strike backwards* as well as downwards."—Comp. Anat. and Phys. and Vertebrates, vol. ii. p. 115.

The following is the account given by M. E. Liais:—"When a bird is about to depress its wing, this is a little inclined from before backwards. When the descending movement commences, the wing does not descend parallel to itself in a direction from before backwards ; but the movement is accompanied by a rotation of several degrees round the anterior edge, so that the wing becomes more in front than behind, and *the descending movement is transferred more and more backwards.* . . . When the wing has completely descended, it is both *further back* and lower than at the commencement of the movement."—"On the Flight of Birds and Insects." Annals of Nat. Hist. vol. xv. 3d series, p. 156.

would be inevitably opened, and the integrity of the wing impaired by a downward and *backward* movement.

*5th.* The disposition of the articular surfaces of the wing (particularly that of the shoulder-joint) is such as to facilitate the downward and *forward* movement, while it in a great measure prevents the downward and *backward* one.

*6th and lastly.* If the wing did in reality strike downwards and *backwards*, a result the converse of that desired would most assuredly be produced, as an oblique surface which smites the air in a downward and *backward* direction (if left to itself) tends to depress the body bearing it. This is proved by the action upon the air of free inclined planes, arranged in the form of a screw.

*The Wing acts as an Elevator, Propeller, and Sustainer, both during extension and flexion.*—The wing, as has been explained, is recovered or drawn off the wind principally by the contraction of the elastic ligaments extending between the joints, so that the pinion during flexion enjoys a certain degree of repose. The time occupied in recovering is not lost so long as the wing makes an angle with the horizon and the bird is in motion, it being a matter of indifference whether the wing acts on the air, or the air on the wing, so long as the body bearing the latter is under weigh; and this is the chief reason why the albatross, which is a very heavy bird,[1] can sail about for such incredible periods without flapping the wings at all. Captain Hutton thus graphically describes the sailing of this magnificent bird:—"The flight of the albatross is truly majestic, as with outstretched motionless wings he sails over the surface of the sea—now rising high in air, now with a bold sweep, and wings inclined at an angle with the horizon, descending until the tip of the lower one all but touches the crest of the waves as he skims over them."[2]

*Birds of Flight divisible into four kinds :—*

*1st.* Such as have heavy bodies and short wings with a rapid movement (fig. 59, p. 126).

---

[1] The average weight of the albatross, as given by Gould, is 17 lbs.—Ibis, 2d series, vol. i. 1865, p. 295.

[2] "On some of the Birds inhabiting the Southern Ocean," by Capt. F. W. Hutton.—Ibis, 2d series, vol. i. 1865, p. 252.

2d. Such as have light bodies and large wings with a leisurely movement (fig. 60, p. 126; fig. 103, p. 186).

3d. Such as have heavy bodies and long narrow wings with a decidedly slow movement (fig. 105, p. 200).

4th. Such as are intermediate with regard to the size of body, the dimensions of the wing, and the energy with which it is driven (fig. 102, p. 183; fig. 106, p. 203; fig. 107, p. 204).

They may be subdivided into those which float, skim, or glide, and those which fly in a straight line and irregularly.

The pheasant, partridge (fig. 59, p. 126), grouse, and quail, furnish good examples of the heavy-bodied, short-winged birds. In these the wing is rounded and deeply concave. It is, moreover, wielded with immense velocity and power.

The heron (fig. 60, p. 126), sea-mew (fig. 103, p. 186), lapwing (fig. 63, p. 138), and owl (fig. 104), supply examples of the second class, where the wing, as compared with the body, is very ample, and where consequently it is moved more leisurely and less energetically.

FIG. 104.—The Cape Barn-Owl (*Stris capensis*, Smith), as seen in full flight, hunting. The under surface of the wings and body are inclined slightly upwards, and act upon the air after the manner of a kite. (Compare with fig. 59, p. 126, and fig. 102, p. 183.)—*Original.*

The albatross (fig. 105, p. 200) and pelican afford instances of the third class, embracing the heavy-bodied, long-winged birds.

The duck (fig. 107, p. 204), pigeon (fig. 106, p. 203), crow and thrush, are intermediate, both as regards the size of the wing and the rapidity with which it is made to oscillate. These constitute the fourth class.

The albatross (fig. 105, p. 200), swallow, eagle, and hawk, provide instances of sailing or gliding birds, where the wing is ample, elongated, and more or less pointed, and where advantage is taken of the weight of the body and the shape of the pinion to utilize the air as a supporting medium. In these the pinion acts as a long lever,[1] and is wielded with great precision and power, particularly at the shoulder.

*The Flight of the Albatross compared to the Movements of a Compass set upon Gimbals.*—A careful examination of the movements in skimming birds has led me to conclude that by a judicious twisting or screw-like action of the wings at the shoulder, in which the pinions are alternately advanced towards and withdrawn from the head in a manner analogous to what occurs at the loins in skating without lifting the feet, birds of this order can not only maintain the motion which they secure by a few energetic flappings, but, if necessary, actually increase it, and that without either bending the wing or beating the air.

The forward and backward screwing action of the pinion referred to, in no way interferes, I may remark, with the rotation of the wing on its long axis, the pinion being advanced and screwed down upon the wind, and retracted and unscrewed alternately. As the movements described enable the sailing bird to tilt its body from before backwards, or

---

[1] *Advantages possessed by long Pinions.*—The long narrow wings are most effective as elevators and propellers, from the fact (pointed out by Mr. Wenham) that at high speeds, with very oblique incidences, the supporting effect becomes transferred to the *front edge* of the pinion. It is in this way "that the effective propelling area of the two-bladed screw is tantamount to its entire circle of revolution." A similar principle was announced by Sir George Cayley upwards of fifty years ago. " *In very acute angles with the current,* it appears that the centre of resistance in the sail does not coincide with the centre of its surface, *but is considerably in front of it.* As the obliquity of the current decreases, these centres approach, and coincide when the current becomes perpendicular to the plane ; hence any heel of the machine backwards or forwards removes the centre of support behind or before the point of suspension."—Nicholson's Journal, vol. xiv. p. 83. When the speed attained by the bird is *greatly accelerated,* and *the stratum of air passed over in any given time enormously increased,* the support afforded by the air to the inclined planes formed by the wings *is likewise augmented.* This is proved by the rapid flight of skimming or sailing birds when the wings are moved at long intervals and very leisurely. The same principle supports the skater as he rushes impetuously over insecure ice, and the thin flat stone projected along the surface of still water. The velocity of the movement in either case prevents sinking by not giving the supporting particles time to separate.

the converse, and from side to side or laterally, it may be represented as oscillating on one of two centres, as shown at fig. 105; the one corresponding with the long axis of the body (fig. 105, a b), the other with the long axis of the wings (c d). Between these two extremes every variety of sailing and gliding motion which is possible in the mariner's compass when set upon gimbals may be performed; so that a skimming or sailing bird may be said to possess perfect command over itself and over the element in which it moves.

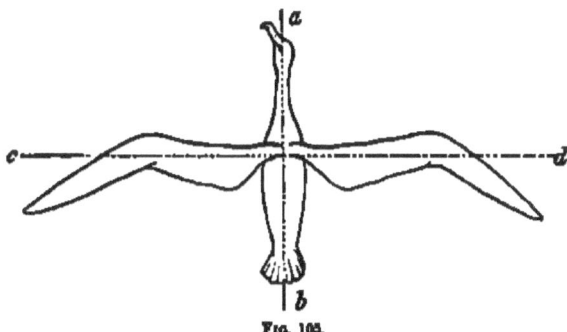

FIG. 105.

Captain Hutton makes the following remarkable statement regarding the albatross:—" I have sometimes watched narrowly one of these birds sailing and wheeling about in all directions for more than an hour, without seeing the slightest movement of the wings, and have never witnessed anything to equal the ease and grace of this bird as he sweeps past, often within a few yards, every part of his body perfectly motionless except the head and eye, which turn slowly and seem to take notice of everything." [1]

> "Tranquil its spirit seem'd and floated slow;
> Even in its very motion there was rest." [2]

As an antithesis to the apparently lifeless wings of the

[1] "On some of the Birds inhabiting the Southern Ocean."—Ibis, 2d series, vol. I. 1865.
[2] Professor Wilson's Sonnet, "A Cloud," etc.

albatross, the ceaseless activity of those of the humming-bird may be adduced. In those delicate and exquisitely beautiful birds, the wings, according to Mr. Gould, move so rapidly when the bird is poised before an object, that it is impossible for the eye to follow each stroke, and a hazy circle of indistinctness on each side of the bird is all that is perceptible. When the humming-bird flies in a horizontal direction, it occasionally proceeds with such velocity as altogether to elude observation.

*The regular and irregular in Flight.*—The coot, diver, duck, and goose fly with great regularity in nearly a straight line, and with immense speed; they rarely if ever skim or glide, their wings being too small for this purpose. The woodpecker, magpie, fieldfare and sparrow, supply examples of what may be termed the " irregular " in flight. These, as is well known, fly in curves of greater or less magnitude, by giving a few vigorous strokes and then desisting, the effect of which is to project them along a series of parabolic curves. The snipe and woodcock are irregular in another respect, their flight being sudden, jerky, and from side to side.

*Mode of ascending, descending, turning, etc.*—All birds which do not, like the swallow and humming-birds, drop from a height, raise themselves at first by a vigorous leap, in which they incline their bodies in an upward direction, the height thus attained enabling them to extend and depress their wings without injury to the feathers. By a few sweeping strokes delivered downwards and forwards, in which the wings are made nearly to meet above and below the body, they lever themselves upwards and forwards, and in a surprisingly short time acquire that degree of momentum which greatly assists them in their future career. In rising from the ground, as may readily be seen in the crow, pigeon, and kingfisher (fig. 102, p. 183), the tail is expanded and the neck stretched out, so that the body is converted into an inclined plane, and acts mechanically as a kite. The centre of gravity and the position of the body are changed at the will of the bird by movements in the neck, feet, and tail, and by increasing or decreasing the angles which the under

surface of the wings makes with the horizon. When a bird
wishes to fly in a horizontal direction, it causes the under
surface of its wings to make a slight *forward* angle with the
horizon. When it wishes to ascend, the angle is increased.
When it wishes to descend, it causes the under surface of the
wings to make a slight *backward* angle with the horizon.
When a bird flies up, its wings strike downwards and *forwards*.
When it flies down, its wings strike downwards and *backwards*.
When a sufficient altitude has been attained, the length of
the downward stroke is generally curtailed, the mere extension and flexion of the wing, assisted by the weight of the
body, in such instances sufficing. This is especially the case
if the bird is advancing against a slight breeze, the effort
required under such circumstances being nominal in amount.
That little power is expended is proved by the endless
gyrations of rooks and other birds; these being continued
for hours together. In birds which glide or skim, it has
appeared to me that the wing is recovered much more
quickly, and the down stroke delivered more slowly, than
in ordinary flight—in fact, that the rapidity with which the
wing acts in an upward and downward direction is, in some
instances, reversed; and this is what we should naturally
expect when we recollect that in gliding, the wings require
to be, for the most part, in the expanded condition. If
this observation be correct, it follows that birds have the
power of modifying the duration of the up and down strokes
at pleasure. Although the wing of the bird usually strikes
the air at an angle which varies from 15° to 30°, the angle
may be increased to such an extent as to subvert the position
of the bird. The tumbler pigeon, *e.g.* can, by slewing its
wings forwards and suddenly throwing back its head, turn
a somersault. When birds are fairly on the wing they have
the air, unless when that is greatly agitated by a storm,
completely under control. This arises from their greater
specific gravity, and because they are possessed of independent
motion. If they want to turn, they have simply to tilt their
bodies laterally, as a railway carriage would be tilted in
taking a curve,[1] or to increase the number of beats given by

[1] "If the albatross desires to turn to the right he bends his head and tail

the one wing as compared with the other; or to keep the
one wing extended while the other is partially flexed.   The
neck, feet, and tail may or may not contribute to this result.
If the bird wishes to rise, it tilts its entire body (the neck
and tail participating) in an upward direction (fig. 59, p. 126;
fig. 102, p. 183); or it rises principally by the action of the
wings and by muscular efforts, as happens in the lark.   The
bird can in this manner likewise retain its position in the
air, as may be observed in the hawk when hovering above
its prey.   If the bird desires to descend, it may reverse
the direction of the inclined plane formed by the body and
wings, and plunge head foremost with extended pinions

Fig. 106.—The Pigeon (*Treron bicincta*, Jerdon), flying downwards and turning
    prior to alighting.   The pigeon expands its tail both in ascending and
    descending.—*Original.*

(fig. 106); or it may flex the wings, and so accelerate its
pace; or it may raise its wings and drop parachute-fashion
(fig. 55, p. 112; *g, g* of fig. 82, p. 158); or it may even fly
in a downward direction—a few sudden strokes, a more
or less abrupt curve, and a certain degree of horizontal
movement being in either case necessary to break the

slightly upwards, at the same time raising his left side and wing, and lowering
the right in proportion to the sharpness of the curve he wishes to make, the
wings being kept quite rigid the whole time.   To such an extent does he do
this, that in sweeping round, his wings are often pointed in a direction nearly
perpendicular to the sea; and this position of the wings, more or less inclined
to the horizon, is seen always and only when the bird is turning."—"On some
of the Birds inhabiting the Southern Ocean."   Ibis, 2d series, vol. i. 1865,
p. 227.

fall previous to alighting (fig. 107, below).    Birds which
fish on the wing, as the osprey and gannet, precipitate
themselves from incredible heights, and drop into the water
with the velocity of a meteorite—the momentum which
they acquire during their descent materially aiding them
in their subaqueous flight.    They emerge from the water
and are again upon the wing before the eddies occasioned
by their precipitous descent have well subsided, in some cases
rising apparently without effort, and in others running along
and beating the surface of the water for a brief period with
their pinions and feet.

*The Flight of Birds referable to Muscular Exertion and Weight.*
—The various movements involved in ascending, descending,

Fig. 107.—The Red-headed Pochard(*Fuligula ferina*, Linn.) in the act of dropping upon the water; the head and body being inclined upwards and forwards, the feet expanded, and the wings delivering vigorous short strokes
in a downward and forward direction.—*Original.*

wheeling, gliding, and progressing horizontally, are all the
result of muscular power and weight, properly directed and
acting upon appropriate surfaces—that apparent buoyancy in
birds which we so highly esteem, arising not from superior
lightness, but from their possessing that degree of solidity
which enables them to subjugate the air,—weight and independent motion, *i.e.* motion associated with animal life, or
what is equivalent thereto, being the two things indispensable
in successful aërial progression.    The weight in insects and
birds is in great measure owing to their greatly developed
muscular system, this being in that delicate state of tonicity

which enables them to act through its instrumentality with marvellous dexterity and power, and to expend or reserve their energies, which they can do with the utmost exactitude, in their apparently interminable flights.

*Lifting-capacity of Birds.*—The muscular power in birds is usually greatly in excess, particularly in birds of prey, as, *e.g.* the condors, eagles, hawks, and owls. The eagles are remarkable in this respect—these having been known to carry off young deer, lambs, rabbits, hares, and, it is averred, even young children. Many of the fishing birds, as the pelicans and herons, can likewise carry considerable loads of fish ;[1] and even the smaller birds, as the records of spring show, are capable of transporting comparatively large twigs for building purposes. I myself have seen an owl, which weighed a little over 10 ounces, lift 2½ ounces, or a quarter of its own weight, without effort, after having fasted twenty-four hours ; and a friend informs me that a short time ago a splendid osprey was shot at Littlehampton, on the coast of Sussex, with a fish 5 lbs. weight in its mouth.

There are many points in the history and economy of birds which crave our sympathy while they elicit our admiration. Their indubitable courage and miraculous powers of flight invest them with a superior dignity, and secure for their order almost a duality of existence. The swallow, tiny and inconsiderable as it may appear, can traverse 1000 miles at a single journey ; and the albatross, despising compass and landmark, trusts himself boldly for weeks together to the mercy or fury of the mighty ocean. The huge condor of the Andes lifts himself by his sovereign will to a height where no sound is heard, save the airy tread of his vast pinions, and, from an unseen point, surveys in solitary grandeur the wide range of plain and pasture-land ;[2] while the bald eagle, nothing daunted by the din and indescribable confusion of the queen of waterfalls, the stupendous Niagara, sits composedly on his

---

[1] The heron is in the habit, when pursued by the falcon, of disgorging the contents of his crop in order to reduce his weight.

[2] The condor, on some occasions, attains an altitude of six miles.

giddy perch, until inclination or desire prompts him to plunge into or soar above the drenching mists which, shapeless and ubiquitous, perpetually rise from the hissing waters of the nether caldron.

Fig. 103.—Hawk and quarry.—*After The Graphic.*

# AËRONAUTICS.

THE VAUXHALL BALLOON OF MR. GREEN.

# AËRONAUTICS.

THE subject of artificial flight, notwithstanding the large share of attention bestowed upon it, has been particularly barren of results. This is the more to be regretted, as the interest which has been taken in it from early Greek and Roman times has been universal. The unsatisfactory state of the question is to be traced to a variety of causes, the most prominent of which are—

1st, The extreme difficulty of the problem.

2d, The incapacity or theoretical tendencies of those who have devoted themselves to its elucidation.

3d, The great rapidity with which wings, especially insect wings, are made to vibrate, and the difficulty experienced in analysing their movements.

4th, The great weight of all flying things when compared with a corresponding volume of air.

5th, The discovery of the balloon, which has retarded the science of aërostation, by misleading men's minds and causing them to look for a solution of the problem by the aid of a machine lighter than the air, and which has no analogue in nature.

Flight has been unusually unfortunate in its votaries. It has been cultivated, on the one hand, by profound thinkers, especially mathematicians, who have worked out innumerable theorems, but have never submitted them to the test of experiment; and on the other, by uneducated charlatans who, despising the abstractions of science, have made the most ridiculous attempts at a practical solution of the problem.

Flight, as the matter stands at present, may be divided into two principal varieties which represent two great sects or schools—

o

1*st*, The Balloonists, or those who advocate the employment of a machine specifically lighter than the air.

2*d*, Those who believe that weight is necessary to flight.
The second school may be subdivided into

    (*a*) Those who advocate the employment of rigid inclined
        planes driven forward in a straight line, or revolving
        planes (aërial screws); and

    (*b*) Such as trust for elevation and propulsion to the
        vertical flapping of wings.

*Balloon.*—The balloon, as my readers are aware, is constructed on the obvious principle that a machine lighter than
the air must necessarily rise through it. The Montgolfier
brothers invented such a machine in 1782. Their balloon
consisted of a paper globe or cylinder, the motor power being
super-heated air supplied by the burning of vine twigs under
it. The Montgolfier or fire balloon, as it was called, was
superseded by the hydrogen gas balloon of MM. Charles
and Robert, this being in turn supplanted by the ordinary gas
balloon of Mr. Green. Since the introduction of coal gas in
the place of hydrogen gas, no radical improvement has been
effected, all attempts at guiding the balloon having signally
failed. This arises from the vast extent of surface which it
necessarily presents, rendering it a fair conquest to every
breeze that blows; and because the power which animates it
is a mere lifting power which, in the absence of wind, must
act in a vertical line. The balloon consequently rises through
the air in opposition to the law of gravity, very much as a
dead bird falls in a downward direction in accordance with
it. Having no hold upon the air, this cannot be employed as
a fulcrum for regulating its movements, and hence the car-
dinal difficulty of ballooning as an art.

Finding that no marked improvement has been made in
the balloon since its introduction in 1782, the more advanced
thinkers have within the last quarter of a century turned
their attention in an opposite direction, and have come to
regard flying creatures, all of which are much heavier than
the air, as the true models for flying machines. An old
doctrine is more readily assailed than uprooted, and accordingly we find the followers of the new faith met by the
assertion that insects and birds have large air cavities in

their interior; that those cavities contain heated air, and that this heated air in some mysterious manner contributes to, if it does not actually produce, flight. No argument could be more fallacious. Many admirable fliers, such as the bats, have no air-cells; while many birds, the apteryx for example, and several animals never intended to fly, such as the orang-outang and a large number of fishes, are provided with them. It may therefore be reasonably concluded that flight is in no way connected with air-cells, and the best proof that can be adduced is to be found in the fact that it can be performed to perfection in their absence.

*The Inclined Plane.*—The modern school of flying is in some respects quite as irrational as the ballooning school.

The favourite idea with most is the wedging forward of a rigid *inclined plane* upon the air by means of a "*vis a tergo.*"

The inclined plane may be made to advance in a *horizontal line*, or made *to rotate* in the form of a screw. Both plans have their adherents. The one recommends a large supporting area extending on either side of the weight to be elevated; the surface of the supporting area making a very slight angle with the horizon, and the whole being wedged forward by the action of vertical screw propellers. This was the plan suggested by Henson and Stringfellow.

Mr. Henson designed his aërostat in 1843. "The chief feature of the invention was the very great expanse of its sustaining planes, which were larger in proportion to the weight it had to carry than those of many birds. The machine advanced *with its front edge a little raised*, the effect of which was to present its under surface to the air over which it passed, the resistance of which, acting upon it like a strong wind on the sails of a windmill, prevented the descent of the machine and its burden. The sustaining of the whole, therefore, depended upon *the speed at which it travelled through the air, and the angle at which its under surface impinged on the air in its front.* . . . The machine, fully prepared for flight, was started from the top of an inclined plane, in descending which it attained a velocity necessary to sustain it in its further progress. That velocity would be gradually destroyed by the resistance of the air to forward flight; it was, therefore, the office of the steam-engine and the vanes it actuated simply to repair the loss of velocity; it was made therefore only of the power and weight necessary for that small effect" (fig. 109). The editor of Newton's Journal of Arts and Science speaks of it thus :—" The apparatus consists of a car containing the goods, passengers, engines, fuel, etc., to which a rectangular frame, made of wood or bamboo cane, and covered with canvas or oiled silk, is attached. This frame extends on either side of the car in a similar manner to the outstretched wings of a bird; but with this difference, that *the frame is immovable.* Behind the wings are two vertical fan wheels, furnished with oblique

Fig. 109.—Mr. Henson's Flying Machine.

vanes, which are intended to propel the apparatus through the air. The rainbow-like circular wheels are the propellers, answering to the wheels of a steam-boat, and acting upon the air after the manner of a windmill. These wheels receive motion from bands and pulleys from a steam or other engine contained in the car. To an axis at the stern of the car a triangular frame is attached, resembling the tail of a bird, which is also covered with canvas or oiled silk. This may be expanded or contracted at pleasure, and is moved up and down for the purpose of causing the machine to ascend or descend. Beneath the tail is a rudder for directing the course of the machine to the right or to the left; and to facilitate the steering a sail is stretched between two masts which rise from the car. The amount of canvas or oiled silk necessary for buoying up the machine is stated to be equal to one square foot for each half pound of weight."

Wenham[1] has advocated the employment of *superimposed planes*, with a view to augmenting the support furnished while it diminishes the horizontal space occupied by the planes. These planes Wenham designates *Aëroplanes*. They are inclined at a very slight angle to the horizon, and are wedged forward either by the weight to be elevated or by the employment of vertical screws. Wenham's plan was adopted by Stringfellow in a model which he exhibited at the Aëronautical Society's Exhibition, held at the Crystal Palace in the summer of 1868.

The subjoined woodcut (fig. 110), taken from a photograph

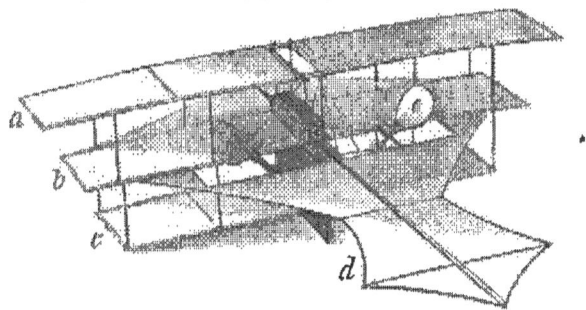

FIG. 110.—Mr. Stringfellow's Flying Machine.

of Mr. Stringfellow's model, gives a very good idea of the arrangement; *a b c* representing the superimposed planes, *d* the tail, and *e f* the vertical screw propellers.

The superimposed planes (*a b c*) in this machine contained a sustaining area of twenty-eight square feet in addition to the tail (*d*).

Its engine represented a third of a horse power, and the weight of the whole (engine, boiler, water, fuel, superimposed planes, and propellers) was under 12 lbs. Its sustaining area, if that of the tail (*d*) be included, was something like thirty-six square feet, *i.e.* three square feet for every pound —the sustaining area of the gannet, it will be remembered (p. 134), being less than one square foot of wing for every two pounds of body.

[1] " Aërial Locomotion," by F. H. Wenham.— *World of Science*, June 1867.

The model was forced by its propellers along a wire at a great speed, but, so far as I could determine from observation, failed to lift itself notwithstanding its extreme lightness and the comparatively very great power employed.[1]

The idea embodied by Henson, Wenham, and Stringfellow is plainly that of a boy's kite sailing upon the wind. The kite, however, is a more perfect flying apparatus than that furnished by Henson, Wenham, and Stringfellow, inasmuch as the inclined plane formed by its body strikes the air at various angles—the angles varying according to the length of string, strength of breeze, length and weight of tail, etc. Henson's, Wenham's, and Stringfellow's methods, although carefully tried, have hitherto failed. The objections are numerous. In the first place, the supporting planes (aëroplanes or otherwise) are not flexible and elastic as wings are, but *rigid.* This is a point to which I wish particularly to direct attention. Second, They strike the air *at a given angle.* Here, again, there is a departure from nature. Third, A machine so constructed must be precipitated from a height or driven along the surface of the land or water at a high speed to supply it with initial velocity. Fourth, It is unfitted for flying with the wind unless its speed greatly exceeds that of the wind. Fifth, It is unfitted for flying across the wind because of the surface exposed. Sixth, The sustaining surfaces are comparatively very large. They are, moreover, passive or dead surfaces, *i.e.* they have no power of moving or accommodating themselves to altered circumstances. Natural wings, on the contrary, present small flying surfaces, the great speed at which wings are propelled converting the space through which they are driven into what is practically a solid basis of support, as explained at pp. 118, 119, 151, and 152 (*vide* figs. 64, 65, 66, 82, and 83, pp. 139 and 158). This arrangement enables natural wings to seize and utilize the air, and renders them superior to adventitious currents. Natural wings work up the air in which they move, but unless the flying animal desires it, they are scarcely, if at all, influenced by winds or currents which are not of their own forming. In this respect they entirely differ from the

[1] Mr. Stringfellow stated that his machine occasionally left the wire, and was sustained by its superimposed planes alone.

balloon and all forms of fixed aëroplanes. In nature, small wings driven at a high speed produce the same result as large wings driven at a slow speed (compare fig. 58, p. 125, with fig. 57, p. 124). In flight a certain space must be covered either by large wings spread out as a solid (fig. 57, p. 124), or by small wings vibrating rapidly (figs. 64, 65, and 66, p. 139).

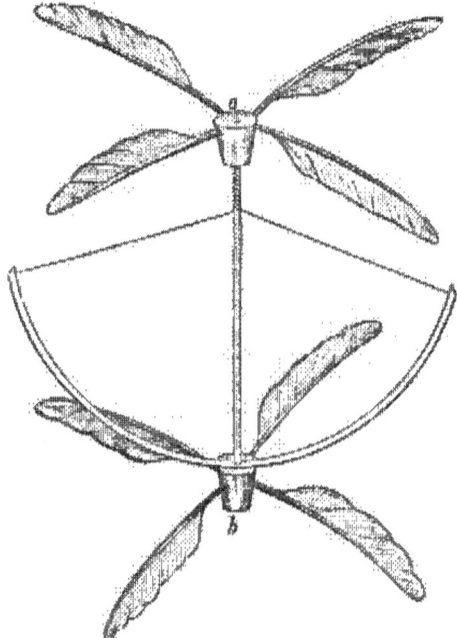

Fɪɢ. 111.—Cayley's Flying Apparatus.

*The Aërial Screw.*—Our countryman, Sir George Cayley, gave the first practical illustration of the efficacy of the screw as applied to the air in 1796. In that year he constructed a small machine, consisting of two screws made of quill feathers (fig. 111). Sir George writes as under :—

"As it may be an amusement to some of your readers to see a machine rise in the air by mechanical means, I will con-

clude my present communication by describing an instrument
of this kind, which any one can construct at the expense of
ten minutes' labour.

"a and b (fig. 111, p. 215) are two corks, into each of which
are inserted four wing feathers from any bird, so as to be slightly
inclined like the sails of a windmill, but in opposite directions
in each set. A round shaft is fixed in the cork a, which ends
in a sharp point. At the upper part of the cork b is fixed a
whalebone bow, having a small pivot hole in its centre to
receive the point of the shaft. The bow is then to be strung
equally on each side to the upper portion of the shaft, and
the little machine is completed. Wind up the string by
turning the flyers different ways, so that the spring of the
bow may unwind them with their anterior edges ascending;
then place the cork with the bow attached to it upon a table,
and with a finger on the upper cork press strong enough to
prevent the string from unwinding, and, taking it away suddenly, the instrument will rise to the ceiling."

Cayley's screws were peculiar, inasmuch as they were superimposed and rotated in opposite directions. He estimated
that if the area of the screws was increased to 200 square
feet, and moved by a man, they would elevate him. Cayley's
interesting experiment is described at length, and the apparatus figured in Nicholson's Journal for 1809, p. 172. In
1842 Mr. Phillips also succeeded in elevating a model by
means of revolving fans. Mr. Phillips's model was made
entirely of metal, and when complete and charged weighed
2 lbs. It consisted of a boiler or steam generator and four
fans supported between eight arms. The fans were inclined
to the horizon at an angle of 20°, and through the arms the
steam rushed on the principle discovered by Hero of Alexan-
dria. By the escape of steam from the arms, the fans were
made to revolve with immense energy, so much so that the
model rose to a great altitude, and flew across two fields
before it alighted. The motive power employed in the present instance was obtained from the combustion of charcoal,
nitre, and gypsum, as used in the original fire annihilator;
the products of combustion mixing with water in the boiler,
and forming gas charged steam, which was delivered at a
high pressure from the extremities of the eight arms. This

model is remarkable as being probably the first which actuated by steam has flown to a considerable distance.[1] The French have espoused the aërial screw with great enthusiasm, and within the last ten years (1863) MM. Nadar,[2] Pontin

Fig. 112. - Flying Machine designed by M. de la Landelle.

d'Amécourt, and de la Landelle have constructed clockwork models (*orthopteres*), which not only raise themselves into the air, but carry a certain amount of freight. These models are

[1] Report on the First Exhibition of the Aëronautical Society of Great Britain, held at the Crystal Palace, London, in June 1868, p. 10.

[2] Mons. Nadar, in a paper written in 1863, enters very fully into the subject of artificial flight, as performed by the aid of the screw. Liberal extracts are given from Nadar's paper in Astra Castra, by Captain Hatton Turner. London, 1865, p. 340. To Turner's handsome volume the reader is referred for much curious and interesting information on the subject of Aërostation.

exceedingly fragile, and because of the prodigious force required to propel them usually break after a few trials. Fig. 112, p. 217, embodies M. de la Landelle's ideas.

In the helicopteric models made by MM. Nadar, Pontin d'Amécourt, and de la Landelle, the screws (*m n o p q r s t* of figure) are arranged in tiers, *i.e.* the one screw is placed above the other. In this respect they resemble the aëroplanes recommended by Mr. Wenham, and tested by Mr. Stringfellow (compare *m n o p q r s t* of fig. 112, with *a b c* of fig. 110, p. 213). The superimposed screws, as already explained, were first figured and described by Sir George Cayley (p. 215). The French screws, and that employed by Mr. Phillips, are *rigid or unyielding*, and strike the air *at a given angle*, and herein, I believe, consists their principal defect. This arrangement results in a ruinous expenditure of power, and is accompanied by a great amount of slip. The aërial screw, and the machine to be elevated by it, can be set in motion without any preliminary run, and in this respect it has the advantage over the machine supported by mere sustaining planes. It has, in fact, a certain amount of inherent motion, its screws revolving, and supplying it with active or moving surfaces. It is accordingly more independent than the machine designed by Henson, Wenham, and Stringfellow.

I may observe with regard to the system of rigid inclined planes wedged forward at a given angle in a straight line or in a circle, that it does not embody the principle carried out in nature.

The wing of a flying creature, as I have taken pains to show, is *not rigid ;* neither does it always strike the air *at a given angle.* On the contrary, it is capable of moving in all its parts, and attacks the air at *an infinite variety of angles* (pp. 151 to 154). Above all, the surface exposed by a natural wing, when compared with the great weight it is capable of elevating, is remarkably small (fig. 89, p. 171). This is accounted for by the length and the great range of motion of natural wings; the latter enabling the wings to convert large tracts of air into supporting areas (figs. 64, 65, and 66, p. 139). It is also accounted for by the multiplicity of the movements of natural wings, these enabling the pinions to create and rise upon currents of their own forming, and to avoid natural currents when not adapted for propelling or sustaining purposes (fig. 67, 68, 69, and 70, p. 141).

If any one watches an insect, a bat, or a bird when dressing its wings, he will observe that it can incline the under surface of the wing at a great variety of angles to the horizon. This it does by causing the posterior or thin margin of the wing to rotate around the anterior or thick margin as an axis. As a result of this movement, the two margins are forced into double and opposite curves, and the wing converted into a *plastic helix* or *screw*. He will further observe that the bat and bird, and some insects, have, in addition, the power of folding and drawing the wing towards the body during the up stroke, and of pushing it away from the body and extending it during the down stroke, so as alternately to diminish and increase its area; arrangements necessary to decrease the amount of resistance experienced by the wing during its ascent, and increase it during its descent. It is scarcely requisite to add, that in the aëroplanes and aërial screws, as at present constructed, no provision whatever is made for suddenly increasing or diminishing the flying surface, of conferring elasticity upon it, or of giving to it that infinite variety of angles which would enable it to seize and disentangle itself from the air with the necessary rapidity. Many investigators are of opinion that flight is a mere question of levity and power, and that if a machine could only be made light enough and powerful enough, it must of necessity fly, whatever the nature of its flying surfaces. A grave fallacy lurks here. Birds are not more powerful than quadrupeds of equal size, and Stringfellow's machine, which, as we have seen, only weighed 12 lbs., exerted *one-third of a horse power*. The probabilities therefore are, that flight is dependent to a great extent on the nature of the flying surfaces, and the mode of applying those surfaces to the air.

*Artificial Wings* (Borelli's Views).—With regard to the production of *flight by the flapping of wings*, much may and has been said. Of all the methods yet proposed, it is unquestionably by far the most ancient. Discrediting as apocryphal the famous story of Dædalus and his waxen wings, we certainly have a very graphic account of artificial wings in the De Motu Animalium of Borelli, published as far back as 1680, *i.e.* nearly two centuries ago.[1]

Indeed it will not be too much to affirm, that to this distinguished physiologist and mathematician belongs almost all the knowledge we possessed of artificial wings up till 1865. He was well acquainted with the properties of the wedge, as applied to flight, and he was likewise cognisant of the flexible and elastic properties of the wing. To him is to be traced the purely mechanical theory of the wing's action. He figured a bird with artificial wings, each wing consisting of *a rigid rod in front* and *flexible feathers* behind. I have thought fit to reproduce Borelli's figure both because of its great antiquity, and because it is eminently illustrative of his text.[2]

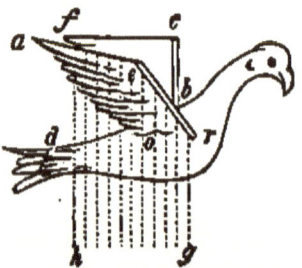

Fig. 113.—Borelli's Artificial Bird.

The wings (*b c f, o e a*), are represented as striking vertically downwards (*g h*). They remarkably accord with those described by Straus-Durckheim, Girard, and quite recently by Professor Marey.[3]

Borelli is of opinion that flight results from the application of an inclined plane, which beats the air, and which has a wedge action. He, in fact, endeavours to prove that a bird wedges itself forward upon the air by the perpendicular vibra-

[1] Borelli, De Motu Animalium. Sm. 4to, 2 vols. Romæ, 1680.

[2] De Motu Animalium, Lugduni Batavorum apud Petrum Vander. Anno MDCLXXXV. Tab. XIII. figure 2. (New edition.)

[3] Revue des Cours Scientifiques de la France et de l'Etranger. Mars 1569.

tion of its wings, the wings during their action forming a wedge, the base of which (c b e) is directed towards the head of the bird; the apex (a f) being directed towards the tail. This idea is worked out in propositions 195 and 196 of the first part of Borelli's book. In proposition 195 he explains how, if a wedge be driven into a body, the wedge will tend to separate that body into two portions; but that if the two portions of the body be permitted to react upon the wedge, they will communicate *oblique impulses* to the sides of the wedge, and expel it, base first, in a straight line.

Following up the analogy, Borelli endeavours to show in his 196th proposition, "that if the air acts obliquely upon the wings, or the wings obliquely upon the air (which is, of course, a wedge action), the result will be *a horizontal transference of the body of the bird.*" In the proposition referred to (196) Borelli states—"If the expanded wings of a bird suspended in the air shall strike the undisturbed air beneath it with a motion *perpendicular to the horizon*, the bird will fly *with a transverse motion* in a plane parallel with the horizon." In other words, if the wings *strike vertically downwards*, the bird will fly *horizontally forwards.* He bases his argument upon the belief that the anterior margins of the wings are *rigid and unyielding*, whereas the posterior and after parts of the wings are *more or less flexible*, and readily give way under pressure. "If," he adds, "the wings of the bird be expanded, and the under surfaces of the wings be struck by the air *ascending perpendicularly to the horizon*, with such a force as shall prevent the bird gliding downwards (*i.e.* with a tendency to glide downwards) from falling, it will be urged *in a horizontal direction.* This follows because the two osseous rods (virgæ) forming the anterior margins of the wings resist the upward pressure of the air, and so retain their original form (literally extent or expansion); whereas the flexible after-parts of the wings (posterior margins) are pushed up and approximated to form a cone, the apex of which (*vide a f* of fig. 113) is directed towards the tail of the bird. In virtue of the air playing upon and compressing the sides of the wedge formed by the wings, the wedge is driven forwards in the direction of its base (c b e), which is equiva-

lent to saying that the wings carry the body of the bird to
which they are attached *in a horizontal direction.*"

Borelli restates the same argument in different words, as
follows :—

"If," he says, "the air under the wings be struck by the
flexible portions of the wings (*flabella,* literally fly-flaps or
small fans) with a motion perpendicular to the horizon, the
sails (*vela*) and flexible portions of the wings (flabella) will
yield in an upward direction, and form a wedge, the point of
which is directed towards the tail. Whether, therefore, the
air strikes the wings from below, or the wings strike the air
from above, the result is the same—the posterior or flexible
margins of the wings *yield in an upward direction,* and in
so doing urge the bird in a *horizontal direction.*"

In his 197th proposition, Borelli follows up and amplifies
the arguments contained in propositions 195 and 196. "Thus,"
he observes, "it is evident that the object of flight is to
impel birds upwards, and keep them suspended in the air,
and also to enable them to wheel round in a plane parallel to
the horizon. The first (or upward flight) could not be accom-
plished unless the bird were impelled upwards by frequent
leaps or vibrations of the wings, and its descent prevented.
And because the downward tendency of heavy bodies is perpendicular to the horizon, the vibration of the plain surfaces
of the wings must be made by striking the air beneath them
in a direction perpendicular to the horizon, and in this manner nature produces the suspension of birds in the air."

"With regard to the second or transverse motion of birds
(*i.e.* horizontal flight) some authors have strangely blundered;
for they hold that it is like that of boats, which, being impelled by oars, moved horizontally in the direction of the
stern, and pressing on the resisting water behind, leaps with
a contrary motion, and so are carried forward. In the same
manner, say they, the wings vibrate towards the tail with a
horizontal motion, and likewise strike against the undisturbed
air, by the resistance of which they are moved forward by a
reflex motion. But this is contrary to the evidence of our
sight as well as to reason ; for we see that the larger kinds
of birds, such as swans, geese, etc., never vibrate their wings

when flying towards the tail with a horizontal motion like
that of oars, but always bend them downwards, and so describe
circles raised perpendicularly to the horizon.[1]

Besides, in boats the horizontal motion of the oars is easily
made, and a perpendicular stroke on the water would be perfectly useless, inasmuch as their descent would be impeded
by the density of the water.   But in birds, such a horizontal
motion (which indeed would rather hinder flight) would be
absurd, since it would cause the ponderous bird to fall headlong to the earth; whereas it can only be suspended in the
air by constant vibration of the wings *perpendicular to the
horizon*.  Nature was thus forced to show her marvellous skill
in producing a motion which, by one and the same action,
should suspend the bird in the air, and carry it forward in a
horizontal direction.   This is effected by striking the air
below perpendicularly to the horizon, but with oblique
strokes—an action which is rendered possible only by the
flexibility of the feathers, for the fans of the wings in the act
of striking acquire the form of a wedge, by the forcing out of
which the bird is necessarily moved forwards in a horizontal
direction."

The points which Borelli endeavours to establish are
these :—

First, That the action of the wing is a wedge action.

Second, That the wing consists of two portions—*a rigid*
anterior portion, and a *non-rigid* flexible portion.   The rigid
portion he represents in his artificial bird (fig. 113, p. 220) as
consisting of *a rod* (*e r*), the yielding portion of *feathers* (*a o*).

Third, That if the air strikes the under surface of the
wing perpendicularly in a direction from below upwards, the
flexible portion of the wing will yield in an upward direction,
and form a wedge with its neighbour.

Fourth, Similarly and conversely, if the wing strikes the

---

[1] It is clear from the above that Borelli did not know that the wings of
birds strike *forwards* as well as downwards during the down stroke, and *forwards* as well as upwards during the up stroke.   These points, as well as the
twisting and untwisting figure-of-8 action of the wing, were first described by
the author.   Borelli seems to have been equally ignorant of the fact that the
wings of insects vibrate in a more or less horizontal direction.

air perpendicularly from above, the posterior and flexible portion of the wing will yield and be forced in an upward direction.

Fifth, That this *upward yielding* of the posterior or flexible margin of the wing results in and necessitates *a horizontal transference* of the body of the bird.

Sixth, That to sustain a bird in the air the wings must strike *vertically downwards,* as this is the direction in which a heavy body, if left to itself, would fall.

Seventh, That to propel the bird in a horizontal direction, the wings must descend in a perpendicular direction, and the posterior or flexible portions of the wings *yield in an upward direction*, and in such a manner as virtually to communicate *an oblique action* to them.

Eighth, That the feathers of the wing are *bent in an upward direction* when the wing *descends*, the upward bending of the elastic feathers contributing to the horizontal travel of the body of the bird.

I have been careful to expound Borelli's views for several reasons :—

1st, Because the purely mechanical theory of the wing's action is clearly to be traced to him.

2d, Because his doctrines have remained unquestioned for nearly two centuries, and have been adopted by all the writers since his time, without, I regret to say in the majority of cases, any acknowledgment whatever.

3d, Because his views have been revived by the modern French school ; and

4th, Because, in commenting upon and differing from Borelli, I will necessarily comment upon and differ from all his successors.

*As to the Direction of the Stroke, yielding of the Wing, etc.*— The Duke of Argyll[1] agrees with Borelli in believing that the wing invariably strikes *perpendicularly downwards*. His words are—" Except for the purpose of arresting their flight birds can never strike except *directly downwards ;* that is, against the opposing force of gravity." Professor Owen in his Comparative Anatomy, Mr. Macgillivray in his British Birds, Mr. Bishop in his article " Motion " in the Cyclopedia of Anatomy

[1] " Reign of Law "—Good Words, 1865.

and Physiology, and M. Linis "On the Flight of Birds and Insects" in the Annals of Natural History, all assert that the stroke is delivered *downwards* and more or less *backwards*.

To obtain an *upward* recoil, one would naturally suppose all that is required is a *downward* stroke, and to obtain an *upward and forward* recoil, one would naturally conclude a *downward and backward* stroke alone is requisite. Such, however, is not the case.

In the first place, a natural wing, or a properly constructed artificial one, cannot be depressed either *vertically downwards*, or *downwards and backwards*. It will of necessity descend *downwards and forwards in a curve*. This arises from its being flexible and elastic throughout, and in especial from its being carefully graduated as regards thickness, the tip being thinner and more elastic than the root, and the posterior margin than the anterior margin.

In the second place, there is only one direction in which the wing could strike so at once *to support and carry the bird forward*. The bird, when flying, is a body in motion. It has therefore acquired momentum. If a grouse is shot on the wing *it does not fall vertically downwards*, as Borelli and his successors assume, but *downwards and forwards*. The flat surfaces of the wings are consequently made to strike downwards and forwards, as they in this manner act as kites to the falling body, which they bear, or tend to bear, *upwards and forwards*.

So much for the direction of the stroke during the descent of the wing.

Let us now consider to what extent the posterior margin of the wing yields in *an upward direction* when the wing descends. Borelli does not state the exact amount. The Duke of Argyll, who believes with Borelli that the posterior margin of the wing is elevated during the down stroke, avers that, "whereas the air compressed in the hollow of the wing cannot pass through the wing owing to the closing upwards of the feathers against each other, or escape forwards because of the rigidity of the bones and of the quills in this direction, it passes backwards, and in so doing *lifts by its force the elastic ends of the feathers*. In passing backwards it communicates

P

to the whole line of both wings a corresponding push forwards to the body of the bird. The same volume of air is thus made, in accordance with the law of action and reaction, *to sustain the bird and carry it forward.*"[1] Mr. Macgillivray observes that " to progress *in a horizontal direction* it is necessary that the downward stroke should be modified *by the elevation in a certain degree of the free extremities of the quills.*"[2]

*Marey's Views.*—Professor Marey states that during *the down stroke* the posterior or flexible margin of the wing yields in *an upward direction* to such an extent as to cause the under surface of the wing *to look backwards*, and make a backward angle with the horizon of 45° *plus* or *minus* according to circumstances.[3] That the posterior margin of the wing yields in a slightly upward direction during the down stroke, I admit. By doing so it prevents shock, confers continuity of motion, and contributes in some measure to the elevation of the wing. The amount of yielding, however, is in all cases very slight, and the little upward movement there is, is in part the result of the posterior margin of the wing rotating around the anterior margin as an axis. That the posterior margin of the wing never yields in *an upward direction* until the under surface of the pinion makes a backward angle of 45° with the horizon, as Marey remarks, is a matter of absolute certainty. This statement admits of direct proof. If any one watches the horizontal or upward flight of a large bird, he will observe that the posterior or flexible margin of the wing never rises during the down stroke to a perceptible extent, so that *the under surface of the wing* on no occasion looks backwards, as stated by Marey. On the contrary, he will find that *the under surface of the wing* (during the down stroke) invariably *looks forwards*—the posterior margin of the wing being inclined *downwards and backwards;* as shown at figs. 82 and 83, p. 158; fig. 103, p. 186; fig. 85 (*a b c*), p. 160; and fig. 88 (*c d e f g*), p. 166.

The under surface of the wing, as will be seen from this

[1] " Reign of Law "—Good Words, February 1865, p. 128.
[2] History of British Birds. Lond. 1837, p. 43.
[3] " Méchanisme du vol chez les Insectes. Comment se fait la propulsion," by Professor E. J. Marey. Revue des Cours Scientifiques de la France et de l'Etranger, for 20th March 1869, p. 254.

account, not only always *looks forwards*, but it forms a true kite with the horizon, the angles made by the kite varying at every part of the down stroke, as shown more particularly at *d, e, f, g; j, k, l, m* of fig. 88, p. 166. I am therefore opposed to Borelli, Macgillivray, Owen, Bishop, M. Liais, the Duke of Argyll, and Marey as to the direction and nature of the down stroke. I differ also as to the direction and nature of the up stroke.

Professor Marey states that not only does the posterior margin of the wing yield *in an upward direction* during the *down stroke* until the under surface of the pinion makes a backward angle of 45° with the horizon, but that during the *up stroke* it yields to the same extent *in an opposite direction*. The posterior flexible margin of the wing, according to Marey, passes through a space of 90° every time the wing reverses its course, this space being dedicated to the mere adjusting of the planes of the wing for the purposes of flight. The planes, moreover, he asserts, are adjusted not by vital and vito-mechanical acts but by *the action of the air alone;* this operating on the under surface of the wing and forcing its posterior margin *upwards* during *the down stroke;* the air during the *up stroke* acting upon the posterior margin of the upper surface of the wing, and forcing it *downwards.* This is a mere repetition of Borelli's view. Marey delegates to the air the difficult and delicate task of arranging the details of flight. The time, power, and space occupied in reversing the wing alone, according to this theory, are such as to render flight impossible. That the wing does not act as stated by Borelli, Marey, and others may be readily proved by experiment. It may also be demonstrated mathematically, as a reference to figs. 114 and 115, p. 228, will show.

Let *a b* of fig. 114 represent the horizon; *m n* the line of vibration; *z c* the wing inclined at an upward backward angle of 45° in the act of making the down stroke, and *z d* the wing inclined at a downward backward angle of 45° and in the act of making the up stroke. When the wing *z c* descends it will tend to dive downwards in the direction *f* giving very little of any horizontal support (*a b*); when the wing *z d* ascends it will endeavour to rise in the direction *g*, as it darts up like a kite (the body bearing it being in motion).

If we take the resultant of these two forces, we have at most propulsion in the direction *a b*. This, moreover, would only hold true if the bird was as light as air. As, however, gravity tends to pull the bird downwards as it advances, the real flight of the bird, according to this theory, would fall in a line between *b* and *f*, probably in *z h*. It could not possibly be otherwise; the wing described and figured by Borelli and Marey is in one piece, and made to vibrate vertically on either side of a given line. If, however, a wing in one piece is elevated and depressed in a strictly perpendicular direction, it is evident that the wing will experience a greater resistance during *the up stroke*, when it is acting *against gravity*, than during *the down stroke*, when it is acting *with gravity*.

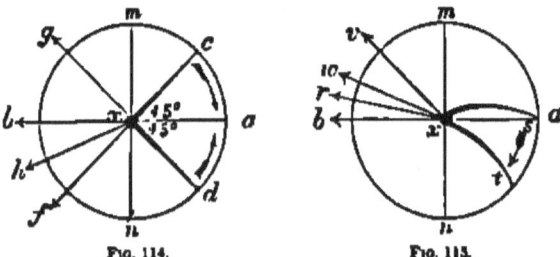

FIG. 114.                          FIG. 115.

As a consequence, the bird will be more vigorously depressed during the ascent of the wing than it will be elevated during its descent. That the mechanical wing referred to by Borelli and Marey is *not a flying wing*, but a mere propelling apparatus, seems evident to the latter, for he states that the winged machine designed by him has unquestionably *not motor power enough to support its own weight.*[1]

The manner in which the natural wing (and the artificial wing properly constructed and propelled) evades the resistance of the air during the up stroke, and gives continuous support and propulsion, is very remarkable. Fig. 115 illustrates the true principle. Let *a b* represent the horizon; *m n* the direction of vibration; *z s* the wing ready to make the down stroke, and *z t* the wing ready to make the up stroke. When the wing *z s* descends, the posterior margin (*s*) is screwed

---

[1] Revue des Cours Scientifiques de la France et de l'Etranger. 8ro. March 20, 1869.

*downwards* and *forwards* in the direction *s, t;* the forward angle which it makes with the horizon increasing as the wing descends (compare with fig. 85 (*a b c*), p. 160, and fig. 88 (*c d e f*), p. 166). The air is thus seized by a great variety of inclined surfaces, and as the under surface of the wing, which is a true kite, looks *upwards* and *forwards*, it tends to carry the body of the bird *upwards* and *forwards* in the direction *x w*. When the wing *x t* makes the *up stroke*, it rotates in the direction *t s* to prepare for the second down stroke. It does not, however, ascend in the direction *t s*. On the contrary, it darts up like a true kite, which it is, in the direction *x v*, in virtue of the reaction of the air, and because the body of the bird, to which it is attached, has a forward motion communicated to it by the wing during the down stroke (compare with *g h i* of fig. 88, p. 166). The resultant of the forces acting in the directions *x v* and *x b*, is one acting in the direction *x w*, and if allowance be made for the operation of gravity, the flight of the bird will correspond to a line somewhere between *w* and *b*, probably the line *x r*. This result is produced by the wing acting as an eccentric—by the upper concave surface of the pinion being always directed upwards, the under concave surface downwards—by the under surface, which is a true kite, darting forward in wave curves both during the down and up strokes, and never making a backward angle with the horizon (fig. 88, p. 166); and lastly, by the wing employing the air under it as a fulcrum during the down stroke, the air, on its own part, reacting on the under surface of the pinion, and when the proper time arrives, contributing to the elevation of the wing.

If, as Borelli and his successors believe, the posterior margin of the wing yielded to a marked extent in *an upward direction* during the *down stroke*, and more especially if it yielded to such an extent as to cause the under surface of the wing to make *a backward angle with the horizon of* 45°, one of two things would inevitably follow—either the air on which the wing depends for support and propulsion would be permitted to escape before it was utilized; or the wing would dart rapidly *downward*, and carry the body of the bird with it. If the posterior margin of the wing yielded in an upward direction to the extent described by Marey during the down stroke, it would be tantamount to removing the fulcrum (the air) on which the lever formed by the wing operates.

If a bird flies in a horizontal direction the angles made by the under surface of the wing with the horizon *are very slight,* but they *always look forwards* (fig. 60, p. 126). If a bird flies upwards the angles in question are increased (fig. 59, p. 126). In no instance, however, unless when the bird is everted and flying downwards, is the *posterior margin* of the wing *on a higher level* than the anterior one (fig. 106, p. 203). This holds true of natural flight, and consequently also of artificial flight.

These remarks are more especially applicable to the flight of the bat and bird where the wing is made to vibrate more or less perpendicularly (fig. 17, p. 36; figs. 82 and 83, p. 158. Compare with fig. 85, p. 160, and fig. 88, p. 166). If a bird or a bat wishes to fly upwards, its flying surfaces must always be inclined upwards. It is the same with the fish. A fish can only swim upwards if its body is directed upwards. In the insect, as has been explained, the wing is made to vibrate in a more or less horizontal direction. In this case the wing has not to contend directly against gravity (a wing which flaps vertically must). As a consequence it is made to tack upon the air obliquely zigzag fashion as horse and carriage would ascend a steep hill (*vide* figs. 67 to 70, p. 141. Compare with figs. 71 and 72, p. 144). In this arrangement gravity is overcome by the wing reversing its planes and acting as a kite which flies alternately forwards and backwards. The kites formed by the wings of the bat and bird always fly forward (fig. 88, p. 166). In the insect, as in the bat and bird, the posterior margin of the wing never rises above the horizon so as to make an upward and backward angle with it, as stated by Borelli, Marey, and others (*c x a* of fig. 114, p. 228).

While Borelli and his successors are correct as to the wedge-action of the wing, they have given an erroneous interpretation of the manner in which the wedge is produced. Thus Borelli states that when the wings descend their posterior margins ascend, the two wings forming a cone whose base is represented by *c b e* of fig. 113, p. 220); its apex being represented by *a f* of the same figure. The base of Borelli's cone, it will be observed, is inclined forwards in the direction of

the head of the bird. Now this is just the opposite of what
ought to be. Instead of the two wings forming one cone,
the base of which is directed *forwards*, each wing of itself
forms two cones, the bases of which are directed *backwards*
and outwards, as shown at fig. 116.

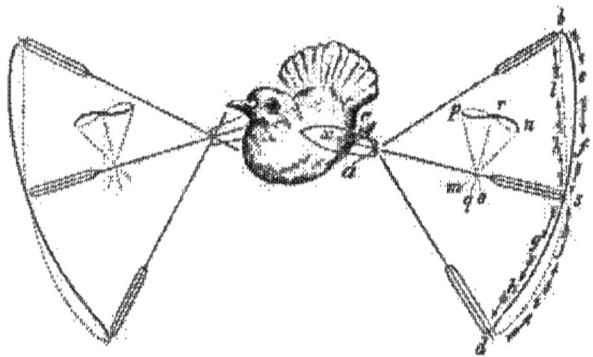

Fig. 116.

In this figure the action of the wing is compared to the
sculling of an oar, to which it bears a considerable resemblance.[1] The one cone, viz., that with its base directed outwards, is represented at *x b d*. This cone corresponds to the
area mapped out by the tip of the wing in the process of *elevating*. The second cone, viz., that with its base directed backwards, is represented at *q p n*. This cone corresponds to the area
mapped out by the posterior margin of the wing in the process
of *propelling*. The two cones are produced in virtue of the
wing rotating on its root and along its anterior margin as it
ascends and descends (fig. 80, p. 149 ; fig. 83, p. 158). The
present figure (116) shows the double twisting action of the
wing, the tip describing the figure-of-8 indicated at *b e f g h d
i j k l;* the posterior margin describing the figure-of-8 indicated at *p r n*. It is in this manner the cross pulsation or wave
referred to at p. 148 is produced. To represent the action of
the wing the sculling oar (*a b, x s, c d*) must have a small scull
(*m n, q r, o p*) working at right angles to it. This follows because

[1] In sculling strictly speaking, it is the upper surface of the oar which is
most effective ; whereas in flying it is the under.

the wing has to elevate as well as propel; the oar of a boat
when employed as a scull only propelling. In order to elevate
more effectually, the oars formed by the wings are made to
oscillate on a level with and under the volant animal rather
than above it; the posterior margins of the wings being made
to oscillate on a level with and below the anterior margins
(pp. 150, 151).

Borelli, and all who have written since his time, are
unanimous in affirming that the horizontal transference of the
body of the bird is due to the perpendicular vibration of the
wings, and to the yielding of the posterior or flexible margins
of the wings in an upward direction as the wings descend.
I am, however, as already stated, disposed to attribute
the transference, 1st, to the fact that the wings, both when
elevated and depressed, *leap forwards in curves*, those curves
uniting to form a continuous waved track; 2d, to the
tendency which the body of the bird has to swing forwards, in a more or less horizontal direction, when once set
in motion; 3d, to the construction of the wings (they are
elastic helices or screws, which twist and untwist when they
are made to vibrate, and tend to bear upwards and onwards
any weight suspended from them); 4th, to the reaction of
the air on the under surfaces of the wings, which always act
as kites; 5th, to the ever-varying power with which the
wings are urged, this being greatest at the beginning of
the down stroke, and least at the end of the up one; 6th,
to the contraction of the voluntary muscles and elastic ligaments; 7th, to the effect produced by the various inclined
surfaces formed by the wings during their oscillations; 8th,
to the weight of the bird—weight itself, when acting upon
inclined planes (wings), becoming a propelling power, and so
contributing to horizontal motion. This is proved by the
fact that if a sea bird launches itself from a cliff with expanded motionless wings, it sails along for an incredible
distance before it reaches the water (fig. 103, p. 186).

The authors who have adopted Borelli's plan of artificial
wing, and who have indorsed his mechanical views of the
action of the wing most fully, are Chabrier, Straus-Durckheim,
Girard, and Marey. Borelli's artificial wing, as already explained (p. 220, fig. 113), consists of *a rigid rod* $(e, r)$ in

front, and *a flexible sail* (*a, o*) composed of feathers, behind. It acts upon the air, and the air acts upon it, as occasion demands.

*Chabrier's Views.*—Chabrier states that the wing has only one period of activity—that, in fact, if the wing be suddenly lowered by the depressor muscles, it is elevated solely by the reaction of the air. There is one unanswerable objection to this theory—the bats and birds, and some, if not all the insects, have distinct elevator muscles. The presence of well-developed elevator muscles implies an elevating function, and, besides, we know that the insect, bat, and bird can elevate their wings when they are not flying, and when, consequently, no reaction of the air is induced.

*Straus-Durckheim's Views.*—Durckheim believes the insect abstracts from the air by means of *the inclined plane* a component force (composant) which it employs *to support* and *direct* itself. In his Theology of Nature he describes a schematic wing as follows :—It consists of a *rigid ribbing* in front, and *a flexible sail* behind. A membrane so constructed will, according to him, be fit for flight. It will suffice if such a sail *elevates* and *lowers* itself successively. It will, of its own accord, dispose itself as an inclined plane, *and receiving obliquely the reaction of the air*, it transfers *into tractile force* a part of the *vertical impulsion it has received.* These two parts of the wing are, moreover, equally indispensable to each other. If we compare the schematic wing of Durckheim with that of Borelli they will be found to be identical, both as regards their construction and the manner of their application.

Professor Marey, so late as 1869, repeats the arguments and views of Borelli and Durckheim, with very trifling alterations. Marey describes two artificial wings, the one composed of a *rigid rod* and *sail*—the rod representing *the stiff anterior margin* of the wing; the sail, which is made of paper bordered with card-board, *the flexible posterior portion.* The other wing consists of a *rigid nervure* in front and behind of thin parchment which supports *fine rods of steel.* He states, that if the wing only elevates and depresses itself, "*the resistance of the air* is sufficient to produce all the other movements. In effect the wing of an insect has not the power of equal resistance in every part. On the anterior margin the extended nervures make it *rigid*, while behind it is fine and *flexible.*

During the vigorous depression of the wing the nervure has the power of *remaining rigid*, whereas the *flexible portion*, being pushed in *an upward direction* on account of the resistance it experiences from the air, *assumes an oblique position*, which causes the upper surface of the wing *to look forwards.*" . . . "At first the plane of the wing is parallel with the body of the animal. It lowers itself—the *front part* of the wing *strongly resists*, the sail which follows it *being flexible yields.* Carried by the ribbing (the anterior margin of the wing) which lowers itself, the sail or posterior margin of the wing being raised meanwhile by the air, which sets it straight again, the sail will take an intermediate position, and *incline itself about* 45° *plus* or *minus* according to circumstances. The wing continues its movements of depression inclined to the horizon, but the impulse of the air which continues its effect, and naturally acts upon the surface which it strikes, has the power of resolving itself into two forces, *a vertical* and *a horizontal force*, the first suffices *to raise* the animal, the second *to more it along.*"[1] The reverse of this, Morey states, takes place during the elevation of the wing—the resistance of the air from above causing the upper surface of the wing *to look backwards.* The fallaciousness of this reasoning has been already pointed

[1] Compare Marey's description with that of Borelli, a translation of which I subjoin. "Let a bird be suspended in the air with its wings expanded, and first let the under surfaces (of the wings) be struck by the air ascending perpendicularly to the horizon with such a force that the bird gliding down is prevented from falling: I say that it (the bird) will be impelled with *a horizontal forward motion*, because the two osseous rods of the wings are able, owing to the strength of the muscles, and because of their hardness, *to resist the force of the air*, and therefore to retain the same form (literally extent, expansion), but the total breadth of the fan of each wing *yields to the impulse of the air* when the flexible feathers are permitted to rotate around the *manubria* or osseous axes, and hence it is necessary that the extremities of the wings approximate each other : wherefore the wings acquire the form of a wedge whose point is directed towards the tail of the bird, but whose surfaces are compressed on either side by the ascending air in such a manner that it is driven out in the direction of its base. Since, however, the wedge formed by the wings cannot move forward unless it carry the body of the bird along with it, it is evident that it (the wedge) gives place to the air impelling it, and therefore the bird *flies forward in a horizontal direction*. But now let the substratum of still air be struck by the fans (feathers) of the wings with a motion perpendicular to the horizon. Since the fans and sails of the wings

out, and need not be again referred to. It is not a little
curious that Borelli's artificial wing should have been
reproduced in its integrity at a distance of nearly two
centuries.

*The Author's Views:—his Method of constructing and applying
Artificial Wings as contra-distinguished from that of Borelli,
Chabrier, Durckheim, Marey, etc.*—The artificial wings which I
have been in the habit of making for several years differ from
those recommended by Borelli, Durckheim, and Marey in
four essential points :—

1st, The mode of construction.

2d, The manner in which they are applied to the air.

3d, The nature of the power employed.

4th, The necessity for adapting certain elastic substances
to the root of the wing if in one piece, and to the root and
the body of the wing if in several pieces.

And, first, as to the manner of construction.

Borelli, Durckheim, and Marey maintain that *the anterior
margin of the wing* should be *rigid ;* I, on the other hand,
believe that no part of the wing whatever should be rigid,
*not even the anterior margin,* and that the pinion should be
flexible and elastic throughout.

That the anterior margin of the wing should not be composed of a rigid rod may, I think, be demonstrated in a
variety of ways. If a rigid rod be made to vibrate by the
hand the vibration is not smooth and continuous; on the
contrary, it is irregular and jerky, and characterized by two
halts or pauses (dead points), the one occurring at the end of
the *up stroke,* the other at the end of the *down stroke.* This
mechanical impediment is followed by serious consequences
as far as power and speed are concerned—the slowing of the
wing at the end of the down and up strokes involving a

acquire the form of a wedge, the point of which is turned towards the tail (of
the bird), and since they suffer the same force and compression from the air,
whether the vibrating wings strike the undisturbed air beneath, or whether,
on the other hand, the expanded wings (the osseous axes remaining rigid)
receive the percussion of the ascending air ; in either case the *flexible feathers
yield to the impulse,* and hence approximate each other, and thus the bird
moves in *a forward direction.*"—De Motu Animalium, pars prima, prop. 196,
1685.

great expenditure of power and a disastrous waste of time. The wing, to be effective as an elevating and propelling organ, should have no dead points, and should be character- ized by a rapid winnowing or fanning motion. It should reverse and reciprocate with the utmost steadiness and smoothness—in fact, the motions should appear as continuous as those of a fly-wheel in rapid motion : they are so in the insect (figs. 64, 65, and 66, p. 139).

To obviate the difficulty in question, it is necessary, in my opinion, to employ *a tapering elastic rod* or *series of rods* bound together for the anterior margin of the wing.

If a longitudinal section of bamboo cane, ten feet in length, and one inch in breadth (fig. 117), be taken by the ex- tremity and made to vibrate, it will be found that a wavy serpentine motion is produced, the waves being greatest when the vibration is slowest (fig. 118), and least when it is most rapid (fig. 119). It will further be found that at the extremity of the cane where the impulse is communi- cated there is *a steady reciprocating movement devoid of dead points.* The continuous movement in question is no doubt due to the fact that the different portions of the cane reverse at different periods—the undulations induced being to an interrupted or vibratory movement very much what the continuous play of a fly-wheel is to a rotatory motion.

*The Wave Wing of the Author.*—If a similar cane has added to it, tapering rods of whalebone, which radiate in an out- ward direction to the extent of a foot or so, and the whale- bones be covered by a thin sheet of india-rubber, an artificial wing, resembling the natural one in all its essential points, is at once produced (fig. 120). I propose to designate this wing, from the peculiarities of its movements, *the wave wing* (fig. 121). If the wing referred to (fig. 121) be made to vibrate at its root, a series of longitudinal ($c\,d\,e$) and transverse ($f\,g\,h$) waves are at once produced; the one series running in the direction of *the length of the wing*, the other in the direction of *its breadth* (*vide* p. 148). This wing further *twists* and *untwists*, figure-of-8 fashion, during the up and down strokes, as shown at fig. 123, p. 239 (compare with figs. 82 and 83, p. 158 ; fig. 86, p. 161 ; and fig. 103, p. 186).

There is, moreover, a continuous play of the wing; the down stroke gliding into the up one, and *vice versâ*, which

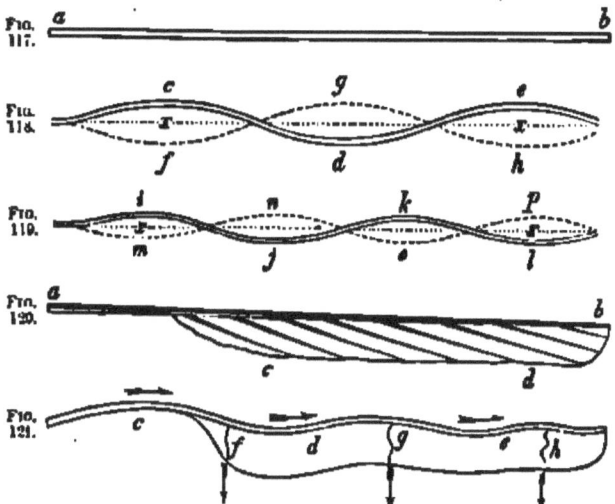

FIG. 117.

FIG. 118.

FIG. 119.

FIG. 120.

FIG. 121.

FIG. 117.—Represents a longitudinal section of bamboo cane ten feet long, and one inch wide.—*Original.*

FIG. 118.—The appearance presented by the same cane when made to vibrate by the hand. The cane vibrates on either side of a given line (*x x*), and appears as if it were in two places at the same time, viz., *c* and *f*, *g* and *d*, *e* and *h*. It is thus during its vibration thrown into figures-of-8 or opposite curves.—*Original.*

FIG. 119.—The same cane when made to vibrate more rapidly. In this case the waves made by the cane are less in size, but more numerous. The cane is seen alternately on either side of the line *x x*, being now at *i* now at *m*, now at *n* now at *j*, now at *k* now at *o*, now at *p* now at *l*. The cane, when made to vibrate, has no dead points, a circumstance due to the fact that no two parts of it reverse or change their curves at precisely the same instant. This curious reciprocating motion enables the wing to seize and disengage itself from the air with astonishing rapidity.—*Original.*

FIG. 120.—The same cane with a flexible elastic curtain or fringe added to it. The curtain consists of tapering whalebone rods covered with a thin layer of India-rubber. *a b* anterior margin of wing. *e d* posterior ditto.—*Original.*

FIG. 121.—Gives the appearance presented by the artificial wing (fig. 120) when made to vibrate by the hand. It is thrown into longitudinal and transverse waves. The longitudinal waves are represented by the arrows *c d e*, and the transverse waves by the arrows *f g h*. A wing constructed on this principle gives a continuous elevating and propelling power. It developes figure-of-8 curves during its action in longitudinal, transverse, and oblique directions. It literally floats upon the air. It has no dead points—is vibrated with amazingly little power, and has apparently no slip. It can fly in an upward, downward, or horizontal direction by merely altering its angle of inclination to the horizon. It is applied to the air by an irregular motion—the movement being most sudden and vigorous always at the beginning of the down stroke.—*Original.*

clearly shows that the down and up strokes are parts of one
whole, and that neither is perfect without the other.

The wave wing is endowed with the very remarkable property that it will fly in any direction, demonstrating more or
less clearly that flight is essentially a progressive movement,
*i.e.* a horizontal rather than a vertical movement. Thus, if
the anterior or thick margin of the wing be directed upwards, so that the under surface of the wing makes a *forward*
angle with the horizon of 45°, the wing will, when made to
vibrate by the hand, fly with an undulating motion *in an
upward direction*, like a pigeon to its dovecot. If the under
surface of the wing makes no angle, or a very small *forward*
angle, with the horizon, it will dart forward in a series of
curves in a *horizontal direction*, like a crow in rapid horizontal
flight. If the anterior or thick margin of the wing be directed
downwards, so that the under surface of the wing makes a
*backward* angle of 45° with the horizon, the wing will describe a waved track, and *fly downwards*, as a sparrow from
a house-top or from a tree (p. 230). In all those movements progression is a necessity. The movements are
continuous gliding *forward movements*. There is no halt or
pause between the strokes, and if the angle which the under
surface of the wing makes with the horizon be properly
regulated, the amount of steady tractile and buoying power
developed is truly astonishing. This form of wing, which
may be regarded as the realization of the figure-of-8 theory
of flight, elevates and propels both during the down and up
strokes, and its working is accompanied with almost no slip.
It seems literally to float upon the air. No wing that is
rigid in the anterior margin can twist and untwist during its
action, and produce the figure-of-8 curves generated by the
living wing. To produce the curves in question, the wing
must be flexible, elastic, and capable of change of form in all
its parts. The curves made by the artificial wing, as has
been stated, are largest when the vibration is slow, and least
when it is quick. In like manner, the air is thrown into
large waves by the slow movement of a large wing, and into
small waves by the rapid movement of a smaller wing. The
size of the *wing curves* and *air waves* bear a fixed relation to
each other, and both are dependent on the rapidity with

which the wing is made to vibrate. This is proved by the
fact that insects, in order to fly, require, as a rule, to drive
their small wings with immense velocity. It is further
proved by the fact that the small humming-bird, in order to
keep itself stationary before a flower, requires to oscillate its
tiny wings with great rapidity, whereas the large humming-
bird (*Patagona gigas*), as was pointed out by Darwin, can
attain the same object by flapping its large wings with a very
slow and powerful movement. In the larger birds the movements are slowed in proportion to the size, and more
especially in proportion to the length of the wing; the cranes
and vultures moving the wings very leisurely, and the large
oceanic birds dispensing in a great measure with the flapping
of the wings, and trusting for progression and support to the
wings in the expanded position.

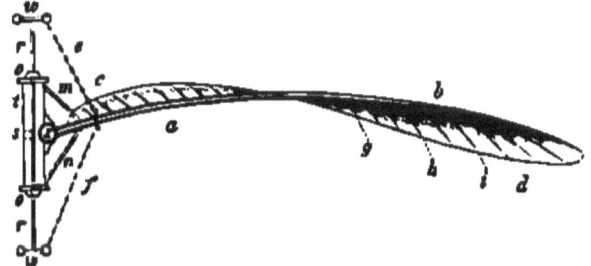

Fig. 122.

Fig. 122.—Elastic spiral wing, which twists and untwists during its action, to
form a mobile helix or screw. This wing is made to vibrate by steam by a
direct piston action, and by a slight adjustment can be propelled vertically,
horizontally, or at any degree of obliquity.
*a*, *b*, Anterior margin of wing, to which the beams or ribs are affixed. *c*, *d*, Posterior margin of wing crossing anterior one. *x*, Ball-and-socket joint at root of
wing; the wing being attached to the side of the cylinder by the socket. *t*,
Cylinder. *r*, *r*, Piston, with cross heads (*v*, *v*) and piston head (*s*). *z*, *o*,
Stuffing boxes. *e*, *f*, Driving chains. *m*, Superior elastic band, which assists in
elevating the wing. *n*, Inferior elastic band, which antagonizes *m*. The alternate stretching of the superior and inferior elastic bands contributes to the
continuous play of the wing, by preventing dead points at the end of the down
and up strokes. The wing is free to move in a vertical and horizontal direction and at any degree of obliquity.—*Original.*

This leads me to conclude that very large wings may be
driven with a comparatively slow motion, a matter of great
importance in artificial flight secured by the flapping of
wings.

*How to construct an artificial Wave Wing on the Insect type.*—The following appear to me to be essential features in the construction of an artificial wing :—

The wing should be of a generally triangular shape.

It should taper from the root towards the tip, and from the anterior margin in the direction of the posterior margin.

It should be convex above and concave below, and slightly twisted upon itself.

It should be flexible and elastic throughout, and should twist and untwist during its vibration, to produce figure-of-8 curves along its margins and throughout its substance.

Such a wing is represented at fig. 122, p. 239.

If the wing is in more than one piece, joints and springs require to be added to the body of the pinion.

In making a wing in one piece on the model of the insect wing, such as that shown at fig. 122 (p. 239), I employ one or more tapering elastic reeds, which arch from above downwards (*a b*) for the anterior margin. To this I add tapering elastic reeds, which radiate towards the tip of the wing, and which also arch from above downwards (*g, h, i*). These latter are so arranged that they confer *a certain amount of spirality* upon the wing ; the anterior (*a b*) and posterior (*c d*) margins being arranged in different planes, so that they appear to cross each other. I then add the covering of the wing, which may consist of india-rubber, silk, tracing cloth, linen, or any similar substance.

If the wing is large, I employ steel tubes, bent to the proper shape. In some cases I secure additional strength by adding to the oblique ribs or stays (*g h i* of fig. 122) a series of very oblique stays, and another series of cross stays, as shown at *m* and *a, n, o, p, q* of fig. 123, p. 241.

This form of wing is made to oscillate upon two centres viz. the root and anterior margin, to bring out the peculiar eccentric action of the pinion.

If I wish to produce a very delicate light wing, I do so by selecting a fine tapering elastic reed, as represented at *a b* of fig. 124.

To this I add successive layers (*i, h, g, f, e*) of some flexible material, such as parchment, buckram, tracing cloth, or even

paper. As the layers overlap each other, it follows that there
are five layers at the anterior margin (*a b*), and only one at
the posterior (*c d*). This form of wing is not twisted upon
itself structurally, but it twists and untwists, and becomes a
true screw during its action.

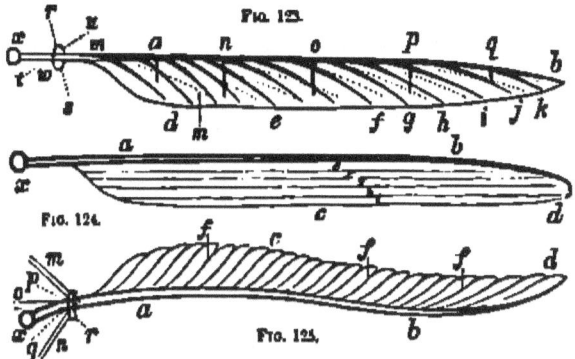

Fig. 123.—*Artificial Wing with Perpendicular (r s) and Horizontal (t u) Elastic
Bands attached to ferrule (w).*

a, b, Strong elastic reed, which tapers towards the tip of the wing.

d, e, f, h, i, j, k, Tapering curved reeds, which run obliquely from the
anterior to the posterior margin of the wing, and which radiate towards the
tip.

m, Similar curved reeds, which run still more obliquely.

a, n, o, p, q, Tapering curved reeds, which run from the anterior margin of
the wing, and at right angles to it. These support the two sets of oblique
reeds, and give additional strength to the anterior margin.

x, Ball-and-socket joint, by which the root of the wing is attached to the
cylinder, as in fig. 122, p. 238.—*Original.*

Fig. 124.—*Flexible elastic wing with tapering elastic reed (a b) running along
anterior margin.*

c, d, Posterior margin of wing. t, Portion of wing composed of one layer
of flexible material. h, Portion of wing composed of two layers. g, Portion
of wing composed of three layers. f, Portion of wing composed of four
layers. e, Portion of wing composed of five layers. x, Ball-and-socket joint
at root of wing.—*Original.*

Fig. 125.—*Flexible valvular wing with india-rubber springs attached to its
root.*

a, b, Anterior margin of wing, tapering and elastic. c, d, Posterior margin
of wing, elastic. f, f, f, Segments which open during the up stroke, and
close during the down, after the manner of valves. These are very narrow,
and open and close instantly. x, Universal joint. m, Superior elastic
band. n, Ditto inferior. o, Ditto anterior. p, q, Ditto oblique. r, Ring
into which the elastic bands are fixed.—*Original.*

*How to construct a Wave Wing which shall evade the super-
imposed Air during the Up Stroke.*—To construct a wing which

Q

shall elude the air during the up stroke, it is necessary to make it valvular, as shown at fig. 125, p. 241.

This wing, as the figure indicates, is composed of *numerous narrow segments (f f f)*, so arranged that the air, when the wing is made to vibrate, opens or separates them at the beginning of the up stroke, and closes or brings them together at the beginning of the down stroke.

The time and power required for opening and closing the segments is comparatively trifling, owing to their extreme narrowness and extreme lightness. The space, moreover, through which they pass in performing their valvular action is exceedingly small. The wing under observation is flexible and elastic throughout, and resembles in its general features the other wings described.

I have also constructed a wing which is self-acting in another sense. This consists of two parts—the one part being made of an elastic reed, which tapers towards the extremity; the other of a flexible sail. To the reed, which corresponds to the anterior margin of the wing, delicate tapering reeds are fixed at right angles; the principal and subordinate reeds being arranged on the same plane. The flexible sail is attached to the under surface of the principal reed, and is stiffer at its insertion than towards its free margin. When the wing is made to ascend, the sail, because of the pressure exercised upon its upper surface by the air, assumes a very oblique position, so that the resistance experienced by it during the *up stroke* is very slight. When, however, the wing descends, the sail instantly flaps in an upward direction, the subordinate reeds never permitting its posterior or free margin to rise above its anterior or fixed margin. The under surface of the wing consequently descends in such a manner as to present a nearly flat surface to the earth. It experiences much resistance from the air during the *down stroke*, the amount of buoyancy thus furnished being very considerable. The above form of wing is more effective during the down stroke than during the up one. It, however, elevates and propels during both, the forward travel being greatest during the down stroke.

*Compound Wave Wing of the Author.*—In order to render

the movements of the wing as simple as possible, I was induced to devise a form of pinion, which for the sake of distinction I shall designate the *Compound Wave Wing*. This wing consists of two wave wings united at the roots, as represented at fig. 126. It is impelled by steam, its centre

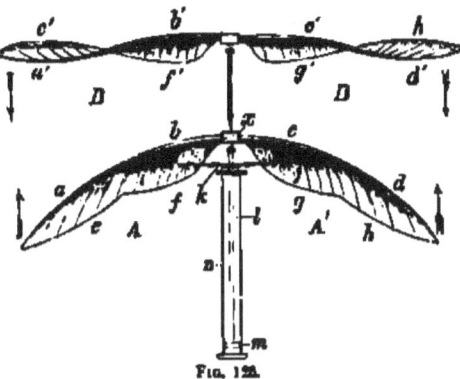

Fig. 126.

being fixed to the head of the piston by a compound joint (*x*), which enables it to move in a circle, and to rotate along its anterior margin (*a b c d; A, A'*) in the direction of its length. The circular motion is for steering purposes only. The wing rises and falls with every stroke of the piston, and the movements of the piston are quickened during the down stroke, and slowed during the up one.

During the up stroke of the piston the wing is very decidedly convex on its upper surface (*a b c d; A, A'*), its under surface being deeply concave and inclined obliquely upwards and forwards. It thus evades the air during the up stroke. During the down stroke of the wing is flattened out in every direction, and its extremities twisted in such a manner as to form two screws, as shown at *a' b' c' d'; e' f' g' h'; B, B'* of figure. The active area of the wing is by this means augmented, the wing seizing the air with great avidity during the down stroke. The area of the wing may be still further increased and diminished during the down and up strokes by adding joints to the body of the wing.

The degree of convexity given to the upper surface of the wing can be increased or diminished at pleasure by causing a cord ($ij$; $A, A'$) and elastic band ($k$) to extend between two points, which may vary according to circumstances. The wing is supplied with vertical springs, which assist in slowing and reversing it towards the end of the down and up strokes, and these, in conjunction with the elastic properties of the wing itself, contribute powerfully to its continued play. The compound wave wing produces the currents on which it rises. Thus during the up stroke it draws after it a current, which being met by the wing during its descent, confers additional elevating and propelling power. During the down stroke the wing in like manner draws after it a current which forms an eddy, and on this eddy the wing rises, as explained at p. 253, fig. 129. The ascent of the wing is favoured by the superimposed air playing on the upper surface of the posterior margin of the organ, in such a manner as to cause the wing to assume a more and more oblique position with reference to the horizon. This change in the plane of the wing enables its upper surface to avoid the superincumbent air during the up stroke, while it confers upon its under surface a combined kite and parachute action. The compound wave wing leaps forward in a curve both during the down and up strokes, so that the wing during its vibration describes a waved track, as shown at $a, c, e, g, i$ of fig. 81, p. 157. The compound wave wing possesses most of the peculiarities of single wings when made to vibrate separately. It forms a most admirable elevator and propeller, and has this advantage over ordinary wings, that it can be worked without injury to itself, when the machine which it is intended to elevate is resting on the ground. Two or more compound wave wings may be arranged on the same plane, or super-imposed, and made to act in concert. They may also by a slight modification be made to act horizontally instead of vertically. The length of the stroke of the compound wave wing is determined in part, though not entirely by the stroke of the piston—the extremities of the wing, because of their elasticity, moving through a greater space than the centre of the wing. By fixing the wing to the head of the piston all gearing apparatus is avoided, and the number of joints and working points reduced—a matter of no small importance when it is desirable to conserve the motor power and keep down the weight.

*How to apply Artificial Wings to the Air.*—Borelli, Durckheim, Marey, and all the writers with whom I am acquainted, assert that the wing should be made to vibrate *vertically.* I believe that if the wing be in one piece it should be made to vibrate *obliquely and more or less horizontally.* If, however, the wing be made to vibrate *vertically,* it is necessary to supply it with a ball-and-socket joint, and with springs at its root (*m n* of fig. 125, p. 241), to enable it *to leap forward in a curve* when it descends, and in another and *opposite curve* when it ascends (*vide a, c, e, g, i* of fig. 81, p. 157). This arrangement practically converts the vertical vibration into *an oblique one.* If this plan be not adopted, the wing is apt to foul at its tip. In applying the wing to the air it ought to have a figure-of-8 movement communicated to it either directly or indirectly. It is a peculiarity of the artificial wing properly constructed (as it is of the natural wing), *that it twists and untwists and makes figure-of-8 curves during its action* (see *a b, c d* of fig. 122, p. 239), this enabling it to seize and let go the air with wonderful rapidity, and in such a manner as to avoid dead points. If the wing be in several pieces, it may be made to vibrate more vertically than a wing in one piece, from the fact that the outer half of the pinion moves forwards and backwards when the wing ascends and descends so as alternately to become a short and a long lever; this arrangement permitting the wing to avoid the resistance experienced from the air during the up stroke, while it vigorously seizes the air during the down stroke.

If the body of a flying animal be in a horizontal position, a wing attached to it in such a manner that its under surface shall look forwards, and make an upward angle of 45° with the horizon is in a position to be applied either vertically (figs. 82 and 83, p. 158), or horizontally (figs. 67, 68, 69, and 70, p. 141). Such, moreover, is the conformation of the shoulder-joint in insects, bats, and birds, that the wing can be applied vertically, horizontally, or at any degree of obliquity

without inconvenience.[1]  It is in this way that an insect
which may begin its flight by causing its wings to make
figure-of-8 horizontal loops (fig. 71, p. 144), may gradually change the direction of the loops, and make them more
and more oblique until they are nearly vertical (fig. 73, p.
144).  In the beginning of such flight the insect is screwed
*nearly vertically upwards;* in the middle of it, it is screwed
*upwards and forwards;* whereas, towards the end of it, the
insect advances in *a waved line* almost horizontally (see
$g', r', s', t'$ of fig. 72, p. 144).  The muscles of the wing are
so arranged that they can propel it in a horizontal, vertical,
or oblique direction.   It is a matter of the utmost importance
that the direction of the stroke and the nature of the angles
made by the surface of the wing during its vibration with
the horizon be distinctly understood; as it is on these that
all flying creatures depend when they seek to elude the upward resistance of the air, and secure a maximum of elevating
and propelling power with a minimum of slip.

*As to the nature of the Forces required for propelling Arti-
ficial Wings.*—Borelli, Durckheim, and Marey affirm that it
suffices if the wing merely elevates and depresses itself by
a rhythmical movement in a perpendicular direction; while
Chabrier is of opinion that a movement of depression only is
required.  All those observers agree in believing that the
details of flight are due to the reaction of the air on the surface of the wing.  Repeated experiment has, however, convinced me that the artificial wing must be thoroughly under
control, both during the down and up strokes—the details of
flight being in a great measure due to the movements communicated to the wing by an intelligent agent.  In order
to reproduce flight by the aid of artificial wings, I find it
necessary to employ a power which varies in intensity at
every stage of the down and up strokes.  The power which

---

[1] The human wrist is so formed that if a wing be held in the hand at an
upward angle of 45°, the hand can apply it to the air in a vertical or horizontal
direction without difficulty.  This arises from the power which the hand has
of moving in an upward and downward direction, and from side to side with
equal facility.  The hand can also rotate on its long axis, so that it virtually
represents all the movements of the wing at its root.

suits best is one which is made to act very suddenly and
forcibly at the beginning of the down stroke, and which gradually abates in intensity until the end of the down stroke, where
it ceases to act in a downward direction. The power is then
made to act in an upward direction, and gradually to decrease
until the end of the up stroke. The force is thus applied
more or less continuously; its energy being increased and
diminished according to the position of the wing, and the
amount of resistance which it experiences from the air. The
flexible and elastic nature of the wave wing, assisted by
certain springs to be presently explained, insure a continuous
vibration where neither halts nor dead points are observable. I obtain the varying power required by a direct piston
action, and by working the steam expansively. The power
employed is materially assisted, particularly during the up
stroke, by the reaction of the air and the elastic structures about to be described. An artificial wing, propelled
and regulated by the forces recommended, is in some
respects as completely under control as the wing of the
insect, bat, or bird.

*Necessity for supplying the Root of Artificial Wings with
Elastic Structures in imitation of the Muscles and Elastic Ligaments of Flying Animals.*—Borelli, Durckheim, and Marey,
who advocate the perpendicular vibration of the wing, make
no allowance, so far as I am aware, for the wing *leaping
forward in curves* during *the down and up strokes.* As a consequence, the wing is jointed in their models to the frame
by a simple joint which moves only in one direction, viz.,
from above downwards, and *vice versâ.* Observation and
experiment have fully satisfied me that an artificial wing,
to be effective as an elevator and propeller, ought to be
able to move not only in an upward and downward direction, but also in a *forward, backward,* and *oblique direction;*
nay, more, that it should be free to rotate along its anterior
margin *in the direction of its length;* in fact, that its movements should be universal. Thus it should be able to rise or
fall, to advance or retire, to move at any degree of obliquity,
and to rotate along its anterior margin. To secure the
several movements referred to I furnish the root of the wing

with a ball-and-socket joint, *i.e.*, a universal joint (see *z* of
fig. 122, p. 239). To regulate the several movements when
the wing is vibrating, and to confer on the wing the various
inclined surfaces requisite for flight, as well as to delegate
as little as possible to the air, I employ a cross system of
elastic bands. These bands vary in length, strength, and
direction, and are attached to the anterior margin of the wing
(near its root), and to the cylinder (or a rod extending
from the cylinder) of the model (*vide m, n* of fig. 122, p.
239). The principal bands are four in number—a superior,
inferior, anterior, and posterior. The superior band (*m*)
extends between the upper part of the cylinder of the
model, and the upper surface of the anterior margin of the
wing; the inferior band (*n*) extending between the under part
of the cylinder or the boiler and the inferior surface of the
anterior margin of the pinion. The anterior and posterior
bands are attached to the anterior and posterior portions of
the wing and to rods extending from the centre of the
anterior and posterior portions of the cylinder. Oblique
bands are added, and these are so arranged that they give to
the wing during its descent and ascent the precise angles
made by the wing with the horizon in natural flight. The
superior bands are stronger than the inferior ones, and are
put upon the stretch during the down stroke. Thus they
help the wing over the dead point at the end of the down
stroke, and assist, in conjunction with the reaction obtained
from the air, in elevating it. The posterior bands are
stronger than the anterior ones to restrain within certain
limits the great tendency which the wing has to leap forward
in curves towards the end of the down and up strokes. The
oblique bands, aided by the air, give the necessary degree of
rotation to the wing in the direction of its length. This
effect can, however, also be produced independently by the
four principal bands. From what has been stated it will be
evident that the elastic bands exercise a restraining influence,
and that they act in unison with the driving power and with
the reaction supplied by the air. They powerfully contribute
to the continuous vibration of the wing, the vibration being
peculiar in this that it varies in rapidity at every stage of the

down and up strokes. I derive the motor power, as has been stated, from a direct piston action, the piston being urged either by steam worked expansively or by the hand, if it is merely a question of illustration. In the hand models the "*muscular sense*" at once informs the operator as to what is being done. Thus if one of the wave wings supplied with a ball-and-socket joint, and a cross system of elastic bands as explained, has a sudden vertical impulse communicated to it at the beginning of the down stroke, the wing darts *downwards and forwards in a curve* (*vide a c*, of fig. 81, p. 157), and in doing so *it elevates* and carries the piston and cylinder *forwards*. The force employed in depressing the wing is partly expended in stretching the superior elastic band, the wing being slowed towards the end of the down stroke. The instant the depressing force ceases to act, the superior elastic band contracts and the air reacts; the two together, coupled with the tendency which the model has to fall downwards and forwards during the up stroke, elevating the wing. The wing when it ascends describes an *upward and forward curve* as shown at *c e* of fig. 81, p. 157. The ascent of the wing stretches the inferior elastic band in the same way that the descent of the wing stretched the superior band. The superior and inferior elastic bands antagonize each other and reciprocate with vivacity. While those changes are occurring the wing is *twisting* and *untwisting* in the direction of its length and developing figure-of-8 curves along its margins (p. 239, fig. 122, *a b, c d*), and throughout its substance similar to what are observed under like circumstances in the natural wing (*vide* fig. 86, p. 161; fig. 103, p. 186). The angles, moreover, made by the under surface of the wing with the horizon during the down and up strokes are continually varying—the wing all the while acting as a kite, which flies steadily *upwards and forwards* (fig. 88, p. 166). As the elastic bands, as has been partly explained, are antagonistic in their action, the wing is constantly oscillating in some direction; there being no dead point either at the end of the down or up strokes. As a consequence, the curves made by the wing during the down and up strokes respectively, run into each other to form a continuous waved track, as represented at fig.

81, p. 157, and fig. 88, p. 166. A continuous movement
begets a continuous buoyancy; and it is quite remarkable to
what an extent, wings constructed and applied to the air
on the principles explained, elevate and propel—how little
power is required, and how little of that power is wasted in
slip.

If the piston, which in the experiment described has been
working *vertically*, be made to work *horizontally*, a series of
essentially similar results are obtained. When the piston
is worked horizontally, the anterior and posterior elastic
bands require to be of nearly the same strength, whereas
the inferior elastic band requires to be much stronger
than the superior one, to counteract the very decided tendency the wing has to fly upwards. The power also requires

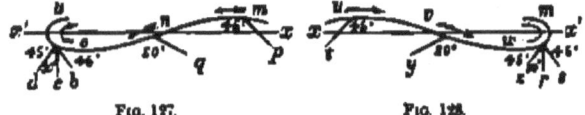

Fig. 127.                          Fig. 128.

Fig. 127.—Path described by artificial wave wing from right to left. *x, x',*
Horizon. *m, n, o,* Wave track traversed by wing from right to left. *p,*
Angle made by the wing with the horizon at beginning of stroke. *q,* Ditto,
made at middle of stroke. *b,* Ditto, towards end of stroke. *c,* Wing in
the act of reversing, at this stage the wing makes an angle of 90° with the
horizon, and its speed is less than at any other part of its course. *d,* Wing
reversed, and in the act of darting up to *n,* to begin the stroke from left to
right (*vide n* of fig. 128).—*Original.*

Fig. 128.—Path described by artificial wave wing from left to right. *x, x',*
Horizon. *u, v, w,* Wave track traversed by wing from left to right. *t,*
Angle made by the wing with horizon at beginning of stroke. *y,* Ditto,
at middle of stroke. *s,* Ditto, towards end of stroke. *r,* Wing in the act
of reversing; at this stage the wing makes an angle of 90° with the horizon,
and its speed is less than at any other part of its course. *s,* Wing reversed,
and in the act of darting up to *m,* to begin the stroke from right to left (*vide
m* of fig. 127).—*Original.*

to be somewhat differently applied. Thus the wing must
have a violent impulse communicated to it when it begins the
stroke from right to left, and also when it begins the stroke
from left to right (the *heavy parts* of the spiral line represented at fig. 71, p. 144, indicate the points where the impulse
is communicated). The wing is then left to itself, the elastic
bands and the reaction of the air doing the remainder of the
work. When the wing is forced by the piston from right to

left, it darts forward in double curve, as shown at fig. 127; the various inclined surfaces made by the wing with the horizon changing at every stage of the stroke.

' At the beginning of the stroke from right to left, the angle made by the under surface of the wing with the horizon ($x\,x'$) is something like 45° ($p$), whereas at the middle of the stroke it is reduced to 20° or 25° ($q$). At the end of the stroke the angle gradually increases to 45° ($b$), then to 90° ($c$), after which the wing suddenly turns a somersault ($d$), and reverses precisely as the natural wing does at $e, f, g$ of figs. 67 and 69, p. 141. The artificial wing reverses with amazing facility, and in the most natural manner possible. The angles made by its under surface with the horizon depend chiefly upon the speed with which the wing is urged at different stages of the stroke; the angle always decreasing as the speed increases, and *vice versâ*. As a consequence, the angle is greatest when the speed is least.

When the wing reaches the point $b$ its speed is much less than it was at $q$. The wing is, in fact, preparing to reverse. At $c$ the wing is in the act of reversing (compare $c$ of figs. 84 and 85, p. 160), and, as a consequence, its speed is at a minimum, and the angle which it makes with the horizon at a maximum. At $d$ the wing is reversed, its speed being increased, and the angle which it makes with the horizon diminished. Between the letters $d$ and $u$ the wing darts suddenly up like a kite, and at $u$ it is in a position to commence the stroke from left to right, as indicated at $u$ of fig. 128, p. 250. The course described and the angles made by the wing with the horizon during the stroke from left to right are represented at fig. 128 (compare with figs. 68 and 70, p. 141). The stroke from left to right is in every respect the converse of the stroke from right to left, so that a separate description is unnecessary.

*The Artificial Wave Wing can be driven at any speed—it can make its own currents, or utilize existing ones.*—The remarkable feature in the artificial wave wing is its adaptability. It can be driven slowly, or with astonishing rapidity. It has no dead points. It reverses instantly, and in such a manner as to dissipate neither time nor power. It alternately seizes and evades the air so as to extract the maximum

of support with the minimum of slip, and the minimum
of force.  It supplies a degree of buoying and propelling
power which is truly remarkable.  Its buoying area is
nearly equal to half a circle.  It can act upon still air,
and it can create and utilize its own currents.  I proved this
in the following manner.  I caused the wing to make a
horizontal sweep from right to left over a candle ; the wing
rose steadily as a kite would, and after a brief interval, the
flame of the candle was persistently blown from right to left.
I then waited until the flame of the candle assumed its
normal perpendicular position, after which I caused the wing
to make another and opposite sweep from left to right.  The
wing again rose kite fashion, and the flame was a second time
affected, being blown in this case from left to right.  I now
caused the wing to vibrate steadily and rapidly above the
candle, with this curious result, that the flame did not incline
alternately from right to left and from left to right.  On the
contrary, it was blown steadily away from me, *i.e.* in the
direction of the tip of the wing, thus showing that the artificial currents made by the wing, met and neutralized each
other always at mid stroke.  I also found that under these
circumstances the buoying power of the wing was remarkably
increased.

*Compound rotation of the Artificial Wave Wing : the different
parts of the Wing travel at different speeds.*—The artificial
wave wing, like the natural wing, revolves upon two centres
(*a b, c d* of fig. 80, p. 149; fig. 83, p. 158, and fig. 122,
p. 239), and owes much of its elevating and propelling,
seizing, and disentangling power to its different portions
travelling at different rates of speed (see fig. 56, p. 120), and
to its storing up and giving off energy as it hastens to and
fro.  Thus the tip of the wing moves through a very much
greater space in a given time than the root, and so also of the
posterior margin as compared with the anterior.  This is
readily understood by bearing in mind that the root of the
wing forms the centre or axis of rotation for the tip, while
the anterior margin is the centre or axis of rotation for the
posterior margin.  The momentum, moreover, acquired by
the wing during the stroke from right to left *is expended in*

*reversing the wing*, and in preparing it for the stroke from left to right, and *vice versâ ;* a continuous to-and-fro movement devoid of dead points being thus established. If the artificial wave wing be taken in the hand and suddenly depressed *in a more or less vertical direction*, it immediately springs up again, and carries the hand with it. It, in fact, describes a curve whose convexity is directed downwards, and in doing so, carries the hand upwards and forwards. If a second down stroke be added, a second curve is formed ; the curves running into each other, and producing a progressive waved track similar to what is represented at *a, c, e, g, i,* of fig. 81, p. 157. This result is favoured if the operator runs forward so as not to impede or limit the action of the wing.

*How the Wave Wing creates currents, and rises upon them, and how the Air assists in elevating the Wing.*—In order to ascertain in what way the air contributes to the elevation of the wing, I made a series of experiments with natural

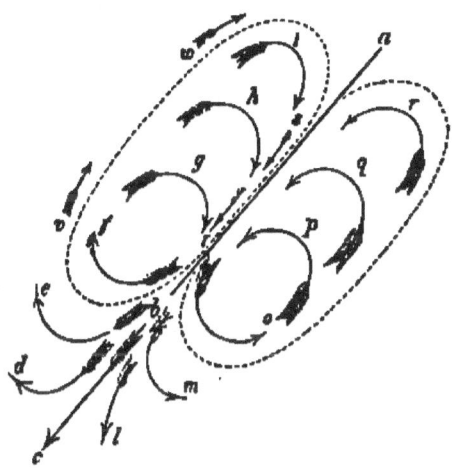

Fig. 139.

and artificial wings. These experiments led me to conclude that when the wing descends, as in the bat and bird, it compresses and pushes before it, in a downward and forward direction, a column of air represented by $a, b, c$ of fig. 129, p. 253.[1] The air rushes in from all sides to replace the displaced air, as shown at $d, e, f, g, h, i$, and so produces a circle of motion indicated by the dotted line $s, t, v, w$. The wing rises upon the outside of the circle referred to, as more particularly seen at $d, e, v, w$. The arrows, it will be observed, are all pointing upwards, and as these arrows indicate the direction of the reflex or back current, it is not difficult to comprehend how the air comes indirectly to assist in elevating the wing. A similar current is produced to the right of the figure, as indicated by $l, m, o, p, q, r$, but seeing the wing is always advancing, this need not be taken into account.

If fig. 129 be made to assume a horizontal position, instead of the oblique position which it at present occupies, the manner in which an *artificial current* is produced by one sweep of the wing from right to left, and utilized by it in a subsequent sweep from left to right, will be readily understood. The artificial wave wing makes a horizontal sweep from right to left, *i.e.* it passes from the point $a$ to the point $c$ of fig. 129. During its passage it has displaced a column of air. To fill the void so created, the air rushes in from all sides, viz. from $d, e, f, g, h, i$; $l, m, o, p, q, r$. The currents marked $g, h, i$; $p, q, r$, represent the reflex or *artificial currents*. These are the currents which, after a brief interval, force the flame of the candle from right to left. It is those same currents which the wing encounters, and which contribute so powerfully to its elevation, when it sweeps from left to right. The wing, when it rushes from left to right, produces a new series of artificial currents, which are equally powerful in elevating the wing when it passes a second time from right to left, and thus the process of making and utilizing currents goes on so long as the wing is made to oscillate. In waving the artificial wing to and fro, I found

---

[1] The artificial currents produced by the wing during its descent may be readily seen by partially filling a chamber with steam, smoke, or some impalpable white powder, and causing the wing to descend in its midst. By a little practice, the eye will not fail to detect the currents represented at $d, e, f, g, h, i, l, m, o, p, q, r$ of fig. 129, p. 253.

the best results were obtained when the range of the wing and the speed with which it was urged were so regulated as to produce a perfect reciprocation. Thus, if the range of the wing be great, the speed should also be high, otherwise the air set in motion by the right stroke will not be utilized by the left stroke, and *vice versâ.* If, on the other hand, the range of the wing be small, the speed should also be low, as the short stroke will enable the wing to reciprocate as perfectly as when the stroke is longer and the speed quicker. When the speed attained is high, the angles made by the under surface of the wing with the horizon are diminished ; when it is low, the angles are increased. From these remarks it will be evident that the artificial wave wing reciprocates in the same way that the natural wing reciprocates ; the reciprocation being most perfect when the wing is vibrating in a given spot, and least perfect when it is travelling at a high horizontal speed.

*The Artificial Wing propelled at various degrees of speed during the Down and Up Strokes.*—The tendency which the artificial wave wing has to rise again when suddenly and vigorously depressed, explains why the *elevator* muscles of the wing should be so small when compared with the *depressor* muscles—the latter being something like seven times larger than the former. That the contraction of the elevator muscles is necessary to the elevation of the wing, is abundantly proved by their presence, and that there should be so great a difference between the volume of the elevator and depressor muscles is not to be wondered at, when we remember that the whole weight of the body is to be elevated by the rapid descent of the wings—the descent of the wing being entirely due to the vigorous contraction of the powerful pectoral muscles. If, however, the wing was elevated with as great a force as it was depressed, no advantage would be gained, as the wing, during its ascent (it acts against gravity) would experience a much greater resistance from the air than it did during its descent. The wing is consequently elevated more slowly than it is depressed ; the elevator muscles exercising a controlling and restraining influence. By slowing the wing during the up stroke

the air has an opportunity of reacting on its under surface.

*The Artificial Wave Wing as a Propeller.*—The wave
wing makes an admirable propeller if its tip be directed
*vertically downwards,* and the wing lashed from side to side
with a sculling figure-of-8 motion, similar to that executed by
the tail of the fish. Three wave wings may be made to act
in concert, and with a very good result; two of them being
made to vibrate figure-of-8 fashion in a more or less horizontal
direction with a view to elevating; the third being turned in
a downward direction, and made to act vertically for the
purpose of propelling.

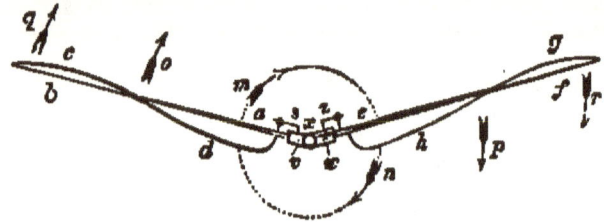

FIG. 130.—Aërial wave screw, whose blades are slightly twisted (*a b, c d,
e f, g h*), so that those portions nearest the root (*d h*) make a greater angle
with the horizon than those parts nearer the tip (*b f*). The angle is thus
adjusted to the speed attained by the different portions of the screw. The
angle admits of farther adjustment by means of the steel springs *r, s,*
these exercising a restraining, and to a certain extent a regulating, influence which effectually prevents shock.

It will be at once perceived from this figure that the portions of the screw
marked *u* and *t* travel at a much lower speed than those portions marked
*o* and *p,* and these again more slowly than those marked *q* and *r* (compare
with fig. 56, p. 120). As, however, the angle which a wing or a portion of
a wing, as I have pointed out, varies to accommodate itself to the speed
attained by the wing, or a portion thereof, it follows that to make the wave
screw mechanically perfect, the angles made by its several portions must
be accurately adapted to the travel of its several parts as indicated above.

*x,* Vertical tube for receiving driving shaft. *v, w,* Sockets in which the
roots of the blades of the screw rotate, the degree of rotation being limited
by the steel springs *r, s. a b, e f,* Tapering elastic reeds forming anterior or
thick margins of blades of screw. *d c, h g,* Posterior or thin elastic margins
of blades of screw. *m n, o p, q r,* Radii formed by the different portions of
the blades of the screw when in operation. The arrows indicate the direction of travel.—*Original.*

*A New Form of Aërial Screw.*—If two of the wave wings
represented at fig. 122, p. 239, be placed end to end, and
united to a vertical portion of tube to form a two-bladed
screw, similar to that employed in navigation, a most powerful
elastic aërial screw is at once produced, as seen at fig. 130.

This screw, which for the sake of uniformity I denominate *the aërial wave screw*, possesses advantages for aërial purposes to which no form of *rigid* screw yet devised can lay claim. The way in which it clings to the air during its revolution, and the degree of buoying power it possesses, are quite astonishing. It is a self-adjusting, self-regulating screw, and as its component parts are flexible and elastic, it accommodates itself to the speed at which it is driven, and gives a uniform buoyancy. The slip, I may add, is nominal in amount. This screw is exceedingly light, and owes its efficacy to its shape and the graduated nature of its blades; the anterior margin of each blade being comparatively rigid, the posterior margin being comparatively flexible and more or less elastic. The blades are kites in the same sense that natural wings are kites. They are flown as such when the screw revolves. I find that the aërial wave screw flies best and elevates most when its blades are inclined at a certain upward angle as indicated in the figure (130). The aërial wave screw may have the number of its blades increased by placing the one above the other; and two or more screws may be combined and made to revolve in opposite directions so as to make them reciprocate; the one screw producing the current on which the other rises, as happens in natural wings.

*The Aërial Wave Screw operates also upon Water.*—The form of screw just described is adapted in a marked manner for water, if the blades be reduced in size and composed of some elastic substance, which will resist the action of fluids, as gutta-percha, carefully tempered finely graduated steel plates, etc. It bears the same relation to, and produces the same results upon, water, as the tail and fin of the fish. It throws its blades during its action into double figure-of-8 curves, similar in all respects to those produced on the anterior and posterior margins of the natural and artificial flying wing. As the speed attained by the several portions of each blade varies, so the angle at which each part of the blade strikes varies; the angles being always greatest towards the root of the blade and least towards the tip. The angles made by the different portions of the blades are diminished in proportion as the

R

speed, with which the screw is driven, is increased. The screw in this manner is self-adjusting, and extracts a large percentage of propelling power, with very little force and surprisingly little slip.

A similar result is obtained if two finely graduated angular-shaped gutta-percha or steel plates be placed end to end and applied to the water (vertically or horizontally matters little), with a slight sculling figure-of-8 motion, analogous to that performed by the tail of the fish, porpoise, or whale. If the thick margin of the plates be directed forwards, and the thin ones backwards, an unusually effective propeller is produced. This form of propeller is likewise very effective in air.

---

## CONCLUDING REMARKS.

FROM the researches and experiments detailed in the present volume, it will be evident that a remarkable analogy exists between walking, swimming, and flying. It will further appear that the movements of the tail of the fish, and of the wing of the insect, bat, and bird can be readily imitated and reproduced. These facts ought to inspire the pioneer in aërial navigation with confidence. The land and water have already been successfully subjugated. The realms of the air alone are unvanquished. These, however, are so vast and so important as a highway for the nations, that science and civilisation equally demand their occupation. The history of artificial progression indorses the belief that the fields etherean will one day be traversed by a machine designed by human ingenuity, and constructed by human skill. In order to construct a successful flying machine, it is not necessary to reproduce the filmy wing of the insect, the silken pinion of the bat, or the complicated and highly differentiated wing of the bird, where every feather may be said

to have a peculiar function assigned to it; neither is it necessary to reproduce the intricacy of that machinery by which
the pinion in the bat, insect, and bird is moved: all that is
required is to distinguish the properties, form, extent, and
manner of application of the several flying surfaces, a task
attempted, however imperfectly executed, in the foregoing
pages. When Vivian and Trevithick devised the locomotive, and Symington and Bell the steamboat, they did
not seek to reproduce a quadruped or a fish; they simply
aimed at producing motion adapted to the land and
water, in accordance with natural laws, and in the presence of living models. Their success is to be measured by
an involved labyrinth of railway which extends to every
part of the civilized world; and by navies whose vessels are
despatched without trepidation to navigate the most boisterous
seas at the most inclement seasons. The aëronaut has a
similar but more difficult task to perform. In attempting to
produce a flying-machine he is not necessarily attempting
an impossible thing. The countless swarms of flying creatures testify as to the practicability of such an undertaking,
and nature supplies him at once with models and materials.
If artificial flight were not attainable, the insects, bats, and
birds would furnish the only examples of animals whose
movements could not be reproduced. History, analogy,
observation, and experiment are all opposed to this view.
The success of the locomotive and steamboat is an earnest
of the success of the flying machine. If the difficulties to
be surmounted in its construction are manifold, the triumph
and the reward will be correspondingly great. It is impossible to over-estimate the boon which would accrue to mankind
from such a creation. Of the many mechanical problems before
the world at present, perhaps there is none greater than that
of aërial navigation. Past failures are not to be regarded
as the harbingers of future defeats, for it is only within
the last few years that the subject of artificial flight has
been taken up in a true scientific spirit. Within a comparatively brief period an enormous mass of valuable data
has been collected. As societies for the advancement of aëronautics have been established in Britain, America, France,

and other countries, there is reason to believe that our
knowledge of this most difficult department of science will
go on increasing until the knotty problem is finally solved.
If this day should ever.come, it will not be too much to
affirm, that it will inaugurate a new era in the history of
mankind ; and that great as the destiny of our race has been
hitherto, it will be quite out-lustred by the grandeur and
magnitude of coming events.

# INDEX.

| | | PAGE |
|---|---|---|
| AERIAL creatures not stronger than terrestrial ones, | | 13 |
| Aërial flight as distinguished from sub-aquatic flight, | | 92 |
| Aëronautics, | | 209 |
| Air cells in insects and birds not necessary to flight, | | 115 |
| Albatross, flight of, compared to compass set upon gimbals, | | 199 |
| Amphibia have larger travelling surfaces than land animals, but less than aërial ones, | | 8 |
| Artificial fins, flippers, and wings, how constructed, | | 14 |
| Artificial wings, Borelli, | | 219 |
| Do. Marey, | | 226 |
| Do. Chabrier, | | 233 |
| Do. Straus-Durckheim, | | 233 |
| Do. how to apply to the air, | | 245 |
| Do. nature of forces required to propel, | | 246 |
| Artificial wave wing of Pettigrew, | | 236 |
| Do. how to construct on insect type, | | 240 |
| Do. how to construct to evade the superimposed air during the up stroke, | | 241 |
| Do. can create currents and rise upon them, | | 243 |
| Do. can be driven at any speed; can make new currents and utilize old ones, | 251, | 255 |
| Do. as a propeller and aërial screw, | | 256 |
| Do. compound rotation of: the different parts of the wing travel at different speeds, | | 252 |
| Do. necessity for supplying root of, with elastic structures, | | 247 |
| Artificial compound wave wing of Pettigrew, | | 242 |
| Atmospheric pressure, effects of, on limbs, | | 24 |
| Axioms, fundamental, | | 17 |
| | | |
| BALANCING, how effected in flight, | | 118 |
| Balloon, | | 210 |
| Bats and birds, lax condition of shoulder-joint in, | | 190 |
| Birds, lifting capacity of, | | 205 |
| Body and wing reciprocate in flight, and each describes a waved track, | | 12 |
| Bones, | | 21 |
| Bones of the extremities twisted and spiral, | 28, | 29 |
| Bones of wing of bat—spiral configuration of their articular surfaces, | | 176 |
| Bones of wing of bird—their articular surfaces, movements, etc., | | 178 |
| Borelli's artificial bird, | | 220 |
| | | |
| CHABRIER's artificial wings, | | 233 |

PAGE

ELYTRA or wing cases and membranous wings, . . . . 170

FEATHERS, primary, secondary, and tertiary, . . . . 160
Fins, flippers, and wings form mobile helices or screws, . . 14
Flight, weight necessary to, . . . . 3, 4, 110, 111, 112, 113
Flight the poetry of motion, . . . . . . 6
Flight the least fatiguing kind of motion, . . . . 13
Flight under water, . . . . . . . 90
Flight of the flying-fish, . . . . . . 98
Flight, horizontal, in part due to weight of flying mass, . . 110
Flight—the regular and irregular, . . . . . 201
Flight—how to ascend, descend, and turn, . . . . 201
Flight of birds referrible to muscular exertion and weight, . 204
Fluids, mechanical effects of, on animals immersed in them, . 18
Fluids, resistance of, . . . . . . . 18
Flying machine, Henson, . . . . . . 212
    Do.        Stringfellow, . . . . . 213
    Do.        Cayley, . . . . . . 215
    Do.        Phillips, . . . . . . 216
    Do.        M. de la Landelle, . . . . 217
    Do.        Borelli, . . . . . . 218
A flying machine possible, . . . . . . 2, 3
Forces which propel the wings of insects, bats, and birds, . 186, 189
Fulcra, yielding, . . . . . . 3, 104, 165

GRAVITY, the legs move by the force of, . . . . 18
Gravity, centre of, . . . . . . . 18

HISTORY of the figure-of-8 theory of walking, swimming, and flying, . 15

JOINTS, . . . . . . . . . 23

KITE-LIKE action of the wings, . . . . . . 98
Kite—how kite formed by wing differs from boy's kite, . . 165

Laws of natural and artificial progression the same, . . 4, 17
Legs, moved by the force of gravity, . . . . . 18
Lever—the wing one of the third order, . . . . 103
Levers, the three orders of, . . . . . . 19
Life linked to motion, . . . . . . . 1
Lifting capacity of birds, . . . . . . 205
Ligaments, . . . . . . . . 24
Ligaments, elastic, position and action of, in wing of pheasant, snipe,
    crested crane, swan, etc., . . . . . . 191
Ligaments, elastic, more highly differentiated in wings which vibrate
    quickly, . . . . . . . . 193
Locomotion, the active organs of, . . . . . 24
Locomotion, the passive organs of, . . . . . 21
Locomotion of the horse, . . . . . . 39
Locomotion of the ostrich, . . . . . . 45
Locomotion of man, . . . . . . . 51

MAREY's artificial wings, . . . . . . 233
Membranous wings, . . . . . . . 170
Motion associated with the life and well-being of animals, . 1
Motion not confined to the animal kingdom, . . . . 2
Motion, natural and artificial, . . . . . . 4

| | PAGE |
|---|---|
| Motion, of uniform, | 17 |
| Motion uniformly varied, | 17 |
| Muscles, their properties, mode of action, etc., | 24 |
| Muscles arranged in longitudinal, transverse, and oblique spiral lines, | 29 |
| Muscles, oblique spiral, necessary for spiral bones and joints, | 31 |
| Muscles take precedence of bones in animal movements, | 29 |
| Muscular cycles, | 26 |
| Muscular waves, | 26 |
| | |
| PENDULUMS, the extremities of animals act as, in walking, | 9, 18, 66, 67 |
| Plane, inclined, as applied to the air, | 211 |
| Pettigrew's method of constructing and applying artificial wings as contradistinguished from that of Borelli, Chabrier, Durckheim, Marey, etc., | 235 |
| Pettigrew's wave wing, | 236 |
| Pettigrew's compound wave wing, | 242 |
| Progression on the land, | 37 |
| Do.   on or in the water, | 61 |
| Do.   in or through the air, | 103 |
| | |
| QUADRUPEDS walk, fishes swim, and insects, bats, and birds fly, by figure-of-8 movements, | 15, 16 |
| | |
| SCREWS—the wing of the bird and the extremity of the biped and quadruped screws, structurally and functionally, | 12 |
| Screws—difference between those formed by the wings and those employed in navigation, | 151 |
| Sculling action of the wing, | 231 |
| Speed attained by insects, | 188 |
| Speed of wing movements partly accounted for, | 190 |
| Spine, spiral movements of, transferred to the extremities, | 33 |
| Sirens-Durckheim's artificial wings, | 233 |
| Swimming of the fish, whale, porpoise, etc., | 66 |
| Swimming of the seal, sea-bear, and walrus, | 74 |
| Swimming of man, | 78 |
| Swimming of the turtle, triton, crocodile, etc., | 82 |
| | |
| TERRESTRIAL animals have smaller travelling surfaces than amphibia, amphibia than fishes, and fishes than insects, bats, and birds, | 8 |
| The travelling surfaces of animals increase as the density of the media traversed decreases, | 7, 8 |
| The travelling surfaces of animals variously modified and adapted to the media on or in which they move, | 34 |
| | |
| WALKING, swimming, and flying correlated, | 6 |
| Walking of the quadruped, biped, etc., | 9, 10, 11 |
| Wave wing of Pettigrew, | 236 |
| Do.   how to construct on insect type, | 240 |
| Do.   how to construct to evade the superimposed air during the up stroke, | 241 |
| Do.   can be driven at any speed, | 251, 245 |
| Do.   can create currents and rise upon them, | 253 |
| Do.   can make new currents and utilize existing ones, | 251, 255 |
| Do.   as a propeller, | 255 |
| Do.   as an aerial screw, | 256 |
| Do.   forces required to apply to the air, | 245, 246 |
| Do.   necessity for supplying root of, with elastic structures, | 247 |

PAGE

Wave wing, *compound*, . . . . . . . 212
Weight necessary to flight, . . . . . . 110
Weight contributes to flight, . . . . . . 112
Weight, momentum, and power to a certain extent synonymous in
   flight, . . . . . . . . . . 111
The wing of the bird and the extremity of the biped and quadruped are
   screws, structurally and functionally, . . . . 12, 136
Wing in flight describes figure-of-8 curves, . . . . 12
Wing during its action reverses its planes and describes a figure-of-8
   track in space, . . . . . . . . 140
Wing when advancing with the body describes looped and waved tracks, 143
Wing, margins of, thrown into opposite curves during extension and
   flexion, . . . . . . . . . . 146
Wing, tip of, describes an ellipse, . . . . . . 147
Wing and body reciprocate in flight, and each describes a wave track, 12
Wing moves in opposite curves to body, . . . . . 168
Wing ascends when body descends, and *vice versâ*, . . . 159
Wing during its vibrations produces a cross pulsation, . . . 148
Wing vibrates unequally with reference to a given line, . . 150, 231
Wing, compound rotation of, . . . . . . . 149
Wing a lever of the third order, . . . . . . 109
Wing acts on yielding fulcra, . . . . . . 8, 104, 165
Wings, their form, etc., all wings screws, structurally and functionally, 136
Wing capable of change of form in all its parts, . . . 147
Wing-area variable and in excess, . . . . . . 124
Wing-area decreases as the size and weight of the volant animal in-
   creases, . . . . . . . . . . 132
Wing, natural, when elevated and depressed must move forwards, . 166
Wing, angles formed by, when in action, . . . . . 167
Wing acts as true kite both during down and up strokes, . . 165
Wing, traces of design in, . . . . . . . 160
Wing of bird not always opened up to same extent in up stroke, . 182
Wing, flexion of, necessary to flight of birds, . . . . 183
Wing flexed and partly elevated by action of elastic ligaments, . 191
Wing, power of, to what owing, . . . . . . 191
Wing, effective stroke of, why delivered downwards and forwards, . 195
Wing acts as an elevator, propeller, and sustainer both during exten-
   sion and flexion, . . . . . . . . 197
Wings, points wherein the screws formed by, differ from those in ordi-
   nary use, . . . . . . . . . . 151
Wings at all times thoroughly under control, . . . . 154
Wings of insects, consideration of forces which propel, . . 186
Wings of bats and birds, consideration of forces which propel, . 189

PRINTED BY T. AND A. CONSTABLE, PRINTERS TO HER MAJESTY,
AT THE EDINBURGH UNIVERSITY PRESS.

# A CLASSIFIED CATALOGUE OF
# HENRY S. KING & CO.'S PUBLICATIONS.

## CONTENTS.

| | PAGE | | PAGE |
|---|---|---|---|
| HISTORY AND BIOGRAPHY | 1 | INDIA AND THE EAST | 19 |
| VOYAGES AND TRAVEL | 5 | BOOKS FOR THE YOUNG, &c. | 21 |
| SCIENCE | 7 | POETRY | 24 |
| ESSAYS, LECTURES, AND COL- | | FICTION | 26 |
| LECTED PAPERS | 12 | THEOLOGICAL | 31 |
| MILITARY WORKS | 15 | CORNHILL LIBRARY OF FICTION | 36 |

## HISTORY AND BIOGRAPHY.

**THE NORMAN PEOPLE,** AND THEIR EXISTING DESCENDANTS IN THE BRITISH DOMINIONS AND THE UNITED STATES OF AMERICA. One handsome vol. 8vo. Price 21s. *[In the Press.*

This work is the result of many years of research into the history of the Norman race in England. It is generally supposed to have become extinct; but careful study has shown that it exists and forms a large part of the English people. In the course of the work the early history of the whole aristocracy is revised, reconstructed, and very many thousands of families are shown to be Norman which have never before been accounted for.

**A MEMOIR OF THE LATE REVEREND DR. ROWLAND WILLIAMS,** With selections from his Note-books and Correspondence. Edited by **Mrs. Rowland Williams.** With a Photographic Portrait. *[In the Press.*

**THE RUSSIANS IN CENTRAL ASIA.** A Critical Examination, down to the present time, of the Geography and History of Central Asia. By **Baron F. Von Hellwald,** Member of the Geographical Societies of Paris, Geneva, Vienna, &c., &c. Translated by **Lieut.-Col. Theodore Wirgman, LL.B.,** late 6th Inniskilling Dragoons; formerly of the Austrian Service; Translator into English verse of Schiller's " Wallenstein's Camp." *[Nearly ready.*

65, Cornhill; & 12, Paternoster Row, London.

### HISTORY AND BIOGRAPHY—*continued.*

**THE GOVERNMENT OF THE NATIONAL DEFENCE.** From the 30th June to the 31st October, 1870. The Plain Statement of a Member. By **Mons. Jules Favre.** 1 vol. Demy 8vo. 10s. 6d.

**BOKHARA: ITS HISTORY AND CONQUEST.** By **Professor Arminius Vámbéry,** of the University of Pesth, Author of "Travels in Central Asia," &c. Demy 8vo. Price 18s.

"We conclude with a cordial recommendation of this valuable book. In the present work his moderation, scholarship, insight, and occasionally very impressive style, have raised him to the dignity of an historian."—*Saturday Review.*

"Almost every page abounds with composition of peculiar merit, as well as with an account of some thrilling event more exciting than any to be found in an ordinary work of fiction."—*Morning Post.*

**THE RELIGIOUS HISTORY OF IRELAND:** PRIMITIVE, PAPAL, AND PROTESTANT; including the Evangelical Missions, Catholic Agitations, and Church Progress of the last half century. By **James Godkin,** Author of "Ireland, her Churches," &c. 1 vol. 8vo. Price 12s.

"For those who shun blue books, and yet desire some of the information they contain, these latter chapters on the statistics of the various religious denominations will be welcomed."—*Evening Standard.*

"Mr. Godkin writes with evident honesty, and the topic on which he writes is one about which an honest book is greatly wanted."—*Examiner.*

**ILÁM ÉN NÁS.** Historical Tales and Anecdotes of the Times of the Early Khalifahs. Translated from the Arabic Originals. By **Mrs. Godfrey Clerk,** Author of "The Antipodes and Round the World." Crown 8vo. Price 7s.

"But there is a high tone about them, a love of justice, of truth and integrity, a sense of honour and manliness, and a simple devotion to religious duty, which however mistaken according to our lights, is deserving of every respect. The translation is the work of a lady, and a very excellent and scholar-like translation it is, clearly and pleasantly written, and

illustrated and explained by copious notes, indicating considerable learning and research."—*Saturday Review.*
"Those who like stories full of the genuine colour and fragrance of the East, should by all means read Mrs. Godfrey Clerk's volume."—*Spectator.*
"As full of valuable information as it is of amusing incident."—*Evening Standard.*

**ECHOES OF A FAMOUS YEAR.** By **Harriet Parr,** Author of "The Life of Jeanne d'Arc," "In the Silver Age," &c. Crown 8vo. 8s. 6d.

"A graceful and touching, as well as truthful account of the Franco-Prussian War. Those who are in the habit of reading books to children will find this at once instructive and delightful."—*Public Opinion.*

"Miss Parr has the great gift of charming simplicity of style; and if children are not interested in her book, many of their seniors will be."—*British Quarterly Review.*

**ALEXIS DE TOCQUEVILLE.** Correspondence and Conversations with NASSAU W. SENIOR from 1833 to 1859. Edited by **Mrs. M. C. M. Simpson.** In 2 vols., large post 8vo. 21s.

"Another of those interesting Journals in which Mr. Senior has, as it were, crystallised the sayings of some of those many remarkable men with whom he came in contact."—*Morning Post.*

"A book replete with knowledge and thought."—*Quarterly Review.*
"An extremely interesting book."—*Saturday Review.*

**JOURNALS KEPT IN FRANCE AND ITALY.** From 1848 to 1852. With a Sketch of the Revolution of 1848. By the late **Nassau William Senior.** Edited by his Daughter, **M. C. M. Simpson.** In 2 vols., post 8vo. 24s.

"The book has a genuine historical value."—*Saturday Review.*
"The present volume gives us conversations with some of the most prominent men in the political history of France and Italy. . . . Mr. Senior has the art of inspiring all men with frankness, and of persuading

them to put themselves unreservedly in his hands without fear of private circulation."—*Athenæum.*
"No better, more honest, and more readable view of the state of political society during the existence of the second Republic could well be looked for."—*Examiner.*

**POLITICAL WOMEN.** By **Sutherland Menzies.** 2 vols. Post 8vo Price 24s.

"Has all the information of history, with all the interest that attaches to biography."—*Scotsman.*
"A graceful contribution to the lighter record of history."—*English Churchman.*

"No author could have stated the case more temperately than he has done, and few could have placed before the reader so graphically the story which had to be told."—*Leeds Mercury.*

**SARA COLERIDGE, MEMOIR AND LETTERS OF.** Edited by her **Daughters.** 2 vols. Crown 8vo. With 2 Portraits. Price 24s. Second Edition, Revised and Corrected.

"We have read these two volumes with genuine gratification."—*Hour.*
"We could have wished to give specimens of her very just, subtle, and concise criticisms on authors of every sort and time —poets, moralists, historians, and philosophers. Sara Coleridge, as she is revealed, or rather reveals herself, in the correspondence, makes a brilliant addition to a brilliant family reputation."—*Saturday Review.*

"These charming volumes are attractive in two ways: first, as a memorial of a most amiable woman of high intellectual mark; and secondly, as rekindling recollections, and adding a little to our information regarding the life of Sara Coleridge's father, the poet and philosopher."—*Athenæum.*
"An acceptable record, and present an adequate image of a mind of singular beauty and no inconsiderable power."—*Examiner.*

**PHANTASMION.** A Fairy Romance. By **Sara Coleridge.**

[*In preparation.*

HISTORY AND BIOGRAPHY—*continued.*

**LEONORA CHRISTINA, MEMOIRS OF,** Daughter of Christian IV. of Denmark: Written during her Imprisonment in the Blue Tower of the Royal Palace at Copenhagen, 1663—1685. Translated by **F. E. Bunnett,** Translator of Grimm's "Life of Michael Angelo," &c. With an Autotype Portrait of the Princess. Medium 8vo. 12*s.* 6*d.*

"A valuable addition to history."— *Daily News.*
"This remarkable autobiography, in
which we gratefully recognise a valuable addition to the tragic romance of history." —*Spectator.*

**THE LATE REV. F. W. ROBERTSON, M.A., LIFE AND LETTERS OF.** Edited by **Stopford Brooke, M.A.,** Chaplain in Ordinary to the Queen. In 2 vols., uniform with the Sermons. Price 7*s.* 6*d.* Library Edition, in demy 8vo, with Two Steel Portraits. 12*s.* A Popular Edition, in 1 vol. Price 6*s.*

**NATHANIEL HAWTHORNE, A MEMOIR OF,** with Stories now first published in this country. By **H. A. Page.** Large post 8vo. 7*s.* 6*d.*

"The Memoir is followed by a criticism of Hawthorne as a writer; and the criticism is, on the whole, very well written, and exhibits a discriminating enthusiasm for one of the most fascinating of novelists."— *Saturday Review.*
"Seldom has it been our lot to meet with a more appreciative delineation of character
than this Memoir of Hawthorne."—*Morning Post.*
"He has done full justice to the fine character of the author of 'The Scarlet Letter.'"—*Standard.*
"A model of literary work of art."— *Edinburgh Courant.*

**LIVES OF ENGLISH POPULAR LEADERS.** No. 1.—STEPHEN LANGTON. By C. **Edmund Maurice.** Crown 8vo. 7*s.* 6*d.*

"Mr. Maurice has written a very interesting book, which may be read with equal pleasure and profit."—*Morning Post.*
"The volume contains many interesting
details, including some important documents. It will amply repay those who read it, whether as a chapter of the constitutional history of England or as the life of a great Englishman."—*Spectator.*

**CABINET PORTRAITS.** BIOGRAPHICAL SKETCHES OF LIVING STATESMEN. By **T. Wemyss Reid.** 1 vol. crown 8vo. 7*s.* 6*d.*

"We have never met with a work which we can more unreservedly praise. The sketches are absolutely impartial."— *Athenæum.*
"We can heartily commend his work." —*Standard.*
"The 'Sketches of Statesmen' are drawn with a master hand."—*Yorkshire Post.*

## VOYAGES AND TRAVEL.

**ROUGH NOTES OF A VISIT TO BELGIUM, SEDAN, AND PARIS,** In September, 1870—71. By John Ashton. Crown 8vo, bevelled boards. Price 3*s.* 6*d.*

This little volume derives its chief interest from the accurate descriptions of the scenes visited during the recent struggle on the Continent.

**THE ALPS OF ARABIA;** or, Travels through Egypt, Sinai, Arabia, and the Holy Land. By William Charles Maughan. 1 vol. Demy 8vo, with Map. Price 10*s.* 6*d.*

A volume of simple "impressions de voyage"—but written in pleasant and interesting style.

**THE MISHMEE HILLS:** an Account of a Journey made in an Attempt to Penetrate Tibet from Assam, to open New Routes for Commerce. By T. T. Cooper, author of "The Travels of a Pioneer of Commerce." Demy 8vo. Illustrated.

**THE PEARL OF THE ANTILLES;** The Artist in Cuba. By Walter Goodman. Crown 8vo. 7*s.* 6*d.*

"A good-sized volume, delightfully vivid and picturesque. . . . Several chapters devoted to the characteristics of the people are exceedingly interesting and remarkable. . . . The whole book deserves the heartiest commendation . . . sparkling and amusing from beginning to end. Reading it is like rambling about with a companion who is content to loiter, observing everything, commenting upon everything, turning everything into a picture, with a cheerful flow of spirits, full of fun, but far above frivolity."—*Spectator.*

"He writes very lightly and pleasantly, and brightens his pages with a good deal of humour. His experiences were varied enough, and his book contains a series of vivid and miscellaneous sketches. We can recommend his whole volume as very amusing reading."—*Pall Mall Gazette.*

**FIELD AND FOREST RAMBLES OF A NATURALIST IN NEW BRUNSWICK.** With Notes and Observations on the Natural History of Eastern Canada. By A. Leith Adams, M.A., &c., Author of "Wanderings of a Naturalist in India," &c., &c. In 8vo, cloth. Illustrated. 14*s.*

"Will be found interesting by those who take a pleasure either in sport or natural history."—*Athenæum.*

"The descriptions are clear and full of interest, while the book is prevented from degenerating into a mere scientific catalogue by many graphic sketches of the rambles."—*John Bull.*

"To the naturalist the book will be most valuable. . . . To the general reader the book will prove most interesting, for the style is pleasant and chatty, and the information given is so graphic and full, that those who care nothing for natural history as a pursuit will yet read these descriptions with great interest."—*Evening Standard.*

"Both sportsmen and naturalists will find this work replete with anecdote and carefully-recorded observation, which will entertain them."—*Nature.*

**TENT LIFE WITH ENGLISH GIPSIES IN NORWAY.** By Hubert Smith. In 8vo, cloth. Five full-page Engravings, and 31 smaller Illustrations, with Map of the Country showing Routes. Price 21*s.*

"If any of our readers think of scraping an acquaintance with Norway, let them read this book. The gypsies, always an interesting study, become doubly interesting, when we are, as in these pages, introduced to them in their daily walk and conversation."—*Examiner.*

"Written in a very lively style, and has throughout a smack of dry humour and satiric reflection which shows the writer to be a keen observer of men and things. We hope that many will read it and find in it the same amusement as ourselves."—*Times.*

VOYAGES AND TRAVEL—*continued.*

**FAYOUM; OR, ARTISTS IN EGYPT.** A Tour with M. Gérôme and others. By J. Lenoir. Crown 8vo, cloth. Illustrated. 7s. 6d.

"A pleasantly written and very readable book."—*Examiner.*

"The book is very amusing. . . . Who-

ever may take it up will find he has with him a bright and pleasant companion."—*Spectator.*

**SPITZBERGEN THE GATEWAY TO THE POLYNIA; OR, A VOYAGE TO SPITZBERGEN.** By Captain John C. Wells, R.N. In 8vo, cloth. Profusely Illustrated. Price 21s.

"Straightforward and clear in style, securing our confidence by its unaffected simplicity and good sense."—*Saturday Review.*

"A charming book, remarkably well written and well illustrated."—*Standard.*

"Blends pleasantly science with adventure, picturesque sketches of a summer cruise among the wild sports and fantastic scenery of Spitsbergen, with earnest advocacy of Arctic Exploration."—*Graphic.*

**AN AUTUMN TOUR IN THE UNITED STATES AND CANADA.** By Lieut.-Colonel Julius George Medley. Crown 8vo. Price 5s.

"Colonel Medley's little volume is a pleasantly written account of a two-months' visit to America."—*Hour.*

"May be recommended as manly, sensible, and pleasantly written."—*Globe.*

**THE NILE WITHOUT A DRAGOMAN.** By Frederic Eden. Second Edition. In one vol. Crown 8vo, cloth. 7s. 6d.

"Should any of our readers care to imitate Mr. Eden's example, and wish to see things with their own eyes, and shift for themselves, next winter in Upper Egypt, they will find this book a very agreeable guide."—*Times.*

"It is a book to read during an autumn holiday."—*Spectator.*

"Gives, within moderate compass, a suggestive description of the charms, curiosities, dangers, and discomforts of the Nile voyage."—*Saturday Review.*

**ROUND THE WORLD IN 1870.** A Volume of Travels, with Maps. By A. D. Carlisle, B.A., Trin. Coll., Camb. Demy 8vo. 16s.

"Makes one understand how going round the world is to be done in the quickest and pleasantest manner."—*Spectator.*

"We can only commend, which we do very heartily, an eminently sensible and readable book."—*British Quarterly Review.*

**IRELAND IN 1872.** A Tour of Observation, with Remarks on Irish Public Questions. By Dr. James Macaulay. Crown 8vo. 7s. 6d.

"A careful and instructive book. Full of facts, full of information, and full of interest."—*Literary Churchman.*

"We have rarely met a book on Ireland which for impartiality of criticism and general accuracy of information could be

so well recommended to the fair-minded Irish reader."—*Evening Standard.*

"A deeply interesting account of what is called a tour of observation, and some noteworthy remarks on Irish public questions."—*Illustrated London News.*

**OVER THE DOVREFJELDS.** By J. S. Shepard, Author of "A Ramble through Norway," &c. Crown 8vo, Illustrated. Price 4s. 6d.

"We have read many books of Norwegian travel, but . . . we have seen none so pleasantly narrative in its style, and so varied in its subject."—*Spectator.*

"Is a well-timed book."—*Echo.*

"As interesting a little volume as could be written on the subject. So interesting and shortly written that it will commend itself to all intending tourists."—*Examiner.*

**A WINTER IN MOROCCO.** By Amelia Perrier. Large crown 8vo. Illustrated. Price 10s. 6d.

"Well worth reading, and contains several excellent illustrations."—*Hour.*

"Miss Perrier is a very amusing writer. She has a good deal of humour, has the

oddity and quaintness of Oriental life with a quick observant eye, and evidently turned her opportunities of sarcastic examination to account."—*Daily News.*

## SCIENCE.

**PRINCIPLES OF MENTAL PHYSIOLOGY.** With their Applications to the Training and Discipline of the Mind, and the Study of its Morbid Conditions. By **W. B. Carpenter, LL.D., M.D., F.R.S., &c.** 8vo. Illustrated. [*Immediately.*]

**THE EXPANSE OF HEAVEN.** A Series of Essays on the Wonders of the Firmament. By **R. A. Proctor, B.A.,** author of "Other Worlds," &c. Small Crown 8vo. [*Shortly.*]

**STUDIES OF BLAST FURNACE PHENOMENA.** By **M. L. Gruner,** President of the General Council of Mines of France. Translated by **L. D. B. Gordon, F.R.S.E., F.G.S., &c.** Demy 8vo. Price 7*s.* 6*d.*

These are some important practical studies by one of the most eminent metallurgical authorities of the Continent.

**A LEGAL HANDBOOK FOR ARCHITECTS.** By **Edward Jenkins** and **John Raymond, Esqrs.,** Barristers-at-Law. In 1 vol. Price 6*s.*

The Publishers are assured that this book will constitute an invaluable and necessary companion for every architect's and builder's table, as well as a useful introduction for architects' pupils to the practical law of their profession. Dedicated by special permission to the Royal Institution of British Architects.

**CONTEMPORARY ENGLISH PSYCHOLOGY.** From the French of **Professor Th. Ribot.** An Analysis of the Views and Opinions of the following Metaphysicians, as expressed in their writings:—

James Mill, A. Bain, John Stuart Mill, George H. Lewes, Herbert Spencer, Samuel Bailey. Large post 8vo.

**PHYSIOLOGY FOR PRACTICAL USE.** By various Eminent writers. Edited by **James Hinton.** 2 vols. Crown 8vo. With 50 illustrations.

These Papers have been prepared at great pains, and their endeavour is to familiarise the popular mind with those physiological truths which are needful to all who desire to keep the body in a state of health. [*In the Press.*]

**THE PLACE OF THE PHYSICIAN.** The Introductory Lecture at Guy's Hospital, 1873-4; to which is added

ESSAYS ON THE LAW OF HUMAN LIFE AND ON THE RELATION BETWEEN ORGANIC AND INORGANIC WORLDS.

By **James Hinton,** Author of "Man and His Dwelling-Place." Crown 8vo. Limp cloth.

SCIENCE—*continued.*

**THE HISTORY OF THE NATURAL CREATION**, Being a Series of Popular Scientific Lectures on the General Theory of Progression of Species ; with a Dissertation on the Theories of Darwin and Goethe ; more especially applying them to the Origin of Man, and to other Fundamental Questions of Natural Science connected therewith. By Professor **Ernst Haeckel**, of the University of Jena. 8vo. With Woodcuts and Plates.
[*In the Press.*]

Second Edition.

**CHANGE OF AIR AND SCENE.** A Physician's Hints about Doctors, Patients, Hygiène, and Society ; with Notes of Excursions for health in the Pyrenees, and amongst the Watering-places of France (Inland and Seaward), Switzerland, Corsica, and the Mediterranean. By **Dr. Alphonse Donné.** Large post 8vo. Price 9s.

"A very readable and serviceable book. . . . The real value of it is to be found in the accurate and minute information given with regard to a large number of places which have gained a reputation on the continent for their mineral waters."—*Pall Mall Gazette.*
"A singularly pleasant and chatty as well as instructive book about health."—*Guardian.*

**MISS YOUMANS' FIRST BOOK OF BOTANY.** Designed to cultivate the observing powers of Children. From the Author's latest Stereotyped Edition. New and Enlarged Edition, with 300 Engravings. Crown 8vo. 5s.

"It is but rarely that a school-book appears which is at once so novel in plan, so successful in execution, and so suited to the general want, as to command universal and unqualified approbation, but such has been the case with Miss Youmans' First Book of Botany. . . . It has been everywhere welcomed as a timely and invaluable contribution to the improvement of primary education."—*Pall Mall Gazette.*

**AN ARABIC AND ENGLISH DICTIONARY OF THE KORAN.** By **Major J. Penrice, B.A.** 4to. Price 21s.

**MODERN GOTHIC ARCHITECTURE.** By **T. G. Jackson.** Crown 8vo. Price 5s.

"The reader will find some of the most important doctrines of eminent art teachers practically applied in this little book, which is well written and popular in style."—*Manchester Examiner.*
"Much clearness, force, wealth of illus-
tration, and in style of composition, which tends to commend his views."—*Edinburgh Daily Review.*
"This thoughtful little book is worthy of the perusal of all interested in art or architecture."—*Standard.*

**A TREATISE ON RELAPSING FEVER.** By **R. T. Lyons,** Assistant-Surgeon, Bengal Army. Small post 8vo. 7s. 6d.

"A practical work thoroughly supported in its views by a series of remarkable cases."—*Standard.*

## FOUR WORKS BY DR. EDWARD SMITH.

I. **HEALTH AND DISEASE,** as influenced by the Daily, Seasonal and other Cyclical Changes in the Human System. A New Edit. 7*s.* 6*d.*

II. **FOODS.** Second Edition, Profusely Illustrated. Price 5*s.*

III. **PRACTICAL DIETARY FOR FAMILIES, SCHOOLS, AND THE LABOURING CLASSES.** A New Edit. Price 3*s.* 6*d.*

IV. **CONSUMPTION IN ITS EARLY AND REMEDIABLE STAGES.** A New Edit. 7*s.* 6*d.*

---

**THE PORT OF REFUGE**; OR, COUNSEL AND AID TO SHIPMASTERS IN DIFFICULTY, DOUBT, OR DISTRESS. By **Manley Hopkins,** Author of "A Handbook of Average," "A Manual of Insurance," &c. Cr. 8vo. Price 6*s.*

SUBJECTS:—The Shipmaster's Position and Duties.—Agents and Agency.—Average.—Bottomry, and other Means of Raising Money.—The Charter-Party, and Bill-of-Lading, Stoppage in Transitu; and the Shipowner's Lien.—Collision.

"Combines in quite a marvellous manner a fullness of information which will make it perfectly indispensable in the captain's bookcase, and equally suitable to the gentleman's library. This synopsis of the law of shipping in all its multifarious ramifications and the hints he gives on a variety of topics must be invaluable to the master mariner whenever he is in doubt, difficulty, and danger."—*Mercantile Marine Magazine.*

"A truly excellent contribution to the literature of our marine commerce."—*Echo.*

"Those immediately concerned will find it well worth while to avail themselves of its teachings."—*Colburn's U.S. Magazine.*

**LOMBARD STREET.** A Description of the Money Market. By **Walter Bagehot.** Large crown 8vo. Third Edition. 7*s.* 6*d.*

"An acceptable addition to the literature of finance."—*Stock Exchange Review.*

"Mr. Bagehot touches incidentally a hundred points connected with his subject, and pours serene white light upon them all."—*Spectator.*

"Anybody who wishes to have a clear idea of the workings of what is called the Money Market should procure a little volume which Mr. Bagehot has just published, and he will there find the whole thing in a nut-shell. . . . The subject is one, it is almost needless to say, on which Mr. Bagehot writes with the authority of a man who combines practical experience with scientific study."—*Saturday Review.*

"Besides its main topic, the management of the reserve of the Bank of England, it is full of the most interesting economic history."—*Athenæum.*

**CHOLERA: HOW TO AVOID AND TREAT IT.** Popular and Practical Notes by **Henry Blanc, M.D.** Crown 8vo. 4*s.* 6*d.*

---

## THE INTERNATIONAL SCIENTIFIC SERIES.

Although these Works are not specially designed for the instruction of beginners, still, as they are intended to address the *non-scientific public*, they are, as far as possible, explanatory in character, and free from technicalities; the object of each author being to bring his subject as near as he can to the general reader.

Th: Volumes already Published are:—

*Third Edition.*

**THE FORMS OF WATER IN RAIN AND RIVERS, ICE AND GLACIERS.** By J. Tyndall, LL.D., F.R.S. With 26 Illustrations. Crown 8vo. 5*s.*

"One of Professor Tyndall's best scientific treatises."—*Standard.*
"With the clearness and brilliancy of language which have won for him his fame, he considers the subject of ice, snow, and glaciers."—*Morning Post.*

"Before starting for Switzerland next summer every one should study 'The forms of water.'"—*Globe.*
"Eloquent and instructive in an eminent degree."—*British Quarterly.*

*Second Edition.*

**PHYSICS AND POLITICS;** OR, THOUGHTS ON THE APPLICATION OF THE PRINCIPLES OF "NATURAL SELECTION" AND "INHERITANCE" TO POLITICAL SOCIETY. By Walter Bagehot. Crown 8vo. 4*s.*

"On the whole we can recommend the book as well deserving to be read by thoughtful students of politics."—*Saturday Review.*

"Able and ingenious."—*Spectator.*
"A work of really original and interesting speculation."—*Guardian.*

*Second Edition.*

**FOODS.** By Dr. Edward Smith. Profusely Illustrated. Price 5*s.*

"A comprehensive résumé of our present chemical and physiological knowledge of the various foods, solid and liquid, which go so far to ameliorate the troubles and vexations of this anxious and wearying existence."—*Chemist and Druggist.*

"Heads of households will find it considerably to their advantage to study its contents."—*Court Express.*
"A very comprehensive book. Every page teems with information. Readable throughout."—*Church Herald.*

*Second Edition.*

**MIND AND BODY:** THE THEORIES OF THEIR RELATIONS. By Alexander Bain, LL.D., Professor of Logic at the University of Aberdeen. Four Illustrations. 4*s.*

**THE STUDY OF SOCIOLOGY.** By Herbert Spencer. Crown 8vo. Price 5*s.*

**ON THE CONSERVATION OF ENERGY.** By Professor Balfour Stewart. Fourteen Engravings. Price 5*s.*

**ANIMAL MECHANICS;** or, Walking, Swimming, and Flying. By Dr. J. B. Pettigrew, M.D., F.R.S.

## LIST OF AUTHORS AND SUBJECTS OF THEIR BOOKS,

### TO BE PUBLISHED IN THE

## INTERNATIONAL SCIENTIFIC SERIES.

**Dr. HENRY MAUDSLEY.**
Responsibility in Mental Disease.

**Prof. E. J. MAREY.**
The Animal Frame.

**{ Rev. M. J. BERKELEY, M.A., F.L.S., and M. COOKE, M.A., LL.D.**
Fungi: their Nature, Influences, and Uses.

**Prof. OSCAR SCHMIDT.**
(University of Strasburg).
The Theory of Descent and Darwinism.

**Prof. W. KINGDOM CLIFFORD, M.A.**
The First Principles of the Exact Sciences
explained to the non-mathematical.

**Prof. T. H. HUXLEY, LL.D., F.R.S.**
Bodily Motion and Consciousness.

**Dr. W. B. CARPENTER, LL.D., F.R.S.**
The Physical Geography of the Sea.

**Prof. WILLIAM ODLING, F.R.S.**
The New Chemistry.

**Prof. SHELDON AMOS.**
The Science of Law.

**W. LAUDER LINDSAY, M.D., F.R.S.E.**
Mind in the Lower Animals.

**Sir JOHN LUBBOCK, Bart., F.R.S.**
The Antiquity of Man.

**Prof. W. T. THISELTON DYER, B.A. B.Sc.**
Form and Habit in Flowering Plants.

**Mr. J. N. LOCKYER, F.R.S.**
Spectrum Analysis.

**Prof. MICHAEL FOSTER, M.D.**
Protoplasm and the Cell Theory.

**Prof. W. STANLEY JEVONS.**
The Logic of Statistics.

**Dr. H. CHARLTON BASTIAN, M.D., F.R.S.**
The Brain as an Organ of Mind.

**Prof. A. C. RAMSAY, LL.D., F.R.S.**
Earth Sculpture: Hills, Valleys, Mountains, Plains, Rivers, Lakes; how they
were Produced, and how they have been
Destroyed.

**Prof. RUDOLPH VIRCHOW,**
(University of Berlin).
Morbid Physiological Action.

**Prof. CLAUDE BERNARD.**
Physical and Metaphysical Phenomena of
Life.

**Prof. A. QUETELET.**
Social Physics.

**Prof. H. SAINTE-CLAIRE DEVILLE.**
An Introduction to General Chemistry.

**Prof. WURTZ.**
Atoms and the Atomic Theory.

**Prof. DE QUATREFAGES.**
The Negro Races.

**Prof. LACAZE-DUTHIERS.**
Zoology since Cuvier.

**Prof. BERTHELOT.**
Chemical Synthesis.

**Prof. J. ROSENTHAL.**
General Physiology of Muscles and Nerves.

**Prof. JAMES D. DANA, M.A., LL.D.**
On Cephalization; or, Head-Characters in
the Gradation and Progress of Life.

**Prof. S. W. JOHNSON, M.A.**
On the Nutrition of Plants.

**Prof. AUSTIN FLINT, Jr. M.D.**
The Nervous System and its Relation to
the Bodily Functions.

**Prof. W. D. WHITNEY.**
Modern Linguistic Science.

**Prof. BERNSTEIN (University of Halle).**
Physiology of the Senses.

**Prof. FERDINAND COHN,**
(University of Breslau).
Thallophytes (Algae, Lichens, Fungi).

**Prof. HERMANN (University of Zurich).**
Respiration.

**Prof. LEUCKART (University of Leipsic).**
Outlines of Animal Organization.

**Prof. LIEBREICH (University of Berlin).**
Outlines of Toxicology.

**Prof. KUNDT (University of Strasburg).**
On Sound.

**Prof. LOMMEL (University of Erlangen).**
Optics.

**Prof. REES (University of Erlangen).**
On Parasitic Plants.

**Prof. STEINTHAL (University of Berlin).**
Outlines of the Science of Language.

**Prof. VOGEL (Polytechnic Acad. of Berlin).**
The Chemical Effects of Light.

# ESSAYS, LECTURES, AND COLLECTED PAPERS.

**IN STRANGE COMPANY**; or, The Note Book of a Roving Correspondent. By **James Greenwood**, "The Amateur Casual." Crown 8vo. 6*s.*

**MASTER-SPIRITS.** By **Robert Buchanan.** Post 8vo, 10*s.* 6*d.*

"*Good Books are the precious life-blood of Master-Spirits.*"—*Milton.*

Criticism as a Fine Art.
Charles Dickens.
Tennyson.
Browning's Marteyneno.
A Young English Positivist.
Hugo in 1872.
Prose and Verse.

Birds of the Hebrides.
Scandinavian Studies:—
1. A Morning in Copenhagen.
2. Bjornen's Masterpiece.
3. Old Ballads of Denmark.

4. Modern Danish Ballads.
Poets in Obscurity:—
1. George Heath, the Moorland Poet.
2. William Miller.

These are some of the author's lighter and more generally interesting Essays on literary topics of permanent interest. His other prose contributions, critical and philosophical, to our literature are included in the collected editions of his works.

**THEOLOGY IN THE ENGLISH POETS.** Being Lectures delivered by the **Rev. Stopford A. Brooke,** Chaplain in Ordinary to Her Majesty the Queen.

**MOUNTAIN, MEADOW, AND MERE**; a Series of Outdoor Sketches of Sport, Scenery, Adventures, and Natural History. By **G. Christopher Davies.** With 16 Illustrations by W. HARCOURT. Crown 8vo, price 6*s.*

**HOW TO AMUSE AND EMPLOY OUR INVALIDS.** By **Harriet Power.** Fcap. 8vo. Price 2*s.* 6*d.*

What Invalids may do to Amuse Themselves.
What Friends and Attendants may do for them.
Articles for comfort in a Sick Room.

Amusement for Invalid Children.
To the Invalid.
Comforts and Employment for the Aged.
Employment for Sunday.

The question, so often put by invalids, "Can you not find me something to do?" is answered at some length in this little book, which takes up a subject but little touched upon in the many manuals for nurses.                                                    [*Just out.*

**STUDIES AND ROMANCES.** By **H. Schutz Wilson.** 1 vol. Crown 8vo. Price 7*s.* 6*d.*

Shakespeare in Blackfriars.
The Loves of Goethe.
Romance of the Thames.
An Exalted Hero.
Two Sprigs of Edelweiss.
Between Moor and Main.
An Episode of the Terror.

Harry Ormond's Christmas Dinner.
Agnes Bernauerin.
"Yes" or "No"?
A Model Romance.
The Story of Little Jenny.
Dining.
The Record of a Vanished Life.

"Vivacious and interesting."—*Scotsman.*
"Open the book, however, at what page the reader may, he will find something to amuse and instruct, and he must be very

hard to please if he finds nothing to suit him, either grave or gay, stirring or romantic, in the capital stories collected in this well-got-up volume."—*John Bull.*

**SHORT LECTURES ON THE LAND LAWS.** Delivered before the Working Men's College. By **T. Leah Wilkinson.** Crown 8vo, limp cloth. 2s.

> "A very handy and intelligible epitome of the general principles of existing land laws."—*Standard.*
> "A very clear and lucid statement as to the condition of the present land laws
>
> which govern our country. These Lectures possess the advantage of not being loaded with superfluous matter."—*Civil Service Gazette.*

**AN ESSAY ON THE CULTURE OF THE OBSERVING POWERS OF CHILDREN,** especially in connection with the Study of Botany. By **Eliza A. Youmans.** Edited, with Notes and a Supplement, by **Joseph Payne, F.C.P.,** Author of "Lectures on the Science and Art of Education," &c. Crown 8vo. 2s. 6d.

> This study, according to her just notions on the subject, is to be fundamentally based on the exercise of the pupil's own powers of observation. He is to see and
>
> examine the properties of plants and flowers at first hand, not merely to be informed of what others have seen and examined."—*Pall Mall Gazette.*

**THE GENIUS OF CHRISTIANITY UNVEILED.** Being Essays by **William Godwin,** Author of "Political Justice," &c. Never before published. 1 vol., crown 8vo. 7s. 6d.

> "Few have thought more clearly and directly than William Godwin, or expressed their reflections with more simplicity and unreserve."—*Examiner.*
>
> "The deliberate thoughts of Godwin deserve to be put before the world for reading and consideration."—*Athenæum.*

**THE PELICAN PAPERS.** Reminiscences and Remains of a Dweller in the Wilderness. By **James Ashcroft Noble.** Crown 8vo. 6s.

> "Written somewhat after the fashion of Mr. Helps's 'Friends in Council.'"—*Examiner.*
> "Will well repay perusal by all thought-
>
> ful and intelligent readers."—*Liverpool Leader.*
> "The 'Pelican Papers' make a very readable volume."—*Civilian.*

**BRIEFS AND PAPERS.** Being Sketches of the Bar and the Press. By **Two Idle Apprentices.** Crown 8vo. 7s. 6d.

> "Written with spirit and knowledge, and give some curious glimpses into what the majority will regard as strange and unknown territories."—*Daily News.*
>
> "This is one of the best books to while away an hour and cause a generous laugh that we have come across for a long time."—*John Bull.*

ESSAYS, LECTURES, ETC.—*continued.*

**THE SECRET OF LONG LIFE.** Dedicated by Special Permission to Lord St. Leonards. Third Edition. Large crown 8vo. 5s.

"A charming little volume."—*Times.*

"A very pleasant little book, cheerful, genial, scholarly."—*Spectator.*

"We should recommend our readers to get this book."—*British Quarterly Review.*

"Entitled to the warmest admiration."—*Pall Mall Gazette.*

**SOLDIERING AND SCRIBBLING.** By **Archibald Forbes**, of the *Daily News*, Author of "My Experience of the War between France and Germany." Crown 8vo. 7s. 6d.

"All who open it will be inclined to read through for the varied entertainment which it affords."—*Daily News.*

"There is a good deal of instruction to outsiders touching military life. In this volume."—*Evening Standard.*

"Thoroughly readable and worth reading."—*Scotsman.*

**THE ENGLISH CONSTITUTION.** By **Walter Bagehot**. A New Edition, revised and corrected, with an Introductory Dissertation on recent changes and events. Crown 8vo. 7s. 6d.

"A pleasing and clever study on the department of higher politics."—*Guardian.*

"No writer before him had set out so clearly what the efficient part of the English Constitution really is."—*Pall Mall Gazette.*

"Clear and practical."—*Globe.*

**REPUBLICAN SUPERSTITIONS.** Illustrated by the Political History of the United States. Including a Correspondence with M. Louis Blanc. By **Moncure D. Conway**. Crown 8vo. 5s.

"A very able exposure of the most plausible fallacies of Republicanism, by a writer of remarkable vigour and purity of style."—*Standard.*

"Mr. Conway writes with ardent sincerity. He gives us some good anecdotes, and he is occasionally almost eloquent."—*Guardian, July 2, 1873.*

**STREAMS FROM HIDDEN SOURCES.** By **B. Montgomerie Ranking**. Crown 8vo. 6s.

"In point of style it is well executed, and the prefatory notices are very good."—*Spectator.*

"The effect of reading the seven tales he presents to us is to make us wish for some seven more of the same kind."—*Pall Mall Gazette.*

"The tales are given throughout in the quaint version of the earliest English translators, and in the introduction to each will be found much curious information as to their origin, and the fate which they have met at the hands of later transcribers or imitators, and much tasteful appreciation of the varied sources from whence they are extracted. . . . We doubt not that Mr. Ranking's enthusiasm will communicate itself to many of his readers, and induce them in like manner to follow back these streamlets to their parent river."—*Graphic.*

# MILITARY WORKS.

**THE GERMAN ARTILLERY IN THE BATTLES NEAR METZ.**
Based on the official reports of the German Artillery. By **Captain Hoffbauer**, Instructor in the German Artillery and Engineer School. Translated by **Capt. E. O. Hollist.**

This history gives a detailed account of the movements of the German artillery in the three days' fighting to the east and west of Metz, which resulted in paralyzing the army under Marshal Bazaine, and its subsequent surrender. The action of the batteries with reference to the other arms is clearly explained, and the valuable maps show the positions taken up by the individual batteries at each stage of the contest. Tables are also supplied in the Appendix, furnishing full details as to the number of killed and wounded, expenditure of ammunition, &c. The campaign of 1870—71 having demonstrated the importance of artillery to an extent which has not previously been conceded to it, this work forms a valuable part of the literature of the campaign, and will be read with interest not only by members of the regular but also by those of the auxiliary forces.

**THE OPERATIONS OF THE FIRST ARMY, UNDER STEINMETZ.** By **Von Schell.** Translated by **Captain E. O. Hollist.** Demy 8vo. Uniform with the other volumes in the Series. Price 10*s*. 6*d*.

**THE OPERATIONS OF THE BAVARIAN ARMY CORPS.** By **Captain Hugo Helvig.** Translated by **Captain G. S. Schwabe.** With 5 large Maps. Demy 8vo. Uniform with the other Books in the Series.

**DRILL REGULATIONS OF THE AUSTRIAN CAVALRY.** From an Abridged Edition compiled by CAPTAIN ILLIA WORNOVITS, of the General Staff, on the Tactical Regulations of the Austrian Army, and prefaced by a General Sketch of the Organisation, &c., of the Country. Translated by **Captain W. S. Cooke.** Crown 8vo, limp cloth.

**THE OPERATIONS OF THE FIRST ARMY UNDER GEN. VON GOEBEN.** By **Major Von Schell.** Translated by **Col. C. H. Von Wright.** Four Maps. Demy 8vo. 9*s*.

*History of the Organisation, Equipment, and War Services of*

**THE REGIMENT OF BENGAL ARTILLERY.** Compiled from Published Official and other Records, and various private sources, by **Major Francis W. Stubbs,** Royal (late Bengal) Artillery. Vol. I. will contain WAR SERVICES. The Second Volume will be published separately, and will contain the HISTORY OF THE ORGANISATION AND EQUIPMENT OF THE REGIMENT. In 2 vols. 8vo. With Maps and Plans. [*Preparing.*

**THE ABOLITION OF PURCHASE AND THE ARMY REGU-LATION BILL OF 1871.** By Lieut.-Col. the Hon. A. Anson, V.C., M.P. Crown 8vo. Price One Shilling.

**THE STORY OF THE SUPERSESSIONS.** By Lieut.-Col. the Hon. A. Anson, V.C., M.P. Crown 8vo. Price Sixpence.

**ARMY RESERVES AND MILITIA REFORMS.** By Lieut.-Col. the Hon. A. Anson. Crown 8vo. Sewed. Price One Shilling.

**VICTORIES AND DEFEATS.** An Attempt to explain the Causes which have led to them. An Officer's Manual. By Col. R. P. Anderson. Demy 8vo. 14*s*.

> "A delightful military classic, and what is more, a most useful one. The young officer should have it always at hand to open anywhere and read a bit, and we warrant him that let that bit be ever so small it will give him material for an hour's thinking."—*United Service Gazette.*

**THE FRONTAL ATTACK OF INFANTRY.** By Capt. Laymann, Instructor of Tactics at the Military College, Neisse. Translated by Colonel Edward Newdigate. Crown 8vo, limp cloth. Price 2*s*. 6*d*.

> "This work has met with special attention in our army."—*Militaria Wochenblatt.*

**THE OPERATIONS OF THE FIRST ARMY IN NORTHERN FRANCE AGAINST FAIDHERBE.** By Colonel Count Hermann Von Wartensleben, Chief of the Staff of the First Army. Translated by Colonel C. H. Von Wright. In demy 8vo. Uniform with the above. Price 9*s*.

> "Very clear, simple, yet eminently instructive, is this history. It is not overladen with useless details, is written in good taste, and possesses the inestimable value of being in great measure the record of operations actually witnessed by the author, supplemented by official documents."—*Athenæum.*
>
> "The work is based on the official war documents—it is especially valuable—the narrative is remarkably vivid and interesting. Two well-executed maps enable the reader to trace out the scenes of General Manteuffel's operations."—*Naval and Military Gazette.*

**ELEMENTARY MILITARY GEOGRAPHY, RECONNOITRING, AND SKETCHING.** Compiled for Non-Commissioned Officers and Soldiers of all Arms. By Lieut. C. E. H. Vincent, Royal Welsh Fusileers. Small crown 8vo. 2*s*. 6*d*.

> "An admirable little manual full of facts and teachings."—*United Service Gazette.*

MILITARY WORKS—*continued.*

## STUDIES IN THE NEW INFANTRY TACTICS. Parts I. & II.

By **Major W. Von Schereff.** Translated from the German by Col. **Lumley Graham.** Price 7*s.* 6*d.*

"Major Von Schereff's 'Studies in Tactics' is worthy of the perusal—indeed, of the thoughtful study—of every military man. The subject of the respective advantages of attack and defence, and of the methods in which each form of battle should be carried out under the fire of

modern arms, is exhaustively and admirably treated; indeed, we cannot but consider it to be decidedly superior to any work which has hitherto appeared in English upon this all-important subject."— *Standard.*

## TACTICAL DEDUCTIONS FROM THE WAR OF 1870—1. By

Captain **A. Von Boguslawaki.** Translated by Colonel **Lumley Graham,** late 18th (Royal Irish) Regiment. Demy 8vo. Uniform with the above. Price 7*s.*

"Major Boguslawski's tactical deductions from the war are, that infantry still preserve their superiority over cavalry, that open order must henceforth be the main principles of all drill, and that the chassepot is the best of all small arms for precision. . . . We must, without delay, impress brain and forethought into the

British Service; and we cannot commence the good work too soon, or better, than by placing the two books ('The Operations of the German Armies' and 'Tactical Deductions') we have here criticised, in every military library, and introducing them as class-books in every tactical school."— *United Service Gazette.*

## THE ARMY OF THE NORTH-GERMAN CONFEDERATION.

A Brief Description of its Organisation, of the different Branches of the Service and their 'Rôle' in War, of its Mode of Fighting, &c. By a **Prussian General.** Translated from the German by Col. **Edward Newdigate.** Demy 8vo. 5*s.*

\*\* The authorship of this book was erroneously ascribed to the renowned General von Moltke, but there can be little doubt that it was written under his immediate inspiration.

## THE OPERATIONS OF THE GERMAN ARMIES IN FRANCE, FROM SEDAN TO THE END OF THE WAR OF 1870—1.

With Large Official Map. From the Journals of the Head-quarters Staff, by **Major Wm. Blume.** Translated by **E. M. Jones,** Major 20th Foot, late Professor of Military History, Sandhurst. Demy 8vo. Price 9*s.*

"The book is of absolute necessity to the military student. . . . The work is one of high merit."—*United Service Gazette.*
"The work of translation has been well done. In notes, prefaces, and introductions, much additional information has been given."—*Athenæum.*
"The work of Major von Blume in its English dress forms the most valuable

addition to our stock of works upon the war that our press has put forth. Major Blume writes with a clear conciseness much wanting in many of his country's historians. Our space forbids our doing more than commending it earnestly as the most authentic and instructive narrative of the second section of the war that has yet appeared."—*Saturday Review.*

## THE OPERATIONS OF THE SOUTH ARMY IN JANUARY AND FEBRUARY, 1871.

Compiled from the Official War Documents of the Head-quarters of the Southern Army. By **Count Hermann Von Wartensleben,** Colonel in the Prussian General Staff. Translated by **Colonel C. H. Von Wright.** Demy 8vo, with Maps. Uniform with the above. Price 6*s.*

MILITARY WORKS—*continued.*

**HASTY INTRENCHMENTS.** By Colonel A. Brialmont. Translated by Lieutenant Charles A. Empson, R.A. Demy 8vo. Nine Plates. Price 6s.

"A valuable contribution to military literature."—*Athenæum.*

"In seven short chapters it gives plain directions for forming shelter-trenches, with the best method of carrying the necessary tools, and it offers practical illustrations of the use of hasty intrenchments on the field of battle."—*United Service Magazine.*

"It supplies that which our own text-books give but imperfectly, viz., hints as to how a position can best be strengthened by means . . . of such extemporised intrenchments and batteries as can be thrown up by infantry in the space of four or five hours . . . deserves to become a standard military work."—*Standard.*

"Clearly and critically written."—*Wellington Gazette.*

**STUDIES IN LEADING TROOPS.** By Colonel Von Verdy Du Vernois. An authorised and accurate Translation by Lieutenant H. J. T. Hildyard, 71st Foot. Parts I. and II. Demy 8vo. Price 7s.

\*\*\* General BEAUCHAMP WALKER says of this work:—"I recommend the first two numbers of Colonel von Verdy's 'Studies' to the attentive perusal of my brother officers. They supply a want which I have often felt during my service in this country, namely, a minuter tactical detail of the minor operations of the war than any but the most observant and for-

tunately-placed staff-officer is in a position to give. I have read and re-read them very carefully, I hope with profit, certainly with great interest, and believe that practice, in the sense of these 'Studies,' would be a valuable preparation for manœuvres on a more extended scale."—*Berlin, June, 1872.*

**THE SUBSTANTIVE SENIORITY ARMY LIST,** Majors and Captains. By Captain F. B. P. White, 1st W. I. Regiment. 8vo, sewed. 2s. 6d.

**CAVALRY FIELD DUTY.** By Major-General Von Mirus. Translated by Captain Frank S. Russell, 14th (King's) Hussars. Crown 8vo, limp cloth. 7s. 6d.

\*\*\* This is the text-book of instruction in the German cavalry, and comprises all the details connected with the military duties of cavalry soldiers on service. The translation is made from a new edition, which contains the modifications intro-

duced consequent on the experiences of the late war. The great interest that students feel in all the German military methods will, it is believed, render this book especially acceptable at the present time.

**DISCIPLINE AND DRILL.** Four Lectures delivered to the London Scottish Rifle Volunteers. By Captain S. Flood Page. A New and Cheaper Edition. Price 1s.

"One of the best-known and coolest-headed of the metropolitan regiments, whose adjutant moreover has lately published an admirable collection of lectures

addressed by him to the men of his corps."—*Times.*

"The very useful and interesting work."—*Volunteer Service Gazette.*

## INDIA AND THE EAST.

**THE ORIENTAL SPORTING MAGAZINE.** A Reprint of the first 5 Volumes, in 2 Volumes, demy 8vo. price 28s.

These volumes contain many quaint and clever papers, among which we may mention the famous Sporting Songs written by S. V. S., of "The Boar, Saddle, Spur, and Spear," &c., &c.—Capt. Mounts, of the Bombay Army; as well as descriptions of Hog Hunts, Fox Hunts, Lion Hunts, Tiger Hunts, and Cheeta Hunts; accounts of Shooting Excursions for Snipe, Partridges, Quail, Toucan, Ortolan, and Wild Fowl; interesting details of Pigeon Matches, Cock Fights, Horse, Tattoo, and Donkey Races; descriptions of the Origin, Regulations, and Uniforms of Hunting Clubs; Natural History of rare Wild Animals; Memoranda of Feats of Noted Horses; and Memoirs and Anecdotes of celebrated Sporting characters, &c., &c.

*[Just out.*

**THE EUROPEAN IN INDIA.** A Hand-book of Practical Information for those proceeding to, or residing in, the East Indies, relating to Outfits, Routes, Time for Departure, Indian Climate, &c. By **Edmund C. P. Hull.** With a MEDICAL GUIDE FOR ANGLO-INDIANS. Being a Compendium of Advice to Europeans in India, relating to the Preservation and Regulation of Health. By **R. S. Mair, M.D., F.R.C.S.E.,** Late Deputy Coroner of Madras. In 1 vol. Post 8vo. 6s.

"Full of all sorts of useful information to the English settler or traveller in India." —*Standard.*
"One of the most valuable books ever published in India—valuable for its sound information, its careful array of pertinent facts, and its sterling common sense. It is a publisher's as well as an author's 'hit,' for it supplies a want which few persons may have discovered, but which everybody will at once recognise when once the contents of the book have been mastered. The medical part of the work is invaluable."—*Calcutta Guardian.*

**THE MEDICAL GUIDE FOR ANGLO-INDIANS.** Being a Compendium of advice to Europeans in India, relating to the Preservation and Regulation of Health. By **R. S. Mair, F.R.C.S.E.,** late Deputy Coroner of Madras. Reprinted, with numerous additions and corrections, from "The European in India."

**EASTERN EXPERIENCES.** By **L. Bowring, C.S.I.,** Lord Canning's Private Secretary, and for many years the Chief Commissioner of Mysore and Coorg. In 1 vol. Demy 8vo. 16s. Illustrated with Maps and Diagrams.

"An admirable and exhaustive geographical, political, and industrial survey." —*Athenæum.*
"The usefulness of this compact and methodical summary of the most authentic information relating to countries whose welfare is intimately connected with our own, should obtain for Mr. Lewin Bowring's work a good place among treatises of its kind."—*Daily News.*
"Interesting even to the general reader, but more especially so to those who may have a special concern in that portion of our Indian Empire."—*Post.*

**TAS-HĪL UL KALĀM;** OR, HINDUSTANI MADE EASY. By **Captain W. R. M. Holroyd,** Bengal Staff Corps, Director of Public Instruction, Punjab. Crown 8vo. Price 5s.

INDIA AND THE EAST—*continued.*

## WESTERN INDIA BEFORE AND DURING THE MUTINIES.
Pictures drawn from Life. By **Major-Gen. Sir George Le Grand Jacob, K.C.S.I., C.B.** In 1 vol. Crown 8vo. 7s. 6d.

> "The most important contribution to the history of Western India during the Mutinies which has yet, in a popular form been made public."—*Athenæum.*

> "Few men more competent than himself to speak authoritatively concerning Indian affairs."—*Standard.*

## EDUCATIONAL COURSE OF SECULAR SCHOOL BOOKS
FOR INDIA. Edited by **J. S. Laurie**, of the Inner Temple, Barrister-at-Law; formerly H.M. Inspector of Schools, England; Assistant Royal Commissioner, Ireland; Special Commissioner, African Settlements; Director of Public Instruction, Ceylon.

### EXTRACT FROM PROSPECTUS.

The Editor has undertaken to frame for India,—what he has been eminently successful in doing for England and her colonies,—a series of educational works, which he hopes will prove as suitable for the peculiar wants of the country as they will be consistent with the leading idea above alluded to. Like all beginnings, his present instalments are necessarily somewhat meagre and elementary; but he only awaits official and public approval to complete, within a comparatively brief period, his contemplated plan of a specific and fairly comprehensive series of works in the various leading vernaculars of the Indian continent. Meanwhile, those on his general catalogue may be found suitable, in their present form, for use in the Anglo-vernacular and English schools of India.

*The following Works are now ready:—*

| | s. d. | | s. d. |
|---|---|---|---|
| **THE FIRST HINDUSTANI READER**, stiff linen wrapper | 0 6 | **GEOGRAPHY OF INDIA**, with Maps and Historical Appendix, tracing the growth of the British Empire in Hindustan. 178 pp. | |
| Ditto ditto strongly bound in cloth | 0 9 | | |
| **THE SECOND HINDUSTANI READER**, stiff linen wrapper | 0 6 | Cloth | 1 6 |
| Ditto ditto strongly bound in cloth | 0 9 | | |

*In the Press.*

| | |
|---|---|
| **ELEMENTARY GEOGRAPHY OF INDIA.** | **FACTS AND FEATURES OF INDIAN HISTORY**, in a series of alternating Reading Lessons and Memory Exercises. |

## EXCHANGE TABLES OF STERLING AND INDIAN RUPEE
CURRENCY, UPON A NEW AND EXTENDED SYSTEM, embracing Values from One Farthing to One Hundred Thousand Pounds, and at rates progressing, in Sixteenths of a Penny, from 1s. 9d. to 2s. 3d. per Rupee. By **Donald Fraser**, Accountant to the British Indian Steam Navigation Co., Limited. Royal 8vo. 10s. 6d.

> "The calculations must have entailed great labour on the author, but the work is one which we fancy must become a standard one in all business houses which have dealings with any country where the rupee and the English pound are standard coins of currency."—*Inverness Courier.*

# BOOKS FOR THE YOUNG AND FOR LENDING LIBRARIES.

**LAYS OF MANY LANDS.** By a **Knight Errant.** Illustrated. Crown 8vo.

Pharaoh Land.    Wonder Land.
Home Land.     Rhine Land.

**SEEKING HIS FORTUNE, AND OTHER STORIES.** Crown 8vo. Four Illustrations. Price 3*s*. 6*d*.

CONTENTS.—Seeking his Fortune.—Oluf and Stephanoff.—What's in a Name?—Contrast.—Onesta.

A series of instructive and interesting stories for children of both sexes, each one enforcing, indirectly, a good moral lesson.

**DADDY'S PET.** By **Mrs. Ellen Ross (Nelsie Brook).** Square crown 8vo, uniform with "Lost Gip." 6 Illustrations.

A pathetic story of lowly life, showing the good influence of home and of child-life upon an uncultivated but true-hearted "navvy."

## THREE WORKS BY MARTHA FARQUHARSON.

Each Story is independent and complete in itself. They are published in uniform size and price, and are elegantly bound and illustrated.

I. **ELSIE DINSMORE.** Crown 8vo. 3*s*. 6*d*.

II. **ELSIE'S GIRLHOOD.** Crown 8vo. 3*s*. 6*d*.

III. **ELSIE'S HOLIDAYS AT ROSELANDS.** Crown 8vo. 3*s*. 6*d*.

The Stories by this author have a very high reputation in America, and of all her books these are the most popular and widely circulated. These are the only English editions sanctioned by the author, who has a direct interest in this English Edition.

**LOST GIP.** By **Hesba Stretton,** Author of "Little Meg," "Alone in London." Square crown 8vo. Six Illustrations. Price 1*s*. 6*d*.

\*\*\* *A HANDSOMELY BOUND EDITION, WITH TWELVE ILLUSTRA-TIONS, PRICE HALF-A-CROWN.*

"Thoroughly enlists the sympathies of the reader."—*Church Review.*  "An exquisitely touching little story."—*Church Herald.*
"Full of tender touches."—*Noncon-*

**THE KING'S SERVANTS.** By **Hesba Stretton,** Author of "Lost Gip." Square crown 8vo, uniform with "Lost Gip." 8 Illustrations. Price 1*s*. 6*d*.

Part I.—Faithful in Little. Part II.—Unfaithful. Part III.—Faithful in Much.

**AT SCHOOL WITH AN OLD DRAGOON.** By **Stephen J. Mac Kenna.** Crown 8vo. 5*s*. With Six Illustrations.

| | | |
|---|---|---|
| "At Ghurnee Villa." | In a Golden Fort. | A Baptism of Frost. |
| Introductory. | A Little Game. | Who Shot the Kafirs. |
| Henry and Amy. | True to his Salt. | John Chinaman and the |
| A Story of Canterbury. | Mother Moran's Enemies. | Middies. |
| A Disastrous Trumpet Call. | Seeks the Syree; or, Sea | |
| A Baptism of Fire. | Horses in Reality. | |

A Series of Stories of Military and Naval Adventure, related by an old Retired Officer of the Army.

BOOKS FOR THE YOUNG, ETC.—*continued.*

**FANTASTIC STORIES.** Translated from the German of **Richard Leander**, by **Paulina B. Granville**. Crown 8vo. Eight full-page Illustrations.

| | | |
|---|---|---|
| The Magic Organ. | The Wishing Ring. | The Dreaming Beech. |
| The Invisible Kingdom. | The Three Princesses with | The Little Hump-Backed |
| The Knight who Grew | Hearts of Glass. | Maiden. |
| Rusty. | The Old Bachelor. | Heavenly Music. |
| Of the Queen who could not | Sepp's Courtship. | The Old Hair Trunk. |
| make Gingerbread Nuts, | Heino in the Marsh. | |
| and of the King who could | Unlucky Dog and Fortune's | |
| not play the Jew's Harp. | Favourite. | |

These are translations of some of the best of Richard Leander's well-known stories for children. The illustrations to this work are of singular beauty and finish.

**THE AFRICAN CRUISER.** A Midshipman's Adventures on the West Coast. A Book for Boys. By **S. Whitchurch Sadler, R.N.** Three Illustrations. Crown 8vo. 3s. 6d.

A book of real adventures among slavers on the West Coast of Africa. One chief recommendation is the faithfulness of the local colouring.

**THE LITTLE WONDER-HORN.** By **Jean Ingelow**. A Second Series of "*Stories told to a Child.*" Fifteen Illustrations. Cloth, gilt. 3s. 6d.

"Full of fresh and vigorous fancy : it is worthy of the author of some of the best of our modern verse."—*Standard.*

"We like all the contents of the 'Little Wonder-Horn' very much."—*Athenæum.* "We recommend it with confidence."—*Pall Mall Gazette.*

*Second Edition.*

**BRAVE MEN'S FOOTSTEPS.** A Book of Example and Anecdote for Young People. By the Editor of "**Men who have Risen.**" With Four Illustrations. By **C. Doyle.** 3s. 6d.

"The little volume is precisely of the stamp to win the favour of those who, in choosing a gift for a boy, would consult his moral development as well as his temporary pleasure."—*Daily Telegraph.*

"A readable and instructive volume."—*Examiner.* "No more welcome book for the schoolboy could be imagined."—*Birmingham Daily Gazette.*

*Third Edition.*

**STORIES IN PRECIOUS STONES.** By **Helen Zimmern.** With Six Illustrations. Crown 8vo. 5s.

"A pretty little book which fanciful young persons will appreciate, and which will remind its readers of many a legend, and many an imaginary virtue attached to the gems they are so fond of wearing."—*Post.*

"A series of pretty tales which are half fantastic, half natural, and pleasantly quaint, as befits stories intended for the young."—*Daily Telegraph.*

*Second Edition.*

**GUTTA-PERCHA WILLIE, THE WORKING GENIUS,** By **George Macdonald.** With Illustrations by **Arthur Hughes.** Crown 8vo. 3s. 6d.

"An amusing and instructive book."—*Yorkshire Post.* "One of those charming books for which the author is so well known."—*Edinburgh Daily Review.*

"The cleverest child we know admires as she has read this story through five times. Mr. Macdonald will, we are convinced, accept that verdict upon his little work as final."—*Spectator.*

**THE TRAVELLING MENAGERIE.** By Charles Camden, Author of "Hoity Toity." Illustrated by J. Mahoney. Crown 8vo. 3s. 6d.

"A capital little book . . . . deserves a wide circulation among our boys and girls."—*Hour.*

"A very attractive story." — *Public Opinion.*

**PLUCKY FELLOWS.** A Book for Boys. By Stephen J. Mac Kenna. With Six Illustrations. Crown 8vo. Price 3s. 6d.

"This is one of the very best 'Books for Boys' which have been issued this year,"—*Morning Advertiser.*
"A thorough book for boys . . . written

throughout in a manly straightforward manner that is sure to win the hearts of the children for whom it is intended,"—*London Society.*

**THE GREAT DUTCH ADMIRALS.** By Jacob de Liefde. Crown 8vo. Illustrated. Price 5s.

"A really good book."—*Standard.*
"May be recommended as a wholesome present for boys. They will find in it numerous tales of adventure."—*Athenæum.*

"Thoroughly interesting and inspiring."—*Public Opinion.*
"A really excellent book."—*Spectator.*

*New Edition.*

**THE DESERT PASTOR, JEAN JAROUSSEAU.** Translated from the French of Eugene Pelletan. By Colonel E. P. De L'Hoste. In fcap. 8vo, with an Engraved Frontispiece. Price 3s. 6d.

"There is a poetical simplicity and picturesqueness; the noblest heroism; unpretentious religion; pure love, and the spectacle of a household brought up in the fear of the Lord. . . . ."—*Illustrated London News.*

"This charming specimen of Eugene Pelletan's tender grace, humour, and high-toned morality."—*Notes and Queries.*
"A touching record of the struggles in the cause of religious liberty of a real man."—*Graphic.*

**THE DESERTED SHIP.** A Real Story of the Atlantic. By Cupples Howe, Master Mariner. Illustrated by Townley Green. Crown 8vo. 3s. 6d.

"Curious adventures with bears, seals, and other Arctic animals, and with scarcely more human Esquimaux, form the mass of

material with which the story deals, and will much interest boys who have a spice of romance in their composition."—*Courant.*

**HOITY TOITY, THE GOOD LITTLE FELLOW.** By Charles Camden. Illustrated. Crown 8vo. 3s. 6d.

"Young folks may gather a good deal of wisdom from the story, which is written in an amusing and attractive style."—*Courant.*
"Relates very pleasantly the history of

a charming little fellow who meddles always with a kindly disposition with other people's affairs and helps them to do right. There are many shrewd lessons to be picked up in this clever little story."—*Public Opinion.*

## POETRY.

**LYRICS OF LOVE FROM SHAKESPEARE TO TENNYSON.** Selected and arranged by **W. Davenport Adams.** Fcap. 8vo, price 3s. 6d.

"He has the prettiest love-songs for maids."—*Shakespeare.*

DEDICATED BY PERMISSION TO THE POET LAUREATE.

**WILLIAM CULLEN BRYANT'S POEMS.** Red-line Edition. Handsomely bound. With Illustrations and Portrait of the Author. Price 7s. 6d.

A Cheaper Edition is also published. Price 3s. 6d.

*These are the only complete English Editions sanctioned by the Author.*

**ENGLISH SONNETS.** Collected and Arranged by **John Dennis.** Small crown 8vo. Elegantly bound, price 3s. 6d.

**HOME-SONGS FOR QUIET HOURS.** By the **Rev. Canon R. H. Baynes,** Editor of "English Lyrics" and "Lyra Anglicana."

Handsomely printed and bound, price 3s. 6d.

**THE DISCIPLES. A New Poem.** By **Harriet Eleanor Hamilton King.** Crown 8vo. 7s. 6d.

The present work was commenced at the express instance of the great Italian patriot, Mazzini, and commemorates some of his associates and fellow-workers—men who looked up to him as their master and teacher. The author enjoyed the privilege of Mazzini's friendship, and the first part of this work was on its way to him when tidings reached this country that he had passed away.

**SONGS FOR MUSIC. By Four Friends.** Square crown 8vo.

CONTAINING SONGS BY

Reginald A. Gatty.        Stephen H. Gatty.
Greville J. Chester.      J. H. E.

**THE POETICAL AND PROSE WORKS OF ROBERT BUCHANAN.** A Collected Edition, in 5 Vols.

Vol. I. Contains.—"Ballads and Romances;" "Ballads and Poems of Life." Vol. II.—"Ballads and Poems of Life;" "Allegories and Sonnets." Vol. III.—"Cruiskeen Sonnets;" "Book of Orm;" "Political Mystics."

*The Contents of the remaining Volumes will be duly announced.*

**THOUGHTS IN VERSE.** Small crown 8vo.

This is a Collection of Verses expressive of religious feeling, written from a Theistic stand-point.

**COSMOS. A Poem.** Small crown 8vo.

Subject.—Nature in the Past and in the Present.—Man in the Past and in the Present.—The Future.

**VIGNETTES IN RHYME.** Collected Verses. By **Austin Dobson.** Crown 8vo. Price 5s.

A Collection of Vers de Société, for the most part contributed to various magazines.

**NARCISSUS AND OTHER POEMS.** By **E. Carpenter.** Small crown 8vo. Price 5s.

**A TALE OF THE SEA, SONNETS, AND OTHER POEMS.** By **James Howell.** Crown 8vo, cloth, 5s.

**IMITATIONS FROM THE GERMAN OF SPITTA AND TERSTEGEN.** By **Lady Durand.** Crown 8vo. 4s.

"An acceptable addition to the religious poetry of the day."—*Current.*

**METRICAL TRANSLATIONS FROM THE GREEK AND LATIN POETS, AND OTHER POEMS.** By **R. B. Boswell,** M.A. Oxon. Crown 8vo.

## POETRY—*continued.*

**ON VIOL AND FLUTE.** A New Volume of Poems, by Edmund W. Gosse. With a Frontispiece by W. B. Scott. Crown 8vo.

**EASTERN LEGENDS AND STORIES IN ENGLISH VERSE.** By Lieutenant Norton Powlett, Royal Artillery. Crown 8vo. 5s.

"Have we at length found a successor to Thomas Ingoldsby? We are almost inclined to hope so after reading 'Eastern Legends.' There is a rollicking sense of fun about the stories, joined to marvellous power of rhyming, and plenty of swing, which irresistibly reminds us of our old favourite."—*Graphic.*

**EDITH (OR, LOVE AND LIFE IN CHESHIRE.** By T. Ashe, Author of the "Sorrows of Hypsipyle," etc. Sewed. Price 6d.

"A really fine poem, full of tender, subtle touches of feeling."—*Manchester News.*

"Pregnant from beginning to end with the results of careful observation and imaginative power."—*Chester Chronicle.*

**THE GALLERY OF PIGEONS, AND OTHER POEMS.** By Theo. Marzials. Crown 8vo. 4s. 6d.

"A conceit abounding in prettiness."—*Examiner.*

"Contains as clear evidence as a book can contain that its composition was a source of keen and legitimate enjoyment. The rush of fresh, sparkling fancies is too rapid, too sustained, too abundant, nor to be spontaneous."—*Academy.*

**THE INN OF STRANGE MEETINGS, AND OTHER POEMS.** By Mortimer Collins. Crown 8vo. 5s.

"Abounding in quiet humour, in bright fancy, in sweetness and melody of expression, and, at times, in the tenderest touches of pathos."—*Graphic.*

"Mr. Collins has an undercurrent of chivalry and romance beneath the trifling vein of good-humoured banter which is the special characteristic of his verse."—*Athenæum.*

**EROS AGONISTES.** By E. B. D. Crown 8vo. 3s. 6d.

"The author of these verses has written a very touching story of the human heart in the story he tells with such pathos and power, of an affection cherished so long and so secretly. . . . It is not the least merit of these pages that they are everywhere illumined with moral and religious sentiment suggested, not paraded, of the brightest, purest character."—*Standard.*

**CALDERON'S DRAMAS.**

THE PURGATORY OF ST. PATRICK.
THE WONDERFUL MAGICIAN.
LIFE IS A DREAM.

Translated from the Spanish. **By Denis Florence MacCarthy.** 10s.

"These translations have never before been published. The 'Purgatory of St. Patrick' is a new version, with new and elaborate historical notes.

**SONGS FOR SAILORS.** By Dr. W. C. Bennett. Dedicated by Special Request to H. R. H. the Duke of Edinburgh. Crown 8vo. 3s. 6d. With Steel Portrait and Illustrations.

An Edition in Illustrated paper Covers. Price 1s.

**WALLED IN, AND OTHER POEMS.** By the Rev. Henry J. Bulkeley. Crown 8vo. 5s.

"A remarkable book of genuine poetry."—*Evening Standard.*

"Genuine power displayed."—*Examiner.*

". . . . . Poetical feeling is manifest here, and the diction of the poem is unimpeachable."—*Pall Mall Gazette.*

"He has successfully attempted what has seldom before been well done, viz. the treatment of subjects not in themselves poetical from a poetic point of view."—*Graphic.*

"Intensity of feeling, a rugged pathos, robustness of tone, and a downrightness of expression which does not shrink from even slang if it seem best fitted for his purpose."—*Illustrated London News.*

**SONGS OF LIFE AND DEATH.** By John Payne, Author of "Intaglios," "Sonnets," "The Masque of Shadows," etc. Crown 8vo. 5s.

"The art of ballad-writing has long been lost in England, and Mr. Payne may claim to be its restorer. It is a perfect delight to meet with such a ballad as 'May Margaret' in the present volume."—*Westminster Review.*

**ASPROMONTE, AND OTHER POEMS.** Second Edition, cloth. 4s. 6d.

"The volume is anonymous, but there is no reason for the author to be ashamed of it. The 'Poems of Italy' are evidently inspired by genuine enthusiasm in the cause espoused; and one of them, 'The Execution of Felice Orsini,' has much poetic merit, the event celebrated being told with dramatic force."—*Athenæum.*

"The verse is fluent and free."—*Spectator.*

## POETRY—*continued.*

**A NEW VOLUME OF SONNETS.** By the Rev. C. Tennyson Turner. Crown 8vo. 4s. 6d.

"Mr. Turner is a genuine poet; his song is sweet and pure, beautiful in expression, and often subtle in thought."—*Pall Mall Gazette.*

"The dominant charm of all these sonnets is the pervading presence of the writer's personality, never obtruded but always impalpably diffused. The light of a devout, gentle, and kindly spirit, a delicate and graceful fancy, a keen intelligence irradiates these thoughts."—*Contemporary Review.*

**GOETHE'S FAUST.** A New Translation in Rime. By the Rev. C. Kegan Paul. Crown 8vo. 6s.

"His translation is the most minutely accurate that has yet been produced . . ."—*Examiner.*

"Mr. Paul evidently understands 'Faust,' and his translation is as well suited to convey its meaning to English readers as any we have yet seen."—*Edinburgh Daily Review.*

"Mr. Paul is a zealous and a faithful interpreter."—*Saturday Review.*

**THE DREAM AND THE DEED, AND OTHER POEMS.** By Patrick Scott, Author of "Footpaths between Two Worlds," etc. Fcap. 8vo. cloth, 5s.

"A bitter and able satire on the vice and follies of the day, literary, social, and political."—*Standard.*

"Shows real poetic power coupled with evidences of satirical energy."—*Edinburgh Daily Review.*

**SONGS OF TWO WORLDS.** By a New Writer. Fcap. 8vo, cloth, 5s. Second Edition.

"These poems will assuredly take high rank among the class to which they belong."—*British Quarterly Review, April 1st.*

"If these poems are the mere preludes of a mind growing in power and in inclination for verse, we have in them the promise of a fine poet."—*Spectator, February 17th.*

"No extracts could do justice to the exquisite tones, the felicitous phrasing and delicately wrought harmonies of some of these poems."—*Nonconformist, March 27th.*

"It has a purity and delicacy of feeling like morning air."—*Graphic, March 16th.*

**THE LEGENDS OF ST. PATRICK AND OTHER POEMS.** By Aubrey de Vere. Crown 8vo. 5s.

"Mr. De Vere's versification in his earlier poems is characterised by great sweetness and simplicity. He is master of his instrument, and rarely offends the ear with false notes. Poems such as these scarcely admit of quotation, for their charm is not, and ought not to be, found in isolated passages; but we can promise the patient and thoughtful reader much pleasure in the perusal of this volume."—*Pall Mall Gazette.*

"We have marked, in almost every page, excellent touches from which we know not how to select. We have but space to commend the varied structure of his verse, the carefulness of his grammar, and his excellent English."—*Saturday Review.*

---

## FICKTION.

**THE OWL'S NEST IN THE CITY.** In 1 vol. Cloth, crown 8vo.

**TWO GIRLS.** By Frederick Wedmore, Author of "A Snapt Gold Ring." In 2 vols. Cloth, crown 8vo.

A powerful and dramatic story of Bohemian life in Paris and in London.

**JUDITH GWYNNE.** By Lisle Carr. In 3 vols. Crown 8vo, cloth.

**MR. CARINGTON.** A Tale of Love and Conspiracy. By Robert Turner Cotton. In 3 vols. Cloth, crown 8vo.

**TOO LATE.** By Mrs. Newman. Two vols. Crown 8vo.

A dramatic love story.

**LADY MORETOUN'S DAUGHTER.** By Mrs. Eiloart. In 3 vols. Crown 8vo, cloth.

FICTION—*continued.*

**HEATHERGATE.** In 2 vols. Cr. 8vo, cloth. A Story of Scottish Life and Character by a new Author.

**THE QUEEN'S SHILLING.** By **Captain Arthur Griffiths,** Author of " Peccavi." 2 vols.

" . . . . A very lively and agreeable novel."—*Vanity Fair.*
" ' The Queen's Shilling ' is a capital story, far more interesting than the meagre sketch we have given of the fortunes of the hero and heroine can suggest. Every scene, character, and incident of the book are so life-like that they seem drawn from life direct."—*Pall Mall Gazette.*

**MIRANDA.** A Midsummer Madness. By **Mortimer Collins.** 3 vols.

" There is not a dull page in the whole three volumes."—*Standard.*
" The work of a man who is at once a thinker and a poet."—*Hour.*

**SQUIRE SILCHESTER'S WHIM.** By **Mortimer Collins,** Author of " Marquis and Merchant," " The Princess Clarice," &c. Crown 8vo. 3 vols.

" We think it the best (story) Mr. Collins has yet written. Full of incident and adventure."—*Pall Mall Gazette.*
" Decidedly the best novel from the pen of Mr. Mortimer Collins that we have yet come across."—*Graphic.*
" So clever, so irritating, and so charming a story."—*Standard.*

**THE PRINCESS CLARICE.** A Story of 1871. By **Mortimer Collins.** 2 vols. Crown 8vo.

" Mr. Collins has produced a readable book, amusingly characteristic. . . . ."—*Athenæum.*
" Very readable and amusing. We would especially give an honourable mention to Mr. Collins's ' revs de mcildt,' the writing of which has almost become a lost art."—*Pall Mall Gazette.*
" A bright, fresh, and original book."—*Standard.*

**WHAT 'TIS TO LOVE.** By the Author of " Flora Adair," " The Value of Fosterstown." 3 vols.

**REGINALD BRAMBLE,** A Cynic of the 19th Century. An Autobiography. One Volume.

" There is plenty of vivacity in Mr. Bramble's narrative."—*Athenæum.*
" Written in a lively and readable style."—*Hour.*
" The skill of the author in the delineation of the supposed chronicler, and the preservation of his natural character, is beyond praise."—*Morning Post.*

**EFFIE'S GAME;** How she Lost and how she Won. By **Cecil Clayton.** 2 vols.

" Well written. The characters move, and act, and, above all, talk like human beings, and we have liked reading about them."—*Spectator.*

**CHESTERLEIGH.** By **Ansley Conyers.** 3 vols. Crown 8vo.

" We have gained much enjoyment from the book."—*Spectator.*
" Will suit the hosts of readers of the higher class of romantic fiction."—*Morning Advertiser.*

**BRESSANT.** A Romance. By **Julian Hawthorne.** 2 vols. Crown 8vo.

" The son's work we venture to say is worthy of the sire. . . . The story as it stands is one of the most powerful with which we are acquainted."—*Times.*
" Pretty certain of meeting in this country a grateful and appreciative reception."—*Athenæum.*
" Mr. Julian Hawthorne is endowed with a large share of his father's peculiar genius."—*Pall Mall Gazette.*
" Enough to make us hopeful that we shall once more have reason to rejoice whenever we hear that a new work is coming out written by one who bears the honoured name of Hawthorne."—*Saturday Review.*

**HONOR BLAKE:** The Story of a Plain Woman. By **Mrs. Keatinge,** Author of " English Homes in India," &c. 2 vols. Crown 8vo.

" One of the best novels we have met with for some time."—*Morning Post.*
" A story which must do good to all, young and old, who read it."—*Daily News.*

FICTION—*continued.*

**OFF THE SKELLIGS.** By **Jean Ingelow.** (Her First Romance.) Crown 8vo. In 4 vols.

"Clever and sparkling."—*Standard.*

"We read each succeeding volume with increasing interest, going almost to the point of wishing there was a fifth."—*Athenæum.*

"The novel as a whole is a remarkable one, because it is uncompromisingly true to life."—*Daily News.*

**SEETA.** By **Colonel Meadows Taylor,** Author of "Tara," "Ralph Darnell," &c. Crown 8vo. 3 vols.

"The story is well told, native life is admirably described, and the petty intrigues of native rulers, and their hatred of the English, mingled with fear lest the latter should eventually prove the victors, are cleverly depicted."—*Athenæum.*

"We cannot speak too highly of Colonel Meadows Taylor's book. . . . We would recommend all novel readers to purchase it at the earliest opportunity."—*John Bull.*

"Thoroughly interesting and enjoyable reading."—*Examiner.*

**HESTER MORLEY'S PROMISE.** By **Hesba Stretton.** 3 vols.

"'Hester Morley's Promise' is much better than the average novel of the day; it has much more claim to critical consideration as a piece of literary work,—not mere mechanism. The pictures of a narrow society—narrow of soul and intellect—in which the book abounds, are very clever."—*Spectator.*

"Its charm lies not so much, perhaps, in any special excellence in character drawing, or construction—though all the characters stand out clearly and are well sustained, and the interest of the story never flags—as in general tone and colouring."—*Observer.*

**THE DOCTOR'S DILEMMA.** By **Hesba Stretton,** Author of "Little Meg," &c., &c. Crown 8vo. 3 vols.

"A fascinating story which scarcely flags in interest from the first page to the last. It is all story; every page contributes something to the result."—*British Quarterly Review.*

**THE ROMANTIC ANNALS OF A NAVAL FAMILY.** By **Mrs. Arthur Traherne.** Crown 8vo. 10s. 6d.

"A very readable and interesting book."—*United Service Gazette,* June 26, 1875.

"Some interesting letters are introduced, amongst others, several from the late King William IV."—*Spectator.*

"Well and pleasantly told. There are also some capital descriptions of English country life in the last century, presenting a vivid picture of England before the introduction of railways, and the busy life accompanying them."—*Evening Standard.*

**JOHANNES OLAF.** By **E. de Wille.** Translated by **F. E. Bunnett.** Crown 8vo. 3 vols.

"The art of description is fully exhibited; perception of character and capacity for delineating it are obvious; while there is great breadth and comprehensiveness in the plan of the story."—*Morning Post.*

**THE SPINSTERS OF BLATCHINGTON.** By **Mar. Travers.** 2 vols. Crown 8vo.

"A pretty story. Deserving of a favourable reception."—*Graphic.*

"A book of more than average merits, worth reading."—*Examiner.*

**A GOOD MATCH.** By **Amelia Perrier,** Author of "Mea Culpa." 2 vols.

"Racy and lively."—*Athenæum.*

"As pleasant and readable a novel as we have seen this season."—*Examiner.*

"This clever and amusing novel."—*Pall Mall Gazette.*

"Agreeably written."—*Public Opinion.*

**THOMASINA.** By the Author of "Dorothy," "De Cressy," etc. 2 vols. Crown 8vo.

"A finished and delicate cabinet picture, no line is without its purpose, but all contribute to the unity of the work."—*Athenæum.*

"For the delicacies of character-drawing, for play of incident, and for finish of style, we must refer our readers to the story itself."—*Daily News.*

"This undeniably pleasing story."—*Pall Mall Gazette.*

**VANESSA.** By the Author of "Thomasina." 2 vols. Crown 8vo. [*Shortly.*

## FICTION—*continued.*

THE STORY OF SIR ED-WARD'S WIFE. By Hamilton Marshall, Author of "For Very Life." 1 vol. Crown 8vo.

"A quiet graceful little story."—*Spectator.*

"There are many clever conceits in it. . . . Mr. Hamilton Marshall can tell a story closely and pleasantly."—*Pall Mall Gazette.*

LINKED AT LAST. By F. E. Bunnett. 1 vol. Crown 8vo.

"'Linked at Last' contains so much of pretty description, natural incident, and delicate portraiture, that the reader who once takes it up will not be inclined to relinquish it without concluding the volume."—*Morning Post.*

"A very charming story."—*John Bull.*

PERPLEXITY. By Sydney Mostyn. 3 vols. Crown 8vo.

"Shows much lucidity—much power of portraiture."—*Examiner.*

"Written with very considerable power, great cleverness, and sustained interest."—*Standard.*

"The literary workmanship is good, and the story forcibly and graphically told."—*Daily News.*

MEMOIRS OF MRS. LÆTITIA BOOTHBY. By William Clark Russell, Author of "The Book of Authors." Crown 8vo. 7s. 6d.

"Clever and ingenious."—*Saturday Review.*

"One of the most delightful books I have read for a very long while. Thoroughly entertaining from the first page to the last."—*Judy.*

"Very clever book."—*Guardian.*

CRUEL AS THE GRAVE. By the Countess Von Bothmer. 3 vols. Crown 8vo.

"*Jealousy is cruel as the Grave.*"

"An interesting, though somewhat tragic story."—*Athenæum.*

"An agreeable, unaffected, and eminently readable novel."—*Daily News.*

Thirty-Second Edition.

GINX'S BABY; His Birth and Other Misfortunes. By Edward Jenkins. Crown 8vo. Price 2s.

Fourteenth Thousand.

LITTLE HODGE. A Christmas Country Carol. By Edward Jenkins, Author of "Ginx's Baby," &c. Illustrated. Crown 8vo. 5s.

A Cheap Edition in paper covers, price 1s.

"Wise and humorous, but yet most pathetic."—*Nonconformist.*

"The pathos of some of the passages is extremely touching."—*Manchester Examiner.*

Sixth Edition.

LORD BANTAM. By Edward Jenkins, Author of "Ginx's Baby." Crown 8vo. Price 2s.

LUCHMEE AND DILLOO. A Story of West Indian Life. By Edward Jenkins, Author of "Ginx's Baby," "Little Hodge," &c. Two vols. Demy 8vo. Illustrated. [*Preparing.*

HER TITLE OF HONOUR. By Holme Lee. Second Edition. 1 vol. Crown 8vo.

"With the interest of a pathetic story is united the value of a definite and high purpose."—*Spectator.*

"A most exquisitely written story."—*Literary Churchman.*

THE TASMANIAN LILY. By James Bonwick. Crown 8vo. Illustrated. Price 5s.

"The characters of the story are capitally conceived, and are full of those touches which give them a natural appearance."—*Public Opinion.*

"An interesting and useful work."—*Hour.*

MIKE HOWE, THE BUSH-RANGER OF VAN DIE-MEN'S LAND. By James Bonwick, Author of "The Tasmanian Lily," &c. Crown 8vo. With a Frontispiece.

FICTION—*continued.*

Second Edition.

**SEPTIMIUS.** A Romance. By **Nathaniel Hawthorne,** Author of "The Scarlet Letter," "Transformation," &c. 1 vol. Crown 8vo, cloth, extra gilt. 9s.

The *Athenæum* says that "the book is full of Hawthorne's most characteristic writing."

"One of the best examples of Hawthorne's writing ; every page is impressed with his peculiar view of thought, conveyed in his own familiar way."—*Post.*

**PANDURANG HARI;** OR, MEMOIRS OF A HINDOO. A Tale of Mahratta Life sixty years ago. With a Preface, by Sir H. Bartle E. Frere, G.C.S.I., &c. 2 vols. Crown 8vo. Price 21s.

"There is a quaintness and simplicity in the roguery of the hero that makes his life as attractive as that of Gusman d'Alfarache or Gil Blas, and so we advise our readers not to be dismayed at the length of Pandurang Hari, but to read it resolutely through. If they do this they cannot, we think, fail to be both amused and interested."—*Times.*

**MADEMOISELLE JOSEPHINE'S FRIDAYS,** and other Stories. By **Miss M. Betham Edwards,** Author of "Kitty," &c. [*Shortly.*

A collection of Miss Edwards' more important contributions to periodical literature.

**HERMANN AGHA.** An Eastern Narrative. By **W. Gifford Palgrave,** Author of "Travels in Central Arabia," &c. 2 vols. Crown 8vo, cloth, extra gilt. 18s.

Reads like a tale of life, with all its incidents. The young will take to it for its love portions, the older for its descriptions, some in this day for its Arab philosophy."—*Athenæum.*

"There is a positive fragrance as of newly-mown hay about it, as compared with the artificially perfumed passions which are detailed to us with such gusto by our ordinary novel-writers in their endless volumes."—*Observer.*

**MARGARET AND ELIZABETH.** A Story of the Sea. By **Katherine Saunders,** Author of "Gideon's Rock," &c. In 1 vol. Cloth, crown 8vo.

**GIDEON'S ROCK,** and other Stories. By **Katherine Saunders.** In one vol. Crown 8vo.

CONTENTS.—Gideon's Rock.—Old Matthew's Puzzle.—Gentle Jack.—Uncle Ned.—The Retired Apothecary.

**JOAN MERRYWEATHER,** and other Stories. By **Katherine Saunders.** In one vol. Crown 8vo.

CONTENTS.—The Haunted Crust.—The Flower-Girl.—Joan Merryweather.—The Watchman's Story.—An Old Letter.

---

A New and Cheaper Edition, in 1 vol. each, Illustrated, price 6s., of

**COL. MEADOWS TAYLOR'S INDIAN TALES** is preparing for publication. The First Volume will be "The Confessions of a Thug," and will be published in December, to be followed by "Tara," "Ralph Darnell," "Tippoo Sultan."

---

## THEOLOGICAL.

**STUDIES IN MODERN PROBLEMS.** A Series of Essays by various Writers. Edited by the **Rev. Orby Shipley, M.A.**

This project secures the supervision of a small number of Clergy and Laity formed of representative men in London, at both Universities, and in the Provinces, who have promised their co-operation editorially, and will act as a Committee of Reference. The first issue will consist of a series of 12 or 13 Tractates, by various writers, of 48 pages each, in a readable type, crown 8vo, at the price of 6*d.*, and will appear fortnightly for six months, by way of trial.

A Single Copy sent post free for 7*d.* . . . . . .
The Series of 13 Numbers sent post free for 7*s.*, or for 7*s. 6d.* if 13 } *if prepaid.*
Additional Copies sent at proportionate rates . . . . .

### PROPOSED SUBJECTS AND AUTHORS.
(AMONGST OTHERS;

**SACRAMENTAL CONFESSION.**
A. H. WARD, M.A.

**RETREATS FOR PERSONS LIVING IN THE WORLD.**
T. T. CARTER, M.A.

**ABOLITION OF THE ARTICLES.**
NICHOLAS POCOCK, M.A.

**CREATION AND MODERN SCIENCE.**
GEORGE GREENWOOD, M.A.

**MISSIONS.** J. EDWARD VAUX, M.A.

**CATHOLIC AND PROTESTANT.**
EDWARD L. BLENKINSOPP, M.A.

**SOME PRINCIPLES OF CERE-MONIAL.** J. E. FIELD, M.A.

**THE SANCTITY OF MARRIAGE.**
JOHN WALTER LEA, B.A.

**RESERVATION OF THE BLESSED SACRAMENT.**
HENRY HUMBLE, M.A.

**CATHOLICISM AND PROGRESS.**
EDMUND G. WOOD, M.A.

**A LAYMAN'S VIEW OF CONFESSION.**
J. DAVID CHAMBERS, M.A.

**UNTIL THE DAY DAWN.** Four Advent Lectures delivered in the Episcopal Chapel, Milverton, Warwickshire, on the Sunday evenings during Advent, 1870. By the **Rev. Marmaduke E. Browne.** Crown 8vo.

**A SCOTCH COMMUNION SUNDAY.** To which are added Certain Discourses from a University City. By **A. K. H. B.**, Author of "The Recreations of a Country Parson." Crown 8vo. Price 5*s.*

**CHURCH THOUGHT AND CHURCH WORK.** Edited by the **Rev. Chas. Anderson, M.A.**, Editor of "Words and Works in a London Parish." Demy 8vo. Pp. 250. 7*s. 6d.* Containing Articles by the Rev. J. Ll. DAVIES, J. M. CAPES, HARRY JONES, BROOKE LAMBERT, A. J. ROSS, Professor CHEETHAM, the EDITOR, and others.

**WORDS AND WORKS IN A LONDON PARISH.** Edited by the **Rev. Charles Anderson, M.A.** Demy 8vo. 6*s.*

"It has an interest of its own for not a few minds, to whom the question 'Is the National Church worth preserving as | such, and if so how best increase its vital power?' is of deep and grave importance." —*Spectator.*

**EVERY DAY A PORTION**: Adapted from the Bible and the Prayer Book, for the Private Devotions of those living in Widowhood. Collected and Edited by the **Lady Mary Vyner.** Square crown 8vo, printed on good paper, elegantly bound.

"Now she that is a widow indeed, and desolate, trusteth in God."

THEOLOGICAL—*continued.*

## WORDS OF HOPE FROM THE PULPIT OF THE TEMPLE CHURCH. By C. J. Vaughan, D.D., Master of the Temple.

*Third Edition.*

## THE YOUNG LIFE EQUIPPING ITSELF FOR GOD'S SERVICE. Being Four Sermons Preached before the University of Cambridge in November, 1872. By the Rev. C. J. Vaughan, D.D., Master of the Temple. Crown 8vo. Price 3s. 6d.

"Has all the writer's characteristics of devotedness, purity, and high moral tone."—*London Quarterly Review.*

"As earnest, eloquent, and as liberal as

everything else that he writes."—*Examiner.*

"Earnest in tone and eloquent in entreaty."—*Manchester Examiner.*

## A NEW VOLUME OF ACADEMIA ESSAYS. Edited by the Most Reverend Archbishop Manning. Demy.

CONTENTS:—The Philosophy of Christianity.—Mystical Elements of Religion.—Controversy with the Agnostics.—A Reasoning Thought.—Darwinism brought to Book.—Mr. Mill on Liberty of the Press.—

Christianity in relation to Society.—The Religious Condition of Germany.—The Philosophy of Bacon.—Catholic Laymen and Scholastic Philosophy.

## WHY AM I A CHRISTIAN? By Viscount Stratford de Redcliffe, P.C., K.G., G.C.B. Crown 8vo. 3s. Third Edition.

"Has a peculiar interest, as exhibiting the convictions of an earnest, intelligent, and practical man."—*Contemporary Review.*

## THEOLOGY AND MORALITY. Being Essays by the Rev. J. Llewellyn Davies. 1 vol. 8vo. Price 7s. 6d.

Essays on Questions of Belief and Practice.—The Debts of Theology to Secular Influences.—The Christian Theory of Duty.—Weak Points in Utilitarianism.—Nature and Prayer.—The Continuity of Creation.—The Beginnings of the Church.—Erastus and Excommunication.—Pauperism as produced by Wealth.—Combinations of Agricultural Labourers.—Communism.

"There is a good deal that is well worth reading."—*Church Times.*

## THE RECONCILIATION OF RELIGION AND SCIENCE. Being Essays by the Rev. T. W. Fowle, M.A. 1 vol., 8vo. 10s. 6d.

The Divine Character of Christ.—Science and Immortality.—Morality and Immortality.—Christianity and Immortality.—Religion and Fact.—The Miracles of God.—The Miracles of Man.—A Scientific Account of Inspiration.—The Inspiration of the Jews.—The Inspiration of the Bible.—The Divinity of Christ and Modern Thought.—The Church and the Working Classes.

"A book which requires and deserves the respectful attention of all reflecting Churchmen. It is earnest, reverent, thoughtful, and courageous. . . . There is scarcely a

page in the book which is not equally worthy of a thoughtful pause."—*Literary Churchman.*

## HYMNS AND VERSES, Original and Translated. By the Rev. Henry Downton. Small crown 8vo, 3s. 6d.

"It is a rare gift and very precious, and we heartily commend this, its fruits, to the pious in all denominations."—*Church Opinion.*

"Considerable force and beauty characterise some of these verses."—*Watchman.*

"Mr. Downton's 'Hymns and Verses'

are worthy of all praise."—*English Churchman.*

"Will, we do not doubt, be welcome as a permanent possession to those for whom they have been composed or to whom they have been originally addressed."—*Church Herald.*

THEOLOGICAL—*continued.*

## MISSIONARY ENTERPRISE IN THE EAST. By the Rev. Richard Collins. Illustrated. Crown 8vo. 6s.

"A very graphic story told in lucid, simple, and modest style." — *English Churchman.*

"A readable and very interesting volume."—*Church Review.*

"It is a real pleasure to read an honest book on Missionary work, every word of which shows the writer to be a man of large heart, far-seeing views, and liberal cultivation, and such a book we have now before us."—*Mission Life.*

"We may judge from our own experience, no one who takes up this charming little volume will lay it down again till he has got to the last word."—*John Bull.*

## THE ETERNAL LIFE. Being Fourteen Sermons. By the Rev. Jas. Noble Bennie, M.A. Crown 8vo. 6s.

"We recommend these sermons as wholesome Sunday reading."—*English Churchman.*

"Very chaste and pure in style."—*Courant.*

"The whole volume is replete with matter for thought and study."—*John Bull.*

"Mr. Bennie preaches earnestly and well."—*Literary Churchman.*

## THE REALM OF TRUTH. By Miss E. T. Carne. Crown 8vo. 5s. 6d.

"A singularly calm, thoughtful, and philosophical inquiry into what Truth is, and what its authority."—*Leeds Mercury.*

"It tells the world what it does not like to hear, but what it cannot be told too often, that Truth is something stronger and more enduring than our little doings, and speakings, and actings." — *Literary Churchman.*

## LIFE: Conferences delivered at Toulouse. By the Rev. Père Lacordaire. Crown 8vo. 6s.

"Let the serious reader cast his eye upon any single page in this volume, and he will find there words which will arrest his attention and give him a desire to know more of the teachings of this worthy follower of the saintly St. Dominick."—*Morning Post.*

"The book is worth studying as an evidence of the way in which an able man may be crippled by theological chains."—*Examiner.*

"The discourses are simple, natural, and unaffectedly eloquent."—*Public Opinion.*

*Fourth Edition.*

## THOUGHTS FOR THE TIMES. By the Rev. H. R. Haweis, M.A., "Author of Music and Morals," etc. Crown 8vo. 7s. 6d.

"Bears marks of much originality of thought and individuality of expression."—*Pall Mall Gazette.*

"Mr. Haweis writes not only fearlessly, but with remarkable freshness and vigour. In all that he says we perceive a transparent honesty and singleness of purpose."—*Saturday Review.*

## SPEECH IN SEASON. A New Volume of Sermons. By the Rev. H. R. Haweis. [*Preparing.*

*Second Edition.*

## CATHOLICISM AND THE VATICAN. With a Narrative of the Old Catholic Congress at Munich. By J. Lowry Whittle, A.M., Trin. Coll., Dublin. Crown 8vo. 4s. 6d.

"We may cordially recommend his book to all who wish to follow the course of the Old Catholic movement." — *Saturday Review.*

THEOLOGICAL—*continued.*

Second Edition.

**SCRIPTURE LANDS IN CONNECTION WITH THEIR HIS-
TORY.** By G. S. Drew, M.A., Vicar of Trinity, Lambeth, Author
of "Reasons of Faith." Bevelled boards, 8vo. Price 10s. 6d.

"Mr. Drew has invented a new method of illustrating Scripture history — from observation of the countries. Instead of narrating his travels, and referring from time to time to the facts of sacred history belonging to the different countries, he writes an outline history of the Hebrew | nation from Abraham downwards, with special reference to the various points in which the geography illustrates the history. . . . He is very successful in picturing to his readers the scenes before his own mind."—*Saturday Review.*

Second Edition.

**NAZARETH : ITS LIFE AND LESSONS.** By the Rev. G. S.
Drew, Vicar of Trinity, Lambeth. Second Edition. In small 8vo, cloth. 5s.

"A singularly reverent and beautiful book."—*Daily Telegraph.*
"Perhaps one of the most remarkable | books recently issued in the whole range of English theology."—*Churchman's Magazine.*

**THE DIVINE KINGDOM ON EARTH AS IT IS IN
HEAVEN.** By the Rev. G. S. Drew, Author of "Nazareth : its
Life and Lessons." In demy 8vo, bound in cloth. Price 10s. 6d.

"Thoughtful and eloquent. . . . Full of original thinking admirably expressed."—*British Quarterly Review.*
"Entirely valuable and satisfactory. . | . . . . There is no living divine to whom the authorship would not be a credit."—*Literary Churchman.*

**SIX PRIVY COUNCIL JUDGMENTS**—1850–1872. Annotated by
W. G. Brooke, M.A., Barrister-at-Law. Crown 8vo. 9s.

THE MOST COMPLETE HYMN BOOK PUBLISHED.

**HYMNS FOR THE CHURCH AND HOME.** Selected and Edited by
the Rev. W. Fleming Stevenson, Author of "Praying and Working."

The Hymn-book consists of Three Parts :—I. For Public Worship.—II. For Family and Private Worship.—III. For Children; and contains Biographical Notices of nearly 300 Hymn-writers, with Notes upon their Hymns.

.\* Published in various forms and prices, the latter ranging from 8d. to 6s. Lists and full particulars will be furnished on application to the Publisher.

*WORKS OF THE LATE REV. F. W. ROBERTSON.*

NEW AND CHEAPER EDITIONS.

**SERMONS.**

Vol. I. Small crown 8vo. Price 3s. 6d.
„ II. Small crown 8vo. Price 3s. 6d.
„ III. Small crown 8vo. Price 3s. 6d.
„ IV. Small crown 8vo. Price 3s. 6d.

**EXPOSITORY LECTURES ON ST. PAUL'S EPISTLE TO
THE CORINTHIANS.** Small crown 8vo. 5s.

**AN ANALYSIS OF MR. TENNYSON'S "IN MEMORIAM."**
(Dedicated by permission to the Poet-Laureate.) Fcap. 8vo. 2s.

WORKS OF THE LATE REV. F. W. ROBERTSON—*continued*.

**THE EDUCATION OF THE HUMAN RACE.** Translated from the German of **Gotthold Ephraim Lessing.** Fcap. 8vo. 2s. 6d.

**LECTURES AND ADDRESSES, WITH OTHER LITERARY REMAINS.** By the late **Rev. Fredk. W. Robertson.** A New Edition, including a Correspondence with Lady Byron. With Introduction by the **Rev. Stopford A. Brooke, M.A.** In One Vol. Uniform with the Sermons. Price 5s. [*Preparing.*

**A LECTURE ON FRED. W. ROBERTSON, M.A.** By the **Rev. F. A. Noble,** delivered before the Young Men's Christian Association of Pittsburgh, U.S. 1s. 6d.

---

# WORKS BY THE REV. STOPFORD A. BROOKE, M.A.

Chaplain in Ordinary to Her Majesty the Queen.

**THE LATE REV. F. W. ROBERTSON, M.A., LIFE AND LETTERS OF.** Edited by **Stopford Brooke, M.A.**, Chaplain in Ordinary to the Queen.

In 2 vols., uniform with the Sermons. Price 7s. 6d.

Library Edition, in demy 8vo, with Two Steel Portraits. 12s.

A Popular Edition, in 1 vol. Price 6s.

**THEOLOGY IN THE ENGLISH POETS.** Being Lectures delivered by the **Rev. Stopford A. Brooke,** Chaplain in Ordinary to Her Majesty the Queen.

*Third Edition.*

**CHRIST IN MODERN LIFE.** Sermons Preached in St. James's Chapel, York Street, London. Crown 8vo. 7s. 6d.

"Nobly fearless and singularly strong. . . . carries our admiration throughout."—*British Quarterly Review.*

*Second Edition,*

**FREEDOM IN THE CHURCH OF ENGLAND.** Six Sermons suggested by the Voysey Judgment. In 1 vol. Crown 8vo, cloth. 3s. 6d.

"A very fair statement of the views in respect to freedom of thought held by the liberal party in the Church of England."—*Blackwood's Magazine.*

"Interesting and readable, and characterised by great clearness of thought, frankness of statement, and moderation of tone."—*Church Opinion.*

*Seventh Edition.*

**SERMONS** Preached in St. James's Chapel, York Street, London. Crown 8vo. 6s.

"No one who reads these sermons will wonder that Mr. Brooke is a great power in London, that his chapel is thronged, and his followers large and enthusiastic.

"They are fiery, energetic, impetuous sermons, rich with the treasures of a cultivated imagination."—*Guardian.*

**THE LIFE AND WORK OF FREDERICK DENISON MAURICE:** A Memorial Sermon. Crown 8vo, sewed. 1s.

---

# THE CORNHILL LIBRARY OF FICTION.

### 3s. 6d. per Volume.

IT is intended in this Series to produce books of such merit that readers will care to preserve them on their shelves. They are well printed on good paper, handsomely bound, with a Frontispiece, and are sold at the moderate price of 3s. 6d. each.

---

**FOR LACK OF GOLD.** By **Charles Gibbon.**

**GOD'S PROVIDENCE HOUSE.** By **Mrs. G. L. Banks.**

**ROBIN GRAY.** By **Charles Gibbon.** With a Frontispiece by **Hennessy.**

**KITTY.** By **Miss M. Betham-Edwards.**

**READY MONEY MORTIBOY.** A Matter-of-Fact Story.

**HIRELL.** By **John Saunders.** Author of "Abel Drake's Wife."

**ONE OF TWO.** By **J. Hain Friswell,** Author of "The Gentle Life," etc.

**ABEL DRAKE'S WIFE.** By **John Saunders.**

**THE HOUSE OF RABY.** By **Mrs. G. Hooper.**

**A FIGHT FOR LIFE.** By **Moy Thomas.**

*OTHER STANDARD NOVELS TO FOLLOW.*

---

# LIST OF AUTHORS AND SUBJECTS OF THEIR BOOKS,

## TO BE PUBLISHED IN THE

## INTERNATIONAL SCIENTIFIC SERIES.

Rev. M. J. BERKELEY, M.A. F.L.S. and M. COOKE, M.A. LL.D.
*Fungi: their Nature, Influences, and Uses.*

Prof. OSCAR SCHMIDT, (University of Strasburg.)
*The Theory of Descent and Darwinism.*

Prof. VOGEL, (Polytechnic Academy of Berlin.)
*The Chemical Effects of Light.*

Prof. W. KINGDOM CLIFFORD, M.A.
*The First Principles of the Exact Sciences explained to the non-mathematical.*

Prof. T. H. HUXLEY, LL.D. F.R.S.
*Bodily Motion and Consciousness.*

Dr. W. B. CARPENTER, LL.D. F.R.S.
*The Physical Geography of the Sea.*

Prof. WILLIAM ODLING, F.R.S.
*The Old Chemistry from the new standpoint.*

Prof. SHELDON AMOS.
*The Science of Law.*

W. LAUDER LINDSAY, M.D. F.R.S.E.
*Mind in the Lower Animals.*

Sir JOHN LUBBOCK, Bart. F.R.S.
*The Antiquity of Man.*

Prof. W. T. THISELTON DYER, B.A. B.SC.
*Form and Habit in Flowering Plants.*

Mr. J. N. LOCKYER, F.R.S.
*Spectrum Analysis.*

Prof. MICHAEL FOSTER, M.D.
*Protoplasm and the Cell Theory.*

Prof. W. STANLEY JEVONS.
*The Logic of Statistics.*

Dr. H. CHARLTON BASTIAN, M.D. F.R.S.
*The Brain as an Organ of Mind.*

Prof. A. C. RAMSAY, LL.D. F.R.S.
*Earth Sculpture: Hills, Valleys, Mountains, Plains, Rivers, Lakes; how they were Produced, and how they have been Destroyed.*

Prof. RUDOLPH VIRCHOW, (University of Berlin.)
*Morbid Physiological Action.*

Prof. CLAUDE BERNARD, (College of France.)
*Physical and Metaphysical Phenomena of Life.*

Prof. A. QUETELET, (Brussels Acad. of Sciences.)
*Social Physics.*

Prof. H. SAINTE-CLAIRE DEVILLE.
*An Introduction to General Chemistry.*

Prof. WURTZ.
*Atoms and the Atomic Theory.*

Prof. DE QUATREFAGES.
*The Negro Races.*

Prof. LACAZE-DUTHIERS.
*Zoology since Cuvier.*

Prof. BERTHELOT.
*Chemical Synthesis.*

Prof. J. ROSENTHAL.
*General Physiology of Muscles and Nerves.*

Prof. JAMES D. DANA, M.A. LL.D.
*On Cephalization: or, Head-Characters in the Gradation and Progress of Life.*

Prof. S. W. JOHNSON, M.A.
*On the Nutrition of Plants.*

Prof. AUSTIN FLINT, Jr. M.D.
*The Nervous System and its Relation to the Bodily Functions.*

Prof. W. D. WHITNEY.
*Modern Linguistic Science.*

Prof. BERNSTEIN, (University of Halle.)
*Physiology of the Senses.*

Prof. FERDINAND COHN, (University of Breslau)
*Thallophytes (Algæ Lichens Fungi).*

Prof. HERMANN, (University of Zurich.)
*Respiration.*

Prof. LEUCKART, (University of Leipsic.)
*Outlines of Animal Organisation.*

Prof. LIEBREICH, (University of Berlin.)
*Outlines of Toxicology.*

Prof. KUNDT, (University of Strasburg.)
*On Sound.*

Prof. LOMMEL, (University of Erlangen.)
*Optics.*

Prof. REES, (University of Erlangen.)
*On Parasitic Plants.*

Prof. STEINTHAL, (University of Berlin.)
*Outlines of the Science of Language.*

☞ For List of Works already Published, see beginning of book.

HENRY S. KING & CO., 65 CORNHILL, AND 12 PATERNOSTER ROW, LONDON.

www.ingramcontent.com/pod-product-compliance
Lightning Source LLC
Chambersburg PA
CBHW060530030726
47498CB00004B/1140